Sue Wilsher grew up in South Essex near a shoe factory and the Thames estuary. The shoe company housed its workers, including Sue's grandparents and mother. Sue based her debut novel, *When My Ship Comes In*, on the history of the area. She now lives in Kent with her husband and two children.

The Copperettes at War

SUE WILSHER

SPHERE

First published in Great Britain in 2019 by Sphere
This paperback edition published by Sphere in 2020

3 5 7 9 10 8 6 4 2

A CIP catalogue record for this book
is available from the British Library.

ISBN 978-0-7515-7087-8

Typeset in Bembo by M Rules
Printed and bound in Great Britain by
Clays Ltd, Elcograf S.p.A.

Papers used by Sphere are from well-managed forests
and other responsible sources.

Sphere
An imprint of
Little, Brown Book Group
Carmelite House
50 Victoria Embankment
London EC4Y 0DZ

An Hachette UK Company
www.hachette.co.uk

www.littlebrown.co.uk

For my Molly

November 1918
East Tilbury, Essex

Young Alfie Pike kicked down his bicycle stand and lifted a crate of groceries out of the front carrier. Now that sugar, flour and butter were on the ration, the deliveries were easier to lift. Even a big house like this one was only allowed to take its fair share and Mr Mercer the grocer couldn't be seen to have favourites. Especially when the customer in this house was in the police. Even if it was only the women's police, the copperettes. This customer would have him down Grays court quick as you like if he was trading unfairly. There was another lady police here too, not really a lady, more like the girls down the bomb factory. Mr Mercer said he didn't know what to think about that.

Alfie got the crate under one arm while he opened the wrought iron gate and, stepping over a bicycle that had fallen over on the front path, made his way round to the side of the house. He rapped at the back door but no one answered. Only the manor houses had maids these days. The lady police had to answer their own doors. He rapped again and thought about Mr Mercer tapping his foot and looking up at the

1

shop clock. It might be worth trying the front door just this once. As he came back round the house, he passed the drawing room window and stopped to look in. His eyes were playing tricks with him. He rubbed at the dusty glass and peered closer and then he started back. There was a woman lying still on the floor. He could see only her legs and feet. A long dark skirt and black boots. Alfie waited a few seconds, his heart beating fast, to make sure she wasn't moving.

Putting the crate of groceries carefully down on the ground, he ran to his bike. He'd hardly kicked the stand back up before he was pedalling like mad down the road to raise the alarm.

1

Aggie

Three Months Earlier

It was hard to know what to do. The girls from cordite were striking for their jobs but the guncotton sheds were safe for now and Aggie hated making a fuss. She stood at the gates of the Greygoose munitions factory, watching as the copperettes in their dark blue military uniforms, long skirts and large felt hats, tried to herd the women workers away to the side to let the men through. When the men had gone on strike the week before, the armed guards had stepped in and some of the workers had ended up at Grays police court. Aggie stayed back and kept quiet.

Pops, a fellow guncotton girl, appeared at Aggie's shoulder. 'Shouldn't we strike with them?' she asked.

Aggie didn't know. 'Will it do any good? They know who they're gonna lay off.'

'Jean said guncotton jobs won't be safe for ever,' said Pops, 'not now the Germans are having to eat their own horses.'

Aggie stared ahead at the copperettes jostling with the workers. Everyone was saying the Germans were on the back foot – they'd pushed ahead without enough supplies and now they were starving. If the Allies got the better of them, there wouldn't be any more need for munitions factories at home.

'Well, my Arnie will be coming home in that case,' she said, knowing that Arnie getting home safe from the front was the priority. While she was making explosives to send to France, he was there in the trenches dodging the Boche's guns. She'd trained herself to think about him only at certain times of the day – it helped to cope with the uncertainty of it all. Pops patted her arm. Aggie didn't want to say that she was terrified of losing her job and going back to service. Munitionettes were better paid than housemaids. But it wasn't just the money; it was the freedom, the camaraderie, doing an important job for King and Country, helping the boys over-seas by making explosives to put in their shells and guns. But everyone wanted the war to end. The slaughter had to stop.

'None of the women's unions are here anyway,' said Pops. 'I don't know what all the fuss was about, telling us to join. When the men came out, their unions were up in arms.'

It was true. The men's unions were upset that they hadn't been consulted about the factory being reduced. The Electricians' Union, the Toolmakers', the Engineers'. It was funny really how they made the government write that law about kicking the women out of the factories when the men came home. And now look, there'd not even be work for the men at Greygoose at this rate, let alone the women.

'Some of the men will get a transfer to another factory, but there's nothing for the women. We're supposed to just go back to what we were doing before the war,' said Aggie.

'Tilda from cordite got a job shipbuilding down the docks,' said Pops.

'They're not gonna need three thousand munitions girls, though, are they?'

'No,' said Pops, 'I don't suppose they will.'

They watched as the copperettes took the cordite girls to one side to give them a talking-to. You could tell they were in cordite, they had yellow skin and orange hair from the poisoning. Aggie's eye twitched involuntarily. She hated the way those police ladies bossed the workers around. They didn't know working women. They thought they did, but they didn't.

Once the cordite girls had been corralled to the side of the gate, the men came through, escorted by the West Kent soldiers who guarded the factory. One of the gunpowder labourers shouted out to the women.

'Go home and watch your children, give the men their jobs back now.'

At this the cordite girls screamed their indignation.

'We've got families to feed,' they yelled. 'My husband was killed in action,' shouted one. 'You get out to fight,' said another. 'You should be on the front line with my husband, not cowering here in the factory.'

At that, the men jeered and shook their fists, some laughing, some angry, some catcalling to put the women in their place. They were doing protected war work at Greygoose, they were exempt from enlisting. They pointed at their badges and the women pointed at their own *On War Service* badges. Aggie felt sick, it wasn't a pleasant sight. The men had never wanted the girls in the factory and now it was everyone for themselves. Aggie had heard all kinds of stories – men hiding the girls' tools, resetting their machines, playing tricks – not to mention the constant leering winks and pinches; there was a lot of that, and more, and nothing done about it.

Mrs Sparrow, the welfare supervisor, stood by the gate watching it all. A tough old bird responsible for all of the girls in the factory, she was keeping tabs on who was making trouble and who wasn't. There was no striking allowed under the Munitions of War Act. With her stood the local women's police sub-inspector – she was the worst of the lot. She looked like a man, her hair was cut short beneath her peaked cap and she wore breeches and tall shining black boots. Whenever there was any trouble from the girls, Mrs Sparrow called on the sub-inspector to sort it out.

'Who are those women, there, hanging around? Get them in, Sergeant Rathbone,' the sub-inspector shouted to one of her sergeants, who Aggie recognised from her village. The sergeant extracted herself from the cordite girls and made her way over to Aggie and Pops.

'Come along now, girls, let's get you into work.'

'Can't we wait a minute to let it blow over?' said Aggie. 'It's a bit much if we just waltz into work past them.'

'Get those shirkers inside, Sergeant Rathbone,' called the sub-inspector.

'Come along,' said Sergeant Rathbone, taking Aggie's arm and steering her towards the gate.

Aggie looked at Pops in exasperation – she hated being accused of shirking.

'They're only afraid for their livelihoods,' said Aggie.

'Well, there'll be plenty of work in service when the factory closes down,' said Sergeant Rathbone. 'Off you go now.' With that she guided Aggie and Pops into the change hut.

Plenty of work in service? Aggie shuddered. She'd worked in service before the war and didn't want to go back to emptying chamber pots at all hours for a fraction of the wage she was on now.

'She's got a cheek saying that to me,' she said, changing into her stiff cotton uniform of white tunic and trousers. 'That sergeant lives in my village. I bet she knows I used to work at Gobions. I've seen her there taking tea with the mistress.'

Gobions. The big manor house on the East Tilbury marshes. Aggie shuddered at the thought of the imperious mistress who would creep around to make sure she was pulling her weight. Aggie would rather face the risk of explosions and poisoning than go back to that kind of humiliation.

'Cheer up,' said Pops, 'you must be used to them by now.'

'Who, the posh patrols?' Aggie shrugged. 'I bet they don't even get paid for patrolling. They don't need the money, just doing their bit for the duration. I wonder what the eight hundred factory workers laid off in March are doing now – being criticised for asking for the dole, I bet.'

The factory girls were doing men's work, just like the copperettes were doing. But in the factory they did long shifts handling toxic materials. They were at risk of being blown up from explosions like the one at Greygoose in 1916 and others at Pitsea and Faversham, not to mention being on the flight path of the German Gotha bombers and Zeppelin airships, one of which had been shot down right by the factory in 1916. They were on the front line at home: the girls behind the men behind the guns. There'd been a special service at St Paul's in April, where the Last Post was played for the munitions workers who'd died in service. They were the ones directly helping the boys abroad to kill the Hun and end the war. And the women police bossed them around like nursery nurses.

'If we drink too much or buy something fancy to wear they say we're indecent, unpatriotic, out of control,' continued Aggie, pulling the pins out of her hair. No metal allowed in the factory: one spark and the whole place could blow.

'One of them pulled Sissy out of the pub for singing the other day,' offered Pops, tucking her long hair into her cap. Caps to be worn at all times. Girls there had been scalped when their hair had caught in the machinery.

'Come on, let's get over there.'

They came out of the change room to see the sergeant waiting there.

'Just a minute,' called the sergeant. 'You'll have to remove that wedding band.'

'Oh, it was wound with thread, it's come off,' said Aggie, annoyed that she hadn't noticed.

'I shall have to confiscate it, I'm afraid. We can have no exposed metal in the factory.'

'I know,' said Aggie, 'I've worked here for two years. I'll just take it off and put it in my bag in the changing room.'

'I'm sorry,' said the sergeant. 'It shouldn't have been brought past the factory gates.' She held out her hand. Either

Aggie missed her shift and forfeited her wages or she gave the sergeant her ring.

Taking it off was a betrayal to Arnie. She removed it and gave it to the sergeant, hating her for it.

'Your name?'

'Agnes Tucker.'

'You can collect your ring from the gatehouse after your shift. A penalty fine will be deducted from your wages.'

'I suppose you're enjoying this, aren't you?' said Aggie.

The sergeant paused. 'Only in as much as I may have just prevented a serious explosion in the factory.'

'You lot,' said Aggie, shaking her head. 'I'd dearly love to tell you what the girls all think of you, but I won't.' She gave the sergeant a stare and walked away.

'Fancy taking your ring,' said Pops, 'when your Arnie's away fighting.'

They walked along the main thoroughfare of the factory grounds. To the right was the safe area, housing the chemical works and administration huts. To the left was the danger area. This was where the cordite was made, and the guncotton and where the acids were mixed. These work sheds were spaced two hundred yards apart and had large mounds of earth piled around them to minimise the level of destruction if one exploded.

The girls walked off the main road onto the raised wooden tramways to the guncotton sheds.

'What would you do if you got laid off then?' said Pops, trying to take Aggie's mind off her ring.

'Dunno, I suppose we've got a bit more time than the cordite girls. We're lucky guncotton is used in torpedoes, not just for making cordite.'

'Yes, but there's talk of the war ending soon, what about then?'

'I dunno, Pops.' They reached their shed and went in through the blackout curtains, pulled on their wellington boots and their face masks, which were black and pointed like beaks and stuffed with cotton-soaked creosote and made them look like strange crows. They'd only had masks for a year or so since one of the cordite girls kicked up a stink at a work tribunal and asked for better safety conditions. Aggie was never sure which made her more lightheaded: the nitric and sulphuric acids or the creosote in the mask.

They greeted their fellow workers and made their way to their batch of four guncotton pans, earthenware pots three feet wide and a foot off the ground. Pops wound the acid tap until the set amount had run into the pots. They took up their long-handled metal forks and began to pitch the washed cotton waste from the Lancashire mills into the pans to mix with the acid.

Aggie didn't know the answer to Pops's question about what she'd do if she lost her job at the factory. 'I bet I could do a better job than that copperette, though,' she said under her breath. She stirred her acid and got on with the task in hand: keeping up production so the boys abroad would have enough explosive to blow the Boche away. Aggie was as nervous as everyone else about the factory closing down. Stirring the acid too vigorously, it splashed up onto her arms. She ran to the hose and doused herself, getting the hateful corrosive off her skin.

'It's all right,' she said to a worried Pops, 'I'll just step out for a bit.'

Standing on the wooden platform outside the hut, she tried to look at her arms but the factory was in darkness. No lights allowed – they were enough of a target for the German Gothas as it was. She blew on her sore skin and let her mind wander to Arnie. His letters were sporadic and he could never say much about what he was doing or where he was. It was nearly four years since he'd enlisted and she'd seen him only a handful of times on leave. Her heart ached when she thought how hard it was now to really picture his face and remember how he would hold her in bed. She was determined not to let the war make strangers of them. Feeling for her wedding band she remembered having to hand it over to that sergeant.

An unfamiliar sound puffed from the guncotton sifting houses two hundred yards away in the darkness. A flash of forbidden light illuminated the sheds. Aggie's stomach lurched. An accident. There was a scream, shouting. All thoughts of acid burns and Arnie forgotten, she grabbed one of the tin fire buckets full of sand from the platform and ran along the wooden tramway towards the noises. She tripped and stumbled, trying to find her footing, and looked up to see why her vision had improved. One of the sifting houses was on fire and had lit up the surrounding area. She ran faster, struggling to carry the heavy sand. Workers streamed out of the hut, calling out. Some of them ran out towards the fire engine shed to raise the alarm. 'Get back,' a man shouted at her, 'it might blow.'

Aggie could feel the heat and smell the burning acid; it stung her nose and got into her throat. Someone inside the shed screamed. She hesitated, then stepped forwards, putting up her arm to shield her face from the heat, and looked around for help but the smoke obscured her vision. She stepped forwards gingerly and stopped when flames reached out of the doorway towards her. A man suddenly stumbled out of the shed, his uniform on fire. He was pulling a woman, half conscious, dragging her to safety, but she was burning. Aggie wanted to help but the heat was too fierce. The man pushed the woman away out onto the marshy ground and he started to flap at his clothes, crying out. Aggie stared in horror. Someone came to the woman with a bucket of water, but the man … She went to him, appalled by the sight of the fire clinging to his clothes and hair. She tipped her bucket at an angle and where the sand landed on him the flames were extinguished. He patted at his face and head to stop the burning. The heat being less intense, she was able to get closer, and dumped the remaining sand on him. The fire on the building lit up his wild eyes. He lay there on the ground, rigid and shaking, his hair and face charred, most of his uniform burned away, the gritty sand mixed with his shining red skin.

The area filled with people coming to help. The copperettes were there, and so was Mrs Sparrow. The welfare supervisor gave Aggie a nod of acknowledgement and she felt herself being pushed to one side. The ambulance team were crouching down to the man. They lifted him gently onto a stretcher and bore him away. Someone tugged at her arm and guided her back to the guncotton mixing shed.

'Sit down here,' said the voice. Aggie looked up to see Pops staring at her. 'Just for a minute and then we'll get you over to the hospital.'

Aggie rested there, her mind suddenly blank but for one thought: the girl, what had happened to the girl?

Pops put her arm around her friend and walked her to the main road, then helped her into a car, which drove her the five minute journey to the hospital in Goosetown, the model village where a lot of the workers lived. The school and shop, the village hall and the dormitory sheds went past the window in a slow blur. A nurse helped her out of the car and took her inside to lie down in a bed. She was propped up with pillows, given a cup of hot, sweet tea. The sugar tasted syrupy and unfamiliar on her tongue – she had given it up since the food shortages.

'I hear you're our hero?' said a nurse, picking up Aggie's arm and pressing her fingers to the pulse.

'Hero?' said Aggie, frowning. 'No, I don't need to be checked. The man, is he all right? The girl, what happened?'

The nurse fixed her expression into one of gentle sympathy. 'You're in shock, you do need to be checked. The man is alive – they've taken him to Orsett hospital. But the girl, I'm afraid she was too badly burned, we lost her.'

Sitting in the Goosetown canteen two days later, Aggie read the newspaper and sipped her tea, her ring finger feeling bare without her wedding band. She'd had lots of pats on the back about saving the guncotton man's life. The poor girl who died hadn't stood a chance. She was too badly burned. But the workers had to carry on, knowing how dangerous their jobs were.

Some of the cordite girls who'd gone on strike the previous week had been given their cards. One week's notice and that was that. Aggie felt for them but knew that they'd be mopping up any of the good jobs going elsewhere and by the time she lost her job at the factory there'd be nothing left but work as a housemaid or taking in washing. Some of the married ones with kids would stay at home but a lot of the working women would have to bring in a wage if they could. The cost of living had gone sky high during the war, it was hard to get a bit of meat anywhere, and separation allowance wasn't enough to live on. There were often little tots begging for food outside the factory gates. At least she and Arnie didn't have any other mouths to feed.

She clenched her jaw and stared down at the front page news. The London police had gone on strike. Twelve thousand men marching down Whitehall for better pay and pensions. It didn't seem right, the policemen going on strike, asking for a twelve per cent war bonus. She supposed the women police would be taking up the slack.

Turning to the Situations Vacant page, she scanned the column. There were a lot of maid positions and not much else, apart from typing, and she didn't know how to. She'd go along to the Labour Exchange, see if there was anything there worth applying for. It was time to jump the sinking ship. The war had been her chance to get on, to do something interesting and worthwhile, and she hated the thought of being stranded. There was talk of women being made to take any position. Once all the men came home, the women wouldn't be needed any more.

Aggie glanced up at the lady volunteers in the canteen. Dressed nicely, hat and hair done to perfection. They were doing their bit for the war, but would slot easily back into their old lives when the men came home. They wouldn't be demanding jobs like the working women had to. These were just another bunch keeping an eye on the factory girls' behaviour. They'd run for a copperette at the drop of a hat if the girls were shouting or fighting about something, if they drank a glass too many at one of the Goosetown dances. Aggie tutted and looked back down at her paper, turned over the page. A job notice jumped out at her.

The Ministry of Munitions has need of women police to take up posts in His Majesty's factories. The Women's Police Service offers the necessary training. An allowance is granted during training and good salaries are offered on appointment.

She read quickly, leaning in closer to the words, her mind racing. She'd had the courage to pull a burning man from a chemical fire, she knew the factory girls and the problems they faced. She wanted to get on and have a good job after the war.

It was perfect. They'd still need police after the war, there was a chance the copperettes would still have a career. It wasn't like the munitionettes, who made explosives. And she wouldn't be patronised by the better-class women any more; she wouldn't be forced back into service. The country had changed, you only had to walk through Stanford high street to see that. Disabled servicemen were selling matches on street corners. There were war widows waiting in shop queues for a bit of mutton to feed the family. And the casualty list in the *Thurrock Gazette* had featured men from Linford, East Tilbury, Stanford and Corringham. Not to mention the number of suicides.

Who knew when the war would end. The soldiers stationed at Tilbury and Coalhouse forts drew factory girls from the area. She'd heard how the copperettes treated these girls, like they were prostitutes trying to corrupt the soldiers, not the other way around. Aggie understood the girls; she'd do a better job of policing them. She knew she could.

Her chair scraped loudly on the floor as she stood up. Grabbing her paper she marched across the marshes to the factory, to the safe area, the admin block, to Mrs Sparrow's office.

'Mrs Sparrow, can I have a word please?' said Aggie, trying to catch her breath.

'Agnes, isn't it?'

'Yes, Agnes, Aggie Tucker,' she said, sitting down at Mrs Sparrow's gesture.

'What is the matter?'

'This,' said Aggie, placing the newspaper showing the advert on the desk.

'This?' The supervisor pulled the paper towards her and frowned.

'Yes, I want to apply for the job.'

Mrs Sparrow smiled. 'This job? The Women's Police Service?'

Aggie nodded. 'I think I can do it.'

'Don't be silly, dear, of course you can't. The Women's Police Service will only take educated ladies of means, not factory girls. They police the factory girls, as well you know.' Mrs Sparrow gave her a patronising smile and looked at the door.

Aggie was not to be put off. 'But you could get me off your books, Mrs Sparrow.' At that, the supervisor looked back at her. 'I know the factory is reducing its staff. I've been a hard worker here, I haven't caused any trouble, and I helped that man in the guncotton fire.' She took a breath. 'I know these girls, Mrs Sparrow, the factory girls and the local girls around here, I know them better than the women police who patronise them. They'd trust me.' The supervisor frowned and laughed. 'And I'm worried about my job here and what I'd do after the war.'

'Oh, you know when the war will end?' said the supervisor in a tone thick with disdain.

'Course not, no, but everyone's saying it'll be soon, aren't they?'

'And you think the Women's Police Service will continue after the war?'

'Well, they might.'

Mrs Sparrow shrugged. 'I suppose they might. There is a higher likelihood of those women having their jobs than the munitions workers, in any case.'

Aggie stayed quiet while Mrs Sparrow thought about it.

'You have been a good worker for the company and you're a bright girl. You haven't been caught up in any of the unrest we've had here. And I saw you help the man in the fire. You were very brave,' she added, sombrely. 'Very brave indeed. I might be able to have a word for you.' Aggie's heart jumped in her chest. 'The Ministry of Munitions funds the WPS here, and of course we work very closely with the Minister. It would be unheard of, mind you, someone from the working classes. The WPS is made up of well-bred, educated women, although some of them are suffragette types, you know,' she added in a lower voice, 'which does lower their respectability in some people's minds.'

Aggie nodded and waited.

'I shall write to the sub-inspector of the local WPS and see what she says. I wouldn't hold your breath, Agnes.'

Aggie whispered thank you and tiptoed out of the office, letting a broad smile spread across her face when she emerged into the sunshine.

2

Mim

'Come along now, girls, let's get you into work.'

Mim took the arm of one of the factory girls hanging around at the Greygoose gates and steered her through, mindful that Sub-Inspector Eglantine Nash was observing her. *These girls, always trying to dodge work. It's the cordite girls refusing to work this week, next week it will be something else*, the sub-inspector had told her.

'Can't we wait a minute to let it blow over?' said the factory girl, who tried to shake Mim away. 'It's a bit much if we just waltz into work past them.'

'Get those shirkers inside, Sergeant Rathbone,' called the sub-inspector.

'Come along,' said Mim, taking the girl's arm and steering her towards the gate.

They are striking for their jobs when the Ministry of Munitions forbids it yet they are happy enough to hang around and shirk their duty at any opportunity.

'They're only afraid for their livelihoods,' said the girl.

'Well, there'll be plenty of work in service when the factory closes down,' said Mim. 'Off you go now.' She sent them into the change hut and stood outside ready to hurry them up. Sometimes it was like looking after children. Most of the girls were all right, but some were insolent and ill-mannered. Mim knew she did a valuable job, keeping the girls on the right moral path, and she preferred doing things her own way when the militant sub-inspector wasn't around barking orders. The two workers came out of the change hut dressed in their cotton whites. Mim looked them over with her expert eye and saw that one of them wore a ring. She had to confiscate it – metal was not allowed past the factory gates, it was a severe explosion hazard. The girls had to wear rubber wellingtons or shoe coverings when they entered the work sheds – even a piece of grit on the sole of a shoe could make a spark and send the whole place up. The girl didn't like handing over her ring, but it wasn't the end of the world, she'd get it back later. She gave Mim a steely look and went off to the shed in the danger area. She needn't have been nasty about what the factory girls said about Mim, who was only doing her job, just as they were. Mim thought she recognised her from East Tilbury village, thought she lived in one of the small houses near the fort. The village was on Mim's patrol area, because of the soldiers stationed at Coalhouse Fort and the local girls who hung around there. She also patrolled Corringham, Stanford and today the factory. It was too much for one sergeant – she had asked for more help but the funding wasn't there.

Walking back to the factory gates, Mim wondered what the factory girls said about her. They probably thought she was a busybody or somesuch.

'Frightful, isn't it?' Constable Firman, one of the regular women officers at the factory, who was full of bluster and lacked confidence when push came to shove, strode over to Mim. 'Mind helping move this lot on?'

Mim nodded. The cordite girls were being held to one side to let the other workers through. With her back rod-straight and her tone crisp to command an air of authority, Mim raised her reedy voice above the noise. She swallowed hard. Sub-Inspector Nash was watching her closely.

'Under the Ministry of Munitions Act 1915, you are forbidden to strike. If you do not return to work immediately, you shall be dismissed.' Mim knew that the altercation would need to be decided by a works tribunal but she needed to clear this lot back to work and avoid any unnecessary fuss. 'Any concerns should be addressed first to Mrs Sparrow, who will refer them to the factory management, and if necessary the ministry, for consideration.'

The cordite girls mumbled amongst themselves and seemed to decide on a course of action. They had made their point for now, at least, and didn't want to lose their jobs prematurely. They scowled at Mim and trudged off to the change huts.

'That shan't be the last of it, if I know these girls,' said Constable Firman, her accent betraying her upper-class credentials.

'Indeed,' said Mim, eyeing the workers. She admired the girls for rolling up their sleeves and doing the hard men's work in the factory while the boys were away fighting. But they were such silly things, so impressionable. Some of them had left home prematurely, without first being married, and were living in local lodgings or here in the factory village, without the guidance of their fathers. They had money in their pockets and didn't hesitate to spend it on gaudy clothes and silly hats and ribbons. Or waste it in the local public houses or the dreaded music halls. The factory girls wanted a good time, they worked hard and they felt justified in lowering their morals. But such an attitude was terribly dangerous. They needed Mim and the other women's police officers to guide them, to show them how to behave.

Mim walked slowly behind the cordite girls to see them into the change hut. Once in, she took a turn around the danger area to look for shirkers. Some of the workers took the change of shift as an opportunity to slip away somewhere and feign a headache. She checked the outhouses around the black powder sheds and found it all in order. She strode along the raised wooden tramway to the cordite drying sheds and around the back to the lavatory. If she stood on tiptoe she could peep over the top of the door. A girl sat on the bowl, fast asleep. She took her umbrella and rapped hard on the door, making the girl wake with a shriek.

'Oh, you bleeder,' said the girl, coming out. 'Oh, that was a rotten trick.'

'How long have you been asleep in there?' said Mim. 'Do you know that it's twenty past six?'

'Is it?' said the girl, looking panicked. 'Oh lord, I need to get home, oh, the kids will need feeding.'

'Kids?' said Mim, thinking the girl looked awfully young.

'My brothers and sisters, miss,' said the girl. 'We're on

our own, that's why I'm doing extra hours, it's only me in work, miss.'

'Sergeant. It's Sergeant Rathbone, not Miss,' sighed Mim. She'd worked hard for her status and liked to be addressed correctly. 'Well, you'll have to come with me to Mrs Sparrow first.'

The girl gave Mim a look of horror. 'Oh, please no, Sergeant Rathbone, I'm sorry I fell asleep. I wasn't in there for long, I promise. I've got to get back.'

Mim had heard it all a hundred times before. It was hard to tell whether they were telling the truth. Lying seemed to be a natural survival instinct for these girls and although Mim often gave them the benefit of the doubt, with the sub-inspector on the factory grounds, she'd have to report this girl. 'What's your name?'

The girl hesitated. 'If you report me, I might lose my job in the next batch laid off. Please don't.' She started to cry.

'Young lady, tears are no good when you have flouted the rules. I will let you go to your family now, but I need to take your name.'

'Polly Greenway,' said the girl, searching Mim's eyes for another chance. But Mim was a professional and had to be seen to take her duty seriously. *If we let our standards slip for this girl, then this girl's standards will slip further as a consequence*, as the sub-inspector was fond of saying.

'Off you go,' said Mim. She'd give the girl's name to the welfare supervisor the next time she saw her. 'And might I advise you to be more particular about your appearance? Your fingernails are black with dirt and it looks as though you haven't run a comb through your hair in a week.'

Polly gave her a look of utter hatred but Mim was used to that by now. Many of the girls didn't observe the fundamental rules of cleanliness and appearance – they were lucky Mim could guide them with a kind word. She headed back onto the main thoroughfare and along to the change huts to make sure the cordite girls weren't in there dreaming up another plan of action. It was a long wooden hut, the walls lined with hundreds of thin lockers, some of which weren't locked, the clothing and shoes spilling out of them. Mim tutted at the mess. The girls took little care about keeping things in a neat order. But they had all gone off to work and Mim was relieved that they had responded to her authority. As she turned to leave, she heard a sound, something falling out of a locker perhaps. She paced down one of the rows and peered into the gloom.

'Is anyone there?' she called.

There was no answer. She made her way to the end of a row to the long washing troughs and saw a girl cowering there in the corner. 'Sorry, Constable,' she said, jumping up and making her way past. But Mim caught her arm.

'What are you doing in here?' said Mim. 'Open your hand.' She gripped the girl's arm and used her most authoritative voice.

'Nothing, Constable,' said the girl, who was scruffy and blonde and had a sly sort of look about her.

'Sergeant. Sergeant Rathbone,' said Mim, for the hundredth time. 'I said, open your hand.'

The girl opened her hand and there in her palm lay four or five of the new one pound notes.

'Thief,' said Mim, and the look on the girl's face told her

she was right. 'And is that a hairpin? Come with me.' Mim took the girl's arm and led her out of the change hut, along the road and to the administration block to Mrs Sparrow's office. Hairpins were forbidden in the factory; those and cigarettes, matches, metal of any kind. And Mim could not abide stealing. The girl went with her readily enough but refrained from the usual arguments that Mim heard.

'What have we here?' said the welfare supervisor.

'A thief, Mrs Sparrow,' said Mim. 'I caught her rifling through the change hut just now.'

'Is this true?' said Mrs Sparrow.

The girl shrugged and Mim felt a shot of despair go through her. The insolence of the girl.

'I need the money. My brother needs medicine. He's back from the war and needs his medicine.'

'Good Lord, you earn a decent wage here. Ella, isn't it?' said Mrs Sparrow, and the girl nodded. 'I shall have to call the local constabulary and I'm afraid you'll find yourself before the magistrate. This is most disappointing, Ella.'

Mrs Sparrow picked up the telephone and asked for a local constable to collect Ella. She locked her into the room next to the office while they waited. Mim would have liked to have escorted the girl to the local police station herself but women police had no powers of arrest.

'A cup of tea?' she asked Mim and Mim nodded gratefully and took a chair opposite Mrs Sparrow's desk.

'Thank you for dispersing the unpleasantness earlier,' said Mrs Sparrow. 'The girls are nervous about their jobs, understandably, but we can't have disorder here. It's preferable if they go back to work for now but next time there's a strike, we'll have to call in the constabulary to start making arrests, else they'll think they have a licence to do it. For now I'll dock their wages and put them on a week's suspension.'

Mim nodded. The Greygoose munitions factory was overseen by the Ministry of Munitions in terms of wages and tribunals and so on, but it was a private establishment and in a remote location, which meant that Mrs Sparrow was self-governing to a large extent and got away with a deal more than if she worked at the Woolwich Arsenal. She'd only involve the women's police service if necessary and meted out her own punishments effectively enough. She was responsible for everything to do with the women workers, from interviews to health checks to discipline and dispersing unrest. She was known for dismissing a worker who was demonstrably undesirable. She was a powerful woman and Mim was a little intimidated by her.

'I am afraid I shall be scraping them off the pavements later and turning them out of shop doorways,' said Mim, sighing. Her evening duties often saw her dealing with drunken factory girls in the streets. Mrs Sparrow nodded and lit the gas on her little stove. 'It's just as well they shan't be able to vote in the next election, the way they behave.'

Mim was beside herself with joy that she was one of the women given the vote in February. That was the advantage of having a husband with property. And luckily she had just turned thirty. It had all aligned for her. Those years of campaigning with the local suffrage society had paid off.

'Their husbands are away,' sighed Mrs Sparrow. 'What else should we expect? There is no one to keep authority.'

'At least if the factory closes, there may be a chance I'll

have my cook and housemaid back,' said Mim, accepting her cup of tea.

'They might be unrecognisable,' said Mrs Sparrow, settling into her chair. 'The things they waste their money on. Silk stockings and taxis, furs and ribbons. Can they ever go back to their pre-war selves?'

'They'll have to. These women need to work to pay the rent. At least they'll be back to a decent existence. I do worry about them, their wayward silliness. If their behaviour matched their new-found taste in clothing . . .'

'They are akin to wild animals let out of a cage,' said Mrs Sparrow. 'A whiff of freedom and money and they are dressing above their station. But their behaviour hardly matches their new appearance. It is a grotesque anomaly. They roll around drunk in the street, they allow themselves to be propositioned by men in uniform, or even initiate the proposition themselves.'

Mim nodded. These were women who would bathe their babies in a frying pan when they settled down. Why were they squandering their money now on furs? All too soon they'd be unable to turn their mattresses for fear of disturbing the nests of fleas and bedbugs beneath. Their crass talk, their trousers and grime. They'd soon be in Orsett workhouse for lack of rent money if they lost their jobs at the factory. Yet Mim would find them in the public houses, drinking their hard-earned money away.

'Well, I must be on my rounds. A quick check of the marshes and I'll be heading back to East Tilbury. How I wish the ministry would fund a constable for me – I am absolutely exhausted, the area is simply too large to patrol alone.' Mim took out her notepad to give Mrs Sparrow the name of the girl she caught sleeping on the lavatory but thought better of it. She'd let her off this time. 'Thank you for the tea, Mrs Sparrow.'

Mim retrieved her bicycle at the factory gates and nodded goodbye to Constable Firman, who was happily patrolling the factory entrance now the protesting workers had gone to their work sheds.

'I'll check the Goosetown marshes on my way out,' called Mim and took the road that led to the company village a half mile away. The wild marshes were a hostile place, blown ragged by the bloated Thames. The workers came from miles around, some commuted from Southend and Barking. Many lived in the colony of dorm huts in the village – there were prostitutes from London and tin miners from Cornwall amongst them. The men and women were kept strictly apart by the company – separate change rooms and separate dorm huts – but they managed to find a way to behave immorally despite this, and that's where Mim and her colleagues came in. She'd often found couples hiding on the marshes tangled in compromising attitudes amongst the thistles, nettles and gorse. She was at a loss to understand why they would want to be out here, with the standing water, the bogs and brambles, just like animals.

She cycled along the main road of the little workers' village, her eye ever searching for improper behaviour. Past the grocer, past the village hall, and back out onto the marshes, to pedal her way over the rough ground to East Tilbury village where she lived. The Thames Haven peninsula was surrounded on three sides by water – Holehaven Creek,

Shell Haven Creek and of course the grey Thames. It was the perfect location for a munitions factory. If it blew it would be contained. The cattle of the eighteen hundreds had been replaced by factories and oil refineries – large petroleum vessels being forbidden past Thames Haven to protect London – there'd be some pretty fireworks if it all went up.

The sun had started its descent and, on cue, Mim's stomach rumbled its discontent. She faced the grim prospect of cooking supper and had planned a pea and haricot soup. She and Bertie had lost their housemaid and their cook to war work. Mim had very little experience of the housekeeping and food shopping that was required of her now and could only hope that more women would turn back to domestic work now there was the threat of the munitions factory closing. Cycling faster, she bumped over the mounds of grass and clods of earth until she came to the main road running up to the village, past the gravel quarries and ploughed barley fields. Her uniform was made of thick worsted wool and she started to perspire in the August warmth as she made her way up the hill, getting off to push her bike. Her house was on the edge of the village, a large detached Victorian pile over three floors with seven bedrooms, a wine cellar and an acre of landscaped grounds. A mansion, some would say, but small compared to Gobions or St Clere's.

Bertie had inherited well and Mim came from a good family of bankers. They had moved to East Tilbury before the war to be near the docks where Bertie dealt in contracts to refurbish passenger liners. Mim had never seen the Yorkshire moors but imagined the Thurrock marshes something like the setting of *Wuthering Heights*, but damper and lower-lying. She hadn't liked the area very well at first but it had grown on her and Bertie had done well. Now with the navy requisitioning passenger ships for the war, Bertie had won contracts to convert liners into hospital ships and even armed boats for the mercantile marine. It was busy business and he was rarely at home. It wasn't often that Mim saw him before eleven o'clock at night. Still, she was lucky he was exempt from conscription, very lucky. He was safe and she thanked God for that.

Pulling into the drive, she parked her bike and let herself into the front door. Sighing, she took off her coat and walked to the kitchen, rolling up her sleeves. The house needed a good clean but she had neither the time nor the inclination. Cooking the meals and washing the dishes was enough. To her surprise, the air-raid siren suddenly sounded from the fort. A long loud whine that was impossible to ignore. She switched into patrol mode and ran outside, grabbing her bicycle. Air raids had dropped off over the recent months – there had been a large and frightful Gotha raid in May, and one Zeppelin had gone over last week – but the searchlights still swept the skies every evening and people continued to fear more bombings. It was part of her duties to tour the area to ensure that all women and children were under cover. It was suppertime and the village was deserted but for a few people running for cover or coming out from houses to pull their children indoors. Mim scanned the roads and gardens and pulled up alongside the Ship public house to look in through the window. Thurrock was a restricted area and public houses were under orders to stop serving drinks at eight o'clock. The punters usually made the most of the time they had at the bar.

Tutting, she pushed in through the door. It seemed that the air-raid siren had not been heard by anyone inside.

'Your attention, please,' she called loudly, the customers and proprietor quietening where they saw her uniform. 'There is an air-raid warning. Would you kindly make your way to the basement of the establishment.'

There were several groans. Three servicemen grabbed their caps and raced out of the door back to the camp at the fort. Mim didn't have time to make sure they all did as she said, or to have a word with the proprietor, who she found exasperating. She had the rest of the village to check. *It's too much*, she muttered to herself. *I need a constable to help me.* Trying to rush away, her foot caught on the pedal of her bike and the chain slipped off. There was no time to put it back on so she trotted away on foot, down to the fort perimeter. Two young women with fancy hats and painted faces were rushing out of the army camp and swore under their breath when they saw Mim.

'What on earth are you doing in there?' demanded Mim. She had seen these two several times in the public house with soldiers and suspected them of hanging around the camp.

'Sorry, miss,' they said and ran away. Ordinarily Mim would have been after them to administer a sharp reprimand and warning but she could hear a loud hum in the sky – it was the Gothas approaching. They hadn't had a raid for some time, and she hoped this wasn't a renewed effort on the part of the Germans. The village was on the flight path to London and with Coalhouse Fort it was an obvious target. But after four years of Zeppelins and the new flying machines, some of the locals were complacent.

'Get inside,' she shouted to a woman who was dashing along the road.

'It's my Marcie, she went out foraging and I can't see her,' said the woman, standing to stare up at the sky.

'How old?' said Mim, frowning.

'Seven,' said the woman, holding her hand at her hip to indicate the child's height.

'Come on,' said Mim, 'I'll look with you.' She knew the woman would refuse to get to safety without her child. They rushed together through the houses and out to the scrubland at the back that led to the chalk quarry. Two German planes went over and the women ducked, as though that would do any good. Mim searched the sky for any sign of more enemy aircraft. The Gothas flew away over the Thames on a course for London.

'Marcie!' the woman called, seeing her daughter in the distance, emerging from behind a tree. 'Oh, there she is,' she said running away towards the child. Mim watched as the woman reached the little girl and pulled her roughly by the arm, her cross voice reaching Mim's ears. The girl started to cry and she gestured to the ground at the greenery she had dropped. The woman softened and picked up the plants with the edge of her apron.

'Nettles,' said the woman with exasperation, when they reached Mim. 'She was collecting nettles for soup.'

The little girl looked at Mim fearfully. She wore a little pin on her lapel that said I EAT LESS BREAD. It was a householder's pledge, something the schoolchildren were encouraged to follow.

Mim smiled at the girl. 'If you hear the siren, run to your mother straight away.'

'Yes, miss,' said the girl.

'And enjoy your soup,' added Mim, turning to walk back to the main road. There was a tug at her skirts. Marcie was there, holding out several nettle stems to her.

'For your soup,' she said.

'Thank you,' said Mim, taking the nettles, glad that she wore gloves. The girl looked pleased. Mim's heart turned over. She imagined the girl as her own child. She'd take her little hand and they'd walk home together, Mim reminding her softly that she was not to go off wandering alone. They would wash the nettles and stir them into the soup, chattering about how they had made a meal without bread and weren't they doing terribly well for the war effort. Mim watched the girl's mother lead the child away by the hand, as though the two were joined, just like the paper-chain dolls Mim made as a child.

At home, Mim sat with a cup of tea in her sitting room. The child had made her pensive. She took her notepad out of her uniform pocket. Something fell to the floor with a ping and rolled underneath the armchair.

'Blast,' she said, retrieving it. The factory girl's wedding ring. She'd forgotten to hand it in at the gate.

3

Aggie

Aggie had been called to Mrs Sparrow's office. The welfare supervisor poured herself a cup of tea, taking her time to give Aggie the news.

'The Ministry of Munitions has agreed to transfer you to the Women's Police Service for training,' she said, stirring her tea slowly, a look of amusement on her face.

Aggie sat forward in her seat, rushing with excitement. 'Have they?'

'Yes, and Sub-Inspector Nash is astonished that you shall be joining them.'

Aggie smiled uncertainly and swallowed.

'This *is* what you wanted?' said Mrs Sparrow.

'Yes,' she whispered. 'Yes, thank you, Mrs Sparrow. When do I start?'

'Forthwith.'

'Now?'

'Yes. There are two other new recruits starting their train-ing today. At the Tilbury Docks headquarters, so you can join immediately. I would have told you last week but I have been away on business.'

You could have told me in a letter, thought Aggie, *instead of telling me the day I start*.

'It's on Dock Road, a few units along from the police sta-tion. Are you a union member?'

The question surprised Aggie. She shook her head.

'You'll need to pay a shilling to join the WSPU, the Women's Social and Political Union. They are behind the WPS.'

'Is that the Pankhursts' one?'

'Ironic, isn't it? Before the war they were setting fire to houses and being locked up in prison, and now they are the ones in uniform. In fact, I do believe the sub-inspector herself was once force-fed in prison.'

Aggie couldn't believe she'd been accepted for training. She was terrified now it was a reality.

'Please don't take this in the wrong way but I shall be glad to get you off my books. There will be another wave of redundancies here very soon.'

Mrs Sparrow looked at Aggie meaningfully. There would be no job to come back to if Aggie failed.

'The Women's Police think our munitions girls very rough. Rough and impressionable and insolent. They are women of high birth, remember. You'll have to be on your guard and do your best to make a good impression. The higher ranks have cropped hair and ride motorcycles, most extraordinary. It's a bitter pill for the local bobbies going around in a pony and trap. Well, good luck,' she said, standing up and holding out her hand. Aggie took it. 'I shall no doubt see you on your patrol training in due course, if you last that long.'

'By the way,' said Aggie. 'One of those police ladies, Sergeant Rathbone, took my wedding ring. I've asked about it but she didn't hand it in.' She wished she could add a comment about good manners and high birth but she held her tongue.

'Oh, an oversight I am sure. I've no doubt that Sergeant Rathbone will return it.'

On the train from Corringham to Tilbury, Aggie wished she was better prepared for the job she was going for. She'd just have to bluff it and hope for the best. Wanting to prove Mrs Sparrow wrong was incentive enough. She got off the train and headed for Dock Road, found the police station and kept walking until she came to a large house-like building with a sign saying WOMEN'S POLICE SERVICE on the front wall. Looking down at herself she decided she looked smart enough in her skirt and jacket. She'd given her boots a surreptitious polish with her handkerchief on the train but they needed a proper clean.

Pushing through the heavy front door she found herself in a large hallway, an open door to her left with a woman in police uniform sitting at a desk. The woman looked up with a small smile.

'Hello, I'm here for my training,' said Aggie, feeling too warm in her jacket.

The officer frowned and shook her head. 'I'm sorry, I thought you said training?'

'Yes, that's right. Mrs Sparrow at Greygoose factory fixed it up with the sub-inspector . . . Nash . . . ' she said, struggling to remember the name.

The officer stared at her, making Aggie squirm. It was clear that no one had told her that Aggie was coming. 'One moment please,' she said. 'Take a seat.'

Aggie sat and waited with her hands in her lap and her back straight until another woman officer came in.

'Good morning, I am Sergeant Wills. I understand you are here for training?'

'Yes, that's right,' said Aggie, and on hearing her accent the first officer looked at the sergeant.

'I'm awfully sorry but we are not expecting you. Did you say that Mrs Sparrow has arranged for you to come?'

'Yes,' said Aggie, frustrated at what was not the best of starts.

The officers turned at the sound of a motorcycle pulling up outside the open front window.

'Ah, here's the sub-inspector now,' said Sergeant Wills. 'We'll have this cleared up in a jiffy.'

In walked a statuesque woman. Tall, lean, immaculate uniform and a flat hat with silver trim, unlike the soup bowl-shaped hats the other women officers wore. Aggie gawped when she took off her hat to reveal a military-style, close-cropped hair style.

'Sub-Inspector,' said the sergeant stepping forwards. 'We have something of an awkward situation. The lady here has come for her training.'

'Ah yes, Mrs Tucker, isn't it?'

With a sigh of relief, Aggie nodded, noticing the look of shock on the sergeant's face.

'But . . .' said the sergeant.

'Yes, indeed,' said the sub-inspector. 'Indeed.' She shook her head at the sergeant. 'This way, if you please, Mrs Tucker.'

Aggie trotted after the long stride of the sub-inspector, through a doorway and into a large room at the back of the building. Two well-dressed women sitting in wooden chairs turned at the sound and stood up slowly.

'Ah, Lady Braithwaite? Mrs Parkington?' The ladies intoned their greetings with cut-glass accents. 'Please, do sit down.'

Aggie joined them, smiling, and the women returned her smile with quizzical glances at her clothes, and her boots, which Aggie positioned beneath her chair out of sight.

Standing before them, the sub-inspector looked formidable in her tall shining boots and breeches. Aggie stayed as still as she could in her chair, but had half a mind to bolt for the door.

'Thank you for enlisting to train with the Women's Police Service,' started the sub-inspector, her voice strong and authoritative. 'If you are not currently a member of the WSPU then please see me at the end. You shall need to rescind membership of any other union – we do ask for loyalty and dedication to our cause.' She paused to wait for dissenters. 'The Commissioner of Police has given us approval to train and deploy women police officers. The Ministry of Munitions have asked us to provide several hundred officers to police their munitions factories and surrounding areas. To date we have trained over one thousand recruits, who have been deployed around the country. This is an extraordinary achievement.'

Lady Braithwaite and Mrs Parkington clapped their gloved hands delicately in muted applause and Aggie joined in.

'Traditionally we have trained only women of high birth who can self-fund their positions, women who have the education to oversee the morals of working women and their children. However, it appears that with the Ministry of Munitions salary attached, we are now attracting women from other areas of society.' The sub-inspector looked directly at Aggie and Aggie felt her face burn red. 'It remains to be seen whether this is beneficial. I am afraid I suspect not.'

The other recruits said nothing but nodded their heads ever so slightly and Aggie looked at her lap.

'As yet we have no official powers of arrest, we are permitted neither handcuffs nor truncheon. We have only the deference our social positions command, and this is not to be underestimated.'

Aggie's face continued to burn at the sub-inspector's implication that she wouldn't get the workers' respect because she didn't have a posh voice.

'Moving on, may I welcome you to Tilbury, affectionately known as Nanny Goat's Island. You shall receive some instructional training here at headquarters but largely you shall be trained on the ground, on patrol around Tilbury. Should you successfully pass the six weeks' training you shall subsequently be informed of your posting, whereupon you will begin a three month probation period on the job, so to speak.'

Aggie wanted to ask where she might be posted but didn't dare – the sub-inspector hardly seemed to want to train her, let alone have her out on patrol.

'As you are no doubt aware,' continued the sub-inspector, taking slow paces up and down with her hands in her breeches pockets, which Aggie thought looked very manly, 'this war has brought many challenges, at home as well as abroad. Women have taken up the mantle and thrown themselves into war work unreservedly, which is commendable, of course. However, many young women have left home prematurely to work in munitions, to live without their families' censorship. The girls are frivolous with their money, spend their social time inappropriately, and have unescorted access to male company. Here in Tilbury we have an encampment of army personnel, which is a veritable honey pot to these girls, and to other girls who choose not to work in a worthy profession but in the oldest and most unworthy – they sell themselves for money.'

Mrs Parkington let out a tiny gasp and the sub-inspector paused to let the awful truth sink in.

'Police work, Mrs Parkington, is not for the faint-hearted. The problems I speak of lead to worse problems still. One of the worst is venereal disease. It is our enemy at home. It can wipe out an army division. It is our duty to police these women, to encourage them to uphold their moral dignity; it is our duty to steer them away from the darkness and into the light.'

Aggie twisted her hands in consternation. The sub-inspector seemed to be implying that the munitions workers were practically as bad as the prostitutes. It was a gross exaggeration.

'We have yet to win over our male colleagues,' said the sub-inspector in grave tones. 'When senior ranks at New Scotland Yard are stating that there will never be official lady police officers, when our own chief constable here at Tilbury is loath to pay our wages or even properly acknowledge us, we must remember that the Ministry of Munitions have asked us to provide officers because our services are urgently needed.'

The sub-inspector paused and clapped her hands together once as though applauding her own speech.

'Our co-founder Margaret Damer Dawson wants us to be able to protect ourselves, wishes us to appear intimidating to criminals,' she went on. 'There is no room for shrinking violets here. This is why you shall learn the art of ju-jitsu, a discipline that will give you the confidence to defend yourselves when necessary. Lady Braithwaite, if you wouldn't mind stepping up?'

With a start, the lady put down her handbag on the seat and stood up. From her enormous adorned hat to her wasp-waisted dress and silk stockings, she was a picture of delicate upper-class finery. Aggie could not imagine her doing ju-jitsu.

'Please remove your hat, Lady Braithwaite,' said the sub-inspector with a hint of impatience, taking off her own.

'Of course,' said the lady, hurriedly unpinning her hat.

'Ju-jitsu is an ancient and noble Japanese martial art that uses the attacker's force against them,' explained the sub-inspector, rolling up her sleeves. 'I shall demonstrate. Lady Braithwaite, attack me.'

Aggie stared with fascination. Surely this well-dressed woman would falter. Lady Braithwaite stood hesitantly before the sub-inspector and glanced nervously at Mrs Parkington, the latter putting a gloved hand over her mouth. The sub-inspector stood waiting, poised for action. Lady Braithwaite raised her gloved hand half-heartedly and stepped towards the sub-inspector, making a feeble punching action. The sub-inspector blocked the offending hand with her arm and, in the blink of an eye, put her other hand on Lady Braithwaite's chest and pulled her down onto the ground, holding her arm back in a painful position to keep her there on the floor.

Aggie and Mrs Parkington looked at one another in alarm.

'A woman of any size can perform this action on a man of any size,' explained the sub-inspector, breathless and bright-eyed. 'Because I used her own weight against her. Thank you, Lady Braithwaite,' she said, releasing her hold and motioning for her ladyship to stand up.

Aggie realised she'd been holding her breath. She hoped she wouldn't be asked to come forward next. Lady Braithwaite stood up, smoothing down her skirt. The sub-inspector turned away to retrieve her hat and to Aggie's astonishment Lady Braithwaite took a rapid step forward and grabbed the sub-inspector from behind. The sub-inspector went rigid and made to turn, trying to explain that the demonstration had ended, but as she pivoted, Lady Braithwaite also turned and reached back to take the top of the sub-inspector's arm. The officer saw the move and reacted, trying to wrest back control. Aggie watched open-mouthed as the two women struggled for a moment, each one digging her heels into the floor and trying to find an advantage. Finally Lady Braithwaite pushed her body into the officer's and pulled her right off the floor, over her own shoulder, to land with an audible thump on the wooden parquet boards.

Lady Braithwaite stood back, allowing the sub-inspector to stand up. 'I say,' said the officer, rubbing her shoulder, 'what in heaven's name?'

'I trained with Edith Garrud in 1914, Sub-Inspector. I would have thought you would have been aware of this?'

The sub-inspector opened her mouth in surprise and then she laughed. 'I was not aware, Lady Braithwaite. I commend your skill, you caught me off guard.'

Aggie could feel herself dissolving into giggles and did her best to frown and concentrate on the herringbone pattern of the parquet flooring. It really was too funny to see these women throwing each other around politely. It was quite different from the women Aggie knew – if there was a fight at the factory it was arms and legs flying in the dust, screeching and wailing with onlookers cheering.

The sub-inspector stood with her hands on her hips to regain her authority. 'This gives you a good idea of the techniques you shall be learning,' she said to Aggie and Mrs Parkington. 'Self-defence is only one aspect of your training. We shall also cover the study of first aid and criminal law, signalling, report writing and court procedure, and of course how to patrol the local area. Tilbury is a bustling port town with a thriving community. There are the usual dockside problems such as the red-light district and multiple nationalities who don't always see eye to eye. Wartime only adds a layer of new challenges. We have encampments of commonwealth soldiers in the open fields to the east of the town and billeted in many houses in the town itself. As is happening all over the country, there are women and men associating inappropriately and a general sense of desperation in the face of the unknown. Our country is grieving for our lost men. Here in Tilbury there are many women widowed, their men based here in the mercantile marine lost at sea. A large number of local men have enlisted, a large number have protected jobs in the docks. And of course, Tilbury is a prime target for German bombers.'

She paused to find her train of thought. 'We are in the thick of things here. Once the boys leave the camps to find entertainment in the town, their commanding officers turn a blind eye. The men in uniform are seen almost as untouchable, immune to the law. Remember that we do not police the men. We are here to oversee women and children and prevent acts of immorality or indecency. Always be mindful that our overarching objective is to be seen as an effective and indispensable force, one that will continue to be needed when this war is over.'

Aggie smiled. It was the first time she felt she'd made the right decision. If these women wanted to make sure there was a women's police service in peacetime then she would have a decent job and not have to go back to domestic service.

'We shall cover a lot of this on the ground. Sergeant Wills, whom you met on arrival, will shortly demonstrate some first aid techniques, then we shall have supper and then I will take you on your first patrol when darkness falls at eight and the criminal classes are out on the streets.'

A flutter of nerves ran through Aggie's body. Criminal classes on the streets in the dark sounded a far cry from the striking factory girls at Greygoose munitions. 'Mrs Tucker, if you wouldn't mind completing some administrative details?' Sub-Inspector Nash motioned for Aggie to follow her to a trestle table set up in the corner.

The sub-inspector pushed a piece of typed paper over to her. 'Please complete this,' she said. Aggie took a seat and read the top of the page. *A Declaration of Loyal Adherence to the Policies of the Women's Social and Political Union.* There followed a summary of the union's policies, a declaration, space for the member's name and address and a line on which to sign.

'Why do I have to sign this?' said Aggie tentatively. 'Aren't they the suffragettes?'

'The WSPU is a suffrage army, yes,' said the sub-inspector testily. 'However, I am sure you are aware that the suffrage campaign ceased when war broke out and that the Representation of the People Act came into force in February. Mrs Pankhurst encourages her members into war work. Only ardent believers in women's enfranchisement should endeavour to become part of the Women's Police Service. I do hope you *are* an ardent believer, Mrs Tucker?'

Aggie remembered what Mrs Sparrow had told her, that the sub-inspector had been jailed and force-fed with the suffragettes before the war. She looked at Aggie with a tinge of bemusement as though goading her to say something ill-informed, stupid or offensive, as though she had used complicated language to put Aggie off, to dissuade her from trespassing into a 'gentlewomen's profession'. But Aggie merely nodded, dipped her pen and wrote her name and address. With only the slightest pause, she signed her name and slid the paper back.

'I see you live in East Tilbury village?' said the sub-inspector, clearly dissatisfied that Aggie had signed the declaration. 'Had you been lodging at the Goosetown colony prior to that?'

'No, me and my husband rent a house in East Tilbury so I used to walk to the factory from there.'

'And your husband is away on service?'

Aggie nodded.

'And you have no children?'

'That's right,' said Aggie stiffly.

'Interesting. I would have thought the troops stationed at Coalhouse Fort would have requisitioned your house for billeting purposes.'

'But I'd have nowhere to live,' said Aggie, frowning.

'Single women live in lodgings together. We do what we must during this war,' stated the sub-inspector, and she wrote something down in a little pad of paper. Aggie wanted to ask her what she was writing; she hoped the sub-inspector wasn't planning to interfere with her living arrangements. That was not something she had signed up for.

'One shilling, please,' said the sub-inspector. 'A token amount for membership to the WSPU.'

Aggie dug in her bag for a shilling and handed it over. A shilling. It seemed symbolic somehow. Her Arnie had taken the King's shilling when he'd enlisted. Now Aggie was handing the same amount back.

'The training period is six weeks,' said the sub-inspector. 'If you are successful, you'll be sworn in under the orders of the local chief constable and will be permitted to wear the WPS uniform, which you shall acquire from Harrods and maintain at your own expense.' Aggie flinched at the idea of buying and cleaning an expensive Harrods uniform. The sub-inspector knew it and smiled. The officer's own uniform was a dark blue military-style belted jacket with silver letters spelling WPS on the shoulders. The sub-inspector wore breeches, presumably for her motorcycle, but the other WPS officers wore a skirt that stopped shockingly short of the ankle, and a white blouse and dark blue tie. It looked well-made and expensive. Aggie couldn't wait to see herself wearing it.

'We advise shooting boots. We have found that dress boots are inadequate in the weather and marshland.' Aggie tried to get a better look under the table but couldn't see what the officer meant by shooting boots. 'We are accused by the public of lacking charm if we appear too manly, and weak and incompetent if too feminine.' She rolled her eyes.

'Should you pass the training, and not everyone does' – *and I very much doubt you will*, Aggie imagined her thinking – 'you shall be placed on a three month probation period, at the end of which time you will be made a fully trained member of the WPS. Not a few recruits have run home with their tail between their legs. It takes a strong and sturdy character to do well here. The working classes show an inherent deference to us; I am at a loss to know how you will cope at all.'

'A couple of weeks back, one of your officers, Sergeant Rathbone, took my wedding ring off me at the factory because the thread had come off and she hasn't given it back.' Aggie did her best to keep a neutral expression.

'Sergeant Rathbone? She is one of our best, I am sure it was an oversight.'

'Yes, I'm sure,' said Aggie. 'I just thought I'd mention it because my husband is away fighting and I'd like my ring back.'

'Yes, yes of course.' The sub-inspector frowned. 'If we could continue? For the duration of the training you will be expected to wear your hair back in a tight bun, dress in dark plain clothing and wear this armband denoting that you are with us. You will be given an umbrella and a lantern to carry when on patrol.' She pushed a folded armband across the table top but kept her finger on it when Aggie reached out.

'There is an allowance made by the Ministry of Munitions of twenty-four shillings per week for the duration of the training period, followed by a salary of two pounds per week should you qualify for constable status.' Keeping her finger on the armband, Sub-Inspector Nash eyed Aggie keenly. 'We have it difficult enough here at the docks, but if you make it through the training you are likely to be posted in the Orsett Rural District, which covers Greygoose munitions. You will effectively be policing the very women you have called your colleagues. Does this not make you reconsider?'

Aggie remembered how she felt as a munitions girl. The sub-inspector's attitude rankled. Aggie knew her place, of course. But still, she returned the officer's stare. This was her chance to do things differently.

'No, it doesn't,' said Aggie in a firm but measured tone. The sub-inspector pursed her lips and released the armband, which Aggie held tightly in her fist.

4

Mim

Mim held her new book in her hands. *Married Love* by Marie Stopes. She glanced at the door of the library but she was being unnecessarily paranoid. Bertie wouldn't be home just yet.

Opening the book to peek at the subtitle, she read: *A New Contribution to the Solution of Sex Difficulties*. Her heart jumped in her chest and she closed it again. Even purchasing the book by mail order had been very courageous of her – she had worried for two weeks that the postwoman or a neighbour would see it. But it had arrived in a discreet wrapping of brown paper and Mim had checked that there was no outward sign of what the parcel contained.

Peeking inside again, she checked the author's credentials. Doctor of Science, Doctor of Philosophy, Fellow of University College, London. There was a preface by a Dr

Jessie Murray, letters from a Professor Starling and a Father Stanislaus St John. It all seemed entirely respectable. It was just that Mim hadn't been brave enough to read it yet.

She felt a shiver of nerves. Her husband Bertie desperately needed a rest. It was why he had resolved not to work on Sunday this week. He was under an intense level of pressure, supplying the navy and mercantile from his shipyard at the docks. He said he wanted to accompany Mim to church on Sunday for the harvest festival service and then spend some time in the Hatchery – what he called his writing shed at the bottom of the garden. He was a keen military historian and had been working on a book about the Boer wars for some time. Mim wanted to take the opportunity of having him to herself.

He wasn't entirely comfortable with Mim working, especially as a policewoman. She wanted to reassure him that she took her duties as a wife very seriously, that above all else she respected her husband and subscribed to the sanctity of marriage and family. She wanted to be a good wife. The best wife. She wanted to please Bertie. She knew women whose husbands didn't allow them to work, wouldn't entertain the idea of women's suffrage, thought it vulgar that women wanted to take responsibility for themselves. Mim was lucky that Bertie allowed her these things. Her father, a man of staunch Edwardian values, would rather have pitched himself into the nearest chalk quarry.

She had joined the diplomatic National Union of Women's Suffrage Societies to campaign for the vote, avoiding the militant suffragettes because she knew Bertie would be less likely to support her, and luckily he had found the NUWSS tolerable. And now women like her had representation. She would be able to vote in the next election and, what's more, the war had afforded her a chance for a career. She hadn't fully realised before how important it was to earn her own money and not rely on the allowance that Bertie gave her.

Bertie had tolerated her joining the union and campaigning quietly for the vote, but the Women's Police Service was harder for him to bear. She wanted to thank him and reassure him. And that was why she had bought the book.

Taking a sharp breath in through her nose, she sat in a comfortable armchair and opened the book to the preface by Dr Jessie Murray. It made difficult reading. It was a frank discussion of the truths of the baser instincts and how, if not addressed in the correct manner, if not aired appropriately but repressed and silenced, they had a negative effect on a marriage.

The author's preface followed and Mim read with trepidation. The words *sex*, *sex-life*, *the art of love*, *sex-attraction*, *sex-ignorance* were mentioned with subtlety and tact but caused Mim's heart to palpitate and her sensibilities to recoil. The author promised to provide the key to a beautiful and happy marriage and at these words, Mim's eyes stung with tears. No one talked about the nuances of marriage. Young girls and boys were not told about it, young women were not told about it. Adults did not discuss it, not even with their spouses. And now this woman, this Marie Stopes, had written a book. It had been published only five months previously and had already been reprinted several times, such was its popularity. The Americans had banned it. And Mim now held it in her hands.

She gripped the volume tightly as she read the author's introduction. Stopes talked about a *glow of spiritual understanding which a solitary soul could never have attained alone . . . each heart begins to hide a sense of boundless isolation . . . secret pain . . . a sense of dull disappointment . . . at her coldness in the marital embrace . . . Only by a reverent study of the Art of Love can the beauty of its expression be realised in linked lives.*

Mim put the book down in her lap. It was a revelation. Never before had she read or heard married life being discussed in such a way. On the one hand it seemed irreverent, unrespectable, but on the other, it was a huge and freeing relief. She and Bertie had an understanding. She allowed him to perform his act when necessary. It was something she shied away from, something she could never imagine initiating. But the simple fact that he sought it out surely meant that if Mim were to be more willing, it would make him happier. From what she had read of Marie Stopes already, it seemed that Mim herself could also be the happier for it, that the repercussions of a happier marriage would mean happier homes, which would even mean a more secure State. She stared at the plain brown cover of the small book and wondered how so simple an object could contain such earth-shattering news.

The author went on to describe a woman's *sex-tide*, which men have over the ages translated as women's unpredictability, *wonderful tides, scented and enriched by the myriad experiences of the human race from its ancient days of leisure and flower-wreathed love-making* . . . Flower-wreathed love-making? Mim baulked at the idea but then warmed to it. Why shouldn't she and her husband be Shakespearean in their romance? In all honesty, she had never fully recovered from the shock of what she had found to be, on her wedding night, her wifely duties. She wondered if anything could have prepared her for such a shock. What if she had read this very book during her courtship? She wasn't sure whether the knowledge of the realities of married life would be reassuring or a terrifying obstacle.

Marie Stopes described women's fundamental pulse, explaining that normal women do have sex impulses, that it is not only depraved prostitutes who seek out the sex act. Normal women's impulses flow and recede like a tide and it is the ignorance of men not knowing when to approach their wives that makes women *a passive instrument for the man's need*. Whereas in men, desire is *always present, ever ready to wake at the lightest call*. Mim wondered at the rationale. A man must always be ready to take his chance to procreate. A woman must see through the necessary machinations of procreation. But how then are the two to live harmoniously if not with mutual understanding?

Mim had never before pondered the subject to such an extent. But something was happening to her as she read. She felt undeniable stirrings in her and instead of repressing them as unnatural, she took a breath and closed her eyes and allowed herself to feel them. She imagined Bertie coming home and felt a flutter of excitement. Her face grew hot as she thought about being close to him.

The book gave an example of a wife yearning, in the heat of passion, for her husband to kiss her breast. Shyly, she had asked him and he had performed the kiss just once, quickly, and never again. Mim wondered. She and Bertie only ever pecked one another's lips or cheek. The thought of his mouth on her body made her feel limp. Dare she ask him?

She heard a key in the lock and the front door pressing

closed. Snapping the book shut, she reached on the tips of her toes to place it on the top shelf out of sight and rushed to see Bertie, blushing with her new knowledge. He removed his hat and smiled at her quizzically.

'What's this, Mimosa?' he said, calling her by her full name in a teasing reprimand. Her hair was blonde and her cheeks pink, which was what had prompted her parents to call her after the mimosa flower. It was also the flower that closes when touched. It had served as an apt description. But she no longer wanted to subscribe to the fate of her name.

'Simply doing the beastly house cleaning,' she lied, taking his hat. 'Did you have a busy day, dear?'

He puffed out his cheeks and took off his coat. 'If the Germans ceased to torpedo our ships I would be out of business.' He laughed, knowing she understood the joke. He was as much a patriot as the next man. 'I wonder if we might eat? I missed luncheon.'

'I shall do my best, as always,' said Mim, smiling and disappearing to the hateful kitchen. She had tried to get a nice cut of meat but had set herself up for failure. There had been rumour of two lambs being distributed by the butcher in Stanford-le-Hope but by the time she had finished her factory patrol, it had all gone. She'd been saving a precious tin of ham and opened it now. There were the last of the tomatoes from the garden, and some potato bread. It would have to do.

Her hands shook as she took the plates through to the dining room. Pouring Bertie a glass of water, she missed the rim and wetted the tablecloth.

'What are you up to, Mim?' said Bertie. 'Are you quite all right?'

'Yes, dear,' she said, sitting down and avoiding his eye. 'I am tired, that is all.'

'I am surprised you are not out on patrol,' he said, with a slight edge to his voice as he forked a piece of ham into his mouth.

'I whizzed round the patrol quickly so as to be able to do the shopping and cleaning,' said Mim, not wanting to talk about her work and put him in a contemplative mood. 'I could do with an early night.'

'Yes, that sounds just the ticket,' he said, leaning back with his eyes closed to chew his ham. 'There was an accident today.'

'Oh?'

'A man fell into the hold of a ship and broke his back. I shall go to the hospital tomorrow.'

'Goodness me, how awful. Does he have family?'

'Three young ones. He'll not walk again, they say.'

The food caught in Mim's throat. They were used to discussing tragedy at dinner. As was everyone in the country. The heavy fog of grief was all around them all of the time. One heard of someone's husband killed in action, or taken prisoner, or coming home with terrible injuries. It felt that the very humanity had evaporated from the earth. They were all making do, waiting, expecting disaster, trembling with the uncertainty of life as it had become. Accidents at home only compounded the terror. Mim was glad Bertie wasn't away fighting. She had the assurance of seeing him, knowing where he was, being certain of his safety. But there were accidents at the docks, it was the nature of the work, during wartime or peace. Bertie was lucky. The owners weren't up cranes or dangling at height on boatswain's chairs, they didn't fall down ships' holds and break their backs. That poor man's wife and children. What would they do now?

They finished their meal in silence, each with their own thoughts. Mim might have regretted the conversation, thinking that it interfered with her plans for a romantic evening with her husband. But it was wartime and one had learned how to live with great sadness, had learned to take pleasure in small things whilst still acknowledging the realities of war.

'I think I shall retire, my dear,' said Bertie with an apologetic smile, wiping his mouth with a napkin and pushing up from his chair.

'Of course, Bertie. I shall be up shortly.' She took the dirty plates to the kitchen sink and ran the water. She had eaten a filling and nutritious meal with her husband at their dining table. Such things were not trifles, they were precious moments to grasp and appreciate. She said a silent prayer of thanks for Bertie being alive and well and there with her.

Mim realised she had wiped the same plate several times. She wanted to go upstairs but was nervous. Reassuring herself that there was no need to do anything if she didn't want to, she climbed the stairs, changed and slipped into bed beside Bertie. He snored softly and she relaxed, relieved. But her mind wandered to the words in the book. *Flower-wreathed love-making.* It was such a tantalising phrase. She nudged into Bertie's side and put her head on his chest. He shifted and grumbled, woke up and looked down at her with surprise.

'You mean the world to me, Bertie Rathbone,' she said, feeling silly at the sentiment.

'You are a funny thing today, Mimosa,' he said, putting his arm around her. 'Are you sure you are quite all right?'

She nodded on his chest, hesitated, and put her hand on his stomach. After a few seconds she felt for the bottom of his pyjama shirt and lay her hand on his bare skin, the touch of the hair on his warm stomach making her own body flutter. His breathing changed. Mim wondered at her own audacity. Never had she initiated the sex act in her life. What must Bertie be thinking? He shifted, put a finger under her chin so that she lifted her eyes to meet his. He was smiling uncertainly, searching her face for an explanation. She smiled back shyly at him and nodded her head ever so slightly. His confusion was swept away in an instant and he leant down to kiss her mouth. She gasped, a stab of pleasure shooting through her groin. He sensed it and rolled on top of her, his body hard against hers, his hand reaching down to lift her nightdress, to pull his pyjamas down. Her body arched, all by itself, the intense arousal making her want to move against him. Never had she experienced such a feeling. And the more she felt it, the more he responded to her. Mim thought about the woman in the book and panicked. How would she manage to ask him? But the very thought of his mouth on her made her feel even more aroused. A whimper escaped her lips and she was simultaneously horrified and joyous. She cast caution aside and tried to move up the pillow, tried to guide his shoulders down. He froze and looked at her. Even in the dim light, she wished he wouldn't look at her face, she was acutely embarrassed. 'Please,' she whispered. She moved him down, pulled up her nightdress higher so it was bunched under her chin, glad that it now hid her face from his. With her hands on the sides of his face, she arched her back until her breast touched his mouth. Her groin exploded with fire.

Someone banged loudly on the front door, the noise rever-berating around the house.

It was as if the air-raid siren had sounded. They both stiff-ened, Bertie rolled off to his side of the bed and pulled his bottoms up, Mim pulled her nightdress down.

'Who the devil?' said Bertie, getting up to put on his dressing gown. He disappeared out of the bedroom door and Mim sank back onto her pillow. She put her hand over her mouth and laughed. She had done it and it had been mar-vellous. Listening to the voices downstairs, she realised the visitor had come for her, there must be a problem of some kind. She got up, slipped down to the hallway unobserved, put on her WPS coat and hat over her night things and went to the door.

'For you,' said Bertie, cross about the disturbance and heading back upstairs.

'Quick, miss,' said a man at the door. He was the worse for being intoxicated with alcohol but looked very anxious.

'What is it?' said Mim, taking out her notebook.

'Fight at the Ship,' he said. 'Two of the bomb girls.'

'All right,' said Mim, tutting. 'I'll be along in a moment.' She rushed upstairs to get dressed. Bertie lay in bed smok-ing his pipe grumpily as she pulled on her uniform. 'Sorry, Bertie, I've got to go out.'

'This is really too much,' he said. 'Surely there is a constable who can go?'

'No, I'm afraid not,' said Mim. She had told him many times that she needed help and was struggling to do her rounds alone. 'I'm sorry, Bertie.'

*

The Ship public house was a ten minute walk from home on the main road through the village but Mim jogged along with the man to get there in five. The pub was an unremarkable structure of plain brick that could have passed for a double-fronted house and sat quite well next to its plain brick neighbouring dwellings. Mim knew to enter the door to the public bar, which was often where the trouble was to be found. Inside, there was a crowd of people cheering and jeering at two women, whom Mim recognised as Greygoose munitions workers, fighting in the centre of the room. They skidded on the sawdusted boards as they jostled and kicked, howling their indignation, their faces scratched and bleeding. One had the other's hair and was holding her head down by it.

'Clear the way,' said Mim in her loudest and most authoritative voice. 'Clear the way immediately.' The crowd parted. 'Step back,' she ordered the fighting women, taking an arm of each roughly and pulling them apart. One of the women lashed out, catching Mim in the stomach and winding her. She gasped for breath but held onto their arms, managing to separate them. They stood up, panting, patting their hair and feeling their wounds. They caught one another's eye and burst into laughter. They were drunk and fell into each other's arms, unable to control their mirth. The punters roared their approval.

'Good heavens,' muttered Mim. Some of these munitions girls had no rational judgement, no sense of decorum. She wrote their names down in her book but knew she could do nothing else but stop the fight. She could have asked someone to run to Stanford-le-Hope to bring one of her male colleagues to make the arrests but it was late and these women were no danger now. 'Be sure that I shall report you to Mrs Sparrow at the factory tomorrow, any sanctions will be administered by her,' said Mim, satisfied that Mrs Sparrow would make them forfeit part of their wages as punishment. Sometimes this was the only way of getting through to these girls.

'Ah, get home,' one of them jeered. 'Get back to your needlework, you old maid.'

Mim didn't engage with them, didn't bother telling them that she wasn't an old maid but in fact was happily married.

'Are you serving alcohol?' she asked the proprietor at the bar, the lecherous and jowly Mr Mercer who wore a permanent sneer and a hand-rolled cigarette stuck to his lip like an appendage.

Mim shuddered at his lewd stare as he took his time to answer her. 'I shut the bar eight o'clock sharp, Sergeant, but my friends like to keep me company for a while afterwards.'

She gave him a curt nod and left for home, not in the mood to check the punters' glasses for intoxicants. Walking back, she thought about Bertie in bed earlier. It had gone unexpectedly well. But now her husband was cross with her because of these silly factory girls.

Bertie stirred when Mim got back into bed. 'You will need to do something about this,' he said to her sleepily.

I know, thought Mim, I do know.

On Monday morning, Mim gathered her resolve and travelled to the WPS headquarters in Tilbury. Sub-Inspector Nash regarded her drily when she asserted her need for a constable to assist her on patrol.

'It is too large an area,' said Mim. 'I need a constable.'

'We are all overworked, Sergeant Rathbone,' said the sub-inspector, testily. 'I really do think you should be able to manage. This work is our very privilege, is it not?'

'Yes, of course, but I can only do what is humanly possible,' said Mim, returning her superior's stare but afraid that it would all backfire. Mim loved her job, she hoped she wasn't jeopardising her position by showing weakness and asking for help.

The sub-inspector paused for thought, picked up some papers from her desk and put them down again. 'I've been to see the commanding officer at Coalhouse Fort. His officers are desperate for billets in the village,' she said, absent-mindedly. Mim wished she wouldn't procrastinate. The sub-inspector was always talking about appeasing the male authorities. It was something the WPS promoted, to garner support for when the war was over. She looked at Mim. 'You know, I am training some recruits at the present time. I think I do have someone for you.'

'That would be wonderful indeed, Sub-Inspector,' said Mim, taken aback.

'But their training has only recently begun. They have received only basic instruction in ju-jitsu, have been on patrol only once and are due to attend a police court session with me tomorrow. If you are as desperate for assistance as you say you are, I could give you a constable but you would need to train her on the job, so to speak.' She looked at Mim and waited for her answer.

Mim considered the offer. It was far from ideal. She needed a trained officer, not to have to spend time finishing a recruit's training. But she supposed it was better than nothing. And it would appease Bertie.

'Thank you, Sub-Inspector, I appreciate your offer. When will you send her?'

'I should think the day after tomorrow, after her court training. There would be the matter of accommodation, though,' she added. 'The constable would need to board somewhere near your village, I think. But what with the problem of the army needing billets, it may be something of a sticking point. And there is no possibility of the WPS funding accommodation. If the higher ranks suspected we are not managing here, they would send someone who could manage.'

Mim did not appreciate the threat. If she didn't accommodate the new recruit herself, her own position would be at risk. It was outrageous after the dedication she had given the WPS. But the sub-inspector knew that every trained WPS officer valued her position with a ferocious passion and she knew that Mim would do anything to keep her job.

'Well, of course we have ample room,' said Mim brightly, feigning enthusiasm. 'We should be happy to accommodate the constable.'

'Well, that's settled it, I shall send her your way in due course,' said the sub-inspector with satisfaction.

Mim left, not knowing if she had come away for the better or for the worse. Now she had to tell Bertie that she had help on her patrol but that they would have a WPS recruit boarding with them for the foreseeable future. There was, however, some comfort in knowing that WPS recruits were women of high social standing and that the new constable would very likely be excellent company. In her new reality of pub brawls and drunken prostitutes, Mim may even have a new friend of higher faculties with whom to share her policing duties.

Back on her bicycle she turned for home but put her foot down to reconsider. Perhaps she'd take her chance whilst in Tilbury and go to see Bertie at work. She headed down Dock Road, steered her way round the hairpin bridge over the railway line and wobbled along to the Manorway entrance to the docks. It was heavily guarded during the war by the military police and the West Kents but this entrance was closest to the dry dock where Bertie worked and most of the guards knew Mim by now. She often saw them in an altogether different frame of mind during the evening when they had enjoyed an alcoholic beverage too many and there was a mutual understanding between them. They would let her through to see Bertie with minimal fuss and she would not report them to their senior officer if they were rather too worse for wear. They didn't like her taking in her bicycle though, so she left it propped against the guard post and walked along the quayside, threading through the work sheds.

There was an enormous liner in the dry dock and the din of the works made Mim's head ache. Shouts of warning rang out as objects were hurled around on deck and thrown overboard to the quayside. Mim jumped back as a beautiful carved fireplace surround crashed down at her feet and splintered apart. 'Careful, miss, the wrecking party's in,' shouted a labourer as he pushed a barrow through. She dove for cover by the dock wall, watching as the guts of the liner were ripped out and thrown over by men wielding crowbars and axes. Panelling and mirrors, luxurious fittings, rugs and furniture. From elsewhere in the docks came the metallic din of rivets being hammered, the shouts of labourers hunched and strained, the groan of cranes lifting loads. The smell of river salt mixed with the men's sweat and the tang of thick black oil, burning coal, and the goods being unloaded: tobacco, grain, rubber. Mim always felt a little uneasy around the men, a little in awe of their strength and ability to make things work, to pull things apart and build things up, the way their thick necks bulged with veins, how their rough hands gripped and grappled, how they did all of this with a laugh and a joke and a cigarette dangling from their lip.

'We're on a bet to get her stripped and armed in ten days.'

Mim turned to see Bertie standing beside her. 'Oh, Bertie,' she said. 'There you are. What a din this all is.'

He nodded and lit a cigarette. 'You might have told me you were coming, Mim. The wreckers are in, it's dangerous.'

'Yes, I can see that,' Mim laughed. 'What will she be, a hospital ship?'

Bertie shook his head. 'An armed cruiser, to see off the Boche in the Channel. They want no wooden fittings at all, because of fire, so she's being stripped back to the metal bulkhead and floorplates.'

'All of those beautiful things, just being thrown over like that,' said Mim. 'Surely they could salvage them?'

'No time,' said Bertie. 'We are up against it. We need to get her fitted with eight 4.7 inch guns.'

'And you are on a bet,' reminded Mim.

'Indeed,' he said with a wink.

Mim smiled. Seeing Bertie at work always made her proud. The docks in wartime were a very different place and a lot of the locals had lost their jobs. Even the native crews of foreign ships were camping in the storage sheds while shipping was disrupted. Bertie's war work, converting passenger liners into hospital ships, armed cruisers and transports, was overseen closely by the War Department, the Royal Navy and the military police but he was able to employ a good number of local men. Previously exempted men up to the age of fifty had been re-examined and called up to serve at home to free the younger ones to go and fight. It was said that three and a half thousand dock workers had gone overseas. The older ones left weren't spring chickens but they were glad to be doing their bit. Bertie and his workers all wore a khaki band on their sleeve to signify that they did important work for the war effort. Despite this, she knew he felt a profound sense of guilt that he wasn't overseas fighting. The days when the injured were transported from the fighting lines to Tilbury on the hospital ships were always hard on him. But she reassured him that without him the German U-boat campaign would prevail, there would be fewer hospital ships, fewer armed cruisers, less food reaching our shores, more men dying from their injuries. And he was saving his workers from death, he was saving their very family lines.

Mim smiled when she saw two women on board hefting a piece of wood panelling. She recognised them from Greygoose munitions. They'd been in black gunpowder and had lost their jobs. It was another reason she was proud of Bertie. He didn't shy from employing women in war work. Mim hoped the women would still be here when the war ended but Bertie told her that society would find it unpalatable, that the government would want women back at home during peacetime.

'And the load of the guns?' Mim saw Bertie flinch and wish she hadn't said it. Three years previously, the HMS *Clan MacNaughton* from Glasgow was converted to an armed merchant cruiser at Tilbury. She had foundered and gone down in a North Atlantic storm. Two hundred and seventy-seven men perished in the sea. Thirty-five of those were local Thurrock men. It had been a devastating accident. Some said the guns fitted to her were too heavy for a passenger ferry, that her buoyancy might have been affected. Bertie had had reservations at the time, but his business partner, Benjamin Proctor, had not.

'Did you need something, my dear, or did you just want to lay eyes on your dashing husband?'

Thankful that he had changed the subject, Mim shook her head and laughed. 'Well, of course I did, but also, I do have some news.'

'Please,' he said, ushering her forward to his little office by the quayside. 'Coffee?' he asked once inside. She shook her head, nervous about telling him.

'I'm to be given a constable,' she said brightly.

'Oh, Mim, that is wonderful news. Just the ticket,' said Bertie putting his hands on her shoulders. 'You're pleased?'

'Yes, yes of course, but as is usually the case with these things, it doesn't come unconditionally.'

'Ah,' said Bertie, sitting in this chair.

'The sub-inspector has said that the constable would need to be billeted with us for the time being.'

Bertie's face fell. 'I see,' he said. 'That is rather more than we bargained for, isn't it, Mim?'

'I should say so, Bertie. I'm awfully sorry, but couldn't we just do it for now?'

'Yes of course, Mim, of course, we've plenty of room and we are fortunate to be together when so many are not.'

Mim sighed with relief. Good old Bertie. She should have known he'd understand.

The door opened and Benjamin Proctor came in.

'Ah, hello, Sergeant, I trust you are well?'

'Quite well, thank you, and you?' He nodded and smiled, looked to Bertie.

'I must get on, my dear,' said Bertie, standing up.

'Yes, and so must I. I shall see you at home.' She kissed his cheek and looked both ways for flying fire surrounds before trotting to retrieve her bicycle.

5

Aggie

With an umbrella hooked over her arm and holding a lantern at hip height, Aggie stood with her fellow recruits and waited nervously to go out on night patrol training. She glanced down at her WPS armband and felt a surge of fear. She'd only have to open her mouth and everyone would know that she wasn't supposed to be there.

Sub-Inspector Nash and Sergeant Wills were talking to the constable who'd man the headquarters while they accompanied the recruits on patrol.

'Once more unto the breach, my friends,' said the sub-inspector, leading the way out. At her words, Mrs Parkington and Lady Braithwaite clutched their umbrellas with expressions of steely determination and Aggie, wondering what she meant, tripped after them.

'We shall nip in to the police station to show our faces,'

said the sub-inspector, heading up Dock Road. 'Three of their constables and the inspector enlisted for service; one of the constables was sadly killed in action and one is missing in action. The station is currently manned by Chief Constable Turnpike and two ordinary constables and that is all. It would be a boon if the WPS were invited to operate from the station, but I am afraid that that invitation has not been forthcoming.'

They climbed the steps to the entrance of the police station and were greeted by a crotchety officer on the front desk.

'Ah, Constable Green, good evening to you,' said the sub-inspector. The constable nodded and waited. 'Could we possibly intrude on the chief's time for a moment, to show him our new recruits?' The sub-inspector appeared unaware of the constable's reluctance to help. He said nothing but got up slowly from his chair and sauntered out to a back office, bringing the chief back with him.

'Sub-Inspector,' said the chief, with a curt nod.

'Good evening, Chief Constable Turnpike. I trust the evening is tolerable thus far?'

'As expected, Sub-Inspector,' he said, giving nothing away.

'Please allow me to introduce our new recruits: Lady Braithwaite, Mrs Parkington and Mrs Tucker.' The chief glanced at the women without much interest but his eye lingered on Aggie for a moment. 'We shall be on night patrol training for the next few hours and shall report to you in the usual way.'

'Very good, Sub-Inspector,' said the chief, turning to go.

As they headed back down Dock Road, Sub-Inspector Nash expressed her impatience. 'Our male colleagues barely tolerate us. But we are not deterred. They know they need us to help keep order and it remains vital that we ingratiate ourselves and maintain as good relations as possible.'

Aggie knew the chief could tell just by looking at her that she was different from the rest. Any one of many little signs would have betrayed her. The size of her hat, the cut of her boot leather, the way she held herself, the expression on her face, the very look in her eye. All different from the women with whom she now stood shoulder to shoulder.

They stopped outside the Alhambra cinema on Dock Road, the thump of an electricity generator sounding through the wall.

'This is part of our regular patrol,' said Sub-Inspector Nash. 'We show ourselves, walk up and down the aisles and deter any untoward behaviour. Look out for couples in the back row and on the balcony.'

Aggie and the others followed her in. The screen flickered in the darkness showing scenes of a character, with large white sideburns, in naval uniform. She mimicked the sub-inspector and held up her lantern as she walked along the aisle. Some of the viewers winced impatiently at the light, some jumped apart from their partner and smoothed their hair, staring intently at the film that they hadn't been watching. The back row was full to capacity with couples entwined. Men in army uniform and young women in showy dresses. At the bob of the women's lanterns they sat back in their seats, nudging those next to them to do the same. The sub-inspector stood for several minutes holding up her lantern and staring along the row. Aggie did the same but felt she was intruding. These people were surely doing no harm. As they walked back down the aisle and out onto the street, she knew everyone inside would assume their previous positions. What difference did it make that the WPS had stood there for a few minutes?

'Our mere presence has a strong effect,' said the sub-inspector as if reading her mind. 'We know that most of them will resume their goings-on the instant our backs are turned. However, one of those girls might reconsider her behaviour, she might decide to make for home before anything unfortunate should happen.'

'I have never seen such a thing in my life,' gushed Mrs Parkington. 'Those young people, in indecorous attitudes. I would never have thought . . . would you, Lady Brathwaite?'

'A very terrible sight, indeed, Mrs Parkington. I am all the more glad to be here to do what I can to help.'

Mrs Parkington looked disappointed at the lack of fervour in Lady Braithwaite's disapproval. She turned to Aggie but hesitated.

'You needn't ask the same of Mrs Tucker,' said the sub-inspector grimly. 'If there is one aspect of the training in which she is ahead, it is the sordid behaviour of the working classes. Is it not, Mrs Tucker?'

'I wouldn't call it sordid behaviour, Sub-Inspector,' said Aggie and immediately wished she hadn't. 'They're just out for the night after a hard slog at work, that's all.'

'Cavorting in a dark cinema?' said Mrs Parkington in a high-pitched whisper. 'You would call this out for the night? The girls' respectability is at risk, indeed already doomed. It is very serious indeed.'

The two recruits and the two officers all peered at Aggie.

'It's good that we're there to remind them not to go any further though,' she said hastily. 'I mean, as long as they keep it innocent they'll be all right.'

The sub-inspector raised her eyebrows at the others and Aggie was very relieved when they continued on their patrol. She made a silent pledge that she wouldn't say anything too 'common' for the rest of the evening.

'We check these clubs on occasion but not on the regular patrol,' explained the sub-inspector, indicating the Irish social club. 'There's the Working Men's Club too. These are frequented by local men, dockers and the like. For those of you who are unfamiliar with the area, there are the large working docks, the dry dock, and a multitude of workshops in the area. Generations of the same family work in the same job; there is a uniformed brass band; it is an area reminiscent of docklands in the north of England. Local men enjoy their alcohol and tobacco at one of their clubs after a day's work and they are largely no trouble. We are more concerned with people in the area for the war, servicemen and the women who flock here with khaki fever, either motivated by innocent excitement or by more salacious endeavours such as prostitution.'

Aggie realised that whatever social life she'd had before the WPS training, she had no longer. As a munitions worker she went to dances and the local pubs with her friends. They hadn't known anything like it before the war when she'd worked in service and had had no free time or spare money. But now that was all gone. She couldn't be seen drinking in pubs or dancing in halls when she was policing others' social behaviour. What would she do for fun now?

'Ah,' said the sub-inspector, stopping. 'This is something to look out for. We have been charged with checking doorways and alleyways, any dark nooks and crannies that are sought out by couples displaying indecent behaviour.'

Aggie followed her gaze and saw a young man and woman in a deep shop doorway. The sub-inspector walked towards them, the recruits in tow, and stood very nearby making a loud cough to clear her throat. The couple stiffened and jumped apart, peering out to see the women there staring at them. They said nothing but scuttled away down the road.

'Occasionally we are challenged but more often than not our mere presence is enough,' said the sub-inspector. Aggie glanced at Mrs Parkington who looked quite pale with shock in the moonlight. 'This is one of several pubs in Tilbury,' said the sub-inspector, stopping at the Ship on Dock Road. 'This is on our regular patrol. The pubs are used by locals but also by sailors and soldiers, and so inevitably by the loose women who seek out the servicemen.'

Aggie felt a shiver of nerves and saw Lady Braithwaite put a comforting hand on Mrs Parkington's arm.

'You'll notice the perambulators,' said the sub-inspector, nodding at three prams lined up outside the pub. They walked over and peered in. One baby in each of two prams and two babies in the third. One of the babies was awake and fretting, the others asleep.

'But where are their mothers?' said Mrs Parkington, ashen-faced.

'Where do you think?' said Sergeant Wills. 'Inside having a drink.'

'No!' exclaimed Lady Braithwaite. 'I can hardly believe it.'

The sub-inspector smiled at the ladies' innocence and looked at Aggie to see her contrasting lack of surprise. Aggie had seen prams outside pubs many times. It didn't shock her.

'Sergeant Wills, would you mind staying with the infants?' said the sub-inspector, leaving the sergeant there and gesturing for the recruits to follow her into the pub. It was half past eight and the pub inside was busy. One quick glance around and Aggie saw several men in uniform, several women with them, men playing cards and sitting at the bar, and when they all turned to see the sub-inspector in her formidable uniform and authoritative stance they sat up a bit straighter, shuffled apart from their companions and quietened down. Aggie felt a strange sense of power but also of discomfort. These people were just out for a drink, they weren't doing any harm.

The sub-inspector walked over to the nook at the end of the bar counter. Behind the frosted glass pane sat three women nursing glasses of what looked like Guinness or stout. When they saw the sub-inspector standing over them they exchanged looks of irritation.

'Good evening, ladies.' They mumbled their greeting back to the sub-inspector. 'I think you may have left your infants unattended on the street outside. It is dark and there are men of uncertain motive walking around. Do you think your children are safe?'

'We're just going,' they said, gulping down the last of their drinks. They got up, grumbling about the sub-inspector poking her nose into their business, how they were having an innocent drink and the babies were all right. They sneered at the recruits as they passed them to leave the pub. The sub-inspector watched them go with satisfaction and caught the proprietor's eye, tapping her wristwatch.

'This is a restricted area. They are not allowed to serve intoxicating liquor after eight o'clock in the evening but they are allowed to keep their doors open until eleven, which is infuriating and makes our work all the harder.'

A woman of around forty rushed over to them in a flurry of shabby skirts, grabbed Aggie's arm, her eyes wide with alarm. 'My girl's gone missing again, miss,' she said.

'Your daughter?' said the sub-inspector, taking out her notepad.

'Yes,' said the woman. 'I'm out of my mind with worry. She keeps going off and I can't find her and she's going to get herself in trouble.'

'Her name?'

'Penny. Penny Crabb. She's skinny, with brown hair and she dresses up tarty for the soldiers,' said Mrs Crabb, looking from one recruit to the next for any help they could give her. 'She's got a funny right eye, sort of down at the corner, but she's a pretty girl.'

'How old is Penny?'

'Sixteen,' said the woman, her voice breaking. 'She's only sixteen, but God help her, she looks older.'

'It's all right, Mrs Crabb, we will find her,' said the sub-inspector. She wrote down Mrs Crabb's address and sent the woman home.

'Good Lord, what can we do to help?' said Lady Braithwaite, once they were back outside the pub.

'It's a common enough occurrence, I'm afraid, Lady Braithwaite,' said the sub-inspector. 'Mothers often come to us for help and we often locate their daughters, sometimes before they are in too much trouble, sometimes in much deeper trouble than we'd hope.'

'The poor woman, I cannot possibly imagine my own daughters in such a terribly wicked and precarious situation,' said Mrs Parkington.

'These are the working classes, may I remind you, Mrs Parkington,' said Sergeant Wills. 'They do things differently.'

Aggie stayed quiet this time. These ladies were very shocked by what they'd seen. But Aggie wasn't shocked. She knew the local girls hung around with the boys in uniform. It was an awful shame when some of them got caught out and their boy wouldn't marry them. None of these women were talking about the boys though. It was only about the girls.

'We'll make our way to the station and we'll look out for Penny Crabb for the remainder of our patrol,' said the sub-inspector. Lady Braithwaite took on a look of fervour, but Mrs Parkington seemed only more anxious. Aggie committed Penny's description to memory and hoped they could find her and get her home if she was in trouble.

'It's quiet tonight,' said Sergeant Wills as they walked onto the station platform. 'It's early yet. Later on there'll be intoxicated people hanging around here, and some will miss their train home and be in trouble.'

'Indeed,' said the sub-inspector. 'When we get a hospital ship docking with wounded soldiers from the war, there are Red Cross detachments driving them in ambulances, putting them on ambulance trains here. We have seen some terrible, unimaginable sights. The poor, poor boys coming home ruined. It is really very difficult. We are always in attendance to help however we can. But not tonight, I am thankful for that.'

Aggie was thankful, too. What if it were Arnie coming home injured and it was her waiting at the station for him? She said a silent prayer that he was safe and well.

'Onwards for a quick patrol of the army camp,' said the sub-inspector.

Aggie was used to being on her feet for twelve hour shifts at the factory, but her fellow recruits seemed to be flagging.

They began tramping across the marshes to the east of the town, Mrs Parkington holding up the back of her skirt to stop it trailing in the mud. A large, tented encampment stretched before them, containing hundreds of white pointed tents. Aggie wondered why they were white when surely they could be clearly seen from the air.

'They hold dances here on occasion,' sighed the sub-inspector, 'much against our advice, I might say. The dance itself is overseen by the army officers and plays out quite respectfully. It is after the dance that the trouble usually starts. Some of the girls who have been let into the camp suddenly vanish into thin air. We catch them the following morning, creeping out over the marshes, and we give them a sound talking-to.

'I have asked Major Brampton, who oversees things here, to put a curfew into place and he is reluctant but not wholly against the idea,' she went on. 'There is no dance tonight as far as we are aware. But we shall go in and have a look around, to see whether Miss Penny Crabb is secreted in there somewhere.'

She approached the armed guards at the entrance to the camp. 'Good evening,' she said. 'Our usual checks, if you wouldn't mind?' The guards let them through without pleasantries and watched their progress into the camp. 'It's no use asking them if they've seen her,' said the sub-inspector, 'they rarely give us useful information. Their boys are beyond reproach.'

The ladies walked to the large wooden mess hut and were greeted with whistles and catcalls when they entered. Several dozen men were lounging around, playing cards and drinking coffee. Aggie saw a sudden flash of yellow in the corner and frowned when it disappeared. The sub-inspector saw it too and gestured for them all to follow her over there. She pulled out a chair and called into the dark beneath.

'Come along, out with you.'

A sly-faced woman in a yellow dress with rouged cheeks and a fur tied at her throat came out from under the table. Aggie peered at her right eye for signs that it was Penny, but knew it couldn't be her. This woman was at least thirty.

The sub-inspector gave the soldiers at the table an icy glare and took the woman's arm to lead her out of the tent.

'Sergeant, escort Martha back to her lodgings, if you will.'

Sergeant Wills nodded grimly and took a firm hold of the woman's arm, marching her back through the camp towards town.

'One of the regular prostitutes,' explained the sub-inspector to the recruits. 'We've had her arrested and convicted before but she pays her fine and comes back on the streets. Now we escort her home and intercept her dealings whenever we see her. What else can one do?'

Mrs Parkington looked like she might be sick. Aggie herself was unsettled by seeing the prostitute in the mess hut with all of those men.

They strolled around the tent looking for other signs of women hiding but found none. They walked around the smaller tents, peering into those with the flaps open, looking at the men sitting outside smoking, but there was no sign of any more women.

'She could be inside one of the tents, but we aren't permitted to go inside, I regret to say. It's no use asking the men, they wouldn't betray their comrades. Contradictory really, given the problem of venereal disease. Syphilis is an especially loathsome disease.'

Aggie felt sure that some of those men were already married and at risk of infecting their wives. It was a disgusting thought.

They left the camp and headed north over the railway sidings to the outskirts of town along Fort Road. 'This is the more salacious part of town,' said the sub-inspector. 'The Daniel Defoe pub is at the centre of the small but busy red-light district. It's an inevitable scene in any docklands, of course, with seamen docking here and looking for entertainment. But the war and the army camp have compounded the problem tenfold, and it is very difficult to uphold the drinking curfew. Recruits, prepare yourselves.'

Aggie winced when Mrs Parkington gripped her arm, as though Aggie were equipped to protect her in such a foul place. The woman's face was taut with worry and there was every chance she might faint. Her waspish waist betrayed a tightly laced corset. It was a wonder she could breathe at all.

As they walked, several young boys stood in a huddle at the roadside, their eyes keenly watching the patrols.

'It is a little late for you to be out, boys,' said the sub-inspector. 'I suggest you go home. Shall I find your mothers?'

The boys, who looked to Aggie to be no more than eleven or twelve, slipped away down a side alley.

'The gangs are more prevalent these days,' said the sub-inspector. 'With their fathers away at war or killed, and mothers working or ill, one sees it more and more. They beg on the streets, selling matches and so on. I once caught a young boy soliciting soldiers on behalf of his mother.'

'In heaven's name, I never expected such a level of wicked-ness and loss of childhood innocence,' said Lady Braithwaite. 'What on earth can be done to save them?'

'Save them?' said Aggie. 'This is how they live. Unless someone's going to give them a load of money to live better, what do you expect them to do?'

'We can talk to them, move them on, persuade them of virtuous behaviour, that is what we do, Mrs Tucker,' said the sub-inspector with distaste.

Aggie said no more. The sub-inspector had taken a dislike to her; she needed to do something to improve her opin-ion of her.

Three drunken soldiers staggered past them along the dirt road, talking and laughing, and disappeared into a nearby house. The sub-inspector stopped the recruits outside.

'Miss Marguerite's delightful establishment,' she said, looking up at the curtained windows. 'We had better go in.'

Aggie's stomach lurched. She'd heard of brothels but had never been near one before. As they walked into the dim entrance a woman of around forty adorned with feathers and fake pearls and with lips painted a bright red danced up to greet them on her high-heeled boots, blocking their way inside.

'Good evening, officers, how lovely to see you,' she said in a mock posh voice. 'May I offer you a drink?'

'Goodness gracious, no thank you, Marguerite. We are looking for a young girl of sixteen, of the name Penny Crabb. She has a deformed right eye. Her mother is extremely worried for her safety. Is she here?'

'Penny, you say? No, no one of that name or appearance is in here, officer.'

'Do I need to look around inside, Marguerite?'

'No, no, no need, she isn't here, Inspector, I know all my . . . friends and she ain't one of them.'

'All right, Marguerite, I do hope you are being frank – you know I can call the chief constable here at a moment's notice, and that it would be twelve months of hard labour for you.'

'Oh yes, officer, no need, tutty bye.'

Marguerite waved a lacy handkerchief at them and disappeared with a flourish back inside. Aggie shuddered. She was glad they didn't need to search the place. She followed the others outside and down an alleyway, looking over her shoulder.

'Look, do you see?' said the sub-inspector, stopping suddenly. 'There, a drug dealer.'

Two men were talking in the shadows. The first one handed something over and scuttled away. The other came out of the shadows and Aggie was shocked to see that it was a soldier in uniform. An injured soldier, one of his sleeves bound flat to his body, an amputee. When he saw the patrols there, he turned on his heel and went the other way, disappearing from view in a moment.

'A soldier?' said Aggie.

'Yes, I am afraid so. They are treated with cocaine and morphine on the front line for their injuries and they return addicted to the stuff. They skulk around the alleyways looking for illicit traders to satisfy their need. It is really a most tragic state of affairs.'

'Addicted?' said Mrs Parkington. 'I was under the impression that these drugs were prescribed by doctors.'

'It is only recently that the dangers of these drugs are becoming apparent,' said the sub-inspector. 'But these men do not fall within our remit.' A movement at the end of the alley caught Aggie's eye, a couple walking together. She increased her pace, following them out onto the main thoroughfare. A young woman with brown hair was on the arm of a soldier, laughing and swaying with drink. Walking faster to catch up with them, her heart beating, she hoped this was her chance to prove her worth to the sub-inspector.

Calling out to the couple, she put on a voice that sounded more like Sergeant Wills' than her own. 'I say,' she called, 'I say there.' The couple stopped and turned around, the smiles dropping from their faces when they saw Aggie's armband and the sub-inspector behind her. 'I say, are you drunk?' said Aggie, hoping the sub-inspector could hear her.

'What?' said the soldier, laughing.

'Are you intoxicated?' said Aggie, looking at the girl, her heart leaping when she saw her drooping right eye. 'Penny Crabb?' she said in her poshest voice. 'Your mother is looking for you.'

But the young girl didn't crumple with shame, or go quietly with the patrols back home. Instead, Penny threw back her head and laughed.

'And who's asking?' she said. 'You're not the police. Get that plum out of your mouth – who do you think you are, asking me if I'm drunk? So what if I am?'

With that, Penny pulled at her companion's arm and they headed off. Aggie fought for something to say but knew her voice would only make it worse. Sub-Inspector Nash strode past, catching up with Penny, speaking to her in soft, grim tones. Aggie could see the girl's face, no longer laughing but sullen and yielding. The soldier stepped back, away from the intimidating policewoman. The sub-inspector took Penny's arm and escorted her away, leaving the soldier angry and alone in the street.

Aggie hung back, with a terrible sense that she was floundering out of her depth. She wasn't made of the right stuff to be a policewoman; no one would respect her, not her colleagues and certainly not the people she was supposed to police. She'd been naive to think she could do it, and especially foolish to think she'd be able to do a better job than the WPS ladies.

'Fancy a drink, miss?' said a man in uniform, coming up close to her, his face shining with sweat and his breath reeking of booze. 'Come on, love, in the Daniel? My treat,' he leered.

'No, thank you,' said Aggie angrily. 'I am a police recruit.'

'A what, love?' he said, frowning with confusion. 'A police . . . ? Ha, that's a good one, now how about that drink?'

Aggie gripped her umbrella and made her way out of the

foul streets, heading towards town. She couldn't face the sub-inspector and didn't go back to the WPS headquarters but instead went to the train station. Mrs Sparrow's face flashed in her mind – the welfare supervisor had been amused by Aggie's plan to join the women police. She'd said Aggie would be most likely to fail and she was right. A train pulled in, spitting soot and smoke and half choking her. Sitting in the carriage, she wrung her hands. The thought of the posh voice she had tried to put on and how Penny Crabb saw through it immediately, how Aggie had challenged the couple, accused them of being drunk, it all made her cringe. It had been unprofessional, nothing like the approach the sub-inspector had taken, and it wasn't how Aggie had intended to deal with the working girls at all. Her desperation to impress the sub-inspector had failed terribly. She'd been a fool to burn her bridges. There was no munitions job for her to go back to now. With angry tears in her eyes, she yanked off her WPS armband and stuffed it into her pocket.

6

Aggie

There was a sharp rap on Aggie's front door early one morning. It had been several days since she'd messed up the WPS training and she'd been fretting at home on her own, making herself feel worse by thinking about Arnie and obsessively looking for letters when the postwoman came. She had relived the moment she had challenged Penny Crabb and the soldier countless times. There had been no word from the sub-inspector, which confirmed that they didn't want her.

Checking her hair in the hallway mirror, she opened the door. To her surprise the sub-inspector was on her doorstep, in her tall polished boots, breeches and cap, her motorcycle parked on the road behind her.

'May I come in?' she asked.

The sub-inspector refused a seat in the front room but looked around with interest.

'I have been to Coalhouse Fort on business and thought I would stop in to see you. Why haven't you been back to training?'

'Why?' said Aggie, thinking it was obvious. 'I messed it up, I didn't think you'd want me.'

'On the contrary. In fact, I've found you a posting. I'm going to have you trained on the job, rather than complete your training in Tilbury.' The sub-inspector peered at Arnie's army photograph propped on the fire surround. 'You are going to have one more day with me, today, in fact, doing courtroom training, and then you shall be posted to the Orsett Rural District. You'll be trained by Sergeant Rathbone, who lives here in East Tilbury village, coincidentally. And you'll be billeted to her house also.' The sub-inspector made to leave, as though no further information was necessary.

'What do you mean, billeted?' said Aggie, recognising the name. Wasn't that the copper who'd taken her wedding ring?

'This house is needed for officer accommodation – that is why I have been to Coalhouse Fort this morning,' said the officer matter-of-factly. 'You shall board with the Rathbones. It's a large house, they have ample room. Mr Rathbone is very busy with the shipbuilding industry at Tilbury Dock and you shall be on patrol most evenings. I shouldn't think you'll disturb one another greatly. We must all face sacrifice in wartime.'

Aggie stared at her as if she were mad. 'I don't think you realise, Sub-Inspector, this is my home. What about when my husband comes back from the war?'

The sub-inspector sighed with impatience. 'We shall cross

that bridge in due course, Mrs Tucker. Now I must get on. Rendezvous at Grays police court. Eleven o'clock sharp.'

Aggie watched from the door as the officer mounted her motorcycle and puttered away down the road. She looked in the other direction towards Coalhouse Fort and frowned. Her house was to be taken over for the war? She went inside to sit down. Several of the houses in the village had been requisitioned so it shouldn't have been such a surprise. But to be told that she'd be lodging with Sergeant Rathbone and to be told that she was still on WPS training . . . A smile formed on her lips. She was still on WPS training. She said it out loud and rushed to get ready. She had to get to Grays police court for eleven o'clock sharp.

Aggie arrived at Grays town hall in plenty of time. Lady Braithwaite was there already and at ten minutes to eleven the sub-inspector pulled up on her motorcycle. There was no sign of Mrs Parkington.

'This is your courtroom training session,' said the sub-inspector, on the steps of the town hall. 'The objective is to sit in session and listen to the proceedings so that if you are ever called to act as witness to a crime you shall know what to do. You'll also gain an understanding of the magistrate's point of view and what we are dealing with. Be under no illusion that you are welcome in court. The judicial system is all-male and rulings are often heavily prejudiced against women.'

Lady Braithwaite nodded grimly and Aggie copied her, knowing nothing about the justice system.

'Should a case of indecency be heard, all women, including ourselves, will be asked to leave the courtroom. We want to stay, I know, but the magistrates will think us abnormal if we choose to subject our delicate ears to such horrors. Remember, we need to be seen to be cooperative. Rebelling against the magistrates will not help our cause.'

She turned to climb the steps, but hesitated.

'I am disappointed, but not surprised, to report that Mrs Parkington has resigned from training. Police work is not for everyone.'

Aggie wasn't shocked either about Mrs Parkington – she had looked quite ill on night patrol in Tilbury – but it gave Aggie a boost to think that she herself was still there when Mrs Parkington had failed.

The women made their way into an already busy courtroom and found seats on the wooden benches, the clerk and attending male constables turning to stare at them.

'This is the petty sessions court,' said the sub-inspector to them in a low voice. 'Held regularly, at least twice per week. Lesser cases are heard here without a jury. More serious cases are referred to the quarter sessions, and the most serious crimes that carry the death penalty are heard at assizes, twice a year on a circuit. Of course, military crimes are heard at courts martial, not here.'

Lady Braithwaite scribbled it all down in a pocket notebook and Aggie wished she'd thought to get one for herself.

'The WPS often give evidence here, but not today. Witnesses must wait outside the courtroom until they are called. Should you be witness to an indecent crime, you must remember to be careful with your descriptions. If you are too graphic you will be accused of indecency yourselves.'

Lady Braithwaite and Aggie exchanged glances.

'On occasion we sit in when we know a woman is on trial or a child is bearing witness, as a show of support,' the sub-inspector went on. 'Of course we have to leave the room in cases of indecency but at the very least the defendant will have noticed our presence. Here come the magistrates now.'

Three men in fine suits came to take their seats behind a slanted wooden bench. They conferred over several papers before calling in the first case. A man was brought before them by a male constable, charged with taking three matches into Greygoose munitions factory where he worked as a labourer in explosives. He held his flat cap against his chest, looking terrified. The magistrates fined him twenty pounds, a month's wages, and sentenced him to prison in the second division for fourteen days.

'The second division, no privileges, solitary confinement,' whispered the sub-inspector. 'They are making an example of him.' Aggie shivered at the thought of it. It seemed clear to her that the man hadn't intended to take the matches into the factory.

Further cases were heard: a butcher fined five pounds for selling pork infected with tuberculosis; a man fined twenty shillings for being found drunk and disorderly; and a man charged with using a forged military certificate and suspected to be a deserter from the army. He was sentenced to three months' hard labour for the forgery and ordered to be handed over to an escort at the end of the sentence.

'He'll be court-martialled and sentenced to death if he's charged with desertion,' explained the sub-inspector. The crowd of onlookers booed the man, threw things at him. Aggie wanted to boo but thought it would look

89

unprofessional. How dare this man desert his comrades when her Arnie was risking life and limb on the front line?

A dishevelled young woman was brought before the bench. She had a similar look about her as the prostitutes Aggie had seen on patrol. She was young but careworn, her hair in disarray, her boots down-at-heel. The chief constable read from his notes. She was a known prostitute and was being charged with such. But the chief constable reported her pleading that she had been raped. At this, the sub-inspector sat up taller, to be seen by the woman. But her eyes were glazed and only half open, she seemed unable to concentrate on what was being said.

'Raped?' scoffed one of the magistrates, smirking at his colleagues. 'Is it indeed possible for a known prostitute to cry rape? This is clearly a ruse to escape conviction.'

The onlookers laughed and the woman looked about her. 'I was raped, by a man in army uniform,' she said and she held up her skirts to show the magistrates her bare legs, which were black and livid with bruises.

The magistrates puffed red with fury. 'All women are to leave the courtroom immediately.'

Aggie stood up with her colleagues and shuffled out of the room into the hall, looking back to see the accused's ashen face. 'I'm surprised they didn't clear the court earlier, before we heard any of this case,' said the sub-inspector.

'Did you see her legs?' said Aggie, appalled. 'She's been attacked – what will they do?'

'She made a mistake in accusing a man in uniform, and in showing them her legs. The bench will have no sympathy. I am sure they will sentence her,' said the sub-inspector.

Aggie felt sick. The prostitute was alone and defenceless. The magistrates could do what they wanted with her.

'Will she be permitted to state the details of her attack?' said Lady Braithwaite, putting a kindly hand on Aggie's arm, her face as wretched as Aggie's own.

'Most certainly not,' said the sub-inspector. 'She has previous convictions. They will say she brought it on herself, that she goaded the man, that the supposed attacker's base desires are no fault of his own.'

'Contemptible,' said Lady Braithwaite. 'When will this country allow women into the professions? This is not justice, not by a long way.'

When they were allowed back into the courtroom the prostitute had gone.

'What was the outcome of the case?' said the sub-inspector, tapping the shoulder of a man sitting in front of her.

'Nine months' hard labour for soliciting, and quite right too,' he replied.

The sub-inspector looked at her recruits knowingly and Aggie bit back her angry tears.

At home the following day, Aggie packed up her bags. She didn't want to leave her possessions in the house when the billeted officer moved in but there was nowhere to store their things. It was odd to think about someone else living there while she boarded with the Rathbones down the road. She'd written to Arnie to tell him, explaining that it would just be for now. She didn't want him to think he didn't have a home to come back to.

With her bags in hand, she knocked on the Rathbones' door

and felt like she was starting a new job in service. Presently, Sergeant Rathbone, in her WPS uniform, answered.

'Yes?' she said, frowning at Aggie's WPS armband.

'Can I have my wedding ring back, please?'

The sergeant stared at Aggie.

'You took it off me when I worked at the factory?'

'Yes, yes, I have it here, as a matter of fact, I do apologise. I'm sorry, but who told you where I live?'

Aggie stepped forward to take the ring, relieved to slip it back on her finger. She considered the sergeant very rude to have kept it all this time.

'I'm the WPS recruit, I've brought my things,' said Aggie, looking down at the bag she held.

Sergeant Rathbone stared at her with the strangest expression, her face seeming to ripple with tension. 'The WPS recruit to board here and be trained by myself?' she said.

'Yes,' said Aggie. 'Sub-Inspector Nash came to see me. Has there been a mistake?'

Sergeant Rathbone took a long breath in through her nose, her lips pinched tightly together. 'I rather think not,' she said curtly. 'Merely skulduggery of the purest form.'

'Is everything all right?' said Aggie, feeling ill at ease.

'You'd better come in,' said Sergeant Rathbone, pursing her lips and holding the door wide for Aggie. For a moment the sergeant stood in her hallway looking at the floor with her hand covering her mouth, as though unsure what to do. As if making a decision, she began to show Aggie around the house.

'This is the library,' she said, and with an afterthought added, 'Do you read?'

Aggie shrugged. 'Not much.'

'The sitting room,' she said with a wave of her arm. 'The kitchen is at the back of the house. I'd rather you didn't use the drawing room, but you are free to use the garden.'

Aggie, struggling with her bags, followed the sergeant upstairs. A lovely sweeping staircase that needed a good clean.

'We have no staff, now,' said Sergeant Rathbone, irritably, as Aggie followed her up a smaller staircase, to what must have been the servant's quarters. 'We lost both our maid and our cook to munitions work. You will be expected to muck in and help with the awful drudge of housework. Cooking, cleaning and so on. And the shopping, of course. I trust you have a ration book with you?' Aggie mumbled yes. 'Our groceries are delivered by Tibble's in Stanford-le-Hope.'

She stopped suddenly, holding the handle of a bedroom door. 'I really am at a loss as to why the sub-inspector would inflict an untrained ... factory girl on me. I am desperate for help on my patrol and now this. It is really beyond the pale. This is your bedroom. You'll have to make it up yourself.'

Aggie was stunned into silence. She wanted to tell Sergeant Rathbone that she hadn't asked to be billeted in someone else's house. She had a perfectly good house herself. The sergeant's disdain only made Aggie feel like an annoying insect caught on the sergeant's shoe. The penny dropped and Aggie realised that the sub-inspector hadn't wanted to finish her training because she didn't think she was up to scratch. She was palming her off onto the sergeant because the sergeant needed help on her patrol.

'Well, that's just bloody marvellous,' she said, suddenly dropping her bags onto the bedroom floor. 'I didn't ask to board with you, you know. I've got my own house down the road, but something tells me that the sub-inspector has arranged all of this to suit herself.'

Sergeant Rathbone regarded Aggie for a moment, sizing her up. 'We all have our duty to do,' she said, and left Aggie there alone.

7

Mim

'Are you familiar with this public house?'

Mim was trying very hard to keep her frustration in check. She stood with her new training recruit, Aggie Tucker, outside the George and Dragon in Linford village. Sub-Inspector Nash had been unsporting, deceitful even, in giving her a dead duck to train. Imagine a factory girl training for the Women's Police Service! These girls were brash, irresponsible. Mim needed a trained constable to help her patrol her large area of East Thurrock. She'd been courteous to Aggie but in no mood to defuse the tension between them. For some reason Aggie had implied that Mim had deliberately kept her wedding ring. How ludicrous. It only confirmed Mim's opinion of the factory girls. They were hard workers, yes, but very silly.

She had asked Aggie what training she'd received. *A bit of this and that*, had been the reply, one patrol around Tilbury, ten minutes of ju-jitsu and one session in court. Not a great deal. Mim personally loathed giving evidence in court, it was like entering the lion's den. She shuddered to think what the male magistrates would make of a girl from the working classes in WPS uniform.

'Yes, I've been in here with the munitions girls.'

Mim bit her tongue. 'In that case you'll know the landlady, a Mrs Rose Rumble?'

Aggie nodded. 'Yes, I know Rose a little bit. My friend Pops, Poppy, boards upstairs. A few munitions girls board here.'

Mim nodded. 'Single girls living together over a pub is not an ideal situation.' She felt she needed to verbalise what would have been obvious to a trainee from a better background. 'Shall we?'

As they crossed the road to the pub, Mim sighed. Two disabled servicemen had taken up position outside the pub. One stood holding a tray of sundries for sale, matches and bootlaces and so on. With the exception of one eye, his face and head was completely covered in bandage. At his feet sat the second man, a double amputee, his left trouser leg rolled up and his right sleeve folded and pinned to his lapel, his crutch lying by his side. They were dressed as smartly as they were able and Mim admired them at least for attempting a respectable living as opposed to taking up residence *inside* the pub, but she failed to see why they brought their many children with them. The youngsters varied in age, sat on the pub window sills swinging their legs, or ran around the forecourt playing games. They should have been in bed at that time. It was no place for children.

Mim was about to administer a soft reprimand when she was surprised to see Aggie approach them.

'Hello, Sid, hello, Arthur, how you bearing up?'

'Hello, Aggie, love,' said the one sitting on the ground. 'What's all this? You're never a copper now?'

Aggie blushed. 'I am, you know. Well, in training anyway. How's the kids?'

'Bored and hungry. We'll be getting them back home soon. The missis'll be in from work now. How's your Arnie getting on?'

'I don't know, he can't say much, but he's still out there and still writing home now and again, so I can be thankful for that. All right, bye, love, bye, Sid.'

The standing man nodded his head, his one eye showing a smile. Mim refrained from reprimanding them.

'Poor loves,' said Aggie quietly, as they walked to the pub door. 'Still holding their heads high though.'

Mim glanced back at the men. They did make a pitiful sight.

Leading the way, Mim pushed open the door to the public bar and entered the thick fog of the smoky pub interior, treading carefully on the damp sawdust strewn about the floor. It was the usual scene. In the public bar sat a scattering of old men, soldiers and young women – some munitionettes, some of lower desirability – a disabled veteran sitting alone at the bar with his crutches propped up next to him, nursing some dregs of porter. Looking through the middle section of the pub to the saloon bar, Mim could see a table of munitionettes and a table of Mr Tunnidge and his committee cronies. It was half past eight in the evening. A good time to patrol, the sale of alcohol being prohibited after eight o'clock. There was a palpable shift in atmosphere when the inhabitants saw them arrive. A few seconds when the punters (as Mim had reluctantly begun to refer to them, but it was a foul word) checked themselves before going back to their conversations.

'Good evening, Sergeant Rathbone,' said the landlady, Mrs Rumble, who stood at the bar putting out glasses. She looked at Aggie's WPS armband with confusion.

'Good evening, Mrs Rumble. May I introduce Trainee Constable Tucker.' Mim couldn't help but say it with some reluctance.

'Hello, Rose,' said Aggie. 'Look at me,' she said, patting her armband.

'Hello,' said Mrs Rumble, seeming to struggle with what to call Aggie. 'What's all this then?'

'Simply that Trainee Constable Tucker is accompanying me on patrol,' interrupted Mim, wanting to keep the exchange professional.

'I see,' said Mrs Rumble. 'That's a turn-up for the books.'

'Indeed,' said Mim, looking about the place. 'Have you anything to report this evening?'

'Nothing worth mentioning, Sergeant,' said Mrs Rumble, giving Aggie a strange look. 'They're still nursing their drinks from earlier, they don't like to leave, it's like a home from home here.'

'It's the best pub around here,' said Aggie smiling. Mim frowned at her. It wouldn't do to be so familiar with the public. 'Oh look, here's Pops coming down now.'

Aggie went to see her friend, who to Mim looked rather

98

ashen-faced. The two were soon deep in conversation, Aggie glancing back over at Mim nervously.

'I know a bit of first-aid,' said Aggie, as Mim approached them.

'Oh no, it's all right, she's all right really,' said the friend Pops, in something of a panic.

'What seems to be the matter?' said Mim.

Aggie and Pops exchanged glances. 'It's just my friend, who boards upstairs, she's feeling a bit out of sorts,' said Pops. 'But she's all right, she wouldn't want a fuss.' She gave Aggie a hard stare.

'We are patrolling upstairs today, so we shall see her in any case,' said Mim brusquely, looking for Aggie to follow her. She walked round to the back of the bar and opened a door that led directly to the stairs.

'I'll come up too,' said the friend Pops loudly. Mim had been doing the job long enough to know when someone was hiding something from her.

All of the first floor had been given over to a munitions hostel. Four rooms, each with two sets of bunk beds. The inhabitants, who must have been on night shift or somewhere kicking up their heels, were all out, but for one of the bottom bunks, the occupant of which was on her side facing the wall and giving a good impression of being asleep.

'Is this your sick friend?' asked Mim of Pops quietly. Pops nodded with obvious anxiety.

Mim leant down and placed her hand on the reclining girl's back. 'I'm awfully sorry, my dear, but are you quite all right?'

'Yes, I'm all right, just a bit off colour,' said the girl, turning just her head.

'Would you mind if I take a look at you? Out you come, please.'

The girl looked at Pops with horror and rolled over, pulled the sheet off herself and stood up with some effort.

'This girl is with child!' exclaimed Mim, looking at her large protrusion with disbelief. At this, the girl started to cry. Mim shook her head and took out her notebook. 'Name, please?'

'Tilly. Tilly Packett,' said the girl miserably.

'Does Mrs Sparrow know about this?'

Tilly shook her head. 'She just thinks I'm sick from the cordite.'

'And your parents?'

'They don't live around here, I came from Bristol to do this job,' said Tilly. 'I'll be all right, I just need to rest.'

Mim was about to snort a rebuff but Aggie stepped forward. 'Hello, Tilly, remember me?'

'Aggie? Course I do,' said Tilly, confused.

'I'm training to be in the police,' said Aggie, smiling and showing her armband. 'We're here to help you, love. Sit down a minute, will you? Now, go like this, I just want to look at your teeth.'

Mim stared as Aggie demonstrated by baring her teeth. She couldn't imagine what she was up to. Tilly shook her head, as though she understood.

'Now come on, love, it's no good you hiding up here all day on your own, is it – you need help.'

Tears ran down Tilly's cheeks. She nodded and showed Aggie her teeth. Aggie looked up at Mim and pointed at a blue line along Tilly's gums.

'Thanks, love,' said Aggie. 'You can lie down now.'

Aggie motioned for Mim to follow her out of the room. On the landing she spoke in hushed tones.

'She's taking lead to try to get rid of the baby. Probably diachylon plaster. They rub it up into pills and swallow it. But that girl must be eight months pregnant. She has to stop it and just have the baby, then think about what to do.'

'Lead?' said Mim, aghast. 'You mean to say she is trying to kill her baby with lead poisoning?'

Aggie nodded. 'You can tell by the blue line along her gums. I've seen it before. It must be making Tilly feel really poorly too.'

'Abortion is against the law,' said Mim, not knowing their legal standing in this case. She knew the girls practised self-abortion by some form or other, but there was never a way of proving they'd done it. Only the abortionists performing illegal operations were imprisoned if caught.

'I know, but don't get her arrested,' said Aggie, 'just make her stop taking it, then she can get the baby sent somewhere if she can't keep it.'

'If it's still alive,' said Mim, reluctant to take any advice from Aggie. 'Miss Packett,' she said, going back into the bedroom, 'I am under the impression that you have been self-administering lead in order to procure a miscarriage.' The friend Pops gave Aggie the most awful glare. Tilly nodded and cried with her head down. 'Where is the lead substance?' asked Mim. Tilly got herself off the bed and opened a chest of drawers. She took out a packet wrapped in brown paper and gave it to Mim. Inside were several large plasters, some of them torn where pieces of the formulation had been picked off.

'You are to take this poison no longer, do you under-stand?' said Mim sternly. 'Abortion is illegal. I could have you arrested. However, if you agree to desist I shall inform the Greygoose munitions doctor to come to your aid. You must bring yourself and your baby back to health. Once you have had the child, we shall help you take the necessary steps.'

'All right, missis,' said Tilly, quietly.

'Who is the father of the child, may I ask?'

Tilly looked at her lap.

'Someone in uniform, I presume?'

Tilly shook her head. 'Someone at work forced me,' she said wretchedly. 'But I'm not saying anything about it, I want to let it lie.'

'Tilly,' said Aggie, holding the girl's hand. 'Who was it? He has to be held to account, else he'll do it to someone else.'

Tilly just shook her head determinedly.

'This is what happens when girls leave home prematurely and have too much freedom,' said Mim. 'I shall send the doctor,' she repeated. 'And I shall ensure that Mrs Sparrow writes to your mother, who I am sure will be devastated.'

Giving the friend Pops a reprimanding stare on her way past, Mim made her way back downstairs into the pub and waited at the bar for the landlady to see her there.

Mim was reluctant to tell Aggie she'd done good work, acknowledge Aggie's diagnosis of the attempted self-abortion, and also of the rape confession. Mim knew it was likely that nothing would come of that if Tilly pressed charges. It wasn't the first time she had heard of the men in authority in the factory taking advantage of the girls. She'd never heard of anyone being held to account for it.

'Ooh lookee,' said a woman, standing up from where she sat with a man in uniform. It was Cecile, a known prostitute in the area. 'Lookee, lookee,' she said, daring to approach Mim, wearing her furs and rouge and silly fancy hat, her hair as black as a gypsy's and green eyes and bad teeth to match. Mim glanced at Aggie with pursed lips.

'Good evening, Cecile, I do hope you are keeping out of trouble? We don't normally see you in this public house.'

At this, Cecile gave a screech of joy. 'Oh, hoity-toity missis, I thought I'd have myself a little bit of a jaunt *ce soir.*'

'Indeed,' said Mim, with a disdainful sigh.

'And who have we got here?' said Cecile, obviously drunk, sliding up to Aggie and peering into her face.

'Constable Tucker in training. A pleasure,' said Aggie.

Cecile's eyes were wide with wonder at the sound of Aggie's voice. 'Constable Tucker in training?' she yelped, hardly able to contain her mirth. 'Fuck a duck, Constable *Tucker?*' she said again, in the most exaggerated, drawn out, working-class way of speaking. 'Well yes, it is a pleasure to meet *you*, a pleasure indeed.' With that, she went back to her table, shrieking with laughter, telling her soldier friend all about it, the two of them laughing and looking round at Aggie.

Mim ground her teeth. It was just the reaction she had expected Aggie to receive. It did Mim's cause no good at all. It was hard enough maintaining respect and order.

'Of course I'd ordinarily reprimand her bad language,' said Mim to Aggie.

At the sound of Cecile's raucous laughter, Mr Tunnidge and his pompous entourage turned around from their conversation at the large corner table in the saloon bar. Mim sighed again. Mr Tunnidge, local landowner, chairman of Linford's War Committee, chairman of Linford's Committee of Public Safety, special police constable (when it suited him) and all round ineffective busybody and leader of ninnies.

'I say, Sergeant Rathbone, I say,' he called through to the public bar. 'The clientele leaves something to be desired in the George and Dragon this evening, wouldn't you say?' He used a clipped and booming voice sufficiently loud for all to hear.

Mim kept her composure. Mr Tunnidge knew that women and children fell within Mim's remit and that he was referring to Cecile the prostitute. Ordinarily women wouldn't be permitted into the public bar but the war had brought many changes. She looked along the bar for Mrs Rumble, but the landlady was still deep in conversation, likely avoiding Mim since she had seen Tilly upstairs.

'Sod off, lumpen toad,' shouted Cecile, 'unless you're after a bit of the other?' she chuckled. 'That one goes a-bed with his boots on,' she told the whole establishment.

'Language, Cecile!' said Mim.

'Good heavens,' growled Mr Tunnidge. 'Please do your duty, Sergeant Rathbone, else someone with the professional faculties will do it for you.'

'If I may interrupt, Mrs Rumble?' said Mim, wanting to get the pub patrol over with. The landlady wiped her rag along the bar as she came. 'What do you know of Tilly Packett, one of your boarders?'

'She's in a bad way and I'm doing her a good turn, that's what I know about her, Sergeant.'

'Why have the authorities not been alerted to her condition?' Mim scrutinised the normally conscientious landlady, keen to keep her pub in order in the absence of her husband serving overseas.

'I know how her present condition came about, Sergeant, and I want to help her.'

'Are you aware she is attempting self-abortion by lead poisoning and half killing herself in the process?'

The landlady chewed her cheek. 'No, but I suspected she might be up to something: she looks dreadfully pale and she is always sleeping.'

'I have confiscated her ... formulation ... and I shall be sending the factory doctor to see her. Please do all in your power to bring the girl back to health, Mrs Rumble. Take her up a glass of Guinness.'

'Of course,' said the landlady, seeming relieved to relinquish her burdensome responsibility. 'Of course.'

'And what, may I ask, is Cecile doing in here?' said Mim. Mrs Rumble shrugged and shook her head as though powerless.

'Right, Cecile, it is time you went home to your children,' said Mim, walking to the prostitute's table and taking the woman's arm. When she protested, Mim took on a firm tone and addressed her soldier companion. 'I do believe you will do what is right to uphold proper moral order here, Private?' The soldier smirked and took up his cap, fixed it on his head and stood up to leave.

'Oh, you're always meddling, aren't you, missis,' drawled Cecile. But she went quietly and let herself be led out of the pub.

'Shall we escort you home?' asked Mim.

Cecile waved her away and started her walk home to the

outskirts of Mucking village, where she lived in a hovel with her six young children. 'Nighty night, Constable *Tucker*,' she called out without turning around.

'That public house is sliding down the path of immorality, I am sorry to say. I am very surprised by Mrs Rumble, I thought better of her,' said Mim, heading home to East Tilbury village.

'She's only trying to help Tilly, I think it's good of her,' said Aggie.

'I shouldn't wonder she's been hiding that girl from me,' said Mim, 'and that she knew about the attempts at miscarriage.' Mim hoped Aggie understood the magnitude of the situation. Mim had been impressed with how she had conducted herself – her knowledge and her ability to talk to the factory girls – perhaps she wasn't such a dead duck after all.

On a fresh autumn evening two days later, Mim took Aggie on patrol in their own village of East Tilbury. The leaves were changing colour – lollipop trees of bright yellow and dark orange showed off like Cecile the prostitute – a reminder that another year of war had passed. Mim said a silent prayer that next autumn would see peacetime. As they took the track out to Able's farm, she scanned the local vegetation for ripe elderberries and sloes but they had all been picked. The hawthorns were sparse. Admittedly, she had brought some of them to her own kitchen. The black nightshade berries remained on the bush and the damp fungus crawled along rotten tree trunks.

The tension between Mim and Aggie still simmered. They made no conversation while walking but both stopped intuitively to watch the gathering of swallows on the farm barn roof. A wretched nag of a horse suddenly cantered out of the farmyard towards them, at which the swallows rose en masse and seemed to conduct an airborne debate as to whether to begin their long flight south for the winter.

'Old Tom,' both women exclaimed at once. Mim had caught Farmer Able's nag on more than one occasion. In the village he was an infamous escapee. She and Aggie went at him in a pincer movement, Aggie grabbing his mane and Mim catching him around the neck. Farmer Able puffed along the track towards them, his clumsy form betraying his tired limbs.

'If you kept a halter on him, he'd be easier to catch, and easier to tie up, more to the point,' said Mim, crossly. The farmer got a rope around the horse's neck to drag him back to the farm.

'Can't say as I blame him much,' he said. 'He's doing the work of five, as am I.'

Mim had read a letter in the *Gazette* from a lieutenant in the third Essex Battery in Palestine reporting the status of the local horses that had gone overseas with them. *Still alive and with the Battery*. At home the farmers were struggling to cope.

'Have you considered my offer of arranging for some Land Girls to come to help you with the farm work?' said Mim, in admiration of the well brought up girls who were working the land up and down the country for the war effort.

'Nope,' said the farmer. 'I'd rather cripples or the German prisoners than have women on my farm.'

'It would cost you less to employ women than unskilled

labourers,' said Mim, hating her own words. The farmer thought women were incapable of farm work, no matter what he'd pay them. Mim knew he employed several local children on the farm and that some of them were doing more hours than they ought. She liked to come by now and again to make her presence known.

'I'm training to be in the police,' said Aggie, when the farmer frowned at her. He harrumphed in response.

'The prisoners of war held in Horndon and South Ockendon are used for farm work there but they don't come as far as East Tilbury,' said Mim to the farmer. 'And I am relieved, as it is hard enough controlling the local girls around the soldiers stationed here, let alone the Germans too.'

'Did you hear that the Germans have got factories where they turn their dead into oils and fertiliser?' said Aggie.

'Yes, I heard it, they all want stringing up,' said Farmer Able. Mim wasn't sure they should be conversing informally with the farmer. The sight of a child no older than ten wheeling a cart of manure across the yard caught her attention.

'Farmer Able, it is late for that child to be working,' she said.

The farmer made a face and called the child over. 'I thought I told you to get home for your tea,' he said, clipping the side of the boy's head. The boy frowned at the obvious injustice and left the cart by the farmer, looking silently at the women police as he made his way out.

'You're here about the game, no doubt?' said the farmer.

'Yes,' said Mim. 'Please do report any untoward behaviour.'

The farmer touched his floppy wide-brimmed hat and wheeled the cart away. Mim and Aggie had come through the farm to check on the football game between the Coalhouse Fort soldiers and the Greygoose munitions girls. It was being held on one of the fields between the fort and the farm.

'I need to get that child into Sunday school,' said Mim, looking down at her muddy boots as they navigated a stile into the field.

'His dad died on the front line,' said Aggie, holding up her skirt as she climbed over. 'I suppose you can't blame his mum for putting him to work, she's got a lot of mouths to feed. And he's better off working long hours for a pittance than be caught up in one of the boy gangs or being sent to beg at the factory gates.'

Again, Mim was struck by Aggie's point of view on matters. More and more parents were being lost to the war, directly or indirectly. Suicide and accidents at home had claimed many mothers. And with the new legislation allowing children to do farm work instead of going to school, it meant they were being used as slave labour.

'Still, the boy needs an education. Sunday school would be better than nothing. I shall go and see Reverend Clow.'

Aggie laughed to herself when they arrived at the make-shift football pitch adjacent to the fort. The sappers had their hands tied behind their backs, to allow for their unfair advantage playing against the munitions girls. Mim ordinarily would find no humour in the mixing of these young people and the potential trouble it could cause, but then one of the men slid over in the mud and couldn't find his footing so had to wait until his teammates pulled him to his feet. Mim supposed it was a moment of frivolity to cheer the dreary dread of war.

'They'll be dancing and drinking later, mind you,' she said. 'We'll be back to check the surrounding area. There'll be several couples hiding in compromising attitudes. There always are.'

'Just a bit of fun,' said Aggie.

'It is our duty to protect these girls from their own impulses,' said Mim, a little sharply, wanting Aggie to understand the girls' peril.

'Yes, I know, like Tilly the other day, I do understand,' Aggie returned curtly.

From the corner of her eye, Mim appraised Aggie. She was watching the football with a smile. Mim regretted her tone and decided to make amends.

'Were you in the football team at the factory?'

'Me? No,' said Aggie, surprised that Mim wanted to make conversation. 'It does look like a lark, though.'

'It does, rather,' agreed Mim, smiling.

'Would you fancy it, then?'

'Me? I don't know, I've never considered it. I was always rather good at hockey at school, and gym.'

'I bet you'd be good then,' said Aggie.

'Perhaps,' said Mim, smiling. 'It does look rather fun,' she said again. 'Speaking of sports, I could show you some ju-jitsu later if you'd like?' Mim had said it with good intentions of training Aggie, but in all honesty she didn't enjoy the more militant methods of the WPS.

Aggie looked dubious. 'You know,' she said, leaning in conspiratorially. 'I couldn't help but laugh when I saw the sub-inspector and Lady Braithwaite fighting each other. That's not the way people around here fight, I can tell you.'

110

'No, I shouldn't think it is,' laughed Mim. 'I'm sure the sub-inspector is a formidable opponent,' she said with an irreverent hint of sarcasm.

'Imagine her in a set-to against Cecile the prostitute,' said Aggie with a cheeky grin.

'Oh, I say, that is rather amusing,' said Mim, feeling an unfamiliar roll of laughter in her stomach. 'I rather fancy Cecile's chances there.'

'Ha ha, me too,' said Aggie. 'You know, I'm not sure I do want the ju-jitsu training – I'm not really one for fighting stuff. Do I have to do it to pass the training?'

'I completely understand,' said Mim, relieved. 'But perhaps we should do some just to show willing?'

'Yes, all right. Oh, look, is that the final whistle?'

'Ah, yes. In that case we shall pop over to check the Ship and then we shall make an appearance in the fort once the dance is in full swing.'

Aggie nodded and climbed back over the stile. She smiled at Mim and they both seemed relieved to have made friends.

'So what does your Bertie think about me moving in, then? Bet he's delighted about that.'

Mim was taken aback at Aggie's candidness. 'Bertie understands the hardships that war brings,' she said, suddenly wishing she'd chosen different phrasing. But Aggie laughed and didn't seem offended. 'What I mean to say . . .'

'Oh, you're all right,' said Aggie, cutting her off. 'I know what you mean.'

'It can't be easy for you, having to board with another family, when your husband is away fighting?' said Mim, nodding at the farmer as they trudged back through the farmyard.

'No, it is a bit strange, but it's a real chance of a lifetime for someone like me.'

'Yes, I suppose it is. And for me too,' Mim added. 'One must take one's chances.'

'Indeed,' said Aggie, with a grin, mimicking her. Mim raised her eyebrows and then laughed at Aggie's audacity, realising she was taking a liking to her unusual new colleague. And frankly, she was relieved to have a companion on her patrol. It was a sight less lonely.

When they entered the Ship, there was a shiver of adjustment as the punters checked themselves. Mim was about to speak to the objectionable victualler Mr Spooner, when Aggie suddenly gripped her arm.

'What on earth is the matter, Aggie?' said Mim, accidentally calling her by her Christian name.

'That's Penny Crabb,' said Aggie. 'Look at her, she's in a terrible state.'

'Who is Penny Crabb?' said Mim, following Aggie's gaze.

8

Aggie

'Who is Penny Crabb?' asked Mim.

In the Ship, Aggie saw the girl Penny, the one who'd gone missing in Tilbury, the one she had confronted. Here Penny was, in the pub, hanging on the arm of a different man. The girl wore more paint this time and her dress almost showed her calves. Her drooping right eye left no doubt it was her, and it was clear that she'd been drinking.

'Her mum reported her missing in Tilbury when I was on patrol there,' Aggie explained. 'We found her in the back streets with a soldier. I tried to talk to her, but I'm afraid I said the wrong thing. The sub-inspector ended up taking her home.'

'I see,' said Mim. 'It is worrying to see her here with the soldiers. This is just the sort of case we can help, before she slips up and does something she can never recover from.'

Mim gave Aggie a nod of encouragement, walking with her.

'Hello, Penny, remember me?' said Aggie.

Penny turned around to see the two women police officers and her face dropped. 'What do you want?' she said rudely.

'We are just on patrol,' said Aggie. 'You're normally in Tilbury, aren't you? That's where you live, isn't it?'

'So what if it is?' said Penny, looking at her companion for help.

'What do you want with Penny?' said the sapper in uniform. 'She hasn't done anything wrong.'

'We are simply patrolling the area,' said Mim, lightly. 'Should you need our assistance, young lady, please do not hesitate to call on us.'

'I'm all right,' said Penny haughtily.

'Yeah, she's all right,' said another man, not in uniform, but with his left arm in bandages, who turned around from his pint of beer at the bar. He placed his good hand on Penny's backside and squeezed it.

'Oi, you,' she cried, jumping away and laughing. But the sapper was offended and stepped forward.

'What do you think you're up to then?' he said, confronting the bandaged man.

'Wally,' Aggie called over to the landlord at the other end of the bar, 'you've got a bit of bother here.'

The landlord, Wally Spooner, looked up from his conversation impatiently. 'It was all right until you lot turned up,' he said. 'Settle down, lads, won't you?'

The bandaged man laughed, which incensed the

114

sapper, whose face turned bright scarlet. 'You apologise to her,' he said.

'Oh come on,' said Penny, pulling the sapper away. 'Isn't it time we went to your dance?'

Aggie watched as Penny and her fellow left the pub. Through the window she saw them mount the sapper's motorcycle and drive away towards Coalhouse Fort.

'Oh dear, they've gone off to the football dance,' said Mim.

'Sorry,' said Aggie. 'I've got it all wrong again, haven't I.'

'No, I don't think so. It's important that she knows we are watching her; it might mean the difference between her getting into trouble or doing the sensible thing. Who is that other fellow, do you know? I haven't seen him before.' Mim nodded over to the bandaged man at the bar.

Aggie shrugged. 'I don't think he's one of the locals. But he's not stationed at the fort either, if he's injured. He must be a casualty. Look at his hands.' The man's hands had livid red scars on them from deep cuts. 'Although my Arnie says cuts like that are a sign that a man is swinging the lead.'

Mim shook her head. 'What does it mean?'

'That he's hurt himself on purpose to get out of serving,' Aggie whispered.

The man had gone back to his drink but his face was angled so as to keep one eye on his surroundings. He suddenly turned to look at Aggie, as though he had heard what she'd said. Her heart lurched and she looked away. 'Are we going to the fort now, then?' she said.

The word about the dance seemed to get around the pub and several of the drinkers left at the same time. Aggie and

Mim walked the short distance. The party-goers gave them a wide berth and Aggie held up her chin, enjoying her new status.

'They won't have the dance inside the fort,' explained Mim. 'It will be in the mess hut in the encampment on the adjacent field, although I expect you know that already. Excuse me, young lady,' she called, as two girls rode bicycles past them. 'Your back light is out. That's a twelve pound and sixpence fine from the magistrate if you don't have it fixed the next time I see you.'

'Yes, sir,' the girl called out merrily as she cycled away.

As they walked they passed Aggie's little house, the windows covered in black-out curtains. It seemed a long time since she had been there with Arnie, a lifetime ago. She imagined someone else warming their hands at the kitchen range. 'What can we do to help Penny stay out of trouble?' she asked.

'I have had some success in finding war work for these girls,' said Mim. 'Greygoose have taken girls under my recommendation. But now they are reducing their workforce, I am not sure what to suggest. Bertie employs some women workers at the dockyard. That is a possibility, I suppose.'

'Yes, that's a good idea. Shall I talk to Penny about it?'

'You could try,' said Mim. 'But perhaps I should first talk to Bertie. He's awfully good but there are only so many workers he can pay. You know, I am always so cross about this every time I pass here.'

Mim had stopped outside St Catherine's church on the hill next to the fort. An old flint church that had been there for centuries.

'The tower, you mean?' asked Aggie, looking at the stump of an unfinished tower at the south-west end.

'Yes, it really is a shame. Poor Reverend Clow,' said Mim.

Aggie knew the story, everyone did. The local vicar had got permission from the War Office to ask the Royal Engineers stationed at the fort to build him a new church tower. They also built a war memorial outside the fort to remember their fallen comrades. Aggie was never sure if they had permission to do that, but still. As she and Mim continued their walk in the dusky light, they saw the remains of the memorial still lying scattered about by the fort wall.

'I remember the explosion,' said Aggie.

'I was invited to the unveiling,' said Mim, sadly. 'It was a proud day. Why the commanding general took offence at not being asked permission to build the memorial is one question. Why he commanded its destruction is quite another.'

The sappers had been ordered to blow the memorial up, and were told to stop work on the church tower. Aggie remembered how disgusted she had felt. It had been in the newspapers at the time, two years previously.

'The sun'll be down soon,' said Aggie.

'Yes, and when darkness falls, our duty calls,' said Mim seriously.

'Is that a WPS motto?'

'No, I do believe I just made it up,' said Mim, smiling.

'When darkness falls, our duty calls. I like it,' said Aggie, nudging Mim in the arm, and then wondering if she was being too friendly. Mim didn't seem to mind. They came up to the entrance to Coalhouse Fort grounds, guarded by armed soldiers. Mim put her hand on Aggie's arm, hanging back to fill her in on the set-up at the fort.

'You may know, the fort is manned by the Royal Garrison Artillery, assigned to the anti-aircraft guns, and the London Electrical Engineers, assigned to the searchlights. Known as the guns and the lights. They live in the fort and some are billeted in local houses – yours, perhaps? But the large encampment in the adjacent field is a transit camp and training centre for other troops going to France. It is the transience of these troops that bothers us – they want a last bit of fun before they go overseas, you understand.'

Aggie nodded and thought she couldn't blame the men for wanting that. It must be terrifying waiting to go to the front line.

'The lights will sweep the sky between nine and ten as usual, unless they have forewarning of a raid. But I expect you know all about that from the factory?'

'Yes, but there haven't been many raids lately.'

Mim nodded. 'Good evening, Sergeant,' she said to the men on duty. 'May I introduce Trainee Constable Tucker? We are here to patrol the dance in the camp.'

The sergeant looked Aggie up and down and let the women through without speaking.

'What's wrong with them?' she said.

'Like most people, they think we are busybodies. They tolerate us patrolling the area around the fort, but inside, they don't want us getting in the way. Our sub-inspector fought to gain access to the dances here. Other than that, we do not enter.'

Aggie stayed close to Mim as they walked the muddy

track to the army camp. Before them lay row upon row of pointed white tents, just as Aggie had seen in Tilbury. Men in uniform stood and sat about smoking and talking. A few light-hearted jeers went up as the women walked through. Mim ignored them, and Aggie copied her, trying not to betray her nervousness. The sound of music could be heard coming from a large wooden hut in the centre of the camp. Young women on the arms of uniformed men laughed and picked their way through the mud in their best shoes.

Inside the mess hut a five-piece band played in one corner. There were a good number of girls inside.

'I can't see Penny,' she said, scanning the room and trying to ignore the dirty looks from the girls.

'No, it is worrying. She must have sneaked off to one of the tents.'

'Aggie?'

Aggie turned to see a girl from the factory who she'd worked with. 'Hello, Doris, how you doing?'

'What this?' said Doris, looking at Mim and frowning. 'You're not one of them, are you?'

'I'm training to be in the women's police.' Aggie couldn't think what else to say on the spot.

'You're never,' said Doris, staring. 'Why would you ever want to spy on your own kind?'

Mim stayed quiet, as though waiting to see what Aggie would say.

'Not spying,' she said, with a nervous laugh. 'We're keeping an eye on things to make sure the local girls don't get into trouble with the soldiers, that's all.'

Doris gave a rude snort. 'We don't need keeping an eye on,

thank you very much.' She turned on her heel back to her group of friends. They put their heads together and looked over at Aggie.

'Not to worry,' said Mim kindly. 'It's as much as one can expect. One is committed to one's duty. Friendships, I'm afraid, must be compromised.'

Aggie was cross with Doris. Didn't the girl understand? Aggie had a chance to patrol the area in a different way, she knew how the working girls were.

'Sorry, I'm just going to have a quick word,' she said and Mim nodded in surprise.

Taking a deep breath, Aggie approached the group of girls. 'How you all doing? How's the factory? I do miss it there,' she said. 'Were you in the football? It looked a lark.'

'What you doing this for, Aggie?' said one of the girls, Pat. 'I can't believe it.'

'It's all right, Pat, I want to do it in my own way, not the way the others do it and I hope it'll give me a job after the war. I'm one of the working girls myself, so I know what it's like to be watched and spied on. These soldiers are allowed to do what they like and it's us girls who get caught out and blamed for everything. I know that.'

'These soldiers?' said Doris. 'You mean like your Arnie, I suppose?'

Aggie swallowed. It was all coming out wrong again. 'Not my Arnie, you know that, Doris. But the young lads, out for a gay time, worried that they're going away to fight and want a bit of a laugh. Sometimes the local girls get caught up in it all and before they know it, it's too late. You know what I mean, I know you do.'

Aggie blushed at what she was implying. But she couldn't think of any other way to say it.

'Sort of,' said Pat. 'I sort of see what you mean, Aggie. But you'd better be careful not to get too big for your boots. You're not better than us just because you're wearing that armband.'

'Course I'm not,' said Aggie. 'Look, have a good time at the dance and I'll see you around.' She smiled at them. Only Doris didn't return the smile.

Mim had been watching her. 'Well done,' she said. 'Now then, where has Penny got to?'

They wandered through the mess hut, watching roving hands on dancing couples and how much punch was being dished out. There was a connecting door at the far end that had a temporary NO ENTRY sign nailed there.

'I think this is the new recreation room that's being built,' said Mim, pushing at the door, which yielded and opened. 'Let's have a little look.'

As they stepped inside the dark room, the whine of the air-raid siren sounded and a great groan rose from the dance-goers behind them. Aggie's heart lurched with panic and she looked to Mim for guidance. 'Wait a minute,' said Mim, peering into the gloom. 'Who is there? Show yourself.' Aggie peered in too. There was what looked like a ping-pong or billiard table covered with a tarpaulin and several new chairs wrapped in straw. She could see no one in there. Mim shrugged and shook her head. 'We'd best get the girls out safely,' she said.

As they came out into the half darkness, the ominous beat of a plane engine could be heard. Aggie's stomach tensed with fear. 'Come on,' she heard herself saying, 'get out of the camp.' She helped Mim to usher the women out of the camp and back onto the village road.

'If you do not live nearby, get to the Ship public house to shelter in the cellar there,' called out Mim.

The girls shuffled forwards down the road, calling to each other. The plane came closer and Aggie saw it caught in the fort's searchlight. The anti-aircraft guns stuttered into life. Everyone started running for the pub, Aggie included. All she could think was the plane would drop a bomb on them all. The plane flew right over them, the girls screamed and ran, some dropped to their knees and covered their heads. 'Get up,' said Aggie, dragging a girl to her feet and pushing her onwards. 'Come on,' she shouted. She looked around, wanting to get her eyes on Penny, but there was no sign of her. Everyone reached the pub in safety. Aggie stayed outside with Mim, watching the road for anyone else out and needing somewhere to shelter. They watched the Gotha bend back round towards the river. Another joined it. Steady fire came from the fort and from the base on the opposite side of the water in Kent; together with the noise from the Gothas it was enough for Aggie to put her hands over her ears.

'If they go north we'll have to get to the factory quickly,' said Mim, watching the sky. The planes flew together over the water and headed west to London. Aggie watched them go, as they receded they got smaller and looked like poisonous wasps disappearing into the darkness. The sound of anti-aircraft guns came from further up the river at Tilbury Fort and Purfleet, then the whine of our own boys' aeroplanes, come to see Fritz off.

'All right,' said Mim. 'All right, they aren't heading for the factory. No bombs dropped. We can stay here for the all-clear.'

Aggie realised she'd been holding her breath and that her chest was thumping. 'I wonder where Penny got to,' she said.

When the all-clear sounded, those sheltering came out onto the street. Someone said the party at the camp was over and the revellers grumbled and hung around in the road.

'This could be difficult,' said Mim. 'Let's disperse them before it gets out of hand.'

Aggie copied Mim and called out, 'The party's over, time to get home.' But when they were ignored, Mim gestured for Aggie to stand back with her.

'I think all we can do is keep an eye on them, they are not ready to go home.'

There was a jeer further up the street and all heads turned, the intoxicated mob moving towards the excitement. Aggie and Mim followed. A group of party-goers were crowded in front of one of the little stone cottages on the main road. They were calling out, 'Yoo-hoo, Mrs Zlin, it's time to go home, we don't want you here,' in sing-song voices. A man in labourer's clothes hopped forwards to rap on the front window and hopped back. As if daring one another, the men and girls took turns to run forward, knocking on the door or window and calling out, 'Boche, go home,' and laughing. But soon the tone took on a sinister note, as though each person in the crowd remembered something personal about the war. Suddenly, they had found a vent for their anger.

The front door opened and Mrs Zlin, who Aggie knew was a charwoman who took in villagers' washing, stood there in what looked like an overcoat hastily thrown on over her nightclothes. She was an ancient widow, less than five feet tall with lines running from her deep-set eyes down her cheeks, like runnels. Her thin grey hair hung loose over her shoulders. She peered out into the darkness, worry etched on her face and holding the doorframe as though for support.

'Germans get out!' someone shouted.

Mrs Zlin's face scrunched in a frown. 'Germans?' she mouthed.

Someone threw a handful of mud, which landed at Mrs Zlin's feet, and she looked at it in surprise. She said something in the accent that betrayed her and the crowd hushed to hear.

'Half German,' she said. 'Half Czech. My husband, he was Czech. I do your washing.'

'Boo,' shouted someone. 'Enemy alien.'

'Let's go and help her,' said Aggie. 'It's only old Mrs Zlin.' Mim nodded and the women stepped forward.

'Disperse, please,' Mim called out. 'It is time to go home.'

'We want her out,' called a girl in a fancy dress. 'What are you defending her for?'

'Mrs Zlin is a villager here, she is no threat,' said Mim.

'Bloody suffragettes,' called out a man in uniform. 'Poking their noses in. My brother was shot by a German – and we've got one living here. Get her out!'

The crowd jeered in agreement.

'I'll not have you persecuting this woman,' said Mim, positioning herself between Mrs Zlin and the crowd. 'Now get back or I shall have you arrested.'

'Arrested?' The crowd laughed and pushed forward.

Aggie felt panic rise in her. The group looked menacing now and it was just her and Mim there to protect the old lady.

'You all know Mrs Zlin,' said Aggie, mustering her courage. 'She doesn't do any harm. You give her your washing, don't you? She knows a lot of you by your flippin' laundry. Now you leave her alone, go on, get away with you.'

Some of the crowd mumbled and quietened at Aggie's words. A couple wandered off. 'Go on, then,' repeated Aggie, looking directly at them. Luckily they did as they were told and drifted away. Aggie and Mim exchanged glances of relief. They turned to the old lady, who had withdrawn into her hallway and was peering up at the policewomen.

'Thank you,' she said, clasping her hands in front of her. Large, arthritic hands that seemed formed into permanent claws by the laundry she had scrubbed.

'Mrs Zlin,' said Mim, 'I don't suppose you would like to come and work for me at my house?'

The old lady's dark eyes fixed on Mim's.

'I mean to say, I have no staff and am in desperate need of a maid, someone to help with the housework. Perhaps it would be safer for you if you were to stay with me?'

Mrs Zlin glanced past Mim out to the front road, as if checking for the mob. She nodded. 'All right,' she said. 'Yes.'

'Thank you,' said Mim, smiling at Aggie. 'Would you like to come now?'

They helped the old lady collect her things. She moved with the panic of a refugee being evicted from her home, checking the stove was out, pulling vests off the clothes line strung across her kitchen. Aggie was sorry for her, she hadn't done anything wrong.

'That was good of you, Mim.'

Mim nodded. 'It serves us both, I cannot deny it. Keeping that house going without help has been torturous.'

Aggie squeezed her new friend's arm. She knew Mim's motive was more to help the old lady than to help herself.

'You know they are calling German measles the Belgian flush? And orchestras aren't allowed to play German music? It has gone too far.'

Aggie nodded her agreement. 'Poor Mrs Zlin, she hasn't harmed anyone.'

'I am not expressing pro-German sentiment, of course I am not. But we were not directly threatened by the Germans at the start, when we declared war. Bertie says we were so intent on going to war with Germany, we used protecting Belgium as an excuse for it. Our politicians wanted this war. Now our men are rotting in German camps, drowning in French mud, being shot in the face, gassed, being blown to pieces so small that they literally disappear, scattered to the winds, inhaled by their comrades . . .'

'They've fought a dirty war,' said Aggie, 'that's why people hate the blighters so much. They gas our boys and torpedo our hospital ships.'

'Yes, of course, but what of the German civilians? By all accounts they are starving to death in their thousands where we complain of having to eat potato bread and dandelion leaves. You're ready, Mrs Zlin?'

Carrying Mrs Zlin's bags, they escorted her down the road

to Mim's house. No one approached them, the revellers had gone home. Aggie could have cried when, upon entering the large house, Mrs Zlin found the kitchen and started to gather up dirty crockery.

'No,' said Mim, gently, touching the woman's arm. 'Please, come, I will show you your room.' The old lady looked confused, shaken. She followed Mim like a child, up the stairs, holding onto the banisters, taking the steps carefully so that both feet had stepped up before attempting the next.

Aggie put the kettle on the stove. She had a pot of tea ready when Mim came down.

'Goodness knows what Bertie will think,' said Mim, taking off her hat and smoothing her hair. 'First you and now old Mrs Zlin. Whatever next, Farmer Able?'

'Oh, Mim, you are a dear,' said Aggie, laughing.

'It's high time I took you to Stanford-le-Hope police station.'

It had been a week since the air raid at Coalhouse Fort and Aggie was helping Mim wash up the breakfast dishes at home. They found that, despite asking Mrs Zlin to help with the housework, they were loath to leave her too much to do. Desperately grateful for being taken in, she already got up at the crack of dawn to scrub the staircase and launder their clothes. Bertie had taken the news of his second lodger calmly and he was so busy at work that he wasn't at home much anyway. 'You'll have met our male colleagues in Tilbury, no doubt?' said Mim.

Aggie nodded. The men police at Tilbury hadn't exactly been welcoming. She expected the same at Stanford. But she was starting to get a thick skin and not mind too much what people thought of her training to be in the police.

'I would say that your training is going very well, wouldn't you?' said Mim, passing her a wet plate.

'Oh, yes,' said Aggie, on the spot. 'Yes, I do.' Policing was a sight better than breathing in poisonous fumes at the factory and she was actually enjoying herself. She liked Mim, too.

'I always say that patrolling is the best training there is. And we have been around most of the area together now. We have done the factory several times, East Tilbury, Linford.'

Aggie nodded. Patrolling the factory was the strangest. Checking women workers going through the factory gates for contraband, looking for shirkers, patrolling Goosetown and the dances, checking on the nursery. She even helped to break up a fight between two women workers. She'd had a mixed response from the girls. Some of them thought it an intrusion, some were encouraged that a girl from the working classes could do a professional job.

'We'll do some of Stanford today,' Mim went on. 'We'll go to Stanford police station, and then I'd like to pop in somewhere ...' She hesitated, wiping her hands on her apron. 'You are welcome to pop in too, but it is not necessary if you'd rather not.'

'Where?'

'The suffrage society,' said Mim, looking sheepish but proud, and turning to put a dish on the dresser. 'Before marriage, I started to train in nursing,' she said, smiling. 'But my father was horrified and I gave it up. Bertie was more tolerant of my interests than my father. I didn't return to nursing once married, of course, but instead I joined the suffragists and became the committee secretary before the war. I wanted to do patrolling work when the war started but because the WPS were active in the area, the suffrage society weren't allowed to have their own patrols here too.'

'So you're not a suffragette then?' Aggie assumed Mim was like the other women police she'd met.

'Goodness, no, I am not. In order to train for the women's police service I had to rescind my NUWSS membership and join the Pankhursts' WSPU.'

'Makes sense,' said Aggie. 'You don't strike me as one of those militant sorts. You're not like the sub-inspector with her cropped hair and motorcycle.'

'I'm still a member of the NUWSS in spirit,' Mim added hesitantly, 'even though my new position means I am detached from my friends in the area. I hold great value in my position as woman police sergeant but I don't hold with a lot of the suffragette ideals. I attended the suffragist Mud March in 1907 and the Great Pilgrimage in 1913,' she said, proudly. 'I helped organise a big suffrage meeting in Grays town at the time. The militancy of the so-called suffragettes only undermined our efforts. This is all between us, you do understand?' Aggie nodded. 'I believe that a quiet campaign is dignified and effective,' Mim went on. 'Frankly, I find the cropped hair, monocles, motorcycles and ju-jitsu all a little alarming.'

'You've got the vote now, haven't you? You must be pleased.' Aggie herself didn't qualify to vote. She was the same age as Mim but Mim's husband was a property owner, Aggie's husband was not.

'Yes, thank goodness, and I'm delighted. I would dearly love women to be permitted entry to the professions now. Imagine there being women judges and magistrates. It would change the justice system dramatically.'

'My Arnie got the vote this year too,' said Aggie. 'But I didn't. Maybe your society will try and get the vote for all women next?'

Mim gave an insincere smile and nodded. 'Shall we go to Stanford? Bicycles?'

'Yes, all right then,' said Aggie, wondering why Mim had avoided her question. Maybe she didn't believe women like Aggie should have the vote.

The roads were quiet. Workers were at work. Children were at school or working on the farms. It was warm for late September, a fine spell of weather and a break from the storms they had had of late.

'Perhaps the Allies will advance while it's dry,' called Mim from her bicycle as they made their way along the lanes to Stanford.

'Hope so,' said Aggie. She'd had a letter from Arnie the day before and had read it aloud to Mim. Reading between his lines of cheery optimism it sounded like he was lucky to be alive. She felt bile rise in her throat at the thought of the shells exploding around him and said another prayer for him to be brought home safely.

'I prayed for Arnie last night,' said Mim with a sympathetic smile. Aggie looked at her friend in amazement. How kind of her to think of Arnie.

'Bertie is very busy, isn't he?'

'Yes, but I am lucky to have him here at all, really.'

Aggie had spent a spare half hour in Mim's library the day before. She had lifted down a book that was slotted into the top shelf and was startled to see that it was called *Married Love*. She read a bit of it, instantly fascinated, and put it back quickly when she heard Mim come down the stairs.

'Yes, I miss my Arnie terribly. Night times are very lonely,' she said, with a glance at Mim, wondering whether she and Bertie had put the book's advice into practice.

'He will be home soon, with any luck,' said Mim. 'The Allies have retaken Passchendaele and there's talk of the Bulgarians withdrawing. With God's good grace—'

'Oh dear, look,' said Aggie. They were on the outskirts of Stanford-le-Hope town, near the chalk quarry. There was a dishevelled-looking man slumped in a ditch. The women jumped off their bikes and rushed to him.

'Sir. Sir!' called Mim, shaking him by the shoulder. The man roused and opened his eyes and the women exchanged glances of relief.

'Are you all right, sir?' asked Aggie, looking to see if she knew the man. He looked vaguely familiar.

'What? Yes,' he said, in a gruff voice.

'Where do you live?'

'Linford,' he said, standing up with some difficulty, grimacing as though in pain and brushing himself off. 'Linford,' he repeated, seeming to wake up. 'I was out drinking in Stanford last night and slept it off here on the way home.'

He looked jittery, his eyes sliding back and forth between the women and in the direction of Stanford. 'Do you need our help to get home?' said Mim.

'No, course not,' he said and trudged off slowly down the road towards Linford, stooping on one side.

Aggie watched him go and Mim started to look around the patch where the man had been sleeping.

'Ah, I thought as much,' she said, picking up something from the grass.

'What is it?' said Aggie.

'Painkilling drugs.' Mim was holding the end of a glass syringe. 'He was injured, did you notice? He probably went to Stanford last night to buy drugs illicitly. It is very sad. Very sad indeed.'

'It's horrible,' said Aggie, remembering when the sub-inspector had pointed out a drug dealer near Tilbury Docks. 'The poor man, as if it wasn't bad enough having to go and fight.'

'Indeed,' said Mim, mounting her bicycle. 'But these men don't want our help and they won't admit they are addicted to the stuff. The government needs to do more for them.'

They pulled up outside Stanford police station and leant their bicycles against the railing. Aggie readied herself for the reception she knew awaited her – a mixture of disdain and loathing. As they entered, a policeman turned to greet them. His face didn't drop with frustration when he saw them. Instead he looked quite cheery.

'Good morning, Sergeant Rathbone. Have you been gifted a constable at long last?' he said, looking at Aggie.

'Good morning, Sergeant Pavey, indeed I have. May I introduce Trainee Constable Tucker?'

'A pleasure,' he said, nodding at Aggie. 'How long have you been in training?'

'Nearly three weeks, now. I worked at Greygoose before that,' she added, seeing his look of confusion.

'Ah, I thought I'd seen you before ...' He paused, sizing up the situation. 'I'll be blowed,' he said, scratching the skin behind his ear. 'What are you up to, Sergeant Rathbone?'

'Not me, Sergeant Pavey. The sub-inspector took her on, and I'm rather pleased she did. Trainee Constable Tucker is a very able colleague.'

'I'll wager she is,' he said, looking visibly shocked. 'You'll help us catch the next POW who makes a run for it, will you?' he joked.

'Have there been any significant events, Sergeant?' asked Mim.

Sergeant Pavey lowered his voice. 'We've had two suicides in the past week, one domestic and one army. And the Peculiars have had some backlash too.'

The Peculiar People, a religious sect, a lot of them conscientious objectors. Aggie wondered that they didn't have more trouble from the other locals.

'We came across a Gerald Green, slumped in a ditch on Butts Lane,' reported Mim. 'He's a drug addict, I am sure of it. He accepted no help though and made his way home.'

'Thank you, I'll make a note of it,' said the sergeant. 'Drugs are taking up a lot of our time now.'

'What's this?' Another officer came into the front desk. He had the flat peaked cap of a higher rank.

'You'll never guess, Chief, they've only made a factory girl into a woman police.'

The chief constable looked as though he'd just sniffed something gone off.

'Is this possible, Sergeant Rathbone?' he asked Mim.

'Yes, indeed,' said Mim tersely.

'Shall we be getting off on patrol, then?' said Aggie, wanting to get out.

'Sergeant Pavey is a decent chap, but the chief constable is as bad as the rest. He has no time for women police officers,' said Mim when they were back on their bikes. 'So I wouldn't take it too personally. We'll just stop off quickly at the society,' she went on, 'if you wouldn't mind too much?'

'No, that's all right,' said Aggie, flattered that Mim wanted her to tag along.

They came to a posh-looking house near the high street. It was hung with green, white and red ribbons. There was a plaque by the front door saying SOUTH ESSEX WOMEN'S SUFFRAGE SOCIETY. Inside, a well-to-do woman greeted Mim affectionately.

'How lovely to see you, Mim. Still doing your patrol duty, I see?'

'Yes. Victoria, may I introduce my new Trainee Constable Tucker.'

'Delighted,' said the woman, taking Aggie's hand in her own white lace gloves.

'Victoria is the president of the local suffrage society,' explained Mim. Aggie smiled and looked around the room. Books and banners were on display and there were piles of leaflets and more coloured ribbons.

'May I offer you some tea?'

'Oh, perhaps we could, that would be lovely, thank you,' said Mim.

Victoria popped her head out of the room to ask someone

to make tea. 'How are things out there?' she said to Mim, motioning for them both to sit down on the brocade sofa.

Mim hesitated and looked at Aggie. 'We can't say too much for confidentiality reasons. But the girls and children need us more than ever. We currently have our eye on one local girl, a frivolous type, at risk of prostitution. The sub-inspector has spoken to her mother. The freedom and the soldier encampments are too much temptation for them to understand or control.'

'These young girls need somewhere to go. Those who don't do munitions work have no leisure facilities of their own. I shall continue my campaign to raise funds for a local girls' club.'

Aggie smiled and nodded, not knowing what to say to this formidable woman. She wanted to say she knew these girls, knew that they deserved to have a good time but maybe could do with a gentle word when push came to shove, but she was too afraid to open her mouth. The tea arrived, carried by another smartly dressed woman, who said hello to Mim. Aggie took her cup and stirred her drink, enjoying the deli-cate scrape of silver on porcelain. She stopped stirring when she saw Victoria looking at her.

'And did you travel far to be here, Constable Tucker? I don't recall hearing the name before.'

'Oh no, I live in East Tilbury, same as Mim, but I've moved in to board with Mim now that I'm training,' said Aggie.

'Ah, I see,' she said, with a delicate frown and glance at Mim. 'Forgive me, but what did you do before joining the WPS?'

'Worked at Greygoose, doing munitions,' said Aggie, biting her top lip and feeling on ceremony.

'Indeed?' said Victoria, her face erupting with confusion and delight.

'And what have you been occupied with, Victoria?' said Mim and Aggie was glad that she had changed the subject.

'Oh, you know, organising my election campaign and so on. Oh, Mim, I am being facetious, I do apologise.'

Both women tittered with laughter and Aggie smiled politely.

'One day, Victoria, and it will be a fine day indeed when you are given that chance.' Victoria gave Mim a grateful smile. 'We'd better be going, I'm afraid. But it has been wonderful to see you.'

Aggie stood up at Mim's signal and they took their leave.

'What was that about an election?' asked Aggie shyly as they walked their bikes down the high street.

'Victoria would dearly love to run in the next local election but of course women are not permitted. We dream of the day when women are allowed into the professions and political system.'

'She's very grand,' said Aggie.

'Yes, I suppose she is. She is a dear friend and an inspiration to me.'

An inspiration. Aggie realised that that was what Mim was to her. 'I'm glad you brought me along,' she said. 'And I'm glad you're training me, Mim. Thank you.'

'We'll have you trained and in WPS uniform yet, Aggie.' Mim smiled and mounted her bicycle.

It was as much in Mim's interest for Aggie to pass her training as it was to Aggie herself. Mim had been tasked with training Aggie and had something to prove to the sub-inspector. Aggie felt a keen sense that they were together in this. It gave her confidence to know that she could trust Mim; it gave her confidence to believe that one day she would put on the WPS uniform and be a factory girl showing she was as good as the society ladies.

9

Mim

Mim and Aggie were laughing. Something funny had happened and the sheer release of being able to let go and to forget the war, to forget the patrol, to simply laugh, was delectable.

Aggie had reminded Mim of something that had happened on patrol earlier that evening. It was very silly but it had tickled them both. Cecile the prostitute had been drunk. They had tried to corral her back home but she had danced away from them down the middle of the road, turned around, bent over and lifted her skirts to show her bare backside. It had stopped Mim and Aggie in their tracks, and they had both blushed red.

And now they were washing up together at the kitchen sink, as had become their habit, and Aggie brought it up and they laughed until tears wetted their cheeks.

'Oh, I am so glad you are here, Aggie.'

Aggie caught her breath. 'Me too.' There was a knock at the front door and they both frowned. It was late. 'It'll be some drama or other,' said Aggie.

'No doubt,' said Mim, going to the door to save Mrs Zlin getting out of bed.

She was still chuckling as she reached to take off the latch and she made a determined effort to greet the visitor with a straight face. If she'd known who was there and what they had come to say, she'd have had no trouble at all extinguishing her joyful demeanour. In fact, nothing else in the world would have squashed her joy in quite as effective a way. Even the face alone of the person at the door would have been sufficient to create such an effect. The face of Benjamin Proctor, Bertie's business partner, was enough to smite the very pleasure from not just Mim, or Aggie, or this house. Not just from East Tilbury village, but from every neighbouring town too, and even from the whole majestic country of Great Britain itself.

Not that Benjamin Proctor showed her his joy-squashing countenance at first. His eyes were cast down at his hat in his hands, as though he was practising the gaze in advance of using it on Mim.

He looked up at her, and there it was. All across his face in thick wattle and daub plaster . . . in electric lights . . . in a prostitute's orange lipstick. It was all there for Mim to see for herself. She almost laughed at the clarity of it. It was so blatantly clear for Mim to know at once, at that first look at Benjamin Proctor's face, that her dear, dear husband Bertie was dead.

*

Get her up . . . bring her in through here . . . on this chair . . . What's happened? . . . Mim? . . . Mim? . . . What's happened? . . . It's Mr Rathbone . . . I'm his business partner . . . he had a terrible accident . . . there was nothing to be done . . . it was instantaneous . . . the men told him not to climb up there . . . he went up to help a fellow hurt . . . he fell, poor chap . . . Bertie? . . . Bertie's dead? . . . Oh no, Mim, oh, Mim . . .

10

Mim

Mim stared at the clock on the mantelpiece. It was half past eleven. One week ago Benjamin Proctor had knocked on her door. He had knocked at the door of her very existence too. She had slammed it shut in his face. Bertie wasn't dead. He had kissed her cheek that very morning when she was still in bed. Up at the crack of dawn as usual. He worked so hard. He never said it, but Mim knew he needed to compensate for not putting on a set of khakis and going overseas to fight the enemy. He was doing his bit for the war, of course he was, he worked all the hours God sent. And he was loath to profit from the war, like so many profiteering mercenaries in the country, squeezing every last shilling they could out of the devastation and horror. Not Bertie. He donated money to the local military hospitals, he bought war bonds, he arranged charity events for war disabled, war widows, he employed women in his shipyard. He was a good man. King and Country needed him, his employees needed him, Mim needed him.

When Benjamin Proctor came knocking on her door one week ago and gave her such an awful fright, she told him to leave. She told him she would tell Bertie what he had done, coming there to scare her. He must have had some sort of personal vendetta, a score to settle. He must have been one of the profiteering mercenaries. Bertie must have found something out about him and he was exacting his revenge by coming to Bertie's house, knocking on Bertie's door, and having the absolute gall to tell Bertie's wife, her, Mim, that he was dead! It was an affront.

Mim stared at the clock on the mantelpiece. It was half past one. She was shaking again. It was really quite disconcerting. Her whole body wracked with sobs that had no sound and no tears. And then it passed.

Please eat something, Mim. You must eat, my dear.

She sighed. Food had no meaning any more. Sustenance. Survival.

We must talk about the funeral, Mim.

Whose funeral? Until she saw Bertie's body she wouldn't entertain the idea. A funeral for somebody who it would transpire was alive and well was ludicrous. Whoever heard of such a thing?

If you come with me, my dear, just into the library, he's there. He's waiting to say goodbye.

Aggie was part of the conspiracy. Why would Bertie want to say goodbye to her? Perhaps he was going overseas for business. She jerked her head and wobbled to standing.

'He's there? He wants to say goodbye?'

Yes, he's there. Come on.

There were tears now, tears of joy and an undignified strangled sound coming out of her. She almost tripped over her skirts as she rushed to the library. It all looked blurry through her tears. There were several figures standing about, who left when she arrived. She felt touches on her arm and heard soft voices as they passed. But where was Bertie? She blinked and looked around. Aggie's hand was on her arm, pulling her gently forward. They stopped at the most curious sight she had seen – and she had seen many a curious sight on her patrols. A coffin in the library. An open coffin on a plinth. She looked at the ceiling and blinked again. The moulding around the electric light fitting was beautifully done. But it swam out of focus. She was shaking again. She gripped the edge of the coffin and felt the silk lining inside. Bertie liked silk, when he could get it. Silk ties and silk socks. They were something of a private indulgence. She took her courage in hand and looked down. Was it him? He looked different. So very pale but with the terrible undertaker's rouge. His mouth looked so set, so determined. She needed to see his eyes but they were closed. She couldn't really be sure that this wasn't a stranger in this coffin in her library. She was shaking so very violently and Aggie was hanging onto her as though she needed ships' scaffolding to keep her upright. And then she noticed it. The stranger in the coffin was wearing Bertie's favourite blue silk tie.

'Who gave it to them?' she suddenly cried into Aggie's face. 'Who gave them his tie?'

Mim stared at the clock on the mantelpiece. It was half past five. There had been a lot of people around her for a long time. She had looked at the ground. She had looked at her hands. She had walked behind the undertaker's hearse, with Aggie pulling her on. She had stood at the graveside.

'You've got him here, at least, haven't you.' Someone had said that to her. 'I didn't get my boy back from France,' the someone said.

Mim looked at the clock and it was half past nine. She started to shake again and Aggie took her upstairs to bed. Her clothes were taken off gently, her shoes removed. Her hair was brushed and she was lain down to sleep.

11

Aggie

Exhausted from sleeping on Mim's bedroom armchair, Aggie got herself dressed and made them both breakfast. Porridge was the best thing. It stayed warm for a while and it usually took some time for Mim to register it was there at her bedside, despite Aggie telling her several times. While Mrs Zlin scrubbed laundry in the scullery, Aggie washed up the pan and her dish by herself in the kitchen, and put on her hat to go to the shops. She needed to finish the shopping before going out on patrol otherwise she wouldn't be able to sit and hold Mim's hand as she fell asleep. Mim had terrible nights, disturbed by bad dreams, talking and muttering in her sleep, reaching out for Bertie. Aggie had taken to sleeping there in the chair to give her arm a reassuring pat and say some soft words of comfort and usually that did the trick and Mim would go back to sleep for a while.

The sub-inspector had written to her. A sergeant from Tilbury would be coming today to continue her training. Aggie had been patrolling by herself the past week. She knew Mim would have done the same. She didn't want to let anyone down and she needed to prove that she was up to the task. Poor Bertie. Death had knocked on the Rathbones' door. It had been so unexpected. Bertie wasn't in the services, he worked here, down the road in Tilbury. He was a big boss, he didn't do dangerous work. But he had seen a man in trouble in the dry dock, he had climbed up to help and he had fallen.

Back from the shop she was sweeping the kitchen floor when there was a knock at the door. It was the Tilbury sergeant come to train her. When she opened the door and saw Sub-Inspector Nash standing there she assumed there had been a set-back, a staffing problem and she would have to wait for her training.

'Good afternoon, Trainee Constable Tucker. If you are ready, we shall commence our patrol.'

'Pardon me, Sub-Inspector. I thought you said in your letter that a sergeant from Tilbury would be training me.'

'Yes, I did say that, didn't I?' said the sub-inspector, removing her leather motorcycle gloves. 'But I have decided that this district needs a little shaking up, so I shall continue your training myself. Now come along.'

She turned and walked back through the garden gate, her tall leather boots buffed and shining, and Aggie's heart sank.

'How is Sergeant Rathbone doing? I shall visit her in a week or two when the rawness of her loss has eased a little.'

'She is as can be expected,' said Aggie, not wanting to

betray the extent of Mim's condition and risk her losing her job. Aggie was surprised and scared by the intensity of Mim's grief. It made her wonder how she would react if Arnie met the same fate. It made her fear even more whether Arnie would return home safely.

The sub-inspector gave a curt nod, appreciating the fortitude of her officers.

'We shall go to Greygoose. The girls are getting up a protest again.' With that, she mounted her motorcycle. Aggie's mind raced. Should she follow on her bicycle and meet the sub-inspector at the factory?

'I'll fetch my bicycle,' she said, turning back to the house.

'Don't be absurd. Jump on the back here.'

Aggie baulked. She'd never been on a motorcycle, or even in a motorcar. They looked like fearful things to her.

'Well, come along,' said the sub-inspector impatiently. Aggie looked down at her long skirt and wondered how she would do it. 'You'll mount side saddle, of course,' said the sub-inspector, kicking at the starter. Aggie grabbed hold of the seat and pulled herself on, gripping tightly and scared to death. The sub-inspector kicked the starter again and the motorcycle roared to life, smoke billowing around them. Aggie wanted to jump off but she was more scared of the sub-inspector than the bike. 'You'll need to hold onto me,' called the sub-inspector as they pulled away. 'And take off your hat else it'll blow off.' All codes of etiquette were swept away in an instant and Aggie took off her hat and grabbed onto her superior's mackintosh cape for dear life.

Luckily the bike wasn't very fast and they puttered along the lanes quite well. Aggie relaxed a little and realised it was quite good. People stared at them as they passed and she was pleased with the looks of awe on their faces.

The guards at the factory let them through the gate and they parked the motorcycle on the inside of the gatehouse. The ride had been exhilarating and Aggie couldn't help but smile.

'What's the state of play?' the sub-inspector asked the woman constable at the gate.

'They are in the Goosetown canteen,' said Constable Firman. 'Refusing to go to work. There have been more laid off this morning.'

'I see. And what are you doing here, may I ask?'

The officer paled. 'I thought I should patrol the entrance, Sub-Inspector.'

'The West Kent guards are here, Constable Firman. I am sure you are needed most where there is trouble with the girls, are you not?'

'Yes, Sub-Inspector, of course,' said Constable Firman, trotting after them as Sub-Inspector Nash and Aggie mounted the motorcycle and drove over to Goosetown where the factory girls lived and took their meals.

As they approached the canteen hut, Aggie's guts twisted with nerves. She hoped it wouldn't be too awkward if any of her factory friends were in there. Sub-Inspector Nash went in first and as soon as the girls saw her a loud jeer went up, screams and boos, and someone threw a currant bun, which caught Aggie on the shoulder as she stepped in at the sub-inspector's side. Aggie jerked away from the missile and looked with dread at the angry faces before her. 'What do you want?' the girls called out. 'We don't want you here, get out of it,' they said.

The sub-inspector remained unshaken. She gave Aggie a look as if to say she had expected the undignified scene.

'What are you doing, Aggie? Going against your own?' Aggie started and looked for the accuser. It was Minnie, a fellow guncotton worker. Aggie shook her head slightly, unable to explain. 'Shame on you!' called another girl, and some others joined in. 'Shame on you.'

'When you have quite finished,' the sub-inspector suddenly bellowed over the din, her voice instantly commanding authority. 'When you have quite finished with this unseemly behaviour, you might hear what I have come to say.'

Aggie looked at her in awe, wishing she could instil respect in the same way.

'Myself and Trainee Constable Tucker are employed by the Ministry of Munitions, as you are yourselves.' The girls quietened down, the scowls on their faces not enough to stop the sub-inspector's speech. 'You are breaking the law by refusing to work.'

'We're not working till our mates have got their jobs back,' shouted out one woman, and the others jeered along in support.

'I have no interest in your terms,' said the sub-inspector. 'If you do not return to work immediately I shall call the chief constable to come to arrest you all. You will appear before Grays police court where you stand a jolly good chance of being sentenced to time in prison with hard labour. You would lose your job here, you would lose any separation allowances allocated for a husband in service. You and your children would become destitute. Orsett workhouse is currently admitting only the sick and insane, however, once the war ends, I am certain there will be a place for you and your families there. You would be separated from your loved ones, of course. It is ten past eleven now,' she said with a glance at the canteen clock. 'Those of you remaining here at a quarter past will be held pending arrival of the chief constable and will then be escorted to Stanford-le-Hope police station.'

Aggie stared at Sub-Inspector Nash. The room had fallen silent. Every woman there stood up and walked out of the canteen, grumbling and cursing. Several of them brushed past Aggie roughly.

At a quarter past eleven there were only the two officers and the volunteer serving women left in the room.

'Right,' said the sub-inspector. 'All they needed was a good telling-off.' She left the canteen with Aggie following in her wake, truly impressed by the power of this formidable woman. 'I know they work hard, I know they are keeping their homes going while their men are away. But they cannot strike. Factory production is paramount.' Aggie nodded even though the sub-inspector wasn't looking at her. They mounted the motorcycle again and headed out onto the lanes.

As they drove back through Linford, a woman flagged them down outside the George and Dragon pub. It was the landlady, Rose Rumble, and she looked uncharacteristically worried.

'Thank the Lord,' she said. 'Something's happened, inside.'

'You might elaborate,' said the sub-inspector, unperturbed and kicking down the stand of the bike.

Aggie slid off the seat and went to Mrs Rumble. 'What is it?' she asked.

'Oh yes, you were with Sergeant Rathbone, weren't you?

You saw Tilly, remember?' she said, lowering her voice and coming very close to Aggie. 'It's Tilly, it's her baby, oh, it's terrible.'

Aggie and the sub-inspector exchanged glances and followed Mrs Rumble inside. They walked through the public bar and up the stairs to the munitions girls' boarding rooms.

'One of the girls was with child,' explained Aggie on the stairs. 'She was trying to ... trying to end the pregnancy. Sergeant Rathbone reported her to the doctor.'

'It came early,' said Mrs Rumble. 'Alive, a miracle.'

They came into Tilly's room. The girl was there sitting on one of the lower bunk beds. There was an unpleasant smell about the place and Aggie's heart raced, looking for the baby.

'Where's the baby, Tilly?' said Aggie, going to the girl.

'Here,' said Mrs Rumble. She opened the bottom drawer of the dresser and the smell was worse. The landlady covered her mouth and nose with one hand and stepped backwards.

Sub-Inspector Nash came forward and looked in. Aggie looked at Tilly's face. The girl was unresponsive, in shock. The sub-inspector lifted a blanket in the drawer and dropped it quickly. 'Do you have a telephone?' she asked.

'No,' said Mrs Rumble.

'Stay here,' said the sub-inspector to Aggie. 'Stay here and let no one or nothing leave the room. I shall ride to the police station.'

'Yes, Sub-Inspector,' said Aggie, feeling sick.

When she left, Aggie sat on the bed with Tilly. She wanted to look in the dresser drawer to confirm her fears but knew it wasn't necessary. Something compelled her to stand up, though, and take a step there, to reach out and pinch the blanket between her finger and thumb, to lift it up. She dropped the blanket and wished she hadn't looked. A tiny baby, grey and lifeless, wearing a white knitted dress. A doll. A doll that had magically come to life and then had fallen down still and silent once more.

'What happened?' whispered Aggie, to no one in particular. Tilly started to cry. 'I've got to go down,' said Mrs Rumble. 'I'm sorry but you are not to leave the room,' said Aggie.

They all fell silent again. Aggie remembered when they had been here last. She had persuaded her friend Pops to let Mim upstairs to see Tilly. Now she wished she hadn't. She regretted telling Mim about what Tilly's blue gums meant, she was trying to prove she was good at her job but if she hadn't said anything perhaps the baby would have miscarried and known no pain.

In due course the sub-inspector returned. 'Sergeant Pavey is bringing the doctor in his pony and trap,' she said. 'Have you established what happened here?' she asked Aggie.

Aggie shook her head and the sub-inspector looked at Mrs Rumble.

'Well, would you kindly enlighten me? What kind of establishment are you running here?'

Mrs Rumble bristled. 'Sergeant Rathbone and this one here knew about the girl's condition,' she said.

'So I understand,' said the sub-inspector. 'But what caused the baby's death? Was the birth declared?' Mrs Rumble sniffed and drew herself up, not wanting to comment. 'Was the baby's birth declared, I asked,' said the sub-inspector sternly to Tilly. Tilly shook her head. 'Then what caused the baby's death?' she said. Tilly didn't answer.

The doctor and Sergeant Pavey knocked and came into the room, the doctor going to the dresser and examining the baby.

'Did you give the baby laudanum?' he asked Tilly. Tilly nodded her head and started to cry again. 'Did you give the baby a lot of it?' Tilly shook her head, in too much of a state to realise what she was being accused of.

'I would say the baby died from laudanum poisoning,' said the doctor.

'Oh, Lord save us and protect us,' said Mrs Rumble, slumping down onto a small wooden chair in the corner.

'What is the girl's surname?' asked Sergeant Pavey gently.

'Packett,' said Mrs Rumble weakly. 'Tilly, Matilda Packett. She's a good girl, she made a mistake, that's all.'

'Miss Matilda Packett, I arrest you for the concealment of the birth of your child and for its wilful murder. You will accompany me to the police station.'

'But how do you know it wasn't an accident?' said Aggie, knowing the scene was incriminating. Why would Tilly have concealed the baby's body?

'That will be decided in court,' said Sergeant Pavey.

Aggie helped the girl to her feet, looked around for her shoes and helped her get them on, got a coat around her shoulders. Tilly didn't protest, she went with the sergeant without a fuss.

'What an awful business,' said Aggie, coming out onto the landing and watching Tilly going down the stairs.

'We shall notify the undertaker,' said the sub-inspector, with a disdainful look at Mrs Rumble. 'I can't help but feel that you have been accomplice to this atrocity. I am certain the Stanford police will want to talk with you further.' Mrs Rumble just looked very sad. Aggie remembered Mim saying that she was a decent, churchgoing woman who was keeping the pub running while her husband was away on service. She had set up the boarding rooms to give the munitions girls somewhere safe and clean to stay. But it had gone horribly wrong. Aggie wondered what she would do now. She gave the landlady a sympathetic smile and followed the sub-inspector out.

'What'll happen to her?' asked Aggie outside the pub. 'What'll happen to Tilly?'

'She'll be sentenced in court, of course.'

'She'll be sent to prison?'

'I should think so,' said the sub-inspector. 'For concealing the birth, if not for murder.'

'I don't think she did,' said Aggie. 'She probably gave laudanum to soothe the baby, I can't believe she'd give it too much on purpose.'

'You'd be surprised what we see in court, Constable Tucker,' said the sub-inspector. 'This is why our work is so important – to prevent these unfortunate situations.'

If Aggie hadn't mentioned the blue gums, Tilly would be back at work now, not on her way to the police station.

'I'm afraid these factory girls are not equipped to take responsibility for themselves,' went on the sub-inspector. 'Tilly Packett lives in a public house, for goodness' sake. It was bound to happen sooner or later. This only validates my petition to implement a liquor ban in this district. Drinking intoxicants only exaggerates their lack of responsibility.'

Aggie bit her tongue. She herself had been a factory girl in the not too distant past and had worked damned hard in a dangerous job and had been happy to serve her country doing so. Poor Tilly had hardly brought it on herself. Aggie had told Mim about the rape but perhaps Mim knew it wasn't worth pursuing the accusation without evidence.

'You may have heard, I have been successful in agreeing a curfew in Tilbury on women of loose character and I am in the process of doing the same here in the Orsett district. I have asked for the power to search homes for deserters but that, as yet, has not been forthcoming. I shudder to think what we should find, but it would be a boon indeed for the WPS here.'

Aggie couldn't help but pull a face and was glad the sub-inspector was looking at her driving gloves. Going into people's houses, invading their privacy? It sounded like an intrusion to her.

'When will they give us the power of arrest?' sighed the sub-inspector, sitting astride her motorcycle. 'It was our fourth anniversary dinner at the Lyceum Club last weekend and everyone agreed we should be given full official status. It was reported in *The Times*.'

Aggie went to get on the back of the bike. 'Oh, could you walk back from here?' said the sub-inspector. 'I need to get over to Tilbury now. I shall call for you tomorrow around ten. Cheerio.'

She puttered away down the road and Aggie started her mile-long walk back to East Tilbury village, lamenting all the way that she had been responsible for the baby's death and for Tilly's arrest. But she needed to pass the training and really, the sub-inspector would know that Aggie had behaved dutifully and this would only help her cause.

Letting herself in to the Rathbones' house, she hoped Mrs Zlin would cook supper. She quite liked the old lady's strange cabbage stews. Mrs Zlin came rushing out of the kitchen when she heard Aggie come in. In her hand she brandished a letter. Aggie's stomach twisted with fear. The War Office's insignia was stamped on the envelope. In an instant she knew it was about Arnie, and panicked and ripped it open but, thank God, a letter meant that Arnie wasn't lost or dead, else she'd have had a telegram. A letter meant something else. She scanned the words, looking for bad news, Mrs Zlin watching her closely. It said he had been injured and was coming home, very soon. She sat down on the hallway chair with a bump. Arnie was coming home.

Aggie woke up and stiffened with anticipation when she remembered that Arnie was coming home today. She imagined meeting him off the boat at Tilbury and was at a loss as to what to expect or what to prepare herself for. Men walked around her patrol area with bandaged faces and limbs missing. Would that be Arnie now?

She busied herself with making Mim's porridge. At the bedroom door, she wondered what to say. She wanted to burst into the room to announce her news, but of course she wouldn't do that. She wanted to ask Mim if Arnie could come and stay with them but how could she when Mim was mourning the loss of her own husband? Arnie had nowhere else to go but here. Their own house had been billeted. But Aggie also didn't want to leave Mim in her sorry condition.

'Good morning, my dear,' she said, opening the curtains. Mim winced and sat up.

'Good morning, Aggie. Are you taking care of me again?' Mim sounded brighter.

'Yes, course I am. That's what friends do for each other, isn't it?'

'Yes, I rather think it is. Thank you,' she said, taking the bowl of porridge.

Aggie pottered around tidying the room, waiting for Mim to pick up her spoon. She sat down in the armchair at the bedside. 'How are you feeling today?'

'A little clearer, I think.' Mim forced a smile as she tried to compose herself.

'I'm glad,' said Aggie. 'You'll be all right. We can look after each other, can't we?'

Mim nodded and swallowed, closed her eyes for a moment, tears falling on her cheeks.

'You know,' said Aggie, 'I know something of loss.' Mim's eyes opened. 'Yes, I've lost children, you see.' Aggie hadn't meant to tell Mim this but it seemed the natural thing to do. 'Three children.' It sounded strange on her lips to say it out loud. She never talked about it. Mim put her hand on Aggie's and squeezed it. 'My first little one, Edward.' Aggie paused, unsure whether she'd be able to continue. 'He died of diphtheria in his first year. And my second, Annie . . . in childbirth, and I nearly went too. But I pulled through. I was stronger than she was. My third . . . my third was Rosie. Rosie went when she was five.' Mim squeezed harder and let go. 'I don't want to add to your pain, Mim, I just want you to know that I know what it's like, that pain you're going through.' Mim let out a big sigh and looked like she might go back to sleep.

'My Arnie's coming—' Aggie started to say.

'We always wanted children,' whispered Mim, the soft words making her flinch. 'But God saw to it that we couldn't.' She shrugged as though there must have been a reason for it. 'We wanted children right up until Bertie went. We never gave up.' She sighed through her nose and looked towards the window. 'Although, we had stopped talking about it. It became something of a ... something of a ...'

Aggie stroked Mim's hand. She'd wondered why Mim had no children but hadn't liked to ask.

'I do think that a woman's monthly blood is so very, awfully, symbolic, don't you?'

'How'd you mean?'

'Each month one waits, as though for a wonderful letter to arrive, but rather than the letter not arriving, one is faced with the most awful kind of butchery, a slaughter that must be washed away and never spoken of. It is quite inhumane.'

'Yes,' said Aggie, understanding. She and Arnie had hoped for more children after Rosie died but none came. And then the war, and then Arnie had to leave.

'There are families in this war that have lost all of their menfolk; their family line has simply stopped. We had none to begin with.'

'Why don't you have a little rest now, Mim, then perhaps get up and have a walk around the garden?'

Mim turned back to Aggie, as though remembering she was there. 'How is Arnie?' she asked.

'He's coming home,' said Aggie quickly, and she started to cry. 'I'm sorry, Mim, he's coming home.'

'Oh, my dear, I'm glad,' said Mim, crying too. 'I am glad, please don't apologise, my dear friend.'

'He's injured. I don't know how bad but he's coming back on a hospital ship today, I'm going to meet him at Tilbury.'

'Thank God he is alive,' said Mim, clutching Aggie's hands. A flicker of fear crossed her face. 'But you'll leave here? You'll need to leave here?'

'Well, Mim, I don't know. He might go to hospital or he might come straight home, I don't know yet. I don't want to leave you like this, Mim ... our house is billeted but we'll find somewhere.'

Mim nodded and looked at Aggie. She forced the most pitiful smile. 'It's all right,' she said. 'He can come here.'

Aggie started to cry again. 'Thank you, Mim.' Mim closed her eyes and turned her head away, tired. Aggie took her cue and, leaving the untouched porridge bowl, went downstairs to the kitchen.

At ten o'clock the sub-inspector knocked at the door.

'He's back,' said Aggie, blurting her news. 'My husband is coming home today.'

'Is he all right?' asked the sub-inspector.

'I don't know but I want to go and meet him off the boat at Tilbury today.'

'Yes, yes of course you must. Do you want to go now? I was going to suggest a ju-jitsu lesson but of course you'll want to go now.'

Aggie bumped across Tilbury marshes on her bicycle, one eye on the distant rain clouds. A kestrel hovered in the sky above her, waiting for her to pass. She wondered what it had spotted in the wetland grasses and whether it would catch its prey. Perhaps a vole or a shrew was crouching scared beneath a clump of brambles. Her heart pounded from the exercise and the thought of seeing Arnie again. A goat willow with black leaves bent away from the river wind reminded her of Mrs Zlin hunched over her washing basket. The clatter of her wheels on the rough ground startled the starlings roosting there – not black leaves but birds – they rose in unison, leaving the tree stripped and bare.

The guards at the docks stopped her to check her WPS card. She was glad to catch her breath. Propping her bike against a wall, she was told to go straight to the railway station, where passengers went when they disembarked. Or, in wartime, where the injured were brought through for the ambulance trains. Aggie was told to wait for Arnie's hospital ship to dock. She wasn't allowed through to the quayside but waited with a small crowd of other women and children at the station terminal, a cavernous hall, its ceiling vaulted with cast iron girders like a ship turned upside down. A brick ticket office stood in the centre, a large clock on top that it was impossible not to check every few minutes. Armed soldiers stood at intervals, men and women in Red Cross uniform waited with cane wheelchairs and stretchers propped against the walls. Some local volunteers had set up a rest stop with a tea urn and plates of sandwiches. There was a sense of anxious anticipation about the place.

For two hours the families waited. Aggie's gaze shifted from the stretchers propped against the wall, to the clock, to the other women, to the stretchers. There was a sudden buzz of activity and authoritative voices calling, and the Red Cross nurses and orderlies jumped to attention and were beckoned through to the landing stage.

Aggie watched the doorway intently and soon the nurses reappeared, this time pushing a man in a wheelchair or holding an arm as a man limped along. Aggie stared. These men looked terrible. They were still in uniform – not the crisp new khaki they had left in, but dirty, bloodied and torn. The men's eyes weren't shining with pride and fear as they had been when they had left on the trains to go to France. Their eyes weren't shining at all. They stared. They stared at nothing, as though there was no joy or fear or any feeling left inside them. Aggie felt sick. The men were bandaged, around the face or around the stump of a missing limb. She scanned each man for a sign it was her husband. The faces all looked the same. What if Arnie's face was bandaged so much that she couldn't make him out? She stepped forward gingerly. A man cried out with pain as he was lifted onto a stretcher. Some of the families came forward with a shout of recognition and Aggie looked for Arnie, her eyes darting from one man to the next. More and more men came through, some walking unaided, some writhing with agony on a stretcher. Aggie moved closer, looking into the face of each one, terrified she wouldn't find him. There was something familiar about one man walking, his face and left arm bandaged. One eye was visible and his hair sprouted from the top of his head. Aggie lurched forward and then stopped, unsure. He saw her and stopped. She ran forward.

'Arnie?'

'Hello, Aggie,' he said.

'Arnie? Is it my Arnie?' Aggie put her hands to her mouth. 'Oh my dear, my dear, you've come back to me.' Arnie held out his good arm and she moved into him carefully, afraid of hurting him. He smelled different but the relief of being near him was overwhelming. 'I can't believe you're here,' she said. 'Thank God, thank God.'

They drew apart and Aggie gingerly put up her hand to his face. 'Are you all right, my love?'

He nodded.

'Come on, let's find out where they want you.'

They waited together for the commanding officer to tell them that Arnie would be going to the auxiliary military hospital at St Clere's Hall in Stanford to be checked and would probably be released to convalesce at home. Arnie was led to a motorised ambulance and Aggie had to say good-bye already.

'I'll see you soon, dear,' she said, not wanting to let go of his hand.

The officers at Tilbury informed Aggie that the sub-inspector was patrolling Greygoose munitions. It was a good forty-five minute cycle ride but a chance to clear her head after seeing Arnie.

'He shan't be at St Clere's long, not if he's walking wounded,' said the sub-inspector at the factory. 'They haven't the room.'

Aggie hoped she was right. She needed to see Arnie, touch him, look at his injuries.

'My husband is coming home,' she told Mrs Zlin later at Mim's house.

'Your husband?' Mrs Zlin clutched Aggie's arm, pulled her in to a strong embrace. 'Good,' she said. 'Good, good.'

The two women made supper together. The old lady didn't talk much but Aggie liked her company. Mim stayed upstairs in bed. Mrs Zlin pointed at the ceiling and shook her head. 'Needs something to do. Too much moping. Get her to work.'

'To work? It's too soon for that, surely?'

Mrs Zlin shrugged. A late knock at the door made them both jump. Aggie tore off her apron and jogged to open it. A VAD nurse stood there on the step with Arnie.

'I shan't come in,' said the nurse brightly. 'I'm needed back straight away. Private Tucker has a severe facial injury that shall need redressing regularly. You can see a doctor or bring him to St Clere's. He also has a clean gunshot wound to the arm but this will heal in time. His medicine is here, but it is to be given strictly according to instructions.'

She gave Arnie an awkward smile and gestured for Aggie to step further outside. 'This medicine is addictive,' she said in a low voice. 'It has become something of a problem. The men need it for the pain, but, well, there are reports of some trying to obtain it without prescription. Your husband has been through a terrible ordeal. So just be careful.' Aggie nodded, alarmed by the nurse's words of caution.

'He needs rest,' said the nurse loudly, going back to Arnie. The nurse looked at Aggie meaningfully. 'Lots of rest, Private Tucker, all right?' Arnie nodded at her and mumbled thank you. She handed Aggie a large brown paper bag. And she handed Aggie her husband. 'Cheerio,' she said, and walked back to the motorised ambulance waiting on the kerb.

'Cup of tea?' said Aggie, leading Arnie into the kitchen, unsure what else to say.

'Please,' he said, taking out a cigarette and lighting it, sitting down at the table.

Aggie wanted to ask him a hundred questions but restrained herself. She put the kettle on and got the cups ready. 'Hungry?' she said.

'No, I'm all right.'

She filled the teapot and stole glances at him. One of his eyes was covered by the bandage, and quite a bit of his face. His arm was bound in a sling. He looked around the room, assessing his new home. Mrs Zlin came in hesitantly, nodded at Arnie and collected the broom from the cupboard.

'You remember Mrs Zlin from the village?' said Aggie. 'She lives here for now.'

Arnie nodded at her and took a puff from his cigarette. The rod of hot water drummed into the teapot and the lid clattered on. The teaspoons scraped and tinkled.

'Whose house is it?' said Arnie.

'The Rathbones. But Mim lost Bertie, her husband, not long ago, he fell down the docks.'

Arnie flinched and pulled on his cigarette.

'I've put a couple of cloves in yours for your head,' she said, giving him his tea.

Aggie sipped her tea too soon and burnt her lips. A silence crept between her and Arnie. 'How are you, love?' she said. 'What happened? I didn't hear anything about it.'

Arnie sniffed. 'No you wouldn't have. We were shelled and shot at.'

'Are you badly hurt?'

He nodded and seemed to be trying to keep his composure. 'I'll need my prescriptions,' he said.

164

'Oh right, yes, you've got some medicine here,' she said, glancing at the brown paper bag.

'I'll need some now then I'll need to see the doctor quite soon to get another prescription.'

'Yes, all right, love.' Aggie smiled but remembered the nurse's words.

She handed the paper bag to him and he rolled up his sleeve. From his pocket he pulled out a small leather pouch, from which he took a needle and syringe. He took out a little glass phial from the paper bag and snapped the head off to draw the liquid into the syringe.

'Do you want me to do it?' said Aggie, as he pulled a rubber band around his arm. But he didn't answer and she watched as he injected himself. In a few seconds he sank back against the chair and sighed.

'That's better, love,' he said. 'It hurts like a bastard. Do you want to see it? It's quite something.'

'What, your face? Hadn't you better keep it covered up, it'll be a job getting the dressing back on, won't it?'

He laughed. 'If you ever take a bullet in the face you know about it, I can tell you. I bet Fritz gave a little cheer when he got me. I shot them right back though. I didn't even flinch, just took aim and fired, used their eye sockets as my target, pop, pop, pop, ha, ha, they didn't see it coming.'

Aggie couldn't see how he could carry on firing a gun when he'd been shot in the face but she didn't like to say so. It was good to hear him talking and happy, she didn't think he'd want to talk about the war.

'It's over now, Arnie, you've done your bit.'

165

'I'd go back,' he said with a wave of his good arm. 'Never mind that, I'd go back tomorrow if they let me.'

'Are these your things?' said Aggie, to change the subject, picking up a dirty khaki-coloured canvas bag. Mrs Zlin was still there in the corner, staring at Arnie. Aggie didn't like the look on her face. She put her hand inside Arnie's bag and drew it out again. There was a greasy woollen thing in there. Pulling it out, she dropped it with disgust on the kitchen floor. A sheepskin covered in mud.

'Got it from a little farm in France,' said Arnie. 'Kept me warm in the trenches. All the lads had them. The only problem was the rats liked them too. Must have liked the smell of them. You'd wake up in the morning and find a rat under each armpit.' He laughed again but Aggie recoiled at the terrible story.

'Mim said you can stay here. We won't have to find somewhere to live. It's good of her.' He gave no answer. 'Arnie, I'm at work on patrol every day but I'll have time to look after you – I have to keep my job going, I'm nearly finished my training.'

He had leant back and closed his eyes, his body sagging into sleep. Mrs Zlin came over to look down at the horrible sheepskin on the floor. She nudged it with the toe of her boot, shaking her head as if to say it'd be going in the bin. Aggie sat down to drink her tea and wondered how bad Arnie's face was. She was glad the medicine had helped him but was relieved he hadn't taken the bandages off to show her. He suddenly woke with a start and grabbed for something that wasn't there.

'What's that?' he hissed. 'Get away.'

Alarmed, Aggie put her hand on his arm to calm him. 'It's just Mim moving around upstairs,' she said.

He glared at her suspiciously and then seemed to relax. He lit up a cigarette and puffed on it as though for oxygen. 'Damn thing itches,' he said, scratching at the bandage on his arm.

'How bad is your arm?' asked Aggie tentatively.

'Well, I've kept it, haven't I?' he said sulkily. 'Damn lucky. The Spanish Lady got some of them. She's come to London too.'

'The Spanish Lady?' said Aggie.

'Flu, Spanish flu. She's a terror, a real terror.' He got up to find the back door to the garden.

'But you're alive,' said Aggie to herself. 'Thank God you're alive.'

Mrs Zlin picked up the sheepskin with her wooden laundry tongs and took it out to the dustbin.

12

Mim

There had been so much talk of death all through the war. In the newspaper, on local people's lips. Mim hadn't fully understood until this point in time that she had been floating. Floating blissfully and ignorantly. Sympathetically, but ignorantly, above it all, all this time. And now she had fallen into the choppy waters with a blacksmith's anvil chained to her ankle. She was drowning, drowning, drowning.

'Mim, Reverend Clow is here to see you.'

Reverend Clow? What could he possibly say to her? Perhaps he had come to explain why God had abandoned them, why he had pitted his sons against his sons. Mim was surprised that Aggie had allowed him entry to her house. Mim had attended St Catherine's in East Tilbury village every Sunday since she had lived there – but the thought of it made her sick now. A passage from Corinthians came to her.

Let your women keep silence in the churches, for it is not permitted unto them to speak; but they are commanded to be under obedience, as also saith the law. And if they will learn anything, let them ask their husbands at home; for it is a shame for women to speak in the church. But her Bertie had gone. She had no husband to learn from. Did this give her licence to speak in church? Very well, she would. She would go there on Sunday, she would stand up and speak, she would scream God's betrayal into the altar.

'Send him away. Tell him not to come again.'

'But, Mim . . . ?'

'No.'

The curtains at the windows were drawn. Photographs of Bertie were turned to the wall. People brought their precious food and made posies out of field poppies and white campion. Mim saw them in little pots around the house. They lasted a day or two before wilting and hanging their heads in sorrow. Aggie took their clothes to the dyeworks in Grays so they had proper mourning colours to wear.

Mim developed a macabre fascination with the roll of honour in the *Grays & Tilbury Gazette*. She followed which local men had died in the war. She pulled out old issues from months before to reread. Mothers in Northumberland Road and Lower Crescent in Linford lost their sons. A boy from the railway cottages in East Tilbury. A Chadwell St Mary son, a chap from Stanford-le-Hope missing in France. A father of two from West Tilbury. A Corringham father of two. A brother from Horndon-on-the-Hill. All dead like Bertie. Mim didn't feel sorrow for them. She felt anger. Anger at the terrible waste of life. The terrible obliteration of families. Anger that the good were not rewarded.

She read that the situation in Germany was so bad that they had stopped their U-boat campaign. After the years of indiscriminate destruction of the Allies' ships hanging heavily on Bertie's conscience, now it had stopped just as Bertie's life was over. There was some kind of irony in it.

She would wake up on the sofa in the drawing room having fallen asleep there hours before. Looking around, she would wonder where everyone was for a split second and then she would remember and her mind would shut down. She would find herself sobbing uncontrollably and then stop suddenly, as if wondering why she was crying. She would wish for sleep at night but lie there in the dark, awake, with a pounding heart and shortness of breath.

Aggie brought her food at mealtimes and then went away again. Sometimes she sat with Mim trying to get her talking. Sometimes Mim was just alone. Often she'd wake up in bed to see Aggie asleep in an armchair at her side. Victoria from the suffrage society came to see her. She was one of the few people permitted entrance. But Mim could not speak. Victoria held her hand and left a piece of paper for her to read. A sermon delivered by Canon Henry Scott Holland on the death of King Edward VII. *Death is nothing at all . . . I have only slipped away into the next room . . . I am I and you are you . . . Whatever we were to each other, that we are still . . .* Mim put it aside. She had heard the sermon before. Reverend Clow had read it a multitude of times in St Catherine's during the war. She used to think it was poignant, comforting, a promise of reunion. But now it only made her angry. It wasn't true.

Aggie had asked her if her husband Arnie could live with them. Mim had wanted to tell Aggie to go. Why on earth would Mim want them there? The sentiment was sordid and uncharitable but she didn't care. Nevertheless, she hadn't the heart to refuse Aggie, who had been such a good friend. So she would let them stay for now.

She was exhausted. There was no reprieve from the eternal burden of loss. Her hair was falling out. She couldn't bear to eat more than a few mouthfuls. It was as if she were dying herself. *At least you've got him here.* Someone had said that to her at Bertie's funeral. Would it have been worse if Bertie's body were rotting away in the putrid green mud of the trenches, or had been feasted upon by French rats, or had been atomised by a shell blast? She didn't know and didn't care. How dare someone say that to her.

When the sun came up she was still wandering the house. She watched from the drawing room window for people going to work and when she saw none, realised it was Sunday. A movement behind her made her turn. It was Arnie. Surprised to see her, he nodded and moved on towards the kitchen. As if reminding her that she had eaten hardly a morsel for two days, she followed him.

'Don't mind me,' he said when she entered the kitchen. 'Want I should get the range fired up?'

She nodded in return. The mornings were chilly in October.

'Couldn't sleep neither?' he asked.

'No,' she said. 'No, I couldn't.'

He moved stiffly, arranging the kindling and sticks in the range with his one good arm. His hair stuck up from his bandaged head.

'You're in pain,' she said, coming near. 'Let me.'

'I can do it,' he said gruffly and she let him be. 'You get the kettle on if you want to do something.'

She was surprised at being spoken to in such a rough way in her own house but she sensed he meant well and filled the kettle at the sink. Before long they both sat at the table with cups of tea. Mim didn't want conversation and it seemed neither did he.

He lit a cigarette and it reminded her of Bertie's pipe. Tears fell down her cheeks and she swiped them away.

'You'll be going to church?' he asked.

She looked at him.

'Ask God if he'll forgive my sins,' he said.

'I'll do no such thing,' she snapped, and he looked at her, surprised. 'You are referring to the war, I think?' He shrugged. 'You've nothing for which to repent,' she said.

They fell silent again. The poor man. What had he had to do over there in France; what atrocities did the war make him commit that he considered sinful and beyond God's forgiveness?

'I'm obliged for the tea,' he said, after draining his cup. He got up and left the room. Mim heard the back door close.

When nine o'clock came round, Aggie caught Mim putting on her coat.

'Going out, Mim? Want me to come with you?'

'No. Thank you, Aggie.' Mim couldn't look her friend in the face. Aggie would know something was up, might guess that Mim was on a wild goose chase. That she was going to face God.

At the church Reverend Clow greeted Mim with enthusiastic sympathy, holding both her hands in his. She did not answer his cooing tones but went into the church and sat down. Where once the interior would have welcomed and warmed her, would have wrapped her in love and gratitude, now she felt its hard flint walls and cold floor, its dampness and rot, its cloying complacency.

From the pulpit, Reverend Clow's patriarchal delivery made her shiver. She wanted to stand up and strike her fist into her hand and ask why God hadn't been at Bertie's side, but she couldn't move. She bowed her head and wondered at the damp patches on the bodice of her coat. She felt small and cold and alone.

The words of the hateful sermon came to her from Reverend Clow's lips and her stomach convulsed with anger. He chose that day to read the dreaded verse; perhaps he had even chosen it for her. *Death is nothing at all. It does not count. I have only slipped away into the next room. Nothing has happened. Everything remains exactly as it was. I am I and you are you . . . Whatever we were to each other that we are still. Call me by my old familiar name. Speak of me in the easy way which you always used. Put no difference into your tone. Wear no forced air of solemnity or sorrow. Laugh as we always laughed at the little jokes we enjoyed together. Play, smile, think of me, pray for me . . .*

She stood defiantly, shaking with rage. Never in her life had she walked out of church. Holding her head high, determined that her departure should be seen as lucid, informed, not in a hunch of sobbed tears, she walked resolutely out.

'You all right, Mim?' asked Aggie when Mim came home and took off her hat and veil. 'Been to church?'

'For what it was worth,' said Mim and hung her hat on its peg with so much determination that she made a dent in it.

'Can I have a quick word before I go out on patrol?' said Aggie, looking rather sheepish. Mim nodded and followed her into the library to sit down.

'I'm glad you're up and about, Mim, I really am.' Aggie chewed her lip and Mim wondered what was coming. With a shot of panic, she thought Aggie was going to leave her and realised how much she relied on her friend. 'I wonder if I can ask you a favour? I mean, you don't have to do it if you're not ready or don't want to.' Aggie waited a second, forming her thoughts. 'It's Arnie. He needs looking after and I can't be here all the time. I want to keep our patrol going so I can finish training and so they don't give it to someone else, because it's our patrol, isn't it.' She said it as though it was fact and not a question. Mim hadn't really given a thought to her job but Aggie's words cut through her grief and she found herself nodding yes, it was their patrol.

'So will you? Help me look after Arnie? He needs taking to the doctor and someone to get his medicines and he needs his meals and everything – well, Mrs Zlin can help with that. He's putting on a front that he's all right but I know he's not.' Aggie stopped, as though the same might apply to Mim. Mim's first thought was how Aggie could ask such a thing of her, when her own husband was dead in the ground. Words could not convey the insensitivity.

But, simultaneously, she found herself saying, 'Yes, all right, Aggie. I'll help.'

Those tiny bright seconds when, after having slept a little in the early hours, Mim woke up and forgot that Bertie was dead. The aching black eternity that followed when she remembered that God had taken him away from her. She heaved long gasping sobs into her pillow and then, as if her reservoir were empty and needed time to replenish, she turned onto her back and opened her eyes. She looked at the hateful drawn curtains and the hateful closed door. She had reason to open neither one.

Aggie's face hovered into her memory. Aggie had asked her to look after Arnie. The thought was almost laughable. She was in no condition to nurse anyone. Nevertheless, it was enough to make her feet find the floor and her hands to push her up from the bed. It was enough to make her go down-stairs to get her own breakfast instead of waiting for Aggie to bring her porridge to her in bed. She found Arnie in the kitchen pacing the floor. When he saw her, he sat down and lit a cigarette.

'Morning,' he said gruffly.

'Good morning,' replied Mim. 'I'm making porridge if you'd care for some?'

'No, I need to get to the doctor for my prescription. Do you know when he opens shop?'

'Nine o'clock, I should think,' said Mim, looking at the kitchen clock that read seven thirty. She jumped when Arnie's palm smacked the wall. He turned away from her stare. 'I'll make us some tea, that should help,' she said. 'Oh, I do have some toothache drops, let me see.' She rummaged in a cup-board. 'It was just before the war, I had a dreadful toothache and these worked splendidly.'

Arnie was at her side in a second and practically snatched them away from her, took one glance at the label and tore open the box with shaking hands, chewing what seemed to be several of the drops at once. By the time the tea was made he seemed calmer and Mim was glad to have been able to help him.

'Much obliged,' he said. 'It hurts like a . . . like anything.'

'That's quite all right,' said Mim. 'Might I accompany you to the doctor? I could do with the fresh air.'

'I know she's asked you to help me,' he said, his one exposed eye looking at her.

'I see,' said Mim, awkwardly.

'I could do with the company,' he said, pulling his bandage away from his upper lip. 'This damned thing needs changing too.'

His facial bandage looked awfully cumbersome. Mim wondered whether she could help him change it at home to save finding the doctor every time. She remembered her nursing study and had learned some first aid as part of her WPS training. She kept the thought to herself. Arnie might not want her to help him in that way.

'You know,' she said tentatively, 'might I try getting a note to Dr Hinton to make a house visit?'

'No,' said Arnie without hesitation, 'I need to see him at nine o'clock sharp.'

'As you wish. I shall go and get myself ready.'

At half past eight, Mim came into the kitchen. 'I have borrowed Farmer Able's pony and trap,' she said, with a rush of satisfaction. 'It's a long walk to Stanford.'

'Righto, let's get on with it,' said Arnie. He had put on his army uniform, which hadn't yet been washed. It was caked with trench mud and what looked like dried blood and it stank to high heaven.

'Oh my goodness,' said Mim, 'we shall need to see to that.'

'I don't think I'm allowed to go out without it till I've been discharged,' said Arnie.

Mim held her tongue. It was hard to believe that he had put on the disgusting uniform.

'Would you care to drive?' she asked him, mindful that his injuries would render him emasculated. But he held up his bandaged arm and gestured that she should do it.

When they arrived at Dr Hinton's surgery, the doctor immediately sent them to the auxiliary military hospital at St Clere's Hall. A nurse took Arnie away to remove his dressing.

'Excuse me,' said Mim. 'Shouldn't I see how it's done, so we can do it at home if necessary?'

Arnie twitched and looked at the floor but he didn't counter her suggestion. 'Yes, all right, if you wish,' said the nurse. 'It's Sergeant Rathbone, isn't it?'

'Yes, and Private Tucker needs some pain medicines too.'

When the nurse removed the dressing, Mim held her breath and tried as hard as she could to keep from squirming. Her stomach turned when she saw Arnie's injury. His left eye and cheekbone were sunken and shattered, his nose was a hole in his face. The flesh was raw, the bandage bloody. It was a travesty of nature. Tears welled in her eyes but she blinked them away and sat up rod-straight. Arnie's good eye swivelled towards her. She gave him a nod and kept her professional demeanour, listening to the nurse's instructions for changing the bandage and dressing the wound. Arnie had also received a gunshot to his arm. When the nurse removed the sling and bandage, Mim saw that the wound was between his shoulder and elbow. He was lucky to have saved his arm from amputation.

'Jolly good,' Mim said in a clipped tone. 'Now, the pain medicine?'

'Yes, of course, I shall fetch the doctor,' said the nurse.

'Looks like I've been shot in the face, doesn't it,' said Arnie with grim sarcasm.

'It will heal in due course,' said Mim.

They waited in silence for the doctor to come.

'Private Tucker?' said the doctor. 'I do apologise for keeping you waiting. It is awfully busy here. I understand you need medicine?'

Arnie nodded. 'Cocaine, doc. The pain is hard to bear.'

Mim stared at him. She knew the servicemen were given such drugs and should have guessed from Arnie's erratic behaviour that he would be taking something like that. On her WPS training she had been warned that some ex-servicemen had become addicts and would seek out back-street drug dealers. Mim remembered seeing pocket cases of cocaine and morphine in Harrods in London not two years previously, sold as gifts to send to the front line, and didn't Ernest Shackleton take cocaine on his trip to the Antarctic, hadn't Queen Victoria herself taken it? For as long as Mim could remember it was a cure for the toothache and now it was gaining an altogether different reputation. In any case, the doctor didn't flinch in prescribing him what he had been taking and Mim certainly would not stand in judgement of this man whose life was irrevocably changed by serving his king and country. He was lucky to be alive.

'And some new needles and syringes, please, doc,' he said. 'Do I have to come back for new prescriptions?'

'Well, officially, yes,' said the doctor. 'But as you have a responsible caretaker, I think it would be all right to administer several now, to save you the journey. Please only fill the prescription each time you need it. Do not keep a stock of this medicine in the house,' he said to Mim carefully. 'It is effective, but highly addictive.'

'What about Private Tucker's discharge? Is there something you could do?'

'Private Tucker will need to appear before a medical board. I will complete the relevant documentation confirming he is unfit for further service. You'll hear from them soon.'

'The next thing we need to do is sort out your discharge,' said Mim on the way home. 'I hope you didn't think me forward to ask the doctor about it. I think you have done quite enough for this war.'

'No, it's all right. I'm obliged to you,' said Arnie.

Mim dropped Arnie off at the house and drove the pony and trap back to Farmer Able. Walking back down the road, she suddenly thought about Bertie's manuscript. He'd been working on a book about the Boer wars. A wave of grief engulfed her. Who would finish his book now? She put her hand to her chest and tried to breathe, looked about, wondered why people weren't gathered in the streets aghast that Bertie Rathbone was dead. She made for home in a fast walk. Shutting the front door she leant against it and closed her eyes.

'Mim?' Aggie was there, her hand on Mim's arm. 'You all right, Mim? Thanks for taking Arnie.'

Mim swallowed and opened her eyes, used her last ounce of energy to nod and give the smallest of smiles. She went upstairs and lay down on the bed, still in her hat and coat. She clutched her stomach and rolled onto her side. *Bertie, Bertie.*

He had gone. Gone and left her there. He'd seen that man in trouble and climbed that ship's mast, he'd played the hero and not left it to one of his other men who climbed masts all the time. He'd damn well slipped and fallen and he'd left her there. Had he thought of her when he climbed it? Had he considered that it might be dangerous, that he might not be qualified for the task? Might God not have eased his way, put out a hand to prevent him from falling? She turned to Bertie's pillow, grabbed it and hit it with her fist. *Damn you, Bertie Rathbone. Damn you for leaving me.*

13

Aggie

Aggie stood at the hallway coat stand, adjusting her hat in the mirror. Today was the day she'd been dreading. Tilly Packett was in Grays police court and Aggie was to be witness against her.

Looking up the stairs, she wondered whether to disturb Arnie to say goodbye. He'd been home for almost three weeks. His restless nights and her late returns home from patrol meant it best that they had their own rooms. She had tried talking to him about his time in the trenches but it depended on his mood. Sometimes he was bouncy with energy, telling big stories about his escapades, which Aggie was never sure were true or made up to protect her from the realities of what he had been through. Other times he was fidgety, paranoid almost. He had got a gun from somewhere and kept it near him at all times. Mrs Zlin was scared of him.

Mim had been marvellous, although Aggie didn't see much of her. She had taken Arnie to his medical hearing and he'd been discharged from service – 'no longer physically fit'. Any fool would know that just by looking at him. Aggie had been there once when Mim had changed the bandages on his face. The sight of it haunted her. She couldn't look at her husband without seeing what lay beneath his dressings.

Inexplicably, thoughts of her lost children grew stronger in her mind. Seeing Arnie like this scared her – she was lucky she hadn't lost him too. Rosie, her little girl, had died in an accident when she'd been out with Arnie before the war. She had always blamed Arnie for Rosie's death, but wild horses wouldn't make her say it. Had he been careless in France? Had he been careless with Rosie too? She hated what the war had done to him and hated blaming him for Rosie. It was easier to go out on patrol and get on with her job than see Arnie and have these thoughts. She loved her husband, she loved him more than anything in the world. Her heart was breaking. Behind closed doors she wept for him. What kind of world was it when a decent man was sent to fight for his country and returned with a smashed face beyond all comparison to his natural self? It wasn't fair.

The medical board had given him one pound in money, a new suit of plain clothes and sent him home. He was told he'd be able to claim a soldier's pension but there was no dis-ability allowance for injuries above the neckline. They said facial injuries didn't stop you from doing manual work like an amputated limb did. Arnie joked later that he'd be better off if he'd lost his arm – he'd have got thirteen shillings a week for a left arm missing below the shoulder and above the elbow. As it was, his left arm was still in a sling and too weak to use.

Patrolling with Sub-Inspector Nash was hard. Aggie missed working with Mim. But she was keen to make a good impression. Today would be her hardest test so far. There was nothing Aggie could do to prevent going to court and being called as witness against Tilly. She had asked the sub-inspector if she would do it instead but had been told that being involved in the case from the start made Aggie the most reliable witness.

Deciding not to disturb Arnie to say goodbye, she let herself out and started walking down the hill. The sub-inspector had offered to collect her and soon came puttering along on her motorcycle, stopping to gather her anxious load. Aggie clung onto the sub-inspector's cape, facing grimly into the wind. Tilly Packett was one of her own. A munitions girl. It made Aggie sick to the stomach to be doing this.

'There's been a case of Spanish influenza in Tilbury,' called the sub-inspector over her shoulder through the wind. 'A man has died. He'd been in London the day before. We think it's contained – he was found—'

'What was that, Sub-Inspector?' shouted Aggie.

'Found dead in his house, so we think it's contained. Schools are being closed in London, the flu is rife there. We need to be on the alert and ready ... If you hear of anything report it immediately.'

'Yes, Sub-Inspector, will do.' Aggie had heard about the Spanish flu in the paper. It had spread across Russia and Europe. Thousands had died. They were calling it an epidemic.

'If you come across someone with symptoms, for goodness' sake cover your mouth. Cover your mouth, I say.'

'Yes, Sub-Inspector.' It was the ultimate smack in the face from God. The Great War had killed hundreds of thousands and now He had sent the Spanish Lady to finish them off.

At Grays police court, the sub-inspector went in and told Aggie to wait outside to be called, but she soon returned. 'Well, that's the nail in her coffin,' she said. 'The magistrate is Mr Speechley – scornful of women in general. Against suffrage, against women police, and he's certainly against young munitions girls who get themselves pregnant.'

Aggie looked at her superior in dismay. 'I don't think I can do it, Sub-Inspector. Tilly didn't kill her baby, it was an accident.'

'That is not for us to decide. You must do it. This is your duty now. And don't forget, your training is just about finished. You shouldn't be seen to make trouble now.'

Shouldn't be seen by who? thought Aggie. You?

'I shall go and sit in now for as long as I'm able, to show our support to the girl. But Mr Speechley will consider this a case of indecency, I should think, and ask all women to leave the courtroom.'

'Why is it a case of indecency?'

'Because Tilly had a child out of wedlock, of course. The fact that she is accused of committing infanticide is secondary to that one fact that has compromised her character.'

'Can't you just stay, won't he let you stay seeing as you're the police?'

The sub-inspector shook her head. 'Two WPS officers once staged a protest in a London court, chaining themselves together to prevent being forced to leave during a case involving a woman. They were arrested.' She paused to let the significance of this register. 'You must realise it is of paramount importance that we maintain good relations with our male superiors. Going against them would only make our work and our progress harder.'

Aggie wondered what Mim would have said about it. Mim had mentioned that the sub-inspector was preoccupied with fawning to the male authority figures in the area.

'If I tried to stay in the courtroom once told to leave, the magistrate would think me abnormal for wanting to stay. He would wonder why a woman would wish to subject her delicate mind to such things. Do you see?'

Aggie shivered and nodded. The sub-inspector had told her this before.

'I'd better get back in. Just wait here to be called.'

Aggie waited. She didn't know how many cases were to be heard before Tilly's. She sat in the corridor picking her nails, trying to think how to avoid having to say anything damaging against Tilly.

'As I thought,' said the sub-inspector coming out. 'He asked me to leave the room.'

Before Aggie had time to speak, the court clerk called her in. She got up unsteadily and walked in through the seated crowd, all men, to see poor Tilly there in the dock, pale and wretched. Aggie felt herself starting to cry at the sight of her but she swallowed and gritted her teeth. Mr Speechley would have even less respect for her if she was crying. Three magistrates sat at the slanted wooden court bench and Aggie wondered which one he was. The one in the middle sat a little straighter, wore a slightly larger moustache. It was he who spoke.

'Who is the attending police witness?'

Aggie came forward. 'Constable Tucker, your honour,' she said.

'Speak up,' he said contemptuously. 'We are not at home in the parlour now.'

'Constable Tucker, your honour,' Aggie said loudly, hating her voice being the only one in the crowded room.

'Well?' said the magistrate, looking at his fellows with raised eyebrows.

'Well, your honour, I was on patrol and the landlady Mrs Rumble, of the pub the George and Dragon, where Tilly lived—'

'The accused, Constable Tucker, the accused.'

'Where the accused lived. I went upstairs and the accused was in her room and the landlady said she'd had her baby and the baby was in the dresser drawer.'

'In what condition was the infant?' said the magistrate.

'It was dead, your honour.'

'And did a doctor attend?'

'Yes, your honour.'

The magistrate sighed with impatience. 'What did he say the likely cause of death was?'

Aggie looked at Tilly. The girl was quivering with fear, her eyes were something Aggie would never forget, staring in absolute terror. How could Aggie say anything else but the truth?

'Laudanum, your honour,' said Aggie quietly.

'Laudanum poisoning?' said the magistrate.

Aggie nodded. 'Yes, your honour.'

'Miss Packett, did you poison your infant child with laudanum?' said the magistrate. Tilly started to sob. 'Please answer the question, we have other cases to hear.'

'I just gave her a bit to calm her, I was worried about the noise,' said the girl in a barely audible whimper.

The magistrate conferred with his two colleagues and banged his gavel down. 'Guilty of concealment of the birth of an infant and sentenced to one month hard labour pending trial at assizes for the charge of wilful murder.'

Tilly dropped to her knees. Aggie tried to get to her but was pushed back by the attending male constable. Another constable went to Tilly and got her away out of the dock. Aggie was told to leave. She made her way out of the courtroom, barely seeing through her tears.

'You look dreadful,' said the sub-inspector.

Aggie didn't stay to talk, she left the courthouse and sat on the steps outside.

'Get up immediately,' said the sub-inspector, following her out. 'You have on your WPS armband and will conduct yourself accordingly.' Aggie stood up and wiped her eyes. 'Come along, we shall have a cup of tea.'

Aggie followed her to a nearby tea shop and sat down. 'It was horrible,' she said. 'I had to tell them about the laudanum then they asked Tilly about it and she said she'd given the baby a bit because she was worried about the noise.'

'She practically confessed. In a police court. You did your duty. Well done,' said the sub-inspector. 'I know it's difficult, of course it is. These girls are very silly and of course the man involved bears no responsibility and is never held to account. This is always seen as the woman's fault, whatever the circumstances leading to the pregnancy. This girl went down a sinful path and whether or not she felt she had no other choice, she is now within the clutches of the patriarchal justice system.'

'She doesn't stand a chance,' said Aggie miserably. 'I heard it was a man at the factory who did it, by the way, he forced her. And now she's going to prison and perhaps even worse if they charge her with murder.'

The sub-inspector put her hand on Aggie's. 'You did well today. This is not an easy job and you have proved yourself. As of now, your training is over. You will be sworn in in due course and will wear the uniform of the Women's Police Service. Congratulations.' She patted Aggie's hand and stood up. 'Now I must be getting on. Would you like me to drop you at East Tilbury?'

Aggie shook her head. 'I'll finish my tea, thanks.'

Two days later and the sub-inspector turned up on Aggie's doorstep carrying a large parcel and hat box.

'I was in London and thought I'd save the bother of sending a written order to Harrods.' She handed the parcel and box to Aggie.

Inside was Aggie's new police uniform. 'You got it from Harrods for me?'

'Yes, we have an appointment tomorrow with Stanford's chief constable to get you sworn in. I thought it would be more ceremonial if you had your uniform.'

'Thank you,' said Aggie, smiling. She held up the dark blue military-style tunic jacket. It smelt new, it felt very expensive and she wondered how much she owed. There were two breast pockets and two side pockets and 'WPS' in silver lettering on the shoulder straps.

'Why don't you go and try it?' said the sub-inspector.

In her bedroom Aggie put on the dark blue skirt, which came to well above the ankle, the shortest she had ever worn, then the manly white cotton shirt, the jacket and, lifting the hat out of its box, she turned to the mirror and placed it on her head. She laughed and cried at the same time. She looked so official, so important, it was hard to believe this was her own reflection. She touched the silver letters on her shoulders, ran her hands over the jacket.

'I don't know how to do the tie,' she said to the sub-inspector downstairs.

'Here,' said her superior, taking it and showing Aggie how to tie the knot. 'You look the part,' she added, standing back to look at her. 'Right, we're needed on patrol. There's been a suicide.'

With that, the sub-inspector turned to leave. Aggie pulled on her boots and followed, used to the officer's abruptness by now. 'Who is it?' she said, on the back of the motorcycle.

'Woman in Linford, hanged herself, found this morning.'

Aggie hoped it wasn't someone she knew. They pulled up outside a house on Lower Crescent road and knocked at the door. A young girl around eight years old answered and called behind her.

'Dad, the police ladies are here.' A man on crutches made his way to the door. He was looking down as he limped, concentrating on his footing. When he looked up, Aggie had to suppress a gasp. The man's lower lip and chin were mutilated. The flesh and bones were exposed and his tongue was hanging there with no jaw to contain it. She thought she might be sick. She suddenly just wanted to cry, to stand there on the man's doorstep and cry for him and for everyone else, including her Arnie, who had been destroyed by this war.

It was a few seconds before anyone spoke. It was the sub-inspector who broke the silence, and Aggie could tell by her strained voice that she found the sight of this man difficult too.

'Mr Stannage?' she asked, looking at the notepad she had pulled from her pocket. The man nodded, his eyes full of pain and humiliation. 'This is Constable Tucker and I am Sub-Inspector Nash. I understand you have suffered a bereavement today?'

He nodded again and gestured with one of his crutches to follow him. He led them into the front room of the tiny house. Aggie was stunned to see a woman hanging from the rafters. She hadn't even been taken down. A rope had been tied to the beam of the ceiling, the other end around the woman's neck. She hung there with her head on one side, resting on her shoulder, as though she had fallen asleep. She wore a smart blouse and a long skirt, but her feet were bare and hanging down, unmoving; she was absolutely still. Aggie wondered what her husband had done when he'd found her, how he had been sure she was dead. A wooden chair lay on its side on the floor.

Mr Stannage couldn't possibly have managed to take the woman down, and the little girl couldn't have either. They had just left her swinging there, it was unspeakably sad.

The sub-inspector rushed to pick up the wooden chair.

190

Aggie got onto it first, desperate to get the poor woman down. She got her arms around the woman's legs and lifted her upwards. On another chair, the sub-inspector got the rope over the woman's head and they almost fell with the weight of her when she was loose. They got her down to the floor. The sub-inspector felt for a pulse but it was obvious that she was dead. The little girl whimpered at the door.

'Please take your daughter into another room, Mr Stannage,' said Aggie. The man looked as though he was in shock. The sub-inspector went upstairs and returned with a threadbare blanket, which she placed over the woman.

'We shall need to inform the undertaker,' she said. 'And Stanford police. Mr Stannage,' she called, going through to find him. 'We are awfully sorry for your loss. Did you find your wife like this?' He nodded and said yes and his tongue flapped upwards with no soft palate to strike. It was a pitiful sight indeed. 'We shall inform the undertaker, Mr Stannage. We are awfully sorry.' The sub-inspector touched the man's arm. Aggie smiled at the little girl and they left the house.

Neither woman shouted a comment on the motorcycle. They rode to Stanford police station, each with their own silent thoughts.

'Do you think she did it because of his injuries?' said Aggie, climbing off the bike.

'Undoubtedly,' said the sub-inspector. 'I've seen it before. It can often be either party who finds it impossible to live with injuries like that.'

Aggie thought of Arnie and shivered. She would never do that to him.

'Good afternoon, Sergeant Pavey.'

'Good afternoon, Sub-Inspector,' said the sergeant looking up from his desk. 'And Constable Tucker.'

Aggie smiled at him. 'We've a suicide to report,' she said.

'Oh?'

'A Mrs Stannage in Lower Crescent Road in Linford,' said the sub-inspector. 'Might the undertaker be informed?'

'Yes, of course,' said Sergeant Pavey, who left them to go into the back office. 'The chief is wondering if you want to be sworn in now, save coming back tomorrow?' he said to Aggie. Her heart jumped and she looked at the sub-inspector.

'Why not?' said Sub-Inspector Nash. 'You have your uniform now. We may as well.'

'Yes, all right, thank you,' said Aggie shyly and still feeling sick from the sight of Mrs Stannage hanging from the ceiling. The sergeant gave her a wink and went to inform the chief constable.

Before she knew it, Aggie was holding a Bible in her hands and swearing allegiance to King and Country. 'Your duties include patrolling the Orsett Rural District to oversee the moral and criminal behaviour of women and children,' said the sub-inspector, reading from her notebook, 'to patrol Greygoose munitions factory and associated train services, to appear in court as witness to crimes, to inform the military and civil police of behaviour of a criminal, immoral or treasonous nature, and to assist the general public at times of air-raid warnings and air strikes.'

'You are employed by the Ministry of Munitions and report to this police station,' continued the chief constable. 'Your police status is unofficial. You have no powers of arrest but may detain individuals under the civil procedure of citizen's arrest. Congratulations.'

He stepped forward to shake her hand, as did Sergeant Pavey and the sub-inspector. Aggie tried to remain calm and professional but inside was bursting. She had done it. She had taken the brave leap of leaving her munitions job to train in the Women's Police Service. She had got onto the training, she had managed to pass, and now here she was, what must have been one of the first, if not *the* first woman from the working classes in a WPS uniform. Her joy dipped into shame when she thought of herself in court the other day giving evidence against Tilly. It had been the price she had paid for her new status.

'There'll be a pay increase too,' said the sub-inspector, patting her on the back on the way out. 'You'll be on two pounds a week now. Nothing compared to what the men get, of course, but still.'

Two pounds a week. A reward for her betrayal. She had started out on this journey with the intention of doing better for girls like her. To be different from the middle-class controlling authorities that were always looking down at the factory girls and policing their morality. She resolved to do better. From then on, she would do things her way, she would look out for the lower classes, she would do what she could for them.

'Don't forget, you're on probation now for three months,' said the sub-inspector. 'Keep things in order and I'm sure you'll pass probation and never look back.'

On their journey back through Stanford on the motorcycle, Aggie saw a poster on the side of the railway station. A picture of several downcast men, some in uniform, some in plain clothes, some on crutches, some with a sleeve pinned to their chest over an amputated arm. DON'T PITY A DISABLED MAN, the poster read, FIND HIM A JOB. Arnie had been discharged from service but was hardly fit for work. Nervous about sharing her good news about the promotion in case it undermined his confidence, Aggie decided that perhaps it would be good for him to find a little job – he'd feel useful and she wouldn't feel so bad about her own job.

When she got home she found Mim changing Arnie's face bandage in the kitchen. Her step faltered. She thought about poor Mr Stannage and his missing jaw. She gave a little wave so as not to disturb them. Arnie's facial injury was higher than Mr Stannage's. It looked like someone had taken a tablespoon and scooped out the flesh from his cheek and nose and his eye was missing, just a hole remained. It was fascinating in a morbid way. This was the second time she had seen it and it wasn't as shocking. The bone was visible in places. It looked awfully raw and painful. No skin to protect or cover. Just the bare flesh and bone, open to the elements.

'How does it feel, dear?' she said.

'It feels like a bastard,' he said. 'Sorry, Mim.' His good eye looked up at his nurse. Mim said nothing but carried on bathing the wound. She applied a dressing and began to wind on the bandage.

'I was thinking,' said Aggie, 'that it might be good if you were to get a little job, Arnie.'

Mim and Arnie looked at her in unison and then looked away. Mim glanced back.

'Your uniform,' she said. 'You've passed your training?'

'Yes,' said Aggie. 'I was sworn in today.'

'Congratulations,' Mim and Arnie said at the same time.

'Thanks. It feels quite strange.' They said nothing further. 'I mean, about Arnie, that it might do you good to get out a bit more. Make you feel like, like, you ...'

'Make me feel like a man again?' Arnie finished for her. She blushed.

'Yes, sort of.'

'I don't know,' he said. 'What do you think, Mim?' Aggie looked away; when he spoke she could see the flesh in his face moving and it made her feel quite queasy.

'Oh, I think you should if Aggie says it's a good idea.'

'All right,' he said glumly, looking at his arm in its sling. 'I don't know what I'd do though.'

'We can have a look,' said Mim. 'Perhaps you could go to the Labour Exchange?'

'Good,' said Aggie. 'Mim, it'll be good when we can go out on patrol together again.' Mim looked at her kindly, as though she'd said something really very silly.

Aggie went upstairs to get changed and looked at herself in the mirror. She certainly did look fine in her new uniform. She turned this way and that, admiring the cut of the expensive cloth. *They might have been happier for me*, she thought. *They hardly said a word about it.*

14

Mim

'You do not really need these bandages any more, Arnie,' said Mim, winding the gauze around his head. 'The wounds have healed sufficiently to benefit from being aired.'

Arnie kept quiet. Mim knew he didn't want to expose his horrific injuries – that he would rather keep them hidden.

'You know,' she said tentatively, 'I have heard of a hospital department in Wandsworth that people refer to as the "tin noses shop".' She took his silence as a sign of interest. 'A professor of sculpture, a Derwent Wood, I believe, makes copper masks for men with facial injuries that look remarkably realistic. I wonder if it is something you would like to consider?'

She placed the used bandages on the table, next to a letter that had arrived for her that morning. Her cousin Matilda in London wishing her well, asking after her health, suggesting she try contacting a spiritualist, who would be able to help her communicate with Bertie. Of all the things. A spiritualist. She couldn't deny that the thought of being able to talk to Bertie was tantalising. Her grief was often paralysing. When with Arnie she sometimes felt short of breath and had to lie down. She still found hair on her pillow and her skirts spun on her waist. Her monthly cycle had stopped too. At best, she wandered the house in a quagmire of gloom. Arnie, a man of few words, was surprisingly good company but she didn't want to infect him with her gloominess, he had enough to worry about. Arnie and Aggie were the most unlikely of friends, she admitted, but strangely she couldn't face anyone else and she didn't want to jeopardise her friendships with them. So she kept her grief inside.

In the newspaper she had read Sigmund Freud proposed that grief does not dissipate with time – that the smallest of things can open up the gaping wound of bereavement at any given moment. She found it fitting but of no comfort. A slip of paper had fallen from Cousin Matilda's letter as she had read it that morning. Matilda had written out the damned sermon that Mim was trying to escape. Was it her cousin's assurance that spiritualism could be bedfellows with Christianity, or was it God's way of telling her to come back to Him? She closed her eyes and said a silent prayer.

I shall come back to you if you let me wake up from this bad dream. I will help Arnie, I will look after him even though it is hard for me. But I will do it if you bring Bertie back. And then I will come back to you.

She decided she would not pursue spiritualism, that she would give God a chance to set things right.

'Would it mean I could go outside and not be stared at?' said Arnie at the suggestion of the tin noses shop.

'I do believe it would, Arnie. And perhaps you might find it easier to find employment too?'

Aggie had persuaded Arnie to get a job. The poor man, all he wanted to do was sleep and hide away. He was traumatised from his time at war and was trying to come to terms with his changed identity, and his sense of having no purpose.

'Would it mean that Aggie would be able to look at me again?' He said it with a hint of bitterness but his honesty only made him more wretched in Mim's eyes.

Mim swallowed. 'Yes, Arnie, I do believe so.'

'What do we do then, go up there?'

'I shall write to the professor,' she said.

It didn't take long to hear a response. Arnie was invited to attend a consultation with the sculpture professor. He said he wanted it to be a surprise for Aggie and not to tell her where they were going. Mim informed Aggie that they were going to a London hospital for Arnie's treatment and left it at that. It wasn't far from the truth.

Travelling to London was an ordeal for both of them. Mim still felt shaky going far from the house and Arnie was terribly self-conscious about his injuries, even though they were covered with bandages. She took his arm and they clung onto each other for support. When they arrived at the Third London General Hospital in Wandsworth and found Derwent Wood's department, everyone was frightfully good.

Unwinding Arnie's bandages, the professor said, 'You are not to worry, I have seen everything and more, I can assure you. I can only thank you for giving your service to this country.'

The professor examined Arnie's wounds. Mim always thought his face looked like a scooped out, half-eaten tapioca pudding. Perhaps her background in nursing had equipped her well to be able to help Arnie. Caring for him was an intimate thing – she imagined it would be the same as helping one's own child. She was becoming fond of Arnie and so caring for him was a labour of fondness, despite his horrific injuries.

The professor spent a long time examining Arnie's face. It occurred to Mim that he might not be able to make Arnie a mask, that there were no guarantees. At last he said, 'Bone restructuring is not required. The wound has healed sufficiently. I can make you a mask.' Mim let out the breath she had been holding. 'Please know that these masks are not suitable for everyone, even when they are made,' he went on. 'Some men find them uncomfortable to wear, they say the mask rubs their wound. Some men feel reborn with the mask, it allows them to have a near normal life, with job and family and so on. If you are willing, I shall make a mould of your face now and will work on the production of the mask for a week or so and call you back in to have it fitted. What say you?'

'Yes please, doc,' said Arnie.

'Ah, yes, I am not a doctor, you see. I am a professor of sculpture,' he said smiling.

'All right, professor, yes, I'd be grateful if you'd make me a mask.'

The professor leant Arnie back in a barber's chair and prepared a bowl of wet clay. He smoothed it over Arnie's face and poor Arnie was left half suffocating while it dried sufficiently well to be taken off. Mim held his hand throughout, watching the surface of the clay turn grey and thinking how like Bertie's face in death it was. When the cast was complete, the professor removed it carefully and placed it over a mannequin mould on his bench.

'Do you have a photograph? From before the injury?' asked the professor. 'We do endeavour to create as much of a previous likeness as possible.'

They left a photograph of Arnie handsome in his army uniform, which Arnie could hardly bear to look at. The contrast between now and then was startling and it occurred to Mim how much one takes for granted. A face, a normal sort of face compared to one that has been shattered by gunshot.

At Fenchurch Street station, Mim waited for Arnie to use the public lavatories. He went in with hanging head and emerged with the pride of the King of England. Mim guessed he must have brought his medicine with him and taken it while in the lavatory. On the journey home, he was high with excitement, talking about keeping his mask secret from Aggie and presenting it to her with a flourish. Mim smiled and nodded, glad to see his spirits lifted. It really would be marvellous if the mask helped him. She watched the fields roll by the window and spoke to God. *You see? Arnie will be reborn and his confidence recovered. That is my side of the bargain. You will send Bertie back to me, that is your side.*

A week later they were back in Wandsworth. The professor showed Arnie his mask and Mim gasped. It was remarkably lifelike. It was made from copper but had been painted to the standard of a fine work of art. It was a puzzle piece to be slotted into Arnie's face to make him whole again. There was no socket to speak of in which to place a glass eye, so the mask covered it and upon the mask was painted a picture of an eye. The professor fitted it on, asked Arnie how it felt, made some adjustments, lightened the skin tone slightly to match Arnie's complexion. By the afternoon, it was ready. When Arnie tried it on, the professor fitted some spectacles over the mask to help hold it on and handed Arnie a hand-held looking glass. His good eye welled up with tears and he couldn't speak. Mim felt choked up too. At a distance one would hardly know this man's face had been blown to smithereens. The mask covered and disguised his smashed nose and cheek, his missing eye. Arnie put the glass down and looked at Mim and that was when the illusion faded. The part of his face covered by the mask didn't move when he smiled, his eye didn't blink. It all stayed still and lifeless. But it was a complete face, nonetheless, it was worth the momentary illusion.

'Thank you, Mim,' he said on the train home. 'This was your idea. Thank you.'

She smiled and hoped God was watching. *I told you I would help him. Now you help me.*

They arrived back home and Arnie was in great anticipation to show his mask to his wife. Aggie was out on patrol, so he sat at the kitchen table and Mim made a pot of tea. As she washed up the cups from the morning, she saw through the kitchen window a thrush land on the back lawn. She watched it hop across the grass. It twitched its head and stopped, pecked out a long, pink earthworm from the soil and dropped it to the ground, watching it squirm under its scrutiny. The thrush pecked the worm's head twice, watched it again, then swallowed it whole and hopped away.

When Aggie came home, she stopped in her tracks and looked with wide eyes at her husband. She put her hands over her mouth. She squinted and came nearer. Arnie smiled and then she hesitated, seeing the thing for what it was. But good old girl, she put on a good front for him.

'Oh, Arnie, it's marvellous, it really is.' She came and kissed her husband on his head and looked at the mask closely. 'How marvellous,' she kept saying.

Mim thought the mask had been a successful endeavour and that she could now help Arnie find a job. As a precaution, and so as not to let him experience undue disappointment, she went to the Labour Exchange in Stanford to enquire after positions and explain Arnie's disabilities. She came away disheartened. Of the jobs available, all required an able-bodied man. Arnie's arm had still not recovered sufficiently for him to use it for manual work. Not wanting to take him bad news, she walked around the small town looking for inspiration. There was a child of around ten years old selling matches on a street corner and it brought to mind the invalided servicemen outside the George and Dragon pub, the ones Aggie had spoken to, the ones with all the children climbing on the public house window sills.

'A job, Arnie,' she said, coming into the house laden with bundles.

He looked up expectantly. 'What is it?'

She pulled out bags of matchboxes, socks and cigarettes that she'd bought at great expense and put them on the table. The good side of Arnie's face dropped. 'Selling matches like a child?' he said.

'It's a start, isn't it? You can do it when you feel up to it and come home when you're tired. When your arm is better you can reconsider your options. You'd be beholden to no employer's rules and regulations. And it's a stepping stone. Who knows who you might meet, who might offer you a better position.'

Arnie rolled a cigarette from his pouch of tobacco and his mouth twitched. Mim knew what he was thinking. He had guessed that she'd been to the Labour Exchange and found that there was no work for him there. He knew that Aggie wanted him to find work.

'All right, Mim, I'll do it,' he said.

'It's my last one,' said Arnie, preparing his medicine syringe. 'Can you get my next prescription, Mim?'

Mim nodded and went to the kitchen dresser. 'Where did I put them?' she said, frowning and rifling through the papers. She was sure the prescriptions were on the top of the pile.

'It's my last one,' said Arnie again.

'Your last one in total?' said Mim, shocked. 'But I haven't been back to the chemist.'

'I went,' said Arnie, preparing his syringe and avoiding her eye.

Mim pulled out a chair at the kitchen table and sat down. She stared at Arnie. He must have been going to the chemist to fill his prescriptions without telling her; he must have been taking a lot more of the medicine than he ought.

'Arnie, the doctor said this medicine is very addictive,' she said cautiously. 'Do you not perhaps think it best to go back to see him, enquire as to alternative pain medication?'

He rolled up his sleeve, applied the tourniquet and injected himself there in front of her. She saw the change come over him almost immediately. His shoulders dropped, his face slackened.

'It's no bother, Mim. I need it. It numbs the pain in my face, my arm and in here.' He tapped his forehead. 'Do you know, Mim, some of the sights I saw?'

She shifted uncomfortably. He was very talkative when he'd had his shot, and spoke in a very different way, rather pompous and rambling. Mim knew it was just the cocaine. The poor man had been through a terrible ordeal.

'You have told me some, Arnie, dear,' she said, trying to soothe him.

'It's a funny thing, Mim, when you see your friend's brains and another chap's guts all in the same day. Sometimes you might see someone's guts mixed up with someone else's brains and a crowd of rats feasting on it all like they was having a king's banquet.'

'Oh, Arnie, please don't,' she said, feeling faint. 'I shall go to the doctor for you. I know you've had a terrible, terrible shock.'

He paused, seeming to settle a little at her words. She wondered whether he spoke to Aggie in the same way. Aggie was out a good deal on patrol, and Mim was grateful to her for the peace of mind that brought, but Arnie needed his wife. He was relying on Mim now and she wasn't sure she was able to do her best for him. He was so desperate for his cocaine that he told her horrific things to provoke a reaction from her, to make her acquiesce and agree to get the medicine. He was manipulating her, but not out of spite, simply because he needed to numb his pain and his memories and because of his need for the damned stuff in his veins.

'Now, how about this new job of yours?' she said brightly, trying to distract him. 'We shall need a wooden tray of some kind in which to display the merchandise. Do you have an idea of where we might get one?' She sank back against her chair, suddenly exhausted from the strain of appearing strong for him but at the same time gaining succour from being in his company. He was helping her too, without really knowing it.

'I can build one,' he said, announcing the fact with excitement and presumption.

'You can? Well, that would be super.'

'We'll go and get my tools from the house and a bit of timber from old Jack, we'll just stop in and ask him, he'll be all right about it. Come on then, Mim,' he said, standing up and going to the front door, picking up his overcoat on his way.

'Now?' she said, hoping he'd go alone. But he wanted her with him. 'I'm coming,' she said.

They knocked at the door of Aggie and Arnie's old house that had been billeted. A man in shirtsleeves answered.

Arnie waited for Mim to speak. 'Good morning. I am Sergeant Rathbone of the Women's Police Service,' she said, hesitating because she was in mourning attire and not her uniform. 'And this is Private Tucker, whose house has been billeted to you. Might we possibly gain entry in order to collect some of Private Tucker's tools?'

The man looked at Arnie, possibly wondering why he couldn't speak for himself. Arnie suddenly saluted and the man saluted in return.

'Of course,' said the man, without introducing himself or asking further questions. 'Where are they?'

'Under the stairs,' said Arnie, going in. 'On service at the fort, are you?' he said, his tone not as bright as it had been at home.

'That's right. Corporal Green, with the Royal Engineers.'

'The Royal Engineers,' said Arnie, on his knees looking through the under-stairs cupboard. 'Perhaps I should have signed up with them, eh, Mim?'

Mim looked down at the floor, embarrassed. Arnie was putting this man's service into question, in light of his own injuries. It was poor etiquette.

Arnie got his armful of tools and left the house, without offering a word of thanks or goodbye to the corporal.

'Good day, Corporal,' said Mim. The man gave her a tight-lipped nod and shut the door.

Arnie traipsed home, his gait dragging. 'These chaps,' he said, almost to himself, 'they don't know they're born. Look at me and look at him.'

'Now then,' said Mim, 'where does this fellow Jack live?'

They deposited the tools at home and went to knock on Jack's door. An old man answered and looked questioningly from Mim to Arnie.

'It's me, you silly old sod,' said Arnie.

'Arnie? When did you get back?'

'Oh, not long,' he replied vaguely. 'I need some wood, you got some?'

'Some wood?' said the old man, scratching his head and staring at Arnie's face. 'You all right, Arnie?'

'Yes, I'm alive, aren't I?' Arnie said it sullenly, his mood had swung since seeing the corporal in his old house. 'I need a bit of timber, let's see what you've got.'

Mim watched as Arnie rifled through a mass of materials in Jack's back garden. He trudged home carrying the pieces of wood without saying a word to Mim. She felt for him. It must have been difficult seeing a man in his house, a healthy, uninjured man with a cosy job at the fort. When they got home he dropped the wood on the hallway floor and sagged against the wall, covering his face with his good hand.

'Arnie, what is it?' said Mim, concerned.

He let out a small strangled sound as if he were sobbing. Alarmed, Mim put a hand on his shoulder. He shook his head. 'I'm all right. It's just this damned mask, it rubs on my wound.'

It wasn't just the mask, Mim knew, but didn't say so. 'Why don't you take it off at home, Arnie? To be more comfortable.'

Arnie shook his head and sniffed. 'I suppose I'd better make this thing then.'

Mim helped him carry the wood and tools out to the back yard. His injured arm hindered him and so she did her best to hold the wood in place where it was needed and between them they managed to fashion a wooden tray by dinner time.

'If we make a hole either side we can thread through some twine to hang it with.'

'Yes, hang it round my neck like a noose,' he mumbled, and Mim pretended she hadn't heard.

They soon had it hanging around Arnie's neck, not so much like a noose but rather more like an usherette selling ices during a theatre interval. They stacked the tray with the socks, matches and cigarettes and Mim stood back, pleased.

'Well, don't you look the part,' she said. Arnie didn't reply.

'What say you stand outside the Ship public house?' she said. 'It's close by and when you're tired you can come home easily.'

He looked like he'd rather shoot himself in the foot but he nodded and left the house. Mim stayed at home and worried about him. It was good for him, she convinced herself, to feel useful and contribute something to society. She wanted him to feel proud of himself, his confidence had taken such a knock. Mrs Zlin came in the back door and stamped her boots on the mat. With a start, Mim realised she was sitting at the kitchen table wringing her hands. She never used to sit in the kitchen, she was there because that was where Arnie liked to sit.

Two hours later he came home. Mim had dozed off on a sofa in the sitting room. She jumped up to see him. One look at his face told her how it had gone. He took off the tray and let it drop to the parquet floor with a slam that startled her.

'I can't do it, Mim, I'm sorry,' he said miserably and went out to the kitchen to roll a cigarette. She sat with him and put her hand over his.

'Was it awful?' she said tentatively.

'Did you go to the chemist?' he said and her heart leapt. She had meant to go earlier but had forgotten and fallen asleep.

'No, I'm sorry, I'll go tomorrow.'

He pressed his lips tightly together and looked at the table. 'Have you got any of those cough things?' he said. She nodded and fetched them. He emptied them into his hand and chewed the lot in one go. Mim took the packet and looked at it. One of the ingredients was cocaine. 'I need my prescription, Mim.'

'I'll go first thing, Arnie,' she said. To her horror he put a hand over his face and let out a dreadful sob. Reaching for his other hand, her throat cracked with emotion. She cried too, for the sheer injustice that had been thrust upon them both. He shuffled towards her awkwardly and they embraced. They held each other as though the one stopped the other from falling to pieces and scattering on the ground.

The next day, Mim came home empty-handed. 'I'm sorry,' she said. 'The doctor said you can't have any more.'

Arnie stood up shakily and looked around as if there was an immediate threat. 'Why did he say it? What did you tell him?'

'Nothing,' said Mim, hurt. 'Nothing at all.'

'What will I do? I need it.' He slumped back down into his chair.

Mrs Zlin bumped through the kitchen with a mop bucket that knocked against Arnie's chair. She tutted as though it was his fault.

'I've had a thought,' said Mim. 'There is a basket works at Orsett. Pound Road. Set up by Colonel Whitmore of Orsett Hall for injured soldiers. It's funded by the Ministry of Labour. What say I ask if you can have a job there?'

Arnie looked at her and chewed the skin on the side of his thumb. He was thinking of only one thing.

'Arnie,' she said, crouching down by his chair. 'Can't you leave this medicine now?'

He shook his head and his one good eye welled with tears. A shroud of dread fell over Mim. Arnie was fragile. If he couldn't have his medicine to cope, perhaps he would stop coping altogether. Perhaps he would take his own life. It was happening frequently around the country. People left alone without their loved ones, men unable to go on living with their horrific memories and injuries. Suicide, and plenty of it.

'I got you these,' she said, taking out a box of cough drops. She had checked that they contained the right sort of stuff that he'd need. He took them from her and shook a few into his palm, throwing them into his mouth. Mrs Zlin tutted again and Arnie looked at her. She scuttled away. He withdrew to his room, taking the box with him.

'Tomorrow, the basket works,' she called to him, but he made no answer.

15

Aggie

The country watched and waited. The Allies had broken through the Hindenburg Line in late September and the Germans were pushed ever further back, with talk of starving troops and the German leadership knowing they had lost the war. Bulgaria signed an armistice with the Allies and withdrew from hostilities. The British and the Belgians pushed forward, forcing the Germans to retreat. The Austro-Hungarian Army was driven out of Italy in their final bloody battle. In late October, Turkey signed an armistice with the Allies and was the second central power to quit the war.

'I rather think we should start wearing masks, don't you? I'll put in an order but I think they might be in short supply.'

The sub-inspector and Aggie had pulled over on the motorcycle to see the troops from the Coalhouse Fort camp marching through East Tilbury village. The men all wore white cotton masks stretched across their noses and mouths.

'It's getting worse,' nodded Aggie.

'They say thousands have died in Britain alone,' said the sub-inspector sombrely. 'One can be fine at breakfast and be dead by suppertime.'

Aggie hadn't yet come across someone in the district with symptoms of Spanish flu, but it gave her a very uneasy feeling.

The troops passed and the women remounted the motorcycle. It was around nine o'clock in the evening. They had been on patrol at Greygoose factory for most of the afternoon, where production had reduced drastically over the past few weeks. More women and men had been laid off. Most had gone quietly. But there was no work for them elsewhere and Aggie was glad she'd decided to get out while she could. More men were coming home from the war. Those injured and in hospital or at home would have inadvertently cast the same shadow over their homes and families as Arnie's return had done. All around the country women were reunited with their menfolk, who had returned different people than had left for war. Many had not returned, the vacuum of grief replacing their presence at home.

But still the war had not ended. Still many, many families did not know for certain whether they would see their loved ones again or in what state they would return to them. Aggie sensed the approach of the end of the war with mixed feelings. It had become everyone's way of life. It had affected everyone, including her. Before the war she'd never have predicted that she'd become a woman police constable and her husband would have a smashed face and be reduced to selling matches for a living. If they could have seen what lay ahead, what would they have done differently?

The sub-inspector had them working all hours. Aggie hadn't had time to see much of Arnie, or of Mim, but she thought they were doing pretty well. Arnie's job selling matches hadn't lasted but now Mim had got him a stint making baskets at home. He did it in Bertie's old writing shed at the bottom of the garden. It wasn't a very manly job but it was better than nothing. Sometimes he went around without his mask on. Aggie didn't know which was worse, the injury or the mask. She dreaded having to kiss him, the thought made her shudder and was always accompanied by a hefty wedge of guilt. In that sense she was glad to be busy at work. It meant she didn't have to face things at home.

A group of boys around twelve or thirteen years old came out of a side alley onto the main road. When they saw the women they exchanged low words and moved along in single file. Aggie tapped the sub-inspector to pull over.

'Good evening, boys,' she said, dismounting. Since Tilly Packet had gone to prison, Aggie was trying her best to do things differently on patrol. 'Out for a walk, are you?'

They relaxed, put their hands in their pockets and kicked at the gravel on the path.

'Do you live in East Tilbury? I don't think I've seen you here before.'

'Stanford,' one of them muttered.

'Oh, Stanford. It's a bit of a walk to get home. Won't your mother be worried?'

'Turn out your pockets,' said the sub-inspector sternly, striding over to the group. 'All of you,' she said.

The boys groaned and pulled things out of their pockets. The sub-inspector went along to each, looking in their hands. There was no obvious contraband.

'Your mothers will be worried,' said the sub-inspector. 'Skulking around the dark streets. I've a good mind to send you to the Cornwall right now and tell your parents about it tomorrow.'

Aggie looked at her colleague. Surely she wasn't serious. The Cornwall was a reformatory school ship moored off Purfleet.

'It's all right, miss,' said one of the boys. 'We'll get home now.'

'See that you do,' said the sub-inspector. 'They need discipline,' she said to Aggie. 'Their fathers are likely away, their mothers working. There is nobody at home to keep them in line. They run around the streets at night committing petty crimes.'

Aggie was disappointed not to have been able to deal with the situation in her own way. She'd have liked to have escorted the boys home, talked to the mother, tried a gentle approach. But the sub-inspector had barged in with her big boots, her big polished shooting boots.

They watched the boys make their way down the hill onto the road to Stanford. A man walked past them, his stride a little in the way of a zigzag. 'Bit of trouble in the pub, Mrs Police,' he slurred, laughing as he went off.

Aggie looked at the sub-inspector and they jumped back on the bike and rode up the hill to the Ship.

'That pub again,' called the sub-inspector. 'It has become a den of immorality. Something needs to be done.'

Aggie wondered whether the curfew, which the sub-inspector had had imposed in Tilbury, had anything to do with the Ship being busier and more like a 'den of immorality' than ever before.

As they approached the pub, Aggie could see a couple entwined in the side return. She glanced at the sub-inspector and went to speak to them. Waiting there for them to notice her, they soon pulled apart. The man was in uniform, she didn't recognise the girl, who looked rather young. Tipping his cap, the man muttered, 'Sorry, miss.'

Aggie saw this as a chance to practise her new method of policing, without the sub-inspector interfering. 'Where do you live?' she said softly to the girl.

'Linford,' came the reply.

'Don't you think it best that you get home now? You're putting yourself at real risk.' She lowered her voice and spoke closely to the girl. 'Of ruining your reputation,' she said. 'If things go too far, you might get in the family way, out of marriage, even catch syphilis.' The girl knew Aggie was right. She nodded. 'And, sir,' Aggie went on, 'can I ask for your chivalry in keeping this girl respectable? A bit of fun for you now could mean a lifetime of misery for her.'

'Yes, miss,' he said. They started to say goodbye when the sub-inspector nudged Aggie aside.

'Off you go then, unless you want us to escort you back home this instant.'

Aggie looked at the sub-inspector who only returned her gaze with a triumphant air. They entered the pub, where the atmosphere was rowdy and loud. *Unseemly*, the sub-inspector would say. A man in uniform was at the bar, banging his fist on the polished wood and losing his balance. 'It's your pub,' he was saying to Wally Spooner, the landlord, 'you do something about it.' Two other men were trying to hold him up but he seemed to be quite floppy and had lost the ability to stand.

'What is all this?' demanded the sub-inspector. 'Do I need to summon Sergeant Pavey?'

Aggie wished Sergeant Pavey was there – it wasn't for the WPS to deal with the men.

'She drugged me,' said the floppy man, turning to face the women. 'Drugged me then robbed me.'

'Who did?' said Aggie.

'Cecile,' he slurred.

'Cecile?' frowned Aggie. 'Are you sure? That's not like her.'

'It was her,' he said. 'You better find her and get my money back.'

'It was,' said another man. 'He was with Cecile.'

Cecile the prostitute. The one who'd given Aggie and Mim a laugh that time when she'd lifted her skirts at them. She was harmless enough. Yes, she brought the area down, but they knew where she lived and knew she worked to support her children.

'That's strange,' said Aggie.

'Yes, it does seem a little odd,' said the sub-inspector. 'She can't be far. Let's get this chap back to camp and then we'll go and find her and sort this out.'

They left the motorcycle where it was, enlisted the help of two of the man's friends and walked him back to the army camp adjacent to the fort.

'Get some black coffee and some bicarbonate of soda and a bucket,' the sub-inspector instructed one of the men when they had reached the mess hut. She mixed the two together and got the soldier to gulp it down. Within seconds he was violently sick in the bucket. 'That should do the trick,' she said. 'Get him off to bed.'

The women left the camp and headed back onto the road, holding their lanterns high and looking out for Cecile. 'Something needs to be done about that public house,' repeated the sub-inspector. 'We might consider patrolling here every night and sorting out a rotation with the officers at the factory and Stanford to enable us to be here more. I heartily wish the general would allow a curfew here. We can only do so much with that awful Mr Spooner.'

They turned down every lane and checked every garden for Cecile in case she was hiding, thinking that they would end up past Linford and into Mucking where she lived before they gave up their search.

They stopped by a small patch of front garden where an old couple were sitting up in what looked like a makeshift bed.

'Good evening,' said Aggie. 'May I ask, why you are sleeping out of doors?'

'We're afraid of the raids,' said the woman matter-of-factly. 'We don't want to be crushed in the house when a bomb lands on us.'

'The German air raids are very infrequent now,' said the

sub-inspector. 'And are likely to stop altogether with the Kaiser desperate for armistice.'

'Why don't you go back inside,' said Aggie kindly, 'much warmer in there.'

'Not until it's over,' said the old man resolutely.

'Do you happen to have seen a woman nearby in the last half hour?' asked the sub-inspector. 'The type of woman you might expect to see consorting with soldiers in the public house.'

'Yes, we saw her,' said the lady. She was about to point in which direction Cecile had gone when they all heard a woman scream. Aggie looked at the sub-inspector and they both ran towards the sound. A young woman came running out of a little alleyway at the side of the rectory opposite St Catherine's. When she saw the policewomen, she called to them. 'Quick, please,' and beckoned them past her and forwards.

Aggie glanced at her as she passed. 'Penny?' It was Penny Crabb, looking like a full-blown prostitute, from her painted face, which didn't disguise her drooping right eye, to the silly flowers and ribbons in her moth-eaten hat.

'There,' said Penny, pointing. 'It's Cecile.' Aggie looked and saw a figure slumped on the ground. Her heart banged in her chest. Please don't let her be dead, she prayed. She crouched down and put her hand on the woman's arm and shook it gently. 'Cecile?' she said. The sub-inspector was there, pressing her finger to Cecile's neck to feel for her pulse.

'She's alive,' she said.

The woman groaned and tried to turn over, wincing

218

with pain. It was Cecile. Even in the dark, Aggie could see the prostitute's gypsy-black hair and green eyes, her bad teeth.

'It's all right, Cecile, it's the police. Where does it hurt?' said Aggie, looking for signs of injury. She held Cecile's shoulder and looked underneath her, held a lantern there. The ground was wet with blood. 'She's bleeding, someone get a doctor. Someone get Sergeant Pavey.'

'I'll go on the motorcycle,' said the sub-inspector racing away, leaving Aggie there with the two women.

'What happened?' she asked Penny, watching them and biting her nails. But Penny shook her head, looking terrified.

'What's all this?' said a man's voice. A tall broad figure approached them.

'Give me your shawl,' she said to Penny. She put it against Cecile's back to try to stop the blood. The man came nearer. He looked familiar and Aggie remembered where she'd seen him. In the Ship that time. The man with the bandaged arm and cut hands.

'Come on,' he said to Penny and took her arm.

'No,' said Penny. 'I'm staying with her.'

Aggie wasn't sure what they were to each other. It looked as though they were together.

'Cecile, it's all right,' said Aggie. 'The doctor's coming.' She peered into the darkness at the sound of approaching footsteps.

'I went to the fort,' said the sub-inspector, out of breath. Several men in khaki ran round, and one of them with a doctor's bag crouched down to examine Cecile and they soon had her up and carried her away. 'They telephoned. Sergeant Pavey is on his way.'

Getting to her feet, Aggie looked for Penny and saw her with the man standing in the shadows a short distance away. 'Penny,' she called. 'Penny Crabb.' She said it with her most authoritative voice and hoped that Penny would heed her, especially now she wore the WPS uniform. The girl pulled her arm away from the man's and came to Aggie. 'What happened here?'

'Sergeant Pavey will soon be here making arrests,' said the sub-inspector unhelpfully.

'Penny,' said Aggie softly. 'Are you all right? Did you see what happened?'

Penny shook her head. 'No, miss, I didn't see, I just heard Cecile scream and went to see what it was. I didn't see anyone else, just Cecile.'

'I see,' said Aggie. 'Well, you'd better wait here for Sergeant Pavey, he'll want to talk to you.'

'She's busy,' said the man, coming forwards to pull Penny away. 'She's got to get home now, her mother's sick.'

'Wait,' said Aggie. 'Just another minute. Penny,' she said to one side, 'who is that man? What have you got yourself into?' She looked at Penny's make-up and clothes. 'What are you doing, Penny? Come with me, I can help you. I can get you a job, a proper job.'

Penny hesitated, but said, 'I'm all right.'

'I would like to escort you home,' said Aggie but the man pulled her away aggressively. Aggie held on tightly to her umbrella in case he tried something and soon she could no longer see them in the dark. 'We know where she lives,' said the sub-inspector. 'Her mother has stopped coming to us in Tilbury trying to find her, but I know her address. I don't know that man, though, do you? He seems a suspicious sort.'

'Yes, I've seen him in the pub before,' said Aggie. 'I think he's an invalided soldier. He had scars on his hands, deep scars, you know?' she said, not sure if the inspector got her meaning about men hurting themselves to dodge service, 'but he was wearing an "On War Service" badge.'

'Frankly, I am rather shocked at Penny's condition,' said the sub-inspector. 'She has embarked upon the road of immorality, I am afraid.'

Aggie remembered her training in Tilbury and the sub-inspector talking about how these girls started off with 'khaki fever', excited to be hanging around the army camps, talking to soldiers. They'd go out drinking with the men, spending time in public houses. They would progress to being the soldier's girl and then they would cross a line that they could never come back from. They would compromise their morality. The family would find out and try to control the situation but the girl would be infatuated, having a gay time and enjoying her new status. And soon, she would be morally questionable. Her reputation would be spoilt. She wouldn't be able to return home. She might start to associate with women who'd come to that way of life earlier and were now entrenched. The young girl would seek support, find a way to live, find herself making a living from the soldiers instead of having a gay time with them. From then on they were branded. Alone. With no legal rights. They were susceptible to venereal disease, alcoholism, they might start taking drugs. There was no way out for them. They couldn't go home, they had disgraced the family. Aggie could see that Penny was on a journey down this lonely road and now she was with this man, who looked rough and dangerous.

Cecile was patched up and transferred to Orsett Hospital. She had been stabbed and knocked about but luckily wasn't in a critical condition. When the sub-inspector and Aggie visited Stanford police station the following day, Aggie was horrified to learn from Sergeant Pavey that the chief constable had arrested Cecile for soliciting.

'But she was attacked by someone. Shouldn't you be looking for the attacker?' she said.

Sergeant Pavey shrugged. 'It's of the chief's opinion that the woman's actions initiated the attack. She was found to have syphilis,' he said, avoiding Aggie's eye. 'She has most likely infected a number of the men. "Beyond help" is the phrase the chief used. She'll rest in hospital and then will find herself at Grays police court.'

Aggie had heard of a sixteen-year-old girl who had recently died of syphilis in Tilbury. 'She's got six children,' said Aggie, almost to herself.

'We'll have to take them to the NSPCC or some such,' said the sub-inspector. 'I've a feeling they will not be seeing their mother in the near future.'

Sergeant Pavey looked at Aggie's horrified face. What would the children do without their mother? 'I'll take you in the trap,' he said.

The sub-inspector had business elsewhere and entrusted

the job to them. Aggie sat with the sergeant as he guided his pony along the lanes to Mucking village where Cecile lived. Aggie could tell he came from a similar background as her. It must have grated when the sub-inspector, with her posh voice, authoritative attitude and her motorcycle arrived in his district. She was from a different world to him and came across as intimidating and presumptuous.

On the outskirts of Mucking they rode along a track and came to a shabby row of hovels. Aggie asked a woman sitting on the ground kneading dough in a tin bowl which door it was and knocked to find four of Cecile's children inside, one around ten and the others younger. They crowded around the door looking like frightened animals, barefoot and dirty. Two more came along from playing in the road when they saw the women police there. It was difficult to tell their ages, they were skinny and had the blank faces of long-term prisoners, one was a girl no more than five years old.

'Your mother is in the hospital,' said Aggie, gingerly. 'She'll be all right, but you'll need to come with me for now until she's better. We're the police, you'll be all right. Come along now. Do you want to bring any of your things?' She peered indoors to see an earthen floor churned into mud from the recent rain and a mangy chicken pecking in the corner. They were living in squalor and Aggie doubted they had any belongings to speak of to bring with them.

She and Sergeant Pavey got the children in the back of the trap and they rode to the children's home in Grays town, silently but for one of the smallest girls whimpering. Aggie felt a heaviness on her heart. Who had attacked poor Cecile? The chief constable didn't seem to care. Cecile would be punished for her profession, no matter what had been done to her. She was branded a loose woman, a moral defective. She'd have no defence in the eyes of the law. Aggie looked behind her at the frightened little rabbits and her heart became heavier still. She was taking Cecile's children away from her. Just as her own children had been taken away, years ago. Aggie was doing the same thing to another woman whom she was supposed to be helping. She wondered whether she was doing any good at all.

16

Mim

The newspapers that Aggie brought home and left on the kitchen table were Mim's contact with the outside world. It was all she was prepared to let in. There had been a false armistice yesterday on the seventh of November. Mim read in the newspaper that the Germans were on their way to discuss terms of the ceasefire and Reuters news had made a mess of it. The whole world celebrated the end of the war before it was over. Mim hadn't celebrated. She didn't know if Arnie had, she hadn't felt like sitting with him the past day or two.

In any case, Arnie was busy working in the Hatchery. It was what Bertie had called his study at the end of the garden, a brick outhouse where he hatched ideas for his books on military history. There was plenty of room in the house, of course, but Bertie had been a busy man and used his time economically – he liked to have his own little space where he could write undisturbed.

Determined to find Arnie a job, Mim had written to the basket works at Orsett. But he wouldn't go. He broke down and apologised to her. His face, his pain ... So she arranged for him to do piecework at home. A veteran soldier came to the house with the materials – willows from their own plantation – and showed Arnie how to make baskets. They made all kinds of baskets but they asked Arnie to make picnic hampers. And that was what he did in Bertie's Hatchery. Mim wondered that there was any longer a market for them. Picnics conjured up images of another life – lazy careless afternoons in the sunshine, roast beef sandwiches and jam tarts. That life had been swallowed up by the war, replaced with food shortages, anxiety and loss. Mim hated the picnic baskets but didn't say so. She hated them for everything they reminded her she no longer had. When she looked out of the kitchen window and saw the lantern on in the Hatchery, she'd think for a second that Bertie was back. She made a pretence of going down there with a cup of coffee, just to check. When she saw it was Arnie, she wasn't disappointed as such, it was just that her bargain with God hadn't worked. Helping Arnie hadn't brought Bertie back, it had only drawn her closer to Arnie. Her logic seemed nonsensical now.

Hers was a joyless existence. At times she felt almost dead herself, unable to express happiness. It was a strange reality, a walking dead. The blues. She understood what that meant now. Even if she wanted to laugh at a memory or something else she couldn't – there was a brick wall. All she wanted to do was slump down. The tears and sadness came easily enough.

Unbidden usually – she had no control over it. What if she stopped drinking tea and water, would that make the tears stop? They had to come from somewhere. Her body was wringing the moisture out of her very sinew to produce tears, more and more tears. They were painful, made her face and throat ache. Bertie wouldn't have wanted it. He would see it as weakness, self-indulgence.

Her name, Mim, Mimosa, after the flower that closes when touched. She was touched. She felt touched by madness. She was closing up. She wanted to close up, to shrink away from the world. Bertie's absence was unending, his existence had simply stopped. She wanted to run away, be separated from the constant reminders of her loss.

She questioned her belief in God over and over again. Sometimes she yearned for her faith, clung to the hope that she would be reunited with Bertie one day. But she was sickened beyond anything she'd known that God had taken him away from her.

When she was with Arnie her grief was there, she was always encased in it, but Arnie's presence let her float above it sometimes. Even so, pleasure was a tenuous memory that might never have existed.

Her relations wrote long letters of support and condolence but she didn't reply. She didn't want to share her misery with anyone but Arnie. Aggie wasn't there any more. Her friendship seemed to have slipped away, under the front door and out onto the streets of the district she patrolled.

Mim knew that Bertie's grave was in St Catherine's churchyard but she was too afraid to go and visit it. *At least you've got him here*, came that voice from the funeral. He hadn't slipped into the liquid mud on the fields of Flanders or been eaten by rats. No, but he was in a wooden box six feet under the earth. The differentiation seemed irrelevant.

She took out the sermon that cousin Matilda had sent her and tried to read it through. *Life means all that it ever meant. It is the same as it ever was. There is absolute and unbroken continuity. What is this death but a negligible accident? Why should I be out of mind because I am out of sight? I am but waiting for you, for an interval, somewhere very near, just round the corner.* More tears. The thought of death was a comfort to her.

Arnie would talk about the war. Mim hated it. The rats in the trenches had swollen faces, he said, and white fur, from eating human meat. They were luminous in the dark. The men would call out for their mothers at night. The brutality of war had stripped them of their British dignity. Mim didn't want to hear these things. She thought her mind would snap.

Arnie was getting worse. He was getting through a box of cough drops every couple of days and Mim was glad he'd stopped with the prescriptions. But the withdrawal was strange, he went through bouts of depression and being very talkative. He was also paranoid. Mrs Zlin had peeped through the Hatchery window one day to see if she could clean and Arnie pulled a gun on her and scared her half to death.

Arnie was getting worse and so was Mim. The grief caused a tightening in her chest and a damp, weighty shroud to fall about her shoulders. It coloured everything. It determined whether she was able, or inclined, to smile. It was the default. Because if she was able to switch on something of her normal self momentarily for the sake of polite conversation with

Aggie or Arnie, immediately that she was alone her shoulders sagged with the weight of the shroud and her mouth was pulled down and she couldn't for the life of her feel any pleasure or see any joy on the horizon. Deep grief had poisoned her. At any moment she could quite easily drop into a chair and weep. She simply felt broken.

Mim had fallen asleep on her bed after luncheon. She roused herself reluctantly and went downstairs. Arnie, she guessed, was in the Hatchery. She wondered whether he'd mind her taking a cup of tea out to him. If she didn't speak to him she was in danger of just going back to bed again. Watching the kettle boil was an acceptable occupation for a few minutes of her time. Something she would never have done before all of this. She wouldn't bother with saucers. Just the cups would do.

It was raining. She didn't mind. In fact, the water on her face reminded her she was still alive. She took her time carrying the tea, watching the raindrops splashing into the hot brown liquid. Arnie looked up from his work. She had startled him, there was panic on his face, on half of his face at least.

He nodded with thanks when she set the tea down. He was making the hateful picnic hampers. Perhaps it was a soothing thing to do. The dextrous manipulation, the monotony.

'I shall go back to work,' she said, surprising herself.

'All right,' he said, as though they had made the decision together. 'Might do you some good.'

Putting on her WPS uniform was a struggle. Every inch of her wanted to get back into bed. But she knew she had to

229

do it or she would only slide further into despair. There were thousands of women in the country mourning as she was. Did they stay in bed or get up and get on with things?

The day was damp and the sky was white. A spectacularly uninteresting sky, with no features to speak of. She wheeled her bike to the road. The sheer effort of pushing off almost made her turn back. She was so lacking in energy now, limp with exhaustion. But she persevered and turned off East Tilbury hill at the Rectory, taking an easy ride past the gravel pits and Bowater Farm, heading for Low Street. The idea was to seek out Aggie and to look for her first in Tilbury. Mim could have bumped across the marshes but was taking the long way round along the roads.

At Low Street station she stopped for breath. There was a scattering of cottages there, some small children played on the dirt road in their pinafore dresses and boots. One of them rolled their wooden hoop in Mim's direction. Perhaps an audacious means of engaging with the strange police lady. Mim caught the hoop as it wobbled past her and held it up for the child to retrieve. 'Go and get it,' called out an older girl, of perhaps nine, who pushed a perambulator, the baby inside sitting up in an enormous white bonnet. The little girl approached Mim gingerly, her woollen pom-pom beret flopping down over one eye. She grabbed the hoop and ran back to the other children. A farmer's cart piled high with hay clopped past, making Mim cover her mouth from the dust. The poor old nag that pulled it looked about ready to drop.

Mim pushed off again, pedalling slowly. She wasn't sure she had the vigour to get to Tilbury but she pushed on and after half an hour was wheeling down Tilbury hill with her hands squeezing the brakes. The sun had started its sneaky descent behind the cover of clouds, and Mim realised it was getting dark. It had never taken her so long to get to Tilbury before. Now she was here she didn't know what to do. She didn't much like the idea of popping into the WPS station – the sub-inspector would expect something of her and Mim was fairly sure she wouldn't be fit for whatever that might be. Instead she continued down Dock Road, turning off towards the fort and onto the red-light district. There was a comfort somehow of being there. A drunk soldier saw her approach and adjusted his footing, two munitions girls staggering out of the Daniel Defoe pub checked themselves when they saw her. She dismounted and walked her bicycle along the dirt road, not needing to speak to anyone but still managing to be useful and keep order.

Turning into a little side street she felt a flutter of nerves. She was more likely to encounter criminal activity down here and she wasn't keen to have to challenge someone's behaviour or call for a male officer to make arrests. She stopped, wondering what to do. It was awfully quiet and dark down this alley. Suddenly she wished she wasn't wearing her uniform, that she hadn't come out, that she was safely tucked up in bed at home. Her heart beat faster, she wiped her upper lip with the back of her hand, pulled at the collar of her blouse and tie. She felt short of breath and wanted to go home.

A man came into the alley up ahead. Mim froze and gripped the handles of her bicycle. She was sufficiently covered by shadow where she stood for him not to notice her. Perhaps he would move away. He looked like an unscrupulous fellow – there was something about his stance, the way his hands were stuffed deep into his jacket pockets, the little movements of his head like a bird watching for danger. Mim stayed still. If she moved now she would attract attention. Her stomach dipped when another man joined him and spoke to him in a low voice. Her scalp prickled with dread when she thought she recognised the form of this second man. He lit a cigarette and the match lit up one side of his face – she could see even from a distance that it was rigid and metallic, without expression. It was Arnie's mask.

Trying to catch her breath, Mim tried to think why Arnie would be there. She had left him at home, but she had taken a long time to cycle to Tilbury, he could easily have run across the marshes in half the time. She watched as the man took something from his pocket, handed it to Arnie, who in turn handed something to the man. They were making an exchange. But of what? Mim's mind ran and landed on the only explanation. Drugs. Arnie was seeking out his drugs illicitly because he could no longer obtain them on prescription. He was committing a crime right in front of her.

Mim gasped and put her hand to her mouth. Her bicycle clanked against the wall and the men's heads turned sharply. The drug dealer leant forward to look, saw Mim there and turned on his heel to run the way he had come. Arnie stared, confusion on his face. He saw it was Mim and his body moved as if he would run. Mim stared back, not knowing what to do or say. Ordinarily she'd have called for a male officer to follow the men, make arrests. Arnie saw her hesitation and he too turned to run, soon disappearing around a corner.

Mim felt sick. She mounted her bicycle and turned back

the way she had come, cycled out onto the fort road and down Dock Road but stopped at Tilbury train station. She hadn't the energy. A train pulled in and she wheeled her bike onto it, getting off at Low Street and walking her bike home, shivering in the darkness. Just the sound of her boots on the road and the jangle of her bicycle chain. The clatter of worries in her mind was loud. She had a terrible dilemma. How she wished she had stayed at home and not seen Arnie. What on earth would she do: flout the law for the sake of her friend, or report him and see him in court? She could countenance neither option. Such was her state of mind that she wanted to pitch herself over the nearest river bank to sink beneath the surface of the numbing, grey water, to just sink without struggle, without flailing her arms for life.

17

Aggie

Aggie was exhausted. Now she was trained, Sub-Inspector Nash had left her to patrol the district by herself. There was too much to do and she couldn't be seen to be struggling – she had to hold the fort for Mim, who was holding the fort at home, looking after Arnie.

The sub-inspector had been in London a fair bit, helping Commandant Damer Dawson, the leader of the WPS, lobby the Home Office for official police status. They were all nervous that the war would end and the government would refuse to recognise the hard work of the women's police service – that they would all be out of a job. The sub-inspector would be back in Thurrock the following day for Cecile's trial at Grays police court. Thankfully, in this case the highest ranking officer at the scene of the crime was required to be witness. It meant Aggie could sit and watch and offer her support to Cecile instead of incriminating her the way she had with Tilly Packett.

In the sub-inspector's absence, Aggie had taken her chance to do things her way. She'd been keeping a close eye on who was in the pubs in East Tilbury and Linford. The local girls and the remaining munitionettes in Greygoose factory were having a gay time and Aggie left them to it but if any of them left with a man, Aggie would be there, following at a distance to make sure nothing untoward happened. If she felt a girl was going too far, on the brink of trouble as she'd seen with Penny Crabb, she'd be there, reminding the girl about her future, and she'd visit the girl's house to talk to her mother. All of this she did quietly, unobtrusively, without lecture, remembering what had inspired her to join the women's police in the first place. She didn't want to treat the working girls the way the educated police treated them.

It was the tenth of November and everyone was waiting for the war to end. There was a palpable sense of being on the brink of salvation but teetering there, not knowing if it would happen. When passing a newsstand it was impossible not to look for the headlines, to scan for the latest word. Only that morning Aggie had stopped by the newsstand at Stanford station when she saw the *Post*'s END OF THE GERMAN EMPIRE headline, but it was a comment on events, not a declaration.

Cycling through Linford she stopped at the George and Dragon. It was just turning eight o'clock, alcohol curfew. As usual, heads turned as she walked in, but it was a sombre atmosphere that reflected how Aggie felt. The punters were waiting for news, too. At the large table in the corner of the saloon bar sat the Linford War Committee and Aggie avoided the eye of Mr Tunnidge, turning to the bar to find Mrs Rumble.

'I say,' said a man's voice behind her. Keeping a neutral face, she turned to see that Mr Tunnidge had walked through into the public bar and was holding his pipe in mid-air as though he'd poke her with it. 'I say, where is Mrs Rumble?' he said.

'I don't know,' said Aggie. 'Who has been keeping the bar?'

'We have been keeping a vigilant eye,' he said, motioning to his table of cronies. 'The landlady excused herself earlier when she was taken ill. She went upstairs and hasn't been seen since. And we have this unfortunate situation here now.' Aggie followed his eye to a nearby table where a woman of questionable reputation sat with two soldiers. The woman had a livid bruised eye. 'What do you propose to do?' he said.

Aggie composed herself under his gaze. 'If you'll excuse me, Mr Tunnidge, I'll go and check on Mrs Rumble.'

'Of course, and what do you propose to do about this?' he said, gesturing to the woman.

Aggie wished he would go away. What could she do about the woman except make her presence known? It was obvious that she was a loose type but she was only talking to the men, after all. She hesitated, wanting to give the impression she was in control. 'If you'll excuse me,' she repeated.

Going up the back stairs of the pub brought flooding back the all too recent memory of Tilly up there with the dead baby. She carried on up past the first floor boarding rooms to the top floor where she assumed Mrs Rumble's rooms would be.

'Mrs Rumble?' she called out, knocking at the door. 'Mrs

Rumble?' There was no reply. She tried the doorknob, which turned, and ventured into a spacious flat that was tidy and feminine. 'Mrs Rumble? It's Constable Tucker,' she called out, enjoying the sound of her official title, no longer 'in training'. She paused at the bedroom door, not wanting to impose. There was no sound from within when she knocked. Opening the door slowly, she called out the landlady's name in a whisper, thinking she must be asleep. Sure enough, the landlady was in bed and Aggie was about to turn away to go downstairs when the stench of excrement reached her. She gagged, putting her hand over her nose and mouth. Stepping closer, she peered over the bedclothes and the world seemed to rock on its pivot. The landlady was dead. Her face blue. A red foam about her mouth. Aggie ran, stumbling down the stairs, out of the pub with Mr Tunnidge calling after her. Outside, she leant over with her hands on her knees, taking deep breaths of air.

She turned back, entered the pub, called out, 'Everybody out. This instant. Everybody out.' Every face turned towards her with a look of horror. She could see they thought it was an air raid, or worse, a ground raid, perhaps the Germans were marching down Linford Road towards them right now, perhaps the papers were wrong, it had all been a ruse, the Germans weren't readying themselves to sign an armistice, they had crept up on Britain's coasts, they had invaded Essex. 'I believe,' she stuttered, trying to find the right words, 'I believe there is a case of the Spanish influenza upstairs. Everybody please leave for your own safety.'

'I say,' said Mr Tunnidge grabbing her arm roughly, 'is it Mrs Rumble?'

Aggie shrugged him off, not answering. He was shoved aside as everyone in the pub pushed their way out in a panic.

'I say,' he called out over the noise, 'hadn't you better contain it? Hadn't you better keep all these people together?'

Her mind raced. She didn't know the protocol. All the sub-inspector had said was look out for symptoms and report them. 'Go for Sergeant Pavey,' she shouted at Mr Tunnidge. 'Go now to Stanford police station.' He nodded and trotted away. 'Everybody,' she shouted to the punters as they started to run down the road, 'everybody stay here, gather outside the blacksmith's. Gather at the forge,' she shouted. Some of the punters stopped, with puzzled faces, some carried on running home. She had to try not to let it spread. Mrs Rumble must surely have infected some of her customers. Aggie didn't know what the incubation period was. She had heard that people turned blue and coughed up bloody froth when they had the flu. They drowned in the fluid in their own lungs. They suffocated and died from lack of oxygen. She was sure it was what Mrs Rumble had died of. The sight of it. It made Aggie want to retch. What a dreadful way to go.

Several of the punters did as they were told and stayed waiting outside the blacksmith's forge opposite the pub. Aggie stayed with them and when Sergeant Pavey arrived she rushed to him.

'It's Rose Rumble,' she said. 'I'm sure it's the Spanish flu. She's upstairs in bed, dead, all blue and red foam at her mouth.'

'Poor Rose,' said Sergeant Pavey, grimacing. 'The chief has given orders to get the punters into the Methodist church, keep them together so it doesn't spread through the district.'

'All right,' she said, glad that Sergeant Pavey was there. They got everyone down the road and into the church, the War Committee included.

'I say, don't you think you are putting us at risk?' said Mr Tunnidge, with a change of heart now he realised he was stuck with the rest of the crowd, including the woman he had complained about in the pub.

'It is a necessary precaution, Mr Tunnidge,' said Sergeant Pavey. 'The incubation period is thought to be three days. You will all stay here for that period until we know there is no contamination.'

'Three days?' snapped Mr Tunnidge in disbelief. 'And if one person here is infected surely we all shall be by then. This is ludicrous. I'll not stay.'

He made to leave but Sergeant Pavey put out an arm and stopped him. 'Mr Tunnidge, in your capacity as Special Constable, may I remind you of your duty? You will be required to take charge here.'

Sergeant Pavey had appealed to Mr Tunnidge's pride and it worked. The man agreed reluctantly and Aggie was able to leave. She thanked God she didn't have to stay in the church. Mr Tunnidge said he knew of other cases of the flu in the district. Aggie thought he'd most likely relish a last chance to lord it over the villagers. When the war ended he'd no longer be a special constable nor the chairman of the War Committee. His status would be dramatically reduced.

'If I were you,' said Sergeant Pavey outside the church, 'I'd keep indoors away from family. It's likely you haven't been infected, but just in case.' Aggie nodded. She returned home and went straight upstairs to her bedroom. She didn't think she'd be infected by a dead woman but still, she wouldn't have wanted to put Arnie or Mim in any danger. In any case it was only a gesture of quarantine, she had to be in court the next morning for Cecile.

Aggie opened her eyes and waited for her vision to come into focus. She listened for any sound but there was only silence. Remembering Rose Rumble the day before she checked for signs of the flu and was relieved to find she felt in fine health. It was the eleventh of November, the day of Cecile's trial. Her stomach turned over as she wondered if there was any chance that Cecile would be given a fair hearing. She dressed quietly and crept downstairs for breakfast. Not wanting to disturb Arnie or Mim and come into contact with them until she knew she wasn't infectious, she cut some bread, the quietest breakfast she could think of.

It was rather wet and cold outside. Aggie cycled to Low Street train station and waited on the platform. When she disembarked in Grays, she put up her WPS umbrella and walked quickly to the police court. At nine o'clock the court clerk allowed entry and she found a seat on the wooden benches near the front, putting her overcoat on the chair next to her for the sub-inspector, in case she arrived before the magistrate.

The courtroom started to fill. The sub-inspector came in out of breath and sat down. 'Still no news,' she said. Aggie looked at her questioningly. 'Armistice.'

No, thought Aggie. Still no news of armistice. Did anyone really believe that the war was coming to an end? It had been the eternal state the past four years, it had been the dreaded, entrenched state that had altered reality and it was difficult to comprehend that they might soon see peacetime.

'No,' said Aggie.

The magistrates filed in. 'Oh, heavens, it's Speechley,' said the sub-inspector, indicating the man in the middle with the large moustache. 'We're doomed. I'd best be off.'

Aggie nodded. The sub-inspector took herself off to the hall outside where witnesses were to wait. The magistrates took their time conferring over their papers and they called the first defendant, a docker accused of stealing coal from Tilbury Docks. For an hour Aggie sat through several petty crimes and her heart leapt when Cecile was brought in. She was shocked by the prostitute's appearance. The side of her face was bruised and she walked stiffly, presumably from the attack. The woman looked as though she'd neither slept nor eaten. Aggie stood up in her place to try to catch Cecile's eye. There were no other women in the room and she wanted to show her support. Cecile was sworn in by the clerk and only then did she lift her eyes to glance around the room. Her gaze fell on Aggie, she frowned and then her face lit with recognition. Aggie did her best to look supportive. She gave a little wave and she smiled. It was unprofessional but she didn't care. Poor Cecile. She'd been attacked and now stood in court. Mr Speechley called for the chief witness and the sub-inspector came to the bench.

'My constable and I were alerted as to a situation in the Ship public house,' she explained to the court. 'On entering the public house we were made aware of a Sapper Burney complaining of being drugged and robbed. It was established that he was referring to the defendant, Cecile Browne.'

'What, may I ask is your occupation?' said Mr Speechley, addressing Cecile with denigration, seeming to notice her appearance suddenly.

'I'm a mother,' replied Cecile, with surprising force.

'Sub-Inspector Nash, please corroborate,' said another of the magistrates.

The sub-inspector was hesitant. Aggie sat up straight, trying to catch her eye. Was this the chance they had of helping Cecile?

'The defendant is a known prostitute in the area,' said the sub-inspector, avoiding Aggie's eye. Aggie struck her thigh with her fist.

'Would all women please leave the courtroom,' said Mr Speechley with a disdainful sigh. 'This is a case of indecency.'

Aggie stayed where she was. She didn't want to leave. Perhaps Mr Speechley would let her stay when he saw her police uniform.

'Constable,' he said, in a loud voice, making her jump. She got up and scurried out of the court into the hall, hating that Speechley wouldn't allow her to stay.

It was agony waiting in the hall. A male police constable was on duty there, blocking access. Aggie stood by the doors, trying to listen to the proceedings. She smiled at the officer. 'No news yet,' she said, 'of the armistice.'

'No,' he said, relaxing a little. 'I expect it won't be long.'

Aggie gave him a friendly nod. Cecile suddenly screeched inside and Aggie stiffened, trying to hear. 'I'm dying to know what's going on,' she said to the constable. He nodded conspiratorially and opened the door a touch to let her slip inside. She took off her large WPS hat so as to be less conspicuous and ducked down to sit at the rear of the courtroom, looking back with a grateful smile at the constable.

Cecile was in a terrible state. 'I was attacked,' she screeched. 'See? He stabbed me here,' she said, pointing to the small of her back, 'and he hit my face. Have you arrested him? It's the captain who did it. Just find the captain.'

'Are you suggesting that a man of the King's army attacked you?' said Mr Speechley with contempt. He shook his head as though a child had told him a tall story to get out of trouble. 'You are a known prostitute. Any harm that comes to you is consequential of your foul occupation. The very sight of you is an offence to this court. Silence,' he said, holding up his hand to stop another tirade. He conferred with his fellow magistrates.

'You are hereby sentenced to six months' hard labour for soliciting and theft.'

Cecile screamed. 'My children, my children. I was attacked.'

Aggie stood up in desperation, wanting to get to Cecile, to help her, but the wretched woman was taken away by the attending constables and Aggie could only listen to her fading cries. Thoroughly demoralised, Aggie sat back down. Another woman sent to prison. The man involved not held to account but scot-free to attack again. She wanted to cry for Cecile but held her tears. She wouldn't let these men see her upset. Where was the sub-inspector? She might have done more to protect Cecile, she might have disguised the fact that Cecile had fallen into prostitution, she should have used her sway to insist on the man being caught and charged. This captain, whoever he was, was a dangerous man at large in their district. Aggie felt sick. What would happen to Cecile's children? They'd end up in the workhouse or an orphanage. She looked at the men around her. The male police, the male magistrates. What chance of justice did a woman like Cecile stand here?

The next defendant was brought in. The attending sergeant was about to read the charges when Mr Speechley held up his hand. A high ranking police officer had entered the courtroom and approached the bench. Aggie sat up. Perhaps something had happened in Cecile's favour, perhaps the attacker had been caught.

Mr Speechley spoke in hushed tones with the police officer and he stood up. Everyone in the court stood too. Aggie wondered what was going on. 'Gentlemen,' said Mr Speechley, who seemed rather unnerved. 'Gentlemen, I have just been informed that the Germans have signed an armistice.' A hush of anticipation spread through the courtroom. Aggie stared at Mr Speechley and held her breath. 'The war has ended,' he said, as though not believing the news himself.

For one second only, Aggie could have heard a pin drop on the floor. And then, a great roar of elation rose up from the crowd. Aggie realised she was roaring too. She cheered with everyone else, and she wept with joy. Shock and joy. Everyone jumped up and patted each other and laughed and started to pour out of the courtroom, to rush through the doors and out into the street, Aggie with them, letting herself be pulled along. She came out into the drizzly day and looked about her in a daze. People were running down the road. She could hear church bells ringing out, peal after peal. Ships' horns rolled off the river, motorcar horns sounded in the streets.

She ran down the steps of the court and walked in the direction of the station. In the far distance she could hear bells and maroon rockets and sirens and wondered if the sounds were coming from London. It was like the charge of a bomb had been lit in the capital and was travelling downriver. It sparked celebration everywhere. One had only to hear the sound of the church bell and know what it meant, the fog-horn of a ship to understand the significance. Air-raid sirens whooped in a new and jubilant fashion, the sound of guns firing came from the forts. The country had been waiting and praying and now it had happened, the anticipation had erupted, it was spilling out onto the streets.

Arnie, she thought. She had to get home to Arnie, and to Mim. Running to the station, she laughed and shouted out with everyone who came near her. *It's over, it's over, it's all over.* Flags and streamers seemed to appear as if they had been there all along but came into view by magic on hearing the news. She gave a thought to poor Mr Tunnidge and the villagers, stuck in quarantine in the village hall – but their relatives would surely call through the windows and tell them the news. The train came, the engine letting out great whoops and pops of steam to announce the end of the war. Aggie climbed aboard and joined in a rousing chorus of 'Land of Hope and Glory' with the other passengers. It was like a dream. She was carried along on the wave of jubilation to alight from the train at Low Street and mount her bicycle. Even cycling up the hard hill, the joy carried her along until she came to Mim's house. A brief attempt at pushing the stand of the bicycle down finished with a reckless throwing it onto the gravel path without a care.

Fumbling for her key, she opened the door with a bang. 'Have you heard?' she shouted out with glee into the hallway. 'Have you heard? It's over, it's all over.'

She ran through into the kitchen where Arnie liked to sit and came up short when she saw Mrs Zlin there at the sink. 'It's over,' she said, rushing to hug the old lady, who turned in surprise. 'The war is over.'

'Is over?'

'Yes,' laughed Aggie. Mrs Zlin clapped her hands and laughed, showing the gaps in her teeth that Aggie hadn't noticed before. 'Where's Arnie? Mim? Have they heard the news?'

'They not down,' said Mrs Zlin, shrugging. 'I not seen.'

Aggie turned to run through the house, up the stairs to Arnie's bedroom. She laughed to see her hands shaking on the door latch. She couldn't wait to tell him the news.

When she opened the door she first saw Arnie's mask lying on the ground at her feet. When she looked up and saw Arnie hanging from the ceiling rafter, her body went into shock. Her hands flew up in front of her, fingers spread apart, her mouth opened in a scream without any sound. She staggered, took a step towards him, shouted his name, grabbed at the wooden chair on its side on the floor, pulled it upright to stand on it. She called his name again, sobbing, held his legs, tried to lift him upwards to take the weight off his neck. He was too heavy. 'Help!' she screamed. 'Help, help.'

Mrs Zlin appeared at the door and shrieked something in German. She ran back out of the room and Aggie clung onto Arnie's legs, trying with all her strength to take his weight without falling off the chair. Mrs Zlin brought Mim, bleary-eyed and confused, buttoning her blouse. 'Oh,' cried Mim. 'Oh, no.' She looked around for something to stand on, pulled the bedside pot cupboard with Mrs Zlin, got it next to Aggie's chair, climbed up, helped lift him. Mim was taller, she held his legs with one arm and reached up to release the noose over Arnie's head. His dead weight collapsed onto them and they fell in a heap, Aggie shrieking with pain when her wrist bent against the floor.

'Arnie,' Aggie sobbed. She held his face, his poor, poor face.

'Let's get him lying straight,' said Mim. They pulled him onto his back. Mim slapped his face and called his name but there was no response. Aggie remembered her first aid training but Mim had already begun the resuscitation procedure, lifting Arnie's arms up over his head and then crossing his arms down over his chest while putting pressure on them.

'Come on, Arnie,' sobbed Aggie. Mim repeated the arm lift over and over again. 'Come on,' shouted Aggie and to her immense relief, Arnie coughed. He put his head to one side and vomited onto the floor.

'On his side,' said Mim. They rolled him onto his side to stop him choking and like a miracle he turned to look at them and he sat up.

'Oh dear God,' said Aggie, pulling him to her chest. 'I thought you'd gone.' She looked at Mim, who was sitting back on her heels, her face white.

'I get water,' said Mrs Zlin, disappearing out of the door.

The women got Arnie up and onto the bed, propped up with pillows. His poor neck was bruised purple from the rope he had used. He closed his eyes as though he couldn't bear the shame of looking at them.

'Why, my dear, why?' said Aggie, crying and holding his hand.

She didn't expect an answer but he said, with a rasping voice, 'Mim knows why.'

'Mim?' Aggie looked at her friend.

'Not now,' said Mim, shaking her head. 'Let him rest.'

'Tell her,' said Arnie, still with his eyes closed.

Mim looked at the ground and Aggie stared at her, utterly confused as to what it could be. Her friend chose her words carefully.

'Arnie shouldn't have worried,' she said slowly. 'He has fallen into drug addiction and needs help, not condemnation.'

'Drug addiction?' said Aggie, frowning. But Mim looked back at the floor and left the room.

18

Mim

Mim's mind was so confused. The trauma of seeing Arnie hanging from the ceiling only splintered her fragile state of mind further. She'd had no sleep. Hour after hour she had lain in bed, wondering what to do for the best. She had decided to tell Aggie about Arnie being addicted to the drugs and thought she would keep the rest to herself. Aggie didn't need to know that Mim had seen him in the backstreets of Tilbury with the drug dealer. Of course, that would mean Mim leaving the policing profession. Something she had fought hard for. With Bertie gone, it was all she had left but she had made the decision to let it go for Arnie's sake. The thought of resuming her pre-war life of Edwardian drawing rooms and polite conversation was not something she could entertain. She walked away from Arnie's room and down the stairs, walked the length of the hallway and out of the front door. Standing there for a moment, she wondered what had happened. The village was in turmoil. It looked apocalyptic. Had her patrol area gone feral in her absence? She blinked and stared.

She stepped down onto the front path and wandered out of the garden gate onto the village road. A soldier rode by on a motorbike holding aloft long streamers coloured red, white and blue. They billowed behind in his slipstream. He seemed to go by in slow motion, the sight was utterly surreal and Mim, as if in a dream, started to walk down the road. The school-children were congregated outside the school house. They were singing the National Anthem. Mim stood to listen. They sang with joyous voices, as did the schoolmaster, and several villagers who were watching. At the end they all cheered for the King, for the army and the navy. Their faces peered sky-wards as a Union flag was raised and they all cheered again, and again when the schoolmaster announced that school was closing early. The children laughed and skipped away.

Mim followed them up the road. Bunting had appeared. She jumped when someone let off a loud firecracker. The world had gone mad. It was lawless and deranged. She'd have been frightened if everyone didn't look so awfully happy. People called out to her. 'It's over, peace at last.' The words filtered into her brain. Peace? Could it be? She realised she could hear several ships' foghorns on the river and church bells ringing in the distance. Could the war be over?

An army motorcar went by, hooting its horn. Men waved flags. Farmer Able rushed over to her, grabbed her hand and shook it, saying something about getting his horses and his farmhands back at last. Outside the Ship, there was more revelry. Merrymakers waved bottles of beer and women danced in the street. More flags, bunting, streamers. A gun went off at the fort, startling everyone and provoking more joy and jubilation. The church bells in the distance rang and rang. The war was over? The concept filtered through into Mim's mind. The war. It had been their constant state of existence for four years. It was as though life before the war was a mythical fairy story, the meaning of peace lost for ever. But people were dancing in the street, soldiers were waving streamers. She let out one sob. She wanted to tell Bertie that the war had ended. He would already have heard, he would be rushing home from the shipyard right now to tell her the news, to celebrate together.

Mim continued walking through the fog of madness until she came to St Catherine's church. A small crowd of villagers had gathered there. Reverend Clow was talking with his flock, going from one person to another, greeting them with a shake of the hand and a soft word. Mim looked up at the unfinished church tower and thought how sad it was that no bells rang there. A hand touched her arm. Reverend Clow was at her side, smiling.

'Sergeant Rathbone,' he said, in a soft voice. 'How delightful to see you. I am very glad you came here on this poignant day.'

Mim looked into his kind face and saw there only love. He put his arm around her shoulder when she started to cry and led her slowly towards the church. She had to stop trying to bargain with God, had to pull herself out of the terrible black despair she had fallen into. She had to accept what had happened.

'Bertie's dead,' she said to the vicar. 'He's gone. He's dead.'

When she said it aloud, it was as if she had suddenly real-ised the words were true and she was ready to believe them.

'Yes,' said Reverend Clow. 'May God be with him.'

Mim clutched the vicar's arm. He led her into the church, past the candles and flowers that had been laid at the door, to the front pew and guided her to sit down. She sat and she waited for the congregation to pour in. These villagers weren't the revellers. They were those who had lost so much in the war. Their dear, loved ones who would be neither celebrating the armistice nor coming home. They wept into their handkerchiefs and comforted one another. Mim saw that she had been selfish. She wasn't alone in her suffering. There was suffering aplenty in her small village, and lots more around the country. Most of these people hadn't been able to bury their loved ones as she had been able to bury Bertie. It was a fundamental need, to lay a dear one to rest. Men who had died in battle would have been left alone in the mud. It was a horrific thought that she couldn't imagine having to live with day after day. She felt ashamed she hadn't been to see Bertie's grave since the funeral. She resolved to go there after the service.

Reverend Clow took the pulpit behind the ornate wooden tracery of the rood screen and spoke to them of the joyous occasion of armistice, of peace restored to their home once more. He spoke of those lost and injured, those left behind. They prayed for hope in the difficult times that lay ahead and they prayed for strength. They prayed for the children who carried the message of God into the future. Mim listened and looked at the precious cloth on the altar, at the three stained glass windows behind it. Tall and thin, she squinted to see them past the screen. She could make out the one on the right, the Good Samaritan, the one in the middle, the Good Shepherd, and she tried to read the inscription that ran across the three at the bottom. *Robert Hamilton Williams ... erected in his memory ... by his widow and son ... 1905.* She remembered the excitement when they had gone in thirteen years previously. Williams, an old local landowner who had spent a good part of his life in America and had fought in the civil war there. Mim liked the fact that his widow had erected the windows in his memory. It was a good legacy to leave. She shook herself out of her reverie when Reverend Clow starting reading the sermon that she had come to despise. She listened now with a new understanding. She was finally ready to accept the words.

What is this death but a negligible accident? Why should I be out of mind because I am out of sight? I am but waiting for you, for an interval, somewhere very near, just round the corner. All is well. Nothing is hurt; nothing is lost. One brief moment and all will be as it was before. How we shall laugh at the trouble of parting when we meet again!

At the end of the service, Mim filed out with the others and shook the vicar's hand. 'I hope to see you again, soon, Mimosa,' he said. She smiled and nodded. Instead of turning left to leave, she turned right into the graveyard. She was appalled to realise she didn't know where Bertie's grave was. She had been in a coma of shock at the funeral and she hadn't had the strength to return before now. Looking around, she saw where the newest headstones were set and walked slowly over to them, her stomach clenched with anxiety. A large oak tree stood there, its leaves the shade of burnt orange. As she walked a wisp of wind blew and the leaves shivered, detached from their branches and trickled down around her. Dozens of leaves, floating slowly down to the earth.

Rathbone, Rathbone, her eyes scanned the inscriptions on the stones. But it was too soon for Bertie to have a stone. The earth hadn't settled. Her heart lurched when she saw it there on a temporary marker, chiselled into a wooden cross. *Bertram Frederick James Rathbone*. She wondered who had laid a posy of dried meadow flowers there. There were two epitaph inscriptions. The first read, *In the Midst of Life We Are in Death*. Mim recognised the line from the Book of Common Prayer and although she had seen it before, it now took on a palpable sense of meaning. She had been faced with death, Bertie's death. Death was inevitable. God would save her from her sins and she too would die. The second inscription read, *No Man is Greater in God's Eyes Than He That Giveth His Life For Others*. Mim put her hand to her chest and wondered who had thought of the epitaph. She had hardly given a thought to Bertie's legacy, she had been angry with him for going up that ship's mast to help a man in trouble, angry at him for putting himself in danger. Yet someone had thought to inscribe that very fact on his headstone and it was true. He *had* given his life for another. Just as the men going into battle overseas had done. Her heart suddenly swelled with pride for her husband. Yes, this was his legacy.

Church bells rang in the distance for the armistice. Perhaps in Stanford or West Tilbury, perhaps in Mucking. Mim turned to look up at St Catherine's half-finished church tower again. 'You know, Bertie,' she said aloud, her throat choking as she spoke to him. 'You know, I do believe I shall build the new church tower in your name and the bells will ring again.'

Mim felt renewed as she made her way back through the village. Accepting Bertie's death was long overdue. She was glad she had visited his grave and glad she had gone to church. Mindful that she still felt compromised, vulnerable, nowhere near her former self, she wanted to find the strength to go home and help her friends. She had wanted to help Arnie and felt she had let him down. She hadn't realised he was still taking those drugs but obtaining them illegally.

Mim let herself into the house and listened for voices.

19

Aggie

'Why didn't you tell me?' said Aggie, sitting on the bed next to Arnie.

'Mim was here,' he said. 'You were at work, you had your job to do.' When he started to cry, she looked at him with despair. He made a pathetic sight.

'That's not the reason,' she said, trying not to show her anger. 'You didn't want to tell me, did you? Why not?'

It looked as though he might cry again and Aggie realised her mistake in asking Mim to look after him. Mim was in no state to look after anyone.

'I was just trying to keep my job going,' she said, tears falling down her face. 'I worked so hard for it and when Bertie died, I thought it was up to me to keep on patrol so they wouldn't take our beat away.'

Arnie nodded and held her hand. 'It's all right.'

'Oh God, Arnie, no it's not. I'm sorry, I'm so, so sorry. What have I done?'

He pulled her to him and they clutched one another, both crying. The poor man, he'd been through hell and his own wife had let him down.

'I've let you down,' she said.

'No, Aggs, this damned war has let us down.' He leant back into the pillow. 'I want it all the time,' he said, the words clearly agony to him. 'It helps me forget.' Aggie nodded, encouraging him to speak. He hadn't told her much at all about the war. 'It was . . . against nature,' he said, struggling to find the words. 'The things I saw, Aggs, were against nature. Terrible, terrible mutilation of men's bodies and minds. Men went mad at the horrors we saw. And we couldn't come home. They told us we'd be shot for desertion if we didn't fight. It was unnatural . . . we ran towards our deaths.' He stopped, exhausted, and Aggie put her hand on his arm. 'The thought of you kept me going, Aggs, you in our little house, waiting for me to come home . . .'

'That's enough,' she said. 'I think you need to see a doctor about all of this. All right?'

The front door slammed downstairs. 'I just need to see Mim,' she said. 'I'll make you a cup of tea.'

Mim was sitting at the kitchen table and Mrs Zlin was filling the kettle with water.

'Thank you, Mim, you saved his life.' Aggie took a chair next to her friend.

'I could have prevented it if I'd realised he was still taking those drugs. Forgive me, Aggie, you asked me to take care of him.'

'Mim, it's you who should forgive me. I didn't know, I've let you both down. I was trying to keep working but it wasn't fair, I shouldn't have asked you to look after Arnie. I thought it would do you good, take your mind off things and give you something to do while you thought about coming back to work, but I was stupid, I shouldn't have asked you. I'm sorry.'

'Oh my goodness, what a mess we have made,' said Mim, wiping her face with her handkerchief. 'What a terrible, terrible mess.'

'It's nothing we can't sort out, Mim,' said Aggie, leaning closer. 'I know we can sort it out.' Mim nodded gratefully. 'I need to get Arnie to the hospital. It's gone too far for me to help him at home.'

'I've been to church, Aggie. Just now, I've been to church.'

Aggie understood her meaning. Church was Mim's medicine. She would be all right now. 'Good, I'm glad,' she said. 'You'll get stronger now. You look better already.'

'Aggie, who chose the epitaph on Bertie's headstone?'

Aggie shook her head, the change of topic confusing her. 'The vicar,' she said. 'The vicar helped choose it. Is it all right?'

'Yes, I think it quite fitting. Thank you for all of your help and friendship when Bertie died. I don't think I could have coped without you.'

'Well, you're back now and we're going to be all right. We'll have to get you to work when you feel ready for it,' said Aggie, standing up to put the kettle on the range. 'Although I don't know what's going to happen to the WPS now the war's over.'

'I don't think so,' said Mim.

'Well, you can think about it later.'

At the police court earlier that day Aggie had been so upset about Cecile being sentenced to prison and it was strange to think she'd had no inkling of what was happening on her own doorstep. The jubilation of the armistice had fizzed away in the background of the day. It seemed such a terrible thing to be celebrating when so many lives had been shattered. But celebrate they should because it was the war to end all wars and they would never suffer the likes of it again.

'To peace,' she said, clinking tea cups with Mim.

'To peace,' said Mim.

It had been ten days since armistice and the country was boiling with change. There were those who thought the Allies should have continued fighting until they gained an unconditional surrender from the Germans, and those who were grateful for the ceasefire agreement, which meant many lives saved. Thousands of men waited overseas for demobilisation, thousands of injured men and prisoners of war came home. Sub-Inspector Nash was needed in Tilbury, the docks being overrun with returning soldiers, and Aggie had been instructed to patrol her district alone. Nothing had yet been said about the future of the WPS. All Aggie could do was continue working and hope that her efforts would not be wasted. At least Mr Tunnidge and the other villagers had been let out of quarantine in the church – thankfully they hadn't caught the flu. That was once less thing to worry about.

Orsett hospital had admitted Arnie for treatment. He would be weaned off the addictive medicine he'd first been given in the trenches. It would be a struggle for him but he had agreed with Aggie that it was for the best. Aggie was desperate to help him. At the hospital they had told her about a new kind of treatment for his facial injury, plastic surgery, and had suggested she write to someone who might see Arnie about reconstructing his face. Much better than him covering it all up with a tin mask.

Mim seemed better each day, now she had accepted Bertie's death and sought support from Reverend Clow. Aggie was looking forward to having her back on patrol. It was very difficult doing it without Mim, especially at Greygoose factory. Two days previously, some of the factory girls had gone up to London to march on Parliament with hundreds of munitions girls from London. They wanted to keep their jobs. But while they had been celebrated during the war for their patriotism and hard work, despite the accusations of extravagance, promiscuity and drunkenness, now at war end they were demonised by the government and the press. They were accused of taking the men's jobs. Wartime regulations changed. If they refused any kind of work, if they insisted on industrial or office work, they wouldn't be able to get the dole. It meant some women had no choice but to take any work for a pittance of a wage not enough to feed their families, no matter whether they were the sole breadwinner. These were the workers who had proved to the government that women were capable of more, the women who, along-side the suffrage campaigners, had won the right for women to vote. Aggie wondered at the irony of women who owned property or whose husbands owned property who had won that right – as usual, the working women were left out and told to get back to where they belonged.

Aggie felt for the factory girls. There were very few left at Greygoose already. The men's unions had gone to court to make sure their pre-war agreement with the government to let women do men's work only for the duration of the war was put into place. Any munitions jobs left after the war would be given to the men. Aggie felt for the men too, especially those invalided by the war. They were competing with the women for jobs in the laundry and suchlike. Aggie clung to her WPS patrol with strong fingers, glad at least that she was still in work. If she'd not taken a leap of courage and left the factory when she did, it would be her back in service working all hours in drudgery for a few shillings.

Mrs Sparrow, the women's welfare supervisor at Greygoose, was indifferent. 'What do we expect?' she said to Aggie. 'Women have no voice in government. They are pawns in the men's games, that is all. I've had my time here. I expect my papers any time soon. I shan't be surprised if the whole factory folds before long.'

'What do you say to the girls?' asked Aggie.

'I tell them to find a job quickly, before they all go. They'll be glad of a job in service in a few months' time when they can't feed their families.'

'The Ministry of Munitions,' said Aggie. 'Have you heard whether the women police will be funded once the factories go?'

Mrs Sparrow shrugged. 'I shouldn't be surprised if all of it went.'

Aggie's heart sank. She hoped the welfare supervisor was wrong.

'In my opinion, you are still needed when there is

depravity on our streets. When prostitutes complain about being attacked by soldiers.'

'Yes,' said Aggie, 'although there's not much we can do when we're not allowed in court to help these women. They are seen as dirt on the magistrates' shoes.'

'Yes, and another one today,' said Mrs Sparrow, tutting.

'Another one?'

'You haven't heard? One of the guncotton girls told me. A loose woman was attacked in Tilbury last night, found this morning.'

Aggie didn't say goodbye but rushed for her bicycle and cycled to Stanford police station to find Sergeant Pavey.

'What happened?' she said, out of breath. 'The attack in Tilbury?'

'Ah, yes,' he said frowning. 'One of the local ones, found in a bad way. Crabb, I think her name was.'

'Penny Crabb?' said Aggie, aghast.

'Yes, that's it,' said Sergeant Pavey. 'She's in Orsett hospital, I think. Do you know of her?'

'Yes. Was the attacker caught?'

'Not that I know of. There was a rumour he's an ex-soldier.'

'We have to catch him,' said Aggie.

Sergeant Pavey looked surprised. 'You know what the chief would say, they are only tarts.'

'Yes, I know, and ex-soldiers are beyond justice,' countered Aggie sarcastically.

'Be careful,' said the sergeant. 'He sounds dangerous.' He turned away to attend to something but Aggie was sure his face had reddened.

'I'm going to Tilbury,' she said.

Aggie cycled to Stanford station and took her bicycle on the train to Tilbury. It was late afternoon and she hoped that some of the girls would be up and about. Cecile had been attacked and sentenced to prison for soliciting. She didn't want the same to happen to Penny Crabb.

Her first stop was the Tilbury WPS office where Sergeant Wills was manning the desk.

'Constable Tucker?' she said. 'Well, don't you look the part.'

'Yes, thank you,' said Aggie, distracted. 'Sergeant Wills, what happened to Penny Crabb last night?'

'Ah yes, another attack. It is a sorry state of affairs. As much as we find prostitution abhorrent, we do not want to see these women in danger. Penny was found injured by the docks. She was bruised and semi-conscious, one arm broken at the wrist. No life-threatening injuries, I am relieved to say.'

'What about the attacker?'

'We don't know. No one seems to know who it might be.'

Frustrated, Aggie thanked the sergeant and left. At least Penny wasn't on death's door – that was a relief. If Sergeant Pavey had heard a rumour about the attacker, she was going to find someone else to ask.

Knocking on the door of the brothel she had seen whilst on training, a woman in tawdry feathers and face paint answered.

'Marguerite?' said Aggie, scanning her memory for the woman's name.

'Yes?' she said, suspiciously, looking behind Aggie for trouble.

'Can I come in? I have a few questions.'

'Yes of course,' she said, with false cheeriness. 'Anything to help the police.'

'Do you know what happened to Penny Crabb?' said Aggie, declining a cup of tea. 'Penny with the funny eye.'

'No, not as such,' said Marguerite. 'Penny has been working for the Captain, as he calls himself. I don't like the man,' she said, screwing up her nose. 'He says he is an ex-serviceman, but I don't know. He has all these cuts on his hands.'

'What?'

'Yes, cuts on his hands, scars. And he is very rough with the girls.'

'He is a pimp?' said Aggie, embarrassed to use the word.

'Of course,' said Marguerite with a smirk. 'I wanted Penny here, but she said she likes the Captain.'

'And Cecile? Did she work for him too?'

'Cecile from Mucking? Yes. You know, it wouldn't surprise me if he was the attacker. I bet he got drunk and knocked them around. It does happen.'

'That bastard,' said Aggie, and Marguerite started and then laughed.

'Yes, are you going to catch him, lady policewoman?'

Aggie ignored the remark. 'Do you know where he lives?'

'No, but Josie might do, I think, let me get her for you.'

Marguerite disappeared up the stairs and returned with a girl in a skimpy dressing gown, old make-up caked under her eyes.

'I know where he lives, but you mustn't tell him I told you,' said the girl. 'He's a mean dog. He wanted me to work for him but I said I wanted to stay with Marguerite. He gave me a shiner for it.'

'Of course,' said Aggie, realising that it wasn't make-up on the girl's face – she had a black eye.

Outside the brothel, Aggie looked at the address, a house on the outskirts of West Tilbury village. She wasn't sure what to do with it. She had no powers of arrest and in any case wouldn't want to attempt to arrest this man by herself. Her first thought was to ask Sergeant Wills at the Tilbury WPS, but what if the sergeant approached the Tilbury constabulary and they didn't like the idea of arresting an ex-serviceman? West Tilbury did come under the Orsett Rural District so she was within her rights to ask Sergeant Pavey at Stanford to assist her, and she felt she could trust him. Without thinking further she got back on the train at Tilbury, alighted at Stanford, and cycled hard to the police station.

'I know who he is and where he lives,' she said.

'Who, the attacker?' said Sergeant Pavey, surprised to see her again so soon.

'Yes, he goes by "the Captain", and he says he's an ex-serviceman. I've seen him at the Ship, he gave me the shivers, rough, scars on his hands. He lives at this address in West Tilbury.'

'And what proof do we have?' said the sergeant, taking the slip of paper.

'He's the pimp for Penny Crabb and was the pimp for Cecile, the prostitute who was attacked a few weeks ago.' She tried not to blush at the language. 'Marguerite and another girl, Josie, in Tilbury told me just now.'

Sergeant Pavey thought for a moment. 'Well, it couldn't hurt to go and talk to him, I suppose. Come on, we'll go in the trap.'

Aggie smiled to herself. This was real police work. And

she wanted to get the man who did this to Cecile and Penny. She wanted to be properly useful.

It was pleasant enough weather as the pony trotted along the lanes. Cold, but dry and clear, and the sun had started to set, lilac and peach blooming across the sky.

'Do you think things will get back to normal now?' said Aggie, making conversation.

'In the district? I shouldn't think so, not yet. There is a lot of trouble with the men coming back. Lots injured and no work for them. Will you be staying on?'

'I don't know. We haven't been told if we're still needed. I hope so.'

'So do I,' said the sergeant, looking straight ahead as he steered the pony. 'The women police are needed around here.'

'Ha, that's something not a lot of men would admit to,' she said, laughing.

It took a while to drive to West Tilbury from Stanford and by the time they arrived at the address it was almost dark. They tied the pony up a couple of houses down so as not to attract attention. Sergeant Pavey knocked at the front door.

A young woman answered and to Aggie's astonishment she saw that it was Tilly. Tilly Packet, the munitions girl who'd had the baby in the George and Dragon pub.

'Tilly?' she said, her voice a pitch higher. 'I thought you were in prison. Do you live here?'

'Oh, it's the lady police who got me banged up. What a lovely surprise. Yes, I've done my month hard labour. You might have noticed how much weight I've lost.'

She did look skinny and bedraggled. 'We might have the wrong house,' Aggie said to Sergeant Pavey. 'Do you live

266

here, Tilly?' Aggie stepped closer and saw that the side of Tilly's face was badly bruised.

'Yes, I live here with my boy,' she said, with an inappropriate swing of her hips.

'Not the Captain?' said Aggie.

The look on Tilly's face told her it was. 'Well, how do you expect me to earn a living and feed myself now? I'm waiting for trial for murder, don't you remember?'

Aggie looked at Sergeant Pavey, who pushed past Tilly to get into the house. Tilly tried to call out a warning but Aggie grabbed her roughly. 'Don't, Tilly,' she warned, close to the girl's face. 'He's dangerous. He's put two girls in hospital already, you'll be the next.' Tilly's confidence left her and she stayed quiet.

The women heard a shout and a scuffle and got out of the way quickly when Sergeant Pavey appeared, grappling with a large man, pushing him towards the front door. The man's hands were in handcuffs. 'Get through there,' said the sergeant, pushing him by force down the garden path and through the gate.

'You drive,' said the sergeant to Aggie, getting into the back of the trap with the man. He put his truncheon across the man's neck and held him still for the duration of the journey. Aggie was terrified, thinking the man would get away, thinking that she had put herself and the sergeant in danger, that they should have brought another male constable with them.

She flicked the reins to keep the pony going, looking back at her cargo nervously. They finally arrived at Stanford police station and the man was locked into the little cell there. 'I've got some explaining to do to the chief,' said the sergeant, 'but I think we're all right. We'll get this chap charged and see him in court soon enough.' Aggie noticed that the sergeant's nose was bleeding.

'He certainly likes to throw his weight around, doesn't he,' she said with distaste. 'Are you hurt?'

'No, it's nothing, I've had worse,' he said grinning. 'You certainly spiced up a dull evening.'

'Do we need . . . should we get Cecile to give evidence in court against him?'

'She's in prison, isn't she?'

'Yes, but can't she be brought out to give evidence?'

'Yes, I suppose so.'

It was all Aggie needed to know.

20

Mim

Mim was feeling a fraction stronger each day. Rediscovering her faith had set her on the right course to mourning Bertie. Her faith in the prospect of heavenly reunion was restored and gave her comfort.

Arnie was coming out of hospital today temporarily, to attend an event in London. It was Aggie's idea, she said it would be good for him, and a way of her and Mim showing him their support. Mim wasn't sure he was ready for something like that but he had agreed to it. Aggie had found out that a number of invalided demobbed servicemen were going to gather in Hyde Park to see the King and they were going to take Arnie. To see the King. It was fitting after what he had been through in the name of the monarch.

Mim bought *The Times* for the train journey. She had suggested to Arnie that he might wear his mask, but he refused, said he'd never wear it again. On the train, there wasn't a single person who didn't take a second horrified look at him, didn't stare at him and then turn away. One woman looking for a seat saw him and covered her daughter's eyes.

'The King will turn away from me, I shouldn't wonder, but I want him to see it,' said Arnie.

'He'll be proud of you, love, just like we all are,' said Aggie, patting his leg and glancing at Mim. Mim could see in Aggie's eyes that this trip might not be filled with the optimism that they had hoped for.

'Perhaps he'll sort out my pension, then,' said Arnie, looking out of the window. 'Seeing as he won't give me a disability allowance.'

There had been controversy in the press surrounding the demobilisation process. Most of the men hadn't yet come home. Families were running out of patience. Lloyd George was trying to tell them that they needed to keep Britain's defences in place until the peace treaty was signed. Armistice was a temporary truce and no one trusted the Germans not to rise up again. But Mim could only imagine the anger building up overseas amongst the men caught up in the bureaucracy after four years of unimaginable horror.

'Perhaps I'll ask him who he thinks might give me a job with a face like this,' said Arnie, turning to look at them.

Mim opened her paper to look for something with which to distract him. She almost cried out when her eyes happened on a story crammed into a corner of page four.

'They've passed a new act,' she announced, scanning the words. 'The Parliament Qualification of Women Act. It allows women over twenty-one years of age to stand for election as a Member of Parliament. I can hardly believe it.'

She looked at Aggie and Arnie jubilantly but they returned her gaze with quizzical expressions. Arnie turned back to the window.

'That's good, Mim,' said Aggie, who seemed not the least bit excited.

'This is what we've been waiting for,' said Mim. 'I'm sure it shan't be long before women are allowed into the professions. This is a most encouraging precedent.'

She hadn't felt such a surge of happiness for the longest time. This was historical progress for women. She wanted to talk to Victoria at the suffrage society immediately, wanted to ask her if she would run for election. Mim would help her campaign. A rush of energy coursed through her. It was better than any medicine.

The coalition had announced that a general election would be held on the fourteenth of December. It would be the first election in which Mim would be able to vote, a hard-won privilege. And now if women were able to run, it increased the stakes of the outcome. What a thrill!

Lloyd George was prioritising demobilisation in his campaign. He knew the country wanted that most before anything. He had promised that serving men would return home to a 'land fit for heroes'. He was also pushing for trial and punishment of the Kaiser. There was no mention of women in the liberal campaign and that was why Mim would vote Labour, the party that had been sympathetic of suffrage throughout. Of course everyone wanted the Kaiser to stand trial for the atrocities committed. It was highly embarrassing that he was the King's first cousin and that the British royal family had had to change their German surname the previous year.

The train pulled into Fenchurch Street station, which was black and grimy with soot. The three friends made their way by bus to Hyde Park, where they were met with the sight of thousands upon thousands of disabled servicemen and their families.

'This is something, eh, Arnie?' said Aggie.

Arnie's good eye swivelled this way and that, taking in the sight of thousands of men like him. Most were out of uniform and dressed in their best suits and hats, standing proud and wearing the silver badge of honourable discharge, as did Arnie. Those in uniform wore wound stripes on their left sleeve, depicting how many times they had been injured in service. Many were sitting in cane wheelchairs, many used crutches, had sleeves or trouser legs pinned back over amputated limbs. Some had bandaged eyes and held a companion's arm for guidance. Some had mutilated faces like Arnie's, some wore the tin masks, their faces expressionless and inanimate. It was a pitiful sight indeed, a macabre circus freak show.

Mim felt sick to her stomach. These poor souls had risked their lives for the people at home. She had read estimates of a million and a half men coming home with a severe physical injury. What would they do now? Unemployment was already a problem and would become much worse when the healthy men were demobbed. These men were unable to do manual work. Mim could only imagine that some of them would turn to drink, drugs, perhaps even to suicide. She wondered, what if Bertie hadn't worked in shipbuilding, what if he had gone to fight and come home an invalid, perhaps blinded? He'd have hated it, he'd no longer have been able to write. The sour truth was that these men were the lucky ones. How many widows were there now in the country? Mim knew that she was only a number to be counted among them.

An army band started to play. There was a ripple of energy through the crowd and Mim stood on tiptoe to see. Several mounted police had entered the park, ahead of the Royal entourage.

'It's the King!' she said. Aggie and Arnie strained to see.

The King was in uniform on horseback, his two sons, the Prince of Wales and the Duke of York, accompanying him, looking proud in their finery. The Queen's open carriage followed. Mim could see Queen Mary and the King's mother, Queen Alexandra, wearing large hats and waving and she felt a compelling sense of patriotism on seeing the Royal family. She wanted to cheer and wave but something stopped her. The atmosphere in the park wasn't celebratory, it was sombre. The disabled men didn't seem pleased to greet their monarch; instead they started to move forwards towards the King in a somewhat menacing manner, Arnie amongst them. Mim and Aggie tried to keep up with him, with a worried glance at one another.

'Where is this land fit for heroes?' someone suddenly shouted loud above the crowds. There was a jeer of agreement. 'Where's our pensions?' someone said. 'Disability pension won't feed my family,' cried another. The King took on a look of alarm. The men pushed forwards to surround his horse, the mounted guards trying to control the crowd.

'What's she smiling at?' shouted a man, pointing at the Queen, who maintained a fixed smile and was still waving. 'Bring our boys home,' came the cries. 'Hang the Kaiser.'

'Arnie,' said Mim and Aggie, trying to pull him away, 'Arnie, come on, get out of it.'

He turned to them, his expression fixed with anger but he reconsidered and let them lead him away.

'You're not strong enough, Arnie,' said Aggie. 'Let's get you home.'

On the train home, Mim wished they hadn't come. What good had it done to see not only Arnie's anger and disappointment but also the anger and disappointment of thousands of men like him? It only undermined any sense of peace he had managed to achieve. She'd been shocked to see the King jostled in that manner, it was most unpatriotic.

She took out her newspaper, this time to distract her own mind. It had been a difficult day for her too. She searched the columns for something heartening to share with her friends. She happened upon a small piece about women patrols and read the contents hungrily. She was very proud of what she had accomplished with the WPS, despite being unable to return to work.

'What does this mean?' she said out loud as she read.

'What is it?' said Aggie.

'The Commissioner of Police, Sir Nevil Macready, has sanctioned the formation of a body of women patrols in London.'

'Really?' said Aggie, sitting forward. 'With official powers?'

'No,' said Mim, reading. 'No, no official powers but paid thirty shillings per week to patrol the streets and open spaces of London the same as regular constabulary and to assist members of the public, especially those of the same sex.'

'Well, that's . . . that's good,' said Aggie. 'It's not as much as we're paid now but it's a job at least. Who are the women?'

'That's just it,' said Mim. 'He's taking women from the women's voluntary patrols, one hundred of them, and discontinuing their previous agreement.'

'And the WPS?' said Aggie.

Mim put the paper down on her lap. 'No mention,' she said. 'Not a single mention of the WPS.'

'What does that mean?' said Aggie, looking worried.

'I don't know.'

'Well, let's get off at Tilbury and see the sub-inspector.'

'All right,' said Mim, wishing she hadn't seen the report. She didn't want to discuss her decision not to return with anyone just yet. They would ask her why, and she hadn't thought what to say.

Mim avoided Aggie's concerned expression and looked out of the window. She had a terrible feeling that the WPS were going to be left out of negotiations on the future of women policing.

'It's bunkum!' said the sub-inspector.

Mim and Aggie had found her at the Tilbury WPS office in a furious mood. Arnie was waiting in the reception area smoking a cigarette.

'Have you spoken to Margaret?' said Mim, giving nothing away about her decision and knowing that the sub-inspector must surely have consulted with the commanders of the WPS.

'I have. And I am afraid the mood is not favourable.

Macready has viciously excluded the WPS from his plans for the Met. We have been politely asked to ...'

The sub-inspector uncharacteristically lost her composure and took a few moments to gather herself. 'We have been politely requested to disband as soon as possible.'

'No!' cried Aggie. 'Mim? No!'

'Have the Ministry of Munitions withdrawn funding?' Mim asked.

The sub-inspector nodded, tight-lipped. 'Yes, I am afraid so. I heard only this morning. There is a rumour that ... if we do not comply, we shall be in jeopardy of being arrested for impersonating the constabulary.'

Mim stared at her colleague in disbelief. 'Impersonating the constabulary? After everything we have contributed, the hard work, the commitment?'

'Insulting beyond words, isn't it?' said the sub-inspector. 'I am still reeling from the news.'

Aggie sank into the nearest chair. Poor Aggie, she had worked so hard, against all the odds, her achievement had been an even more extraordinary one. It would be a hard blow for all of them, but for Aggie the stakes were higher. Without the protection of an assured income, she would have to look for other work, and would likely find herself in domestic service. And with Arnie out of work it would be especially difficult for them financially. Unemployment was already high, the cost of living at record levels, the country plunged into terrible debt.

'What will you do, Eglantine?' Mim asked the sub-inspector, her title suddenly irrelevant.

'Margaret thinks that those of us who can self-fund should

do so for now. We shall petition Macready and hope for some concession, I suppose.'

'All right. Do keep us posted. We need to get Mr Tucker back to the hospital. We have been to London today and it was rather an ordeal for us all.'

'To London? I have been avoiding going. Influenza is rife there now,' said the sub-inspector vaguely. 'Very well, Mim, Aggie, thank you for your service, I am really at a loss as to what to say at the present moment. I shall see you very soon.'

Two days after the visit to London, Mim woke up with a head full of plans. She had two meetings arranged for the day and it took at least one full minute before she thought about Bertie and that was real progress. As usual she sank back into her pillow and wept for him, but the utter despair that had held her in its clutches released her and she sat up and got out of bed into the chill of the room to make a fire. Distraction was the best course of action. Only eighteen days until the election, she thought, a shiver running through her. She visualised herself with the men at the polling booth and used that as something to look forward to, to get her through the day in a good frame of mind. Setting the kindling and coal, she lit the fire and sat back, rubbing her temples with her fingertips. She had a slight headache from the weeping, the smoke from the fire stung her eyes and her chest and the fire didn't seem to be taking the chill off the room very effectively. She stood up to dress and face the day, thinking that what she needed was some warm gruel and a hot cup of tea.

Mrs Zlin was downstairs bustling about. 'Good morning,' said Mim, dropping into a kitchen chair.

'You want tea?' said the old lady.

'Thank you, yes. I am meeting Reverend Clow today to discuss the new church tower.' Mrs Zlin nodded. The vicar had been delighted at the suggestion that Mim fund the tower in memory of Bertie. In the afternoon she planned to see Victoria at the suffrage society. If Victoria hadn't already considered the idea, Mim had a notion to persuade her to run in the election.

Aggie came clopping down the stairs and popped her head into the kitchen. 'Morning,' she said, 'sorry, can't stop to chat, I'm going to court.'

'Good luck!' called Mim, wondering that Aggie wore her WPS uniform despite the news from the sub-inspector. Aggie disappeared down the hall but came back.

'Are you seeing Victoria today?' she said.

'Yes, this afternoon.'

'Put a good word in for me, will you?'

'Yes, of course,' said Mim. Aggie turned back to smile and wave before she rushed out. It was the vile attacker's trial that morning at Grays police court. Penny Crabb was testifying against him. The poor girl had been attacked. Mim felt sure it would go the same way as it had done with Cecile and result in a charge of soliciting but Aggie was hopeful for a better outcome. Mim hoped that her friend wouldn't be disappointed.

Mim readied herself to leave. November was almost over and it had been chilly of late but she felt she didn't want her coat. The day had taken a turn for the warmer. In fact she took off her neck scarf too, it really was decidedly warm. Walking along the village main road, she welcomed the river breeze and the salty tang in the air. It would be wonderful to hear church bells ringing in the village and every time they rang the villagers would think of Bertie Rathbone and how he had died to save another. *In the midst of life we are in death.* The epitaph came to her mind. Yes, death was ever-present in life. Once that fact was understood there was no returning to the blissful ignorance of youth.

'Good morning, Mimosa, are you quite well?' said Reverend Clow, guiding her to the sitting room in the rectory.

'Yes, quite well, thank you, Reverend. It is unseasonably warm today, is it not?'

'Oh,' laughed the vicar, 'I have topped up the fire, my poor circulation the probable cause.'

The room was stifling but Mim was loath to say so. 'Have you had any thoughts about the tower?' she asked.

'Yes, I am rather excited about it, to tell the truth. I have consulted the powers that be and it is all tickety-boo. You say that you are able to meet the entire cost of the project?' The vicar looked bashful, clearly uncomfortable discussing the use of Mim's inheritance.

'Oh yes, I'd be delighted to. Bertie would have been proud to, I am sure of it.'

'Quite so. Very well, so to the plans.'

They spent a pleasant hour looking at the plans that had been drawn up in 1917 when the Royal Engineers had started work on the tower. It still angered Mim that they had been ordered to stop work by the Ministry of War. Reverend Clow didn't quite compare the ungenerous view to that of the Dutch who fired a cannon from the Thames at the tower in the sixteen hundreds, knocking it down, but he may have implied it. They agreed to meet again soon and to begin tendering contractors as and when the opportunity arose. When Mim pushed herself up from the armchair she felt rather heavy about the legs and thought that the trip to London two days previously must have taken its toll on her muscles, weak from inactivity during the course of her bereavement. All the more reason to push on and force her legs back to working, she thought.

After a brief luncheon at home, Mim made her way to Stanford on her bicycle, stopping frequently to catch her breath and laughing at herself at becoming so lacking in physical fitness.

'Mim, how delightful to see you looking so well,' said Victoria – rather uncertainly, Mim thought. She had made it to the suffrage society office in Stanford but was perspiring awfully and felt rather embarrassed about it.

'Forgive me, Victoria,' she said, out of breath. 'I am unused to the exercise.'

'I quite understand,' said her friend, taking her arm and leading her to a cosy sitting room. 'Now, what news? I know you must have heard about the new act and that is why you have come?' She grinned wickedly.

'Ah, you have found me out,' said Mim, with a smile. 'Yes, isn't it awfully exciting? What do you propose to do with it?'

'I shall run,' announced Victoria, smacking her lap with both hands. 'If the party allow it. What do you think?'

'Oh, Victoria, how wonderful, I shall help you campaign, of course.'

'I am delighted to hear it. But Mim, before we discuss the campaign, I was awfully sorry to hear of the WPS and their exclusion from the new Metropolitan police team. What does this mean for you here?'

'It is rather bad news, Victoria. The Ministry of Munitions have withdrawn their funding and the police commissioner is set against the WPS, he does not like their history.'

'Neither do we, Mim.'

Mim nodded. She was a suffragist at heart and believed, as did Victoria, that women's enfranchisement would have occurred before the start of the war if the militant 'suffragettes' hadn't poisoned the campaign with their ridiculous toffee hammers and hunger strikes.

'Mim, come back to the society. There may be an opportunity to make a plea to fund a patrol.'

'Ah, thank you, Victoria, but I am not quite ready, I hope you understand?' Mim didn't want to discuss her secret resignation just yet. 'However, it is a splendid idea for my colleague and dear friend Constable Aggie Tucker, whom you met. But for now, I have only so much energy. I am still rather delicate, I am afraid. I would dearly love to help you and then I shall consider my options.'

'Very well. I am honoured to have you on board. And I should be delighted to assist you in your honourable career when the opportunity arises to do so.'

The women discussed the campaign over tea but all the while Mim felt progressively groggier, as though she were coming down with a cold. It was really rotten luck, now that she was feeling invigorated by the two new projects she had embarked upon. She excused herself, saying she would return soon. Mounting her bicycle outside, she could barely bring herself to push off. She did so unsteadily and was grateful for the downward sloping road that led out of the town. At any slight incline along the Mucking lanes though, she had to get off the bike and push, leaning on it for support. She didn't get back on but pushed the bike all the way home from Linford, struggling up the hill to East Tilbury village, almost sobbing with the exertion of it.

Letting the bicycle fall on its side on her front path, she made her way inside the house, heading for the sofa in the drawing room. She had the most frightful shivers and wondered how the temperature could have dropped so drastically since morning. On the sofa she laid her head back against a cushion, shivering violently, pulling her overcoat around her tightly. Straining to listen for Mrs Zlin, to ask for some hot tea, she remembered the old lady had gone out on a shopping errand. She started to cough, a strange cough that didn't start small but was immediately painful and loud. Her head craned up from the cushion with the force of it and when it stopped she lay back down feeling quite frightened. She tried to remember if she'd had anything similar over the years but couldn't follow a train of thought, her mind wandering. Suddenly she tore off her overcoat and her jacket, ripped away her blouse and lay there in only her slip and skirt. She had a fever and it came on as suddenly as the shivers left her. She coughed again, the pain of it causing her to curl forward as though cradling her lungs.

Whimpering, she closed her eyes, wanting to go to the kitchen dresser to look for some aspirin, but she hadn't the energy to get up. Bertie was there in her mind's eye. He was holding onto something that caught in the wind. A ship's sail, no, a mast, no, a Union flag. His face twisted with fear as he tried to keep hold but he was slipping. Mim grimaced and shrank back. Bertie flailed for life, screamed out for help. Mim shook her head, tried to shake the image away but it was strong. She opened her eyes and tried to sit up but the cough came again and shook her body violently.

Mim started to cry, gasping for air. She wiped her mouth and looked at her hand with horror. It was smeared red with a foaming blood. As she looked at her hand, her gaze ran the length of her bare arm and she squinted, wondering at the light in the room. Her skin seemed to be a pale blue colour and, looking at her other arm, it too was blue. She coughed again, the force of it ripping her lungs and making her gasp again for breath. Clutching her arms to her chest, she slipped off the sofa onto the floor, unable to get up again. She lay there sobbing and struggling to breathe, calling out to Bertie, who was looking at her, the torn flag in his hands. *Bertie*, she tried to call but her voice was barely a whisper, *help me, Bertie*.

21

Aggie

Aggie lay in bed with a hundred things spinning around her mind. It was all giving her a headache. She'd woken up earlier than usual, unable to get warm in the chilly November morning but thinking it wasn't worth the coal or the bother to make up a fire when she was going out this morning.

Sergeant Pavey had secured a trial at police court for the attacker, whose name he had discovered was John Parren. Parren had been charged with police brutality and with grievous bodily harm. Penny Crabb was coming out of the hospital to testify against him and Aggie wanted to be there in court to show her support. She was also hoping that Sergeant Pavey would be able to bring Celine out of jail to bear witness but she'd had no confirmation about this. She got out of bed, pausing for a moment as her brain banged in her head, and went to the wash stand to splash some water on her face half-heartedly. It only made her feel colder.

Her WPS uniform hung on the front of her closet. She looked at it, felt the expensive cloth of the jacket, brushed some specks away from the skirt. Her disappointment at the probable fate of the WPS was a bitter pill to swallow. She had worked so hard. It couldn't all just fizzle out to nothing before she'd had a chance to prove herself. Sub-Inspector Nash had said that the Ministry of Munitions funding had been rescinded, which meant that Aggie was no longer employed by them. But Aggie was going to court and wanted to look the part. She needed some armour. *To hell with it*, she thought. *To hell with the consequences.* Taking the uniform down, she put it on, looking at herself in the glass and feeling her chest inflate with pride. It may be the last time she'd ever wear it. She had to prove her worth while she was still wearing the uniform of the WPS; she had to prove it to herself and to everyone else who didn't think a working girl could do the job of an educated lady. She needed to show that women from the working classes were more than just factory girls and maids. If she could help Penny and get this Captain character put away, then she would certainly have proved herself. If none of it went her way, then she'd have lost her job and shown she wasn't very good at it either.

Time was getting on, she'd have to miss breakfast. In any case, she felt sick with nerves. Clopping down the stairs she popped her head into the kitchen where she could hear voices, to say a quick goodbye to Mim and Mrs Zlin.

'Morning,' she said, 'sorry, can't stop to chat, I'm going to court.'

'Good luck!' called Mim. Aggie made for the hallway but remembered something and turned back.

'Are you seeing Victoria today?'

'Yes, this afternoon,' said Mim.

'Put a good word in for me, will you?'

'Yes, of course,' said Mim. Aggie gave a wave before rushing out. She smiled at the sight of Mim. Her friend was on the mend, thank goodness. Aggie hoped that Victoria at the suffrage society might find a way for her and Mim to keep their patrol. The new women patrols in London were linked to the suffragist campaigners, they weren't suffragettes like the WPS commanders. With Mim's contacts it might mean they could get funding for a patrol in Thurrock.

Riding her bike to Low Street Station, she started to sweat profusely and wondered if it was because she was so nervous about Penny being in court. The last time that vile man had attacked a prostitute, she had ended up in jail. It would be a travesty of justice if that happened again. Aggie had done all she could to make it a fair hearing. She had visited Penny in hospital. Her injuries were worse than Aggie had thought. She had a broken arm and two broken ribs.

'Who did this to you, Penny?' she had asked.

Penny was reluctant to say. 'I don't know, it was dark.'

'Penny, you can trust me,' said Aggie, putting her hand on the girl's. 'I'm from around here, I'm looking out for our girls. Whoever did this to you should be in jail. He'll only do it to someone else.' Penny looked at her uncertainly, her right eye drooping more than usual. 'Was it the Captain?' Penny nodded, her eyes full of fear. 'Good, that's good, Penny, because he did it to Cecile too. You know Cecile?'

Penny nodded. 'But Cecile was put in prison for soliciting and I don't want that to happen to you, too. I want this man to go to jail instead. See?'

'Yes,' said Penny. 'But if he doesn't go to jail, he'll get me again.'

'Then we have to make sure of it, don't we? We have to have courage, Penny. Women like us have got something to prove. If we see an opportunity we have to seize it quickly before it disappears.' Penny seemed to know that Aggie didn't mean prostitutes and police officers, but women born without a future paved with advantage.

Aggie had been glad she'd gone to see Penny. In court the girl might otherwise have denied she'd known her attacker. Aggie hoped she would stick to her guns today.

Cecile too. Aggie had gone all the way to Chelmsford to see Cecile in jail to ask her if she'd bear witness in court against the Captain if it could be arranged to get her there.

'I don't know,' said Cecile, looking scared. 'He's a mean one. He'll wait for me to get out and then he'll find me. I've got my kids to think of.'

'Cecile, there's a chance he'll do that anyway,' said Aggie. 'And he's already hurt someone else. Penny Crabb, do you know her?'

'Penny, with the eye?' said Cecile, touching the edge of her own eye. 'Yes, she's working for him too. She's only a young thing. What did he do?'

'Bashed her around and left her on the street, just like he did with you, Cecile. He needs putting away, and you can help do it.'

Aggie left the jail not certain if Cecile would have the

courage to speak against the Captain. But Sergeant Pavey had promised to try to get her to the hearing and now Aggie could only hope for the best.

Getting off the train at Grays, Aggie looked at the station clock and hurried along to the police court. Inside, it was full of spectators. She scanned the faces for the sub-inspector but could see only two other women, most likely family of the defendants. Aggie thought one of them looked like Penny's mother, Mrs Crabb, and remembered those months ago when she had appealed to the sub-inspector to help her find her daughter. She might not know that Penny had fallen further into prostitution – it would be a humiliating shock indeed to hear it said in court. Aggie threaded her way through, to squeeze in on a seat that was very near the witness stand. She wanted to be in plain sight of Penny and Cecile. The men seated either side of her eyed her warily. She kept her eyes straight ahead.

By now Aggie was used to being in the courtroom. She watched as the magistrates filed in and took their seats at the bench. It was Mr Speechley again. Still, there were two other magistrates to make their opinion known. The first defendant was brought in by a male constable. Aggie scanned the room again for the sub-inspector or for Sergeant Pavey, neither of whom she could see. The clerk declared that the defendant was a painter's labourer from Linford. He was charged with stealing half a pound of paint worth twopence from P & O Company at Tilbury Docks and remanded on bail to the Petty Session.

Aggie sat up straight. Sergeant Pavey was bringing in a man by his arm. He looked like John Parren, the Captain.

Aggie tried to get a look at his hands because the scars were the thing that she remembered most about him. The clerk announced his name and read the charges. Ex-Captain John Parren, charged with police brutality and grievous bodily harm. He was placed in the dock and Sergeant Pavey described the case history.

'I attended the defendant's home in West Tilbury and arrested him on suspicion of the bodily harm of two women in Tilbury – a Miss Penny Crabb and a Miss Cecile Browne.'

'But this is a man of the military, is he not?' said Mr Speechley in an impatient manner. 'On what evidence did you make the arrest?'

'Sir, the women's associates provided the information.'

'Associates? What do you mean?'

Aggie looked on with alarm. When Speechley found out that the girls were prostitutes it would colour his judgement of the case.

'Sir, the injured parties are known for soliciting in the area.'

'Prostitutes?' said Speechley, incredulous. 'Sergeant Pavey, we have known one another for a long time and I never thought I would have cause to caution you on wasting the court's time, but I shall be speaking with your chief constable at the soonest opportunity. It is an affront to this man who has served his country. I am bound to dismiss this case.'

Aggie wanted to stand up and shout no, but she held her tongue. He couldn't dismiss the case, not yet.

'Sir, if I may,' said Sergeant Pavey, looking visibly shaken. 'There are several witnesses on hand . . .'

The magistrates conferred, the two either side of Speechley nodding their heads.

'Bring them in,' said Speechley as though he could hardly be bothered to utter the words.

The attending officer, a Sergeant Fitzgerald, came in.

'Sir, I found a Miss Penny Crabb in a state of injury on Dock Road in Tilbury on the night of the twenty-second of November. I enquired as to what happened and she said she didn't know because it was dark.'

Mr Speechley waved Sergeant Fitzgerald away as though swatting a fly. Aggie strained to see who would be brought in next. It was Penny and the poor thing looked in a terrible way. She walked with difficulty to the bench, her drooping right eye giving her the look of a wretched case, and the clerk stated her name and took her oath. Aggie sat up as tall as she could to catch Penny's eye. The girl looked terrified but there was a flicker of relief when she saw Aggie there among the spectators. Aggie gave the girl nods and smiles of encouragement. But Penny spotted her mother there and baulked.

'Please state your occupation,' said Mr Speechley.

Penny hesitated. 'I'm out of work, sir,' she said.

'A likely story. You are under oath. Have you solicited unseemly services to men in the locality?'

Penny looked at the floor and nodded. Mrs Crabb cried out in anguish.

'Would all women leave the court,' said Mr Speechley.

Mrs Crabb and another woman shuffled their way along their benches and left, the pitiful whimpers of Mrs Crabb fading away. Aggie remained in her seat.

'All women,' said Mr Speechley, staring directly at her. Aggie said nothing but remained where she was. Every man in the place looked in her direction, Sergeant Pavey included. 'Clerk?' said Speechley.

Aggie stood up and the clerk stopped in his tracks. 'I am in my rights to stay,' said Aggie. 'Sir, I know you want me to leave, but you can't make me leave, I haven't done anything wrong. It is up to me to judge if the morality of the case is too much for me.'

There was absolute silence in the court and all heads turned to Speechley, whose face had turned an unpleasant shade of purple. He seemed about to bark an order to the clerk to remove Aggie by force but one of the other magistrates put a hand on his arm and spoke into his ear.

'I find it hard to believe that any virtuous woman would wish to subject herself to the indecency of a case such as this,' he said, after a moment's consideration. 'Constable Tucker, I understand?' Aggie nodded. 'Why any virtuous woman would involve herself in the immorality of police work is beyond my comprehension. Are you married, Constable Tucker?' Aggie replied that she was. Mr Speechley acted surprised to hear it. 'Do you have children, may I ask?'

'No, sir, I do not.'

'Ah,' he said, knowingly. 'I thought as much. It takes a particular type of woman to want to do work of this nature. An abnormal type, cold, masculine.'

He let his words echo around the room, doing his utmost to humiliate Aggie into leaving. She wouldn't leave. He could say what he liked about her. She wouldn't tell him that she had had children and that they had all died. What would be the point in that?

'You strike me as an uneducated woman, might I say,

which is unusual in the women's police service. This leads me to wonder, what was your previous occupation?'

'I worked in munitions, sir.'

'Ah, yes, of course, yes of course. The more intelligence I receive the more sense this makes. Being a woman of the lower classes you naturally have less restraint, you naturally are less responsible for your actions. Yes,' he said, nodding at his colleagues. 'But what I do not understand, Constable Tucker, is that why, when Commissioner Macready, a most sensible man, has ordered the dissolution of the Women's Police Service, you are still here in this court wearing your uniform.' He gave an unkind sort of laugh, looking at the other spectators. 'But I shall permit you to remain for the present time.'

Aggie sat back down, her heart banging in her chest. She wiped her forehead with the back of her hand and it came away wet. Stealing a glance at Mr Speechley she immediately averted her eyes as he was looking straight at her. When Aggie looked at Penny, the girl was staring at her with disbelieving eyes. Aggie nodded and smiled at her. Standing up to Speechley had, she hoped, also given Penny some confidence.

'Your occupation, Miss Crabb, renders you an unreliable source. What say you?'

'He, the Captain, him,' she said, pointing to Parren, 'he was my pimp and he knocked me around and broke my ribs and my arm.'

'Your *pimp*?' said Mr Speechley. 'This is becoming farcical. Captain Parren, I am sure you are quite beside yourself with incredulity but please humour us and tell the court whether or not you have ever seen this woman before now?'

'No, sir, I have not,' said Parren, speaking for the first time.

'Sergeant Fitzgerald, what was the state of Miss Crabb's clothing when you found her?'

'In disarray, sir,' said the sergeant, coming forward.

'As though she might have been in a compromising attitude with a man, perhaps?'

'Perhaps. However—'

'Take her away,' said Mr Speechley, 'and hold her in remand to be charged with soliciting. We do so need to remove this filth from our streets.'

Aggie bit her lips together tightly, watching as they took Penny away. The girl looked back at Aggie with alarm and Aggie forced another smile and nod.

'Well, Sergeant Pavey, this is going awfully well, is it not?' said Mr Speechley sarcastically. 'Who, pray tell us, will be called next? This is a pretty jolly for police court, I must say. You wouldn't see the likes of it at assizes.'

Cecile came next. When she saw Parren she blanched but she took her place and Aggie caught her eye with an encouraging wave, grateful to Sergeant Pavey for managing to get her there.

'Really, Constable Tucker, you do seem to be on remarkably good terms with these women. It does make me wonder that the Women's Police Service lasted as long as it did. Now, tell me, what do we have here? From the looks of you I'd say another prostitute?'

Cecile looked like she might give the magistrate a piece of her mind. She looked at Aggie with indignation. Aggie shook her head and signalled with wide eyes that Cecile should keep calm.

'I am a mother of six, sir,' said Cecile.

A magistrate consulted his notes and showed them to Mr Speechley.

'Ah!' he said. 'You are currently serving a sentence for soliciting. I thought I recognised you. Well, Sergeant Pavey, you have excelled yourself. You have brought this woman from Chelmsford gaol to bear witness in this lowly police court case. This is the stuff of the music hall, is it not?'

Sergeant Pavey's face contorted with all manner of things but he remained quiet.

'Do you know this man?' said Mr Speechley to Cecile.

Cecile looked at Aggie and Aggie nodded her head with great energy.

'Yes, sir. He's the one who knocked me about.'

'This is absurd,' said Mr Speechley. 'These women are of no use in the witness stand against men who have fought for their King and Country. They are morally deficient, they are—'

Cecile took another look at Aggie and blurted out, 'Sir, he's a deserter, he told me, sir.'

Aggie clutched her hands together. Was it true? How she hoped it was true.

'A deserter?' said Mr Speechley.

'He was in France and he took another man's name who was missing and he got home.'

The magistrates conferred. Aggie didn't know what else she could do but stand up and make her presence known.

'Sit down, Constable Tucker,' said Mr Speechley. 'Your lack of good manners betrays your lack of education. This court shall reconvene in one hour.'

With that, the magistrates stood up and filed out of the court, leaving everyone there wondering what was happening.

'What are they doing?' Aggie said, when she managed to get over to Sergeant Pavey.

'They are sending an urgent telegram to the War Office,' he said. 'Did anyone say this before, that he's a deserter?'

'No,' said Aggie, shrugging. 'But what if it's true? He's done for, isn't he?'

'I should think so. It's the death penalty for desertion. If there's anything Speechley hates more than prostitutes, it's a deserter – he'll have his guts for garters.'

Aggie took her seat and waited. It was two hours before the magistrates came back in. Speechley's face was like thunder.

When everyone was seated and Parren was back in the box, Speechley spent some moments looking down at his hands clasped on the bench before him. Aggie was sure he was composing himself.

'The defendant shall be held on remand pending court martial,' said Speechley, 'where he shall stand trial for desertion in the face of the enemy whilst serving King and Country.'

A hush of whispers ran through the spectators and a single cheer went up. It was Aggie. She cheered with all her heart and Speechley looked at her with something like indifference. He took a deep breath through his nose. 'Court adjourned.'

Aggie caught Sergeant Pavey's eye – he raised his eyebrows and gave the smallest of shrugs. They were both wondering whether Penny was going to be charged with soliciting. Aggie couldn't care less about Speechley's opinion of her. She had done her job and done it well. She had refused to leave the court, she had gained the trust of prostitutes and a male sergeant, she was the working class copperette who had achieved something that others could not have done.

The intensity of the hearing had taken all of her energy. She said goodbye to Sergeant Pavey and made her way to the station. Her headache was still pounding and she felt weak with the exertion of the day. It would have been nice to tell Arnie about the court case but he was still in the hospital. She hoped that Mim was back from her appointment with the suffrage society so that she could share the good news with her friend at home. And then Aggie would rest. She felt a deep desire to fall into bed and sleep.

At Low Street station Aggie retrieved her bicycle but laughed at herself when she hardly had the energy to pedal. She made it home entirely exhausted. Pulling open the garden gate, she frowned. Mim's bike was on its side on the garden path as though it had been thrown there, or perhaps Mim had had some good news and had rushed inside to tell it. Aggie pushed the stand of her own bike down and picked up Mim's bike for her, standing it next to her own. Going to the front door, she glanced sideways and saw a wooden box of groceries there beneath the drawing room window. Frowning, she looked around for the delivery boy from Tibble's grocery. There was no sign of him or of his bicycle. Aggie went to retrieve the box, bent to pick it up and as she did saw through the window into the drawing room. She dropped the box with a clatter, the contents rolling out onto the ground, and ran to the front door. Fumbling for her key, she got the door open and rushed inside, skidded into the drawing room and fell to her knees with a cry.

Mim was on the floor. One leg was bent at the knee and sideways as though she had fallen and not been able to right herself. She was in just her slip and skirt, her jacket and blouse discarded beside her. Mim. Her dear friend Mim. Aggie reached out towards her, her hand hovering above Mim's skin, which was a purplish blue colour. The colour of the Spanish Lady. Aggie's hand shook an inch away. She touched Mim's cold arm and drew her hand back. Mim's mouth was smeared with pale red. Her eyes were open and fixed on the wall as though she looked at something there.

22

Aggie

Aggie rushed out of the house into the street for help, startled when a motorised ambulance pulled up at the kerb.

'I'm a doctor,' said a man getting out of the driver's seat. 'The delivery boy from Tibble's came for me.'

'The drawing room,' said Aggie, pointing. He nodded and pulled a white cotton mask across his face and went into the house. He wasn't inside long.

'It's the Spanish flu,' he said, coming out. 'Don't let anyone in there. I shall inform the undertaker.'

Aggie sat on the kerb and cried.

'Have you been exposed?' the doctor asked her. 'How do you feel?'

'I've had a headache today and felt hot,' said Aggie, realising with alarm that she might also be infected.

'Get into the back,' said the doctor, 'and put this on.' He

handed her a mask to wear and he dropped her at West Tilbury village hall, which was being used as a quarantine holding area. She was told by a nurse in a mask to lie down on a camp bed. Several others were in bed too, some coughing into their masks. Aggie thought this was the worst place for her to be. Surely if she wasn't already infected, she would be if she stayed here. She thought about Mr Tunnidge and his complaints about being shut into the Methodist church for quarantine. After three days they had all been let out with no one succumbing to the flu.

But Aggie's fever became worse over the coming hours, punctuated by chills that made her body shake. Her mind was addled with strange thoughts that she couldn't control. She saw Arnie's face and Mim's face, one mutilated, one deathly and staring. They swam in her mind when she tried to sleep. She saw her daughter Rosie at five years old, just before she died. Saw her going off for a walk with Arnie and turning back to wave and smile. Aggie saw herself running after her, dragging her back to the house, telling Arnie not to go. She saw Rosie in the water by the fort, floating and still, and Arnie running and running and not saving her. Aggie's very bones were frozen as though she'd never feel warm again. But she was hot, so hot that her throat was swollen and her lungs couldn't gasp air. A nurse sat her up to drink, to eat, but she could only sip, only take the smallest bite. Her body had broken, it was heavy and immobile, it ached and refused to work. Only her mind raced fast, running round and round and not letting her rest.

And then she opened her eyes and looked about her and wondered what day it was.

'Ah, you are come back to us,' said a nurse, coming to feel Aggie's pulse. 'You gave us quite a fright.'

'How long ...' said Aggie, feeling weak just uttering the words, but seeing that there were more beds in the room than when she had arrived, more patients.

'You were out for three days,' said the nurse. 'But you are lucky, you have fought off the virus, you are strong.'

Aggie sank back onto her pillow. She didn't feel strong, but thank God she was alive.

There was a shout from another nurse, with a patient who was coughing uncontrollably. Aggie's nurse rushed to assist her colleague. They held the woman up while she coughed, wiping away what looked like blood. The woman wheezed and gasped for air, her eyes bulging. She shivered and fell limp. The nurse tried to jerk her awake, called her name, but the woman didn't respond. Feeling for the pulse, the nurse shook her head with a grim expression and pulled the bed sheet over the woman's face.

Aggie turned away. She remembered that Mim had gone and tears came to her eyes. Had Mim met with the same end? She had been alone, alone and coughing up blood like that and unable to call for help. Aggie let out a sob; she wanted to cry for her friend but felt so awfully weak. Mim was with Bertie now, they were reunited. Aggie fell asleep knowing that that was what her friend wanted most of all.

On waking, she thought that Arnie would be wondering where she was and why she hadn't visited him in hospital. But she was too weak to move. Taking the nurse's advice, she drank lots of water and did her best to eat and after another day in the village hall she was allowed to leave. She got a lift with the doctor, this time in his own transport – she clutched the side of the cab as the horse clopped through the lanes towards Orsett.

In the hospital, when Arnie saw her come into the ward, he looked as though he'd been afraid he'd never see her again.

'Where have you been? I've been out of my wits with worry,' he said, grabbing her hand.

'I've had the flu, the Spanish flu, I've been in quarantine. It's been terrible, Arnie.' As she told him she broke into tears, the magnitude of what had happened hitting her suddenly. 'I think I nearly died,' she said, sitting on the edge of the bed, weak with the exertion of walking.

'Oh, love,' he said. 'Oh I'm so glad, I'm so glad, what would I have done if I'd lost you?'

He seemed to melt with sadness at the news – he was still very fragile. The other news she had brought might be too much for him to bear but she couldn't keep it from him.

'Arnie,' she said, clutching his hands, 'Mim had it too.' Aggie tried to be strong but the tears rolled down her face. Arnie looked at her, terrified. 'She wasn't strong enough, Arnie, she's gone.'

He shook his head. 'No,' he said. 'Not Mim.' He covered his face with his hands. 'Not Mim,' he said, his voice muffled and choked.

Making her way home wearily, Aggie let herself into Mim's house. She walked around the rooms, but not even Mrs Zlin was there. On the kitchen table she found a letter addressed to her. It was from Mim's mother. *Sergeant Pavey of the local constabulary has informed me that you, too, have been stricken by the dreaded influenza,* she wrote. *I do hope you make a good recovery.* She must have wondered whether Aggie would be alive to read the letter. *The house will be sold forthwith. Please know that you are at liberty to stay for a week or two while you look for other accommodation. Mimosa's funeral is to be held at St Catherine's church on Sunday the first of December.* In two days' time.

Next to it there was a note scrawled on a corner of brown paper bag. *I gone home. HZ.* Mrs Zlin. Aggie hoped she had gone of her own choice and not been asked to leave. She would check in on her later.

Before leaving Orsett hospital the doctor had told her that Arnie was being discharged the following day. The hospital needed the bed, there were so many men coming back from the war needing medical attention. They had weaned him off the cocaine and morphine and now he needed rest. Aggie hoped that the news of Mim's death wouldn't set him back – she'd have to keep a close eye on him. She wondered where on earth they were going to live.

After an eerie night in the empty house, which she had spent tossing and turning, Aggie got up feeling worse than she had the previous day. She cycled slowly to Stanford to speak to the local billeting officer. Understanding her situation, and in view of the fact that some of the men from the fort had been demobbed, he agreed to rehouse the officer currently residing in her house, and to let her and Arnie move back in. It came as a huge relief and was just the thing Arnie would need to start feeling settled. When she got back to the house, Arnie was there being dropped off by a motorised hospital ambulance. He and Aggie smiled at one another uncertainly, as if something had changed between them.

'How are you feeling, love?' said Aggie, taking his arm as they walked to the front door.

'Not bad,' he said with a brave smile. They gravitated naturally to the kitchen and Aggie put the kettle on. She remembered washing up with Mim when they had been on patrol together, before Bertie's accident and before Arnie had come home. It felt like a hundred years ago.

'Have you still got pain?' she said, sitting down at the table with Arnie and pushing his cup of tea towards him. 'Is it all right without the medicine?'

'It's not too bad,' he said and sipped his tea as though to avoid her question.

'I went to see the billeting officer this morning,' she said.

'Oh, yes?'

'He said we can get back into our house next week. That's good, isn't it?'

'Yes, I suppose it is.'

'We can't stay here, the family are going to sell it,' she said, thinking he'd be happier about it.

'Yes, I imagine they will,' he said vaguely. Aggie wondered if he was missing Mim, they had spent a lot of time together. She didn't want to upset him by asking about it. It seemed they both felt a little lost. Mim had been their common denominator since Arnie had come home from the war, and now they had to face each other without her. It wasn't the only thing that Aggie wanted to talk about but she daren't, he was too fragile. To her surprise, he said it himself.

'I thought about Rosie a lot in the trenches.'

Aggie started, put down her cup in its saucer a little too firmly. 'Did you?' She was so surprised that he had brought it up.

He nodded and swallowed, avoided her eye. 'I always think about her, but in the trenches you sort of cling on to your memories like they will keep you alive.'

'Yes,' she said.

'Do you remember that red doll she had?'

'Yes, course I do.'

'I always see it, floating on the river. I remember it floating there when I realised she'd gone in and I was trying to get to her.'

Aggie ground her teeth together, trying not to cry.

'I saw her go under and couldn't get to her in time. But it's that damned doll that haunts me, it just bobbed there on the surface like it was mocking me.' He looked up at her and his poor broken face crumpled and the tears ran down the runnels and troughs there now. 'I'm sorry, Aggs, I can't tell you how sorry I am. I was thinking in the trenches how I never said sorry to you and I wanted to stay alive so I could say it.'

Aggie broke too. She reached forward for his hands and grabbed them. She couldn't blame him for Rosie's death. It might have happened just as easily on her watch. Children run off, they don't sense danger, they do things like go too near to the river's edge. It wasn't Arnie's fault that she'd lost two children before Rosie, that Edward was caught by diphtheria and that Annie died in childbirth. It wasn't his fault that Rosie was Aggie's little angel, the one who had survived, the one who made up for her other losses. And it wasn't his fault that Rosie had slipped at the river's edge. He was left with the heavy burden of guilt. He didn't need her blame too.

'I'm sorry too, my love,' she said. 'I'm sorry I've never been able to let it go.'

23

Aggie

'Arnie, what do you think about this?' said Aggie the following day. 'Remember that surgeon they told you about at the hospital?'

'Yes,' he said. 'In Kent, wasn't it?'

'I talked to the doctor about it when I came to see you at Orsett. He said this surgeon in Kent, Sidcup, is very good. He rebuilds men's faces. With operations, so it's your proper face, not a mask. I want to write to him, Arnie.'

'Yes, all right,' said Arnie after hesitating for a moment.

Aggie walked to Linford to post her letter to the surgeon. The sky was unusually blue for December, the sun warm on her face, despite the cold pinch about her ears and nose. She wondered when she'd have gone back to the patrol, how long she'd have convalesced after the flu. She missed being in uniform and riding about on her bike to check all was well.

People who passed her nodded or tipped their hat, looking quizzically at her normal clothes.

Her letter safely deposited at the post office, she turned about and headed home. Going past the George and Dragon, she looked up and saw her old munitions friend Pops at the window. She waved. Pops hesitated before waving back. Aggie knew Pops blamed her for Tilly going to prison. She beckoned Pops to come down and was relieved when her friend disappeared from the window and a minute later appeared from around the side of the public house.

'Not in uniform then?' said Pops, in an offhand way.

'Nope. I'm out of a job,' said Aggie. 'How about you?'

Pops let out a long sigh and her face relaxed as though she hadn't wanted to be hostile in the first place. 'Me too. I think they've got rid of most of the munitions girls now. I miss it, I really do.'

'Sorry to hear that, Pops. It's a hard time now. Is your dad back?'

Pops winced with pain. 'No, Aggs, he was killed, he's not coming back.'

'Oh no, Pops, I'm so sorry.'

The friends embraced. 'This damned war,' said Pops, pulling back and wiping her eyes. 'I heard about your police friend, too. The flu?'

Aggie nodded. 'Yes, and it nearly got me, too, but I came out of it.'

'Thank God, Aggie.' Pops shook her head. 'As if the war wasn't bad enough, the flu too, it beggars belief.' She paused as though thinking how to phrase something. 'I saw your Arnie a couple of weeks ago.' She looked meaningfully at

Aggie as if just laying eyes on Arnie was enough to explain everything.

'Yes, it's been hard and won't get much easier, I don't think,' said Aggie, not wanting to go into it much more. 'So have you looked for work, then? Is there anything about?'

'Nothing like what I've loved doing the past three years. We've been told at the Labour Exchange that if we don't take the work they've got then we won't get the new dole the government are giving. It's a pittance at seven shillings a week but better than nothing when you're holding out for a decent job. That means doing anything they've got. Marge from guncotton refused to do a char job for three shillings a week and got her dole taken away. It's not right.'

'Three shillings a week?' said Aggie, frowning. 'You can't live on that.'

'No, I know, but the government want the men to have their jobs back. I understand that, of course, but what about all the women who are the breadwinners, all the ones whose men haven't come home or won't be coming home, the ones who are supporting their families themselves? Like me, I'm supporting my mum, my granddad, my sisters.' She broke off, clearly upset. 'We've had a taste of something else during this war, we've shown everyone what we can do and now it's being taken away from us. I just feel like I've been robbed or something.'

'I know how you feel,' said Aggie. 'I thought I'd be in with a chance of a good job after the war if I joined the police. But the same thing has happened to me. You were right, I might as well have stayed in munitions. Some women patrols are being kept on in London but there's no money from the government for me any more. I need to get down to the Labour Exchange. I'm just having a few days to get my strength back after the flu.'

'I'm sorry to hear that, Aggie. We've had our differences lately, but I know you worked hard. You know what people are saying? That the munitions girls should have saved the good money they were earning to live on after the war. Bloody cheek. Some of us went up to London on that march. There were banners saying "Shall Peace Mean Starvation?" Some people were shouting out to us that we're parasites and blacklegs.' Pops laughed wryly. 'I tell you what, how are we supposed to feed ourselves? A lot of us haven't got husbands and probably won't have now. And the men who are around are stuck in camps waiting to be demobbed. It's a bloody mess.'

'I can't believe it's come to this, Pops, after everything the munitions girls have done for the country. When we were needed for war work, all the reasons for keeping us down were suddenly swept away, but now, we're being told to get back to where we belong. It's not fair to show us what we can do and then take it all away.'

'I know, I feel like leaving this bloody country. There's a circular going round, asking women to emigrate to the New World. I'm thinking about it.'

'You've got somewhere to live for now though?' said Aggie, looking up at the pub and hoping that Pops wouldn't go abroad. Aggie would never see her again if she did that.

'For the time being. We're keeping the pub going for Rose but when her husband comes back we think he'll want us out.'

'Yes, poor Rose. And how about Tilly? Is she all right now that awful chap she was working for has gone?'

'Tilly?' said Pops, as though she was surprised Aggie would have the cheek to mention her. 'No, Tilly is still earning her money the way she has been since coming out of prison.'

'Oh, I thought, now that Parren is ... well, did you hear, he's got the death sentence?' Aggie had heard the outcome of Parren's court martial. He was proven to be a deserter and they made an example of him. Pops nodded but seemed unwilling to acknowledge the part Aggie had played in his downfall. 'I thought Tilly would get out of it all.'

'Nope,' said Pops, raising her eyebrows. 'She hangs around with that Penny girl. The two of them are a right old state.'

Aggie's heart sank. Tilly and Penny both soliciting? It was difficult news to hear. If she still had her job she'd be straight on her bicycle looking for them, but she couldn't do that now. 'God, I wish there was something else they could do,' she said.

'There's no work for decent folk, let alone girls with a reputation. And what with the men in the camps waiting for demob, there's plenty of the other kind of work for them.' Pops looked at Aggie meaningfully as if to say Tilly's bad reputation was Aggie's fault. Aggie felt the blame keenly and wished there was some way of helping Tilly.

'All right, well, I'd better be getting back to Arnie. Bye, Pops.'

Aggie smiled at her friend as she walked away, glad that they had made up. But then a shot of panic went through her. What was she going to do for work? They couldn't exist on Arnie's basket-making for long. The sub-inspector had told her that there was no chance of her being put forward for the London patrols because she was still on probation and there were many more experienced WPS officers who would be in front of her in the queue if the chance came up. She'd end up having to go back to service. Not at Gobions, though, she hoped not. She shivered at the thought of the mistress holding up a dusty finger in her face.

24

Aggie

When the family turned up for Mim's funeral, Aggie felt like an intruder in the house. She and Arnie, dressed in their best, stayed in a corner of the kitchen. Aggie served teas and was treated as the maid by family members who didn't know her. Arnie could take only so many stares and went up to his room.

The hearse arrived and the family followed it up the hill to St Catherine's, Aggie and Arnie trailing behind. Their friendship hadn't lasted long but Aggie felt a strong kinship with Mim – they had connected on a level that not many would understand. They had lived and worked together, they had patrolled together. It was an unusual friendship that would never have developed during peacetime. A working woman and an educated woman. The war had thrown a lot of lives into disarray. Her friendship with Mim was one of the good things to come out of it.

Reverend Clow was visibly moved when he gave the service. *Mimosa was a good woman*, he said, *a dutiful woman, a woman who looked to God for guidance.* He gave a beautiful reading that moved Aggie to tears. It started, *Death is nothing at all. It does not count. I have only slipped away into the next room. Nothing has happened. Everything remains exactly as it was. I am I and you are you, and the old life that we lived so fondly together is untouched, unchanged. Whatever we were to each other, that we are still . . .*

At the graveside, Aggie saw Victoria from the suffrage society and when they were back at the house and she found herself serving teas again, she took a cup to Victoria.

'Hello,' she said. 'We met, I was—'

'On patrol with Mim, yes, I remember, Aggie, how are you?'

Aggie didn't remember Victoria using her Christian name before, only Constable Tucker.

'I'm all right. I miss Mim very much.'

'Yes,' said Victoria simply. 'Yes.'

'Mim was happy about the new act, she was going to help you with your campaign.'

Victoria smiled, tears springing to her eyes. 'It was very important to her, to me too. But alas, I have not been chosen to run as Labour candidate, it seems the time is not right for that here. I could run independently but we have been given a ludicrously short amount of time to campaign and I have decided I shall support the Labour candidate, and that is what Mim would have done too, I am sure of it. They are in favour of improving women's rights.'

'Shame, about you not running,' said Aggie. 'But still. I wish Mim could have voted. She was looking forward to that.'

Victoria only nodded, pinching her lips together, trying to keep her composure. 'We have fought for a long time for the right to vote. It is terribly sad that Mim will not have her chance.'

Victoria sipped her tea and Aggie turned to go.

'Mim spoke very highly of you, Aggie,' said Victoria. 'What is happening with your policing job now?'

'I've lost my job,' said Aggie, feeling empty. 'The commissioner is funding some women's patrols in London but the WPS have been asked to disband. The Ministry of Munitions funding has been stopped, so . . . '

'It is ironic that the WPS have been left out of negotiations. If we'd only had the opportunity to have our own women's patrols in this area, then you might still have a position. As it is, the WPS were active here, and now, because of their militant affiliations, they have been cast aside.'

Aggie shrugged. She didn't know what to say.

'Do you miss it? Being on patrol?'

'Very much.'

'In my opinion you are still very much needed in this area. I wonder whether there is an opportunity now for us to fund a position, or to help fund a position, in collaboration with the local constabulary.'

'What do you mean?' said Aggie, her stomach turning over.

'I mean to say, I want to help you. As I said, Mim spoke very highly of you and I think I should like to do something in her honour.'

Aggie nodded, hardly believing her ears.

'Mim said you gave her a valuable insight into the lives and minds of working women. She was set on the idea that it is the higher classes who should effect change for the lower classes. So that is what I should like to do.'

'What's this?' said Aggie, picking up a letter from the kitchen table addressed to her. The funeral guests had gone and Arnie had come back downstairs. He shrugged and lit a cigarette.

Aggie opened the envelope and took out the page.

Dear Mrs Tucker,
     Please be advised that we, Messrs Green and Ball, are acting executors of the last will and testament of Mrs Mimosa Elizabeth Rathbone upon her untimely death. We are bound to inform you that Mrs Rathbone has bequeathed to you an amount of two hundred pounds. Please find enclosed the personal banker's cheque for said amount. May we take this opportunity to wish you our sincere condolences. Should there be any cause for enquiry, please write to the address above.

Aggie sat down and read the letter again. 'Mim's left me some money, two hundred pounds.'

'What?' said Arnie.

'Two hundred pounds. From Mim.'

Arnie started to cry. Aggie got up to put her arm around him. Mim couldn't have guessed that she'd die now. She must have rewritten her will on Bertie's death and included Aggie in it. 'She's just thinking of us, that's all,' said Aggie. 'We don't have to worry now, we'll be all right.'

*

Another letter arrived the following day, from the face surgeon in Kent. The letter said that Arnie could come and be seen at the hospital.

'Let's go today,' said Aggie. 'I don't want to wait. Let's get the ball rolling.'

'If you think so, Aggs.'

'I do. Let's go after breakfast. Don't look so worried. We'll get the Tilbury ferry across to Kent then a train to Sidcup.'

When they arrived at Queen's Hospital, Aggie's nerves set in and she could tell that Arnie felt the same. They were shown into a waiting room and told the surgeon would come to see them when he was out of theatre.

'He's a busy man,' said the nurse kindly.

They waited for an hour and a half, Arnie becoming increasingly restless.

'Harold Gillies,' said a man in a white doctor's coat, holding out his hand to Arnie first and then to Aggie. 'How do you do, my dears.'

He looked at Arnie for a moment before sitting down next to him. 'What happened?' he said.

'I was shot in the face, in France,' said Arnie, blood rushing to the uninjured skin under the doctor's scrutiny.

'May I?' said the doctor, waiting for Arnie to nod his consent before putting his hands on Arnie's face to examine it. 'Yes,' he said. 'Yes, I see.' And finally, he said, 'Yes. I am very glad you came to me. I do believe I can help you.'

Aggie felt tears spring to her eyes. The doctor patted Arnie's arm affectionately and stood up. 'Did you bring a bag of things with you? Good. You'll be with us for several months, at least.'

Arnie turned to Aggie in alarm, but she gave him a reassuring nod.

'It takes time, you see,' said Dr Gillies. 'We shall need to perform several operations, with healing time in between. It will be a painful ordeal, I put you under no illusions, but it will be worth it. We've a good bunch of lads here, all in it together, and we're all in good spirits. Have you a photograph of yourself before the accident?' Arnie confirmed that he had. 'And we shall need to discuss what kind of nose you should like,' said the doctor with a twinkle in his eye.

Aggie followed them out of the waiting room and down a hall into a large ward. The doctor hadn't prepared her for what was there and it took all of her courage to keep from running out.

The following day their old house became vacant and Aggie could move in. It felt strange leaving Mim's house, and the ghost of Mim's memory. But it also felt like a positive move. Aggie and Arnie needed to be back in their own home. They had a lot of rebuilding to do, in more ways than one. As Aggie started the first of several trips down the road shifting their bags of things, she thought about the hospital. She had stayed long enough for Arnie to be shown to his bed and to settle him in but she couldn't wait to leave. It was hard not to look around her at the monstrous faces of mutilated men, hard not to baulk at the tongues lolling down jawless cavities streaming with saliva, at the fleshy holes where there should have been an eye, a nose, at raw burns and burnt exposed bones. 'There's a cinema here,' said one chap brightly, whose eyelids had burnt away, 'and a chapel and a half-decent canteen.' Aggie smiled and nodded, gripping Arnie's arm, wondering how he felt, if it was a comfort to be amongst these men who had suffered so like himself. She said goodbye to him, said she'd see him again soon, wished him luck, told him to write. And she got out of there, walking fast, then trotting, and she ran down the road, disgusted, nauseated, wholly aghast at being confronted with the horror of war, of what these men had endured.

The billeted officer had left the house in a pretty good state but Aggie wanted to clean it anyway. She set to work with bucket and rag, washing surfaces, sweeping out fires, sluicing the floors and blacking the range. Finally she made up the bed and flopped down on it, exhausted. Arnie was going to be away for several months, the doctor had said. Aggie wondered what he would look like when he came home. She wouldn't hope for his face to be reconstructed to its former self, but it might be something nearer to what it had been and it might be easier for them both to get back to a normal life.

She wondered about his state of mind. He hadn't really talked very much about his experiences in the war and she didn't really expect him to. Trying to put herself in his shoes, she wondered, would she be full of hate about being forced to fight and to come home as changed and traumatised as he was? Would she be able to find a way to live peacefully or would she forever carry the hatred with her? Getting up, she went into the second bedroom. She hadn't cleaned it yet, it was difficult to go in there. She understood something of carrying hate with her. She had borne a hatred of Rosie's death. Although she knew she would carry it for ever, she now knew that it would be only a part of her existence – it would no longer define her, she would be able to find peace in other ways too.

25

Aggie

Dear Aggie,

I do hope this is not an imposition. I have taken the liberty of speaking with my superiors in London and with the local Watch Committee. I am delighted to tell you there is a possibility of one position being funded for a women's patrol here in Thurrock. The Watch Committee wish to meet with you. They next convene, and I am afraid it is very short notice for you, on Monday 9th December, ten o'clock at Stanford police station. I thought it best to take the first available opportunity. I do hope you can be there, Aggie. If not, please let me know at your earliest convenience.

Yours ever sincerely
Victoria

When Aggie collected the last of their bags from Mim's house and saw the letter from Victoria, she was quite overcome with emotion. It was as though it was Mim's parting gift to her. A chance to get a job as a police officer, it was everything she hadn't dared to hope for. The meeting was today. Aggie wasn't sure what to wear and could only think that her WPS uniform would be the best thing. She brushed it off carefully and sipped a cup of tea, too nervous to eat breakfast.

Cycling to Stanford, she enjoyed being out in uniform again. She tried to think what she would say to the committee, wondered whether she would need to prove herself or whether Victoria had already arranged it and this was simply a formality. Either way she didn't want to muck it up. This was her chance to get the job she wanted. If this didn't turn out well, she'd be back scrubbing someone else's floors.

At Stanford police station, Sergeant Pavey was chatting with a group of formal-looking men in suits and uniforms. He saw her and came over.

'Just putting in a good word for my favourite lady constable,' he said, beaming.

'I'm so nervous,' said Aggie. 'I don't want to muck it up. Oh, gracious, is that Mr Tunnidge? What's he doing here?' She swallowed; the last time she had seen Mr Tunnidge she had quarantined him against his will in Linford Methodist church. It wasn't the best of omens.

'You'll be all right, just tell them about the work you've been doing,' said Sergeant Pavey as though he really had faith in her.

Looking back at him, she went into the committee room,

where she was asked to sit at the foot of the table. The men took their seats, including the chief constable from Stanford, who had never expressed any kind of appreciation for the WPS. On the contrary, he had always been quite hostile towards them. Half expecting Victoria to be there, and hoping she would be, the last chair, at the head of the table, was taken up by one of the men and Aggie's stomach clenched with nerves. It was the magistrate, Mr Speechley.

'Good morning, Constable Tucker,' said a man at the side of the table. Aggie recognised him as being one of the other magistrates from Grays police court. 'We are here today to interview you for the position of first-class reserve woman constable.' He looked at his notes to confirm the rank and Aggie shot a glance at Mr Tunnidge, who had coughed into his hand rather disapprovingly. An interview? It sounded as though they would be considering other women for the job. Her mind raced with the other WPS officers in Thurrock, including the sub-inspector herself.

'Ah, Constable Tucker, is it?' said Mr Speechley, suddenly seeming to recognise her. 'I do believe you recently refused to leave my courtroom when instructed?' He frowned at her through his large eyebrows and waited for her response. What on earth was she supposed to say?

'Yes, sir,' she stuttered. 'For the sake of the woman who'd been attacked by the army deserter, sir.'

Mr Tunnidge shuffled forward in his chair as though his posture would encourage the committee to condemn her. Mr Speechley held her in his stare. 'Ah, but you were not aware at the time that the man Parren was an army deserter, were you?'

Feeling on trial herself, she shook her head and looked at Tunnidge who did actually smile at her discomfort. 'No, sir, but I was worried that Penny Crabb would be sentenced to jail time when she wasn't in the wrong.'

'What concern is it of yours? The woman is a known prostitute in the area.'

Aggie took a deep breath. All eyes were on her. 'I think I can help her get out of that, sir. She fell into that trade very recently and I know her mother. It would be a shame if she was jailed and then returned to the trade, sir.'

Mr Speechley stared at her, thinking about her response. 'I think we can all agree,' he said to his colleagues, 'that a female police presence is exactly what we need here.'

Aggie looked at him in disbelief. Was he on her side?

Mr Tunnidge looked as though a dog had eaten his Christmas dinner. He harrumphed his disagreement but didn't dare openly contradict the magistrate.

'A female police presence that is unafraid of the cases of indecency we so often see in this area,' he went on. 'I admit, I have not always been of this mind. To think of a lady is to think of someone to be shielded from such things. The Women's Police Service has always, in my mind, been something of an abnormal presence associated with our honourable male constabulary. However, I am willing to concede that Constable Tucker here has shown herself worthy of the position. Her actions helped the discovery of a deserter of the army, the lowest of the low, and I would like to see Constable Tucker on the streets of Thurrock to help tackle the immorality and indecency of cases of women and children.'

Aggie could have cried with joy. The other men around

the table nodded along to Mr Speechley's words, murmuring their agreement. Mr Tunnidge's face was in all kinds of contortions.

'It is proposed, Mr Speechley,' said the chief constable, 'that we take on Constable Tucker on a year's contract, to test the waters, as it were.'

Mr Speechley nodded. 'Yes, good. Would you kindly outline her duties, Chief Constable?'

'Constable Tucker,' said the chief, addressing her directly, with no hint of hostility, 'your duty shall be to prevent acts of immorality or indecency, to deal with prostitutes and runaway children, to prevent the unlawful practice of fortune telling, to patrol public houses, other entertainment establishments, railway stations and known areas of iniquity in the Thurrock area, six days per week, ten hours per day, with your base here at Stanford-le-Hope station. You shall also assist male colleagues when required and notify male colleagues of any unlawful activity which does not fall within your own specified role.'

'Good. Mr Pound, would you kindly describe the terms of the post,' said Speechley.

A man in a smart suit who Aggie didn't recognise addressed her. 'Constable Tucker, you shall be paid the sum of thirty-five shillings per week plus a uniform allowance of nine pounds per year. You shall order a female version of the Essex constabulary uniform to be made. In the meantime please continue to wear your current uniform but without the identifying insignia. You shall have no official powers of arrest, nor will you be permitted to carry a truncheon or handcuffs. Your position shall start forthwith. You have already been sworn in for your current position, there is no need to do so again. You will be issued with an Essex Constabulary badge to fix to your hat.'

Aggie smiled and nodded, not knowing what she was expected to say. 'Thank you,' she said.

'It is regretful that Constable Tucker is married, Mr Speechley,' said Mr Tunnidge, speaking at last and managing to contain his resentment.

'Ah, yes, regretful indeed,' said Speechley. 'Should you become with child, of course you shall entirely rescind your role. Homemaking in that instance would be your priority, naturally.' Aggie nodded, it was to be expected. She stole a glance at Mr Tunnidge, not daring to smile and give him his comeuppance.

'Constable Tucker, are these terms to your satisfaction?' said Speechley.

26

Aggie

My dearest Arnie

I hope you are very well? Please write when you know about your first operation. I've got some good news. I have got my police job back. It's not with the WPS but with the local police, based in Stanford but patrolling all round Thurrock. I'm the only woman police officer here, it's a real turn up. I've got some more good news for you. We are back in our old house and I've brought all of our things from Mim's. It's all nice and ready for you to come home to. So please write here when you can. I've been thinking, Arnie, about things. And about what to do with Mim's inheritance money. I know we will give some to the hospital for your treatment and I'm very, very glad to do so. There is something I would like to do with the rest of the money and I hope you agree with it because I wouldn't do it without your say-so, of course. I would like us to start up a small business for some of the local women who need a job, especially some of the women who have got themselves into trouble and will find it very hard to earn their keep. I am thinking of a little laundry shop. Once it is up and running it should earn its own keep, if not more. Arnie, I know this is hard but can I ask you please if two of the women I speak of could board in our second bedroom until they are in a better position? Please write soon as I would like to get it started if you agree with it. The business would be in your name, of course.

   With all my love and best wishes, darling Arnie.

   Your loving wife, Aggie

My darling Aggie

   My heart is full. The men here are ever so good. I am at home for now, and my first operation is scheduled today. The men say it is painful but that I can endure it and go on to enjoy having a more normal looking face. I do this for you as much as for me, my dear. I am so glad for your news, and ever so proud of you and of course I trust you to use the inheritance money as you see fit. Mim would be proud of you too, I know she would. Let us do this for her memory. Perhaps I could help with the laundry business when I am fit again? You'll need someone to do collections I shouldn't wonder. We could get a little horse and cart maybe.

   With love and best wishes

   Your, Arnie.

   p.s. yes, please do offer the room to the two women for now.

27

Aggie

The silver WPS lettering on the shoulders of Aggie's uniform came off with a struggle. The letters had been sewn on thoroughly, the stitches had gone over and over, to make sure they stayed on for a long time. Aggie snipped at them with her sewing scissors. Pulling them off was satisfying and she wasn't sure why. She was sad about the WPS disbanding. They had given her a chance of something new. But she was very proud of securing her own policing position without them. Perhaps that's why it gave her so much satisfaction. She liked to think that her working background had given the Watch Committee confidence that she wouldn't shrink from her duty, perhaps that her background had meant a good relationship with Sergeant Pavey, who wasn't intimidated by her as he may have been by the likes of the sub-inspector.

She pulled out the little knot from the back of the fabric

and rubbed at the material to hide any stitching holes. They wanted her to have a new uniform but for now this would do. Today was a big day for her. She would be starting the first patrol of her new job. Her area straddled the Orsett Rural and Tilbury Urban districts. Ultimately Tilbury Docks would be part of her patrol area but for the present time she would need to tread carefully. She didn't know the situation with the Tilbury WPS. Her first port of call today would be the sub-inspector and her stomach fluttered with nerves at the thought of it. She set to work sewing the official Essex constabulary badge to the front of her hat.

Today was the fourteenth of December – election day. As she dressed, a cold hand squeezed her heart as she thought how much Mim had looked forward to this day. Aggie had read in the paper that Christabel Pankhurst was a candidate, and a few other women. She tried not to think about it, she had a job to do. She missed Arnie – she could have done with his support today. He would have his first vote today, too, but he'd only had his operation a couple of days ago so he'd have to forfeit it this time. Too nervous to eat breakfast, Aggie mounted her bicycle and set off through the lanes to Tilbury.

As she rode down Lansdowne Road, she passed the polling station set up in the school. With a start, she saw both Sergeant Green from Tilbury police station and Sergeant Wills from Tilbury WPS standing outside. They were not talking to each other but Sergeant Wills was in conversation with a woman who was smartly dressed and looked as though she had come to vote. It was confirmation that the WPS were still patrolling Tilbury, something that Aggie had hoped would not be the case. She didn't stop at the polling station but rode past with a nod at Sergeant Wills who stared as she went by. Her stomach turned over again when she turned onto Dock Road and saw the sub-inspector's motorcycle parked outside the WPS office.

There was no one manning the front desk and Aggie wondered whether to go through to the back when the sub-inspector came along holding some papers. She looked up with surprise at Aggie, took in Aggie's uniform, her gaze lingering on the shoulders where the WPS insignia once was and on the official constabulary badge on Aggie's hat.

'Sergeant Tucker,' said the sub-inspector.

'Hello, Sub-Inspector.'

'I heard your news,' said the sub-inspector, putting the papers on the desk and looking down at them as if not wanting to meet Aggie's eye.

'Yes. I wanted to stop by to see you and find out . . .'

'Whether we are still here?'

'Sort of,' said Aggie, feeling uncomfortable. 'I'm funded by Essex Constabulary and my patrol area takes in Tilbury. But of course, I shan't need to come here very much if the WPS is still . . .'

'Still in operation?'

Aggie nodded.

'Well, yes we are, for the present time at least. Does that answer your question?'

'I'm glad,' said Aggie, not wanting to fall out with her.

The sub-inspector scrutinised Aggie as though to judge her sincerity. Aggie wasn't sure herself if she meant it and tried to keep her face from revealing any clues. The sub-inspector seemed satisfied – she relaxed and sat on the edge of the desk.

'In his wisdom, the Home Secretary ordered Macready, the Commissioner of Police to recruit women into the Metropolitan police force without specifying from where he should find them. Macready, being anti-WPS and an annoying little man, has chosen to source those women from the patrols and not us. We hope that the next waves of recruitment will spread a wider net and some of us shall be considered. In the meantime, we are funding ourselves as a voluntary service and shall carry on until we are no longer able or until we are told to, rather than advised to, stop.'

Aggie nodded. 'Well, I hope that you are considered, Sub-Inspector, it would be a terrible waste otherwise.'

'He is really only enforcing the WPS dissolution in London,' said the sub-inspector, ignoring her. 'A couple of us have been deployed regionally where the chief constable is sufficiently wise to understand that we are needed. Unfortunately Chief Constable Turnpike here at Tilbury is not. Sufficiently wise.'

Aggie held her tongue.

'Sir Leonard Dunney, Inspector of Constabulary, *is* sufficiently wise to know that we are needed regionally and so we can only hope that sense prevails. As is usual we wait for the word of a man to seal our fate.'

'Yes,' said Aggie.

'I haven't yet voted,' said the sub-inspector, suddenly on her feet. 'Would you accompany me?'

'Yes, of course.'

'Did you see the advertisement in *The Times* yesterday?' said the sub-inspector as they walked side by side down Dock Road.

'No.'

'It was remarkable. There is a new service, orchestrated by the government I'll bet my hat on it, for the training of war wives, you know, women demobbed from munitions or wives of soldiers and so on, to, now let me see, the wording was, yes, "to perfect themselves in household accomplishments which will make the homes of the future ideal for family life."' She gave a wry laugh. 'They are telling us to get back to where we belong, in the home. It is really beyond belief after everything we have shown them we are capable of during this war.'

Aggie could see why the country would need the women in the home and the men to have what jobs there were available, in general. But yes, she agreed with the sub-inspector's sentiment; it rankled, it belittled what they had achieved, and it was almost as if they were being told to forget all of that because it wasn't convenient any more, despite there being many women outside the normal 'family life' now.

On Lansdowne Road, the sub-inspector paused outside the polling station. 'Are you coming in? Or have you voted in Linford?' Her question seemed to lack sincerity somehow.

Aggie frowned. 'No, I can't vote, I didn't get the vote.'

'You didn't? Ah, yes, of course, the property criterion. Ah well, I shall say goodbye then. It really is quite the exciting time.' She made to leave but then added, 'You know, our eminent co-founder, Mary Allen, believes that only educated women make effective police women.'

The sub-inspector smiled and turned away. It was as good as a slap in the face. She had done this purposely to remind Aggie that she wasn't equal to her. Aggie's heart pounded with anger in her chest. Her mind ran fast, there was just time for her to say something in reply, before the sub-inspector disappeared into the school.

'Yes, I had better be off on my patrol,' she called out, 'there is such a large area to cover now.' She forced a smile and gave the sub-inspector a wave, who smirked back at her and disappeared inside.

Aggie rode away with her head held high. She hadn't wanted to reduce her accomplishments to a silly tit-for-tat with the sub-inspector, but really, the woman was impossible.

28

Aggie

Rethinking her direction, Aggie turned down Calcutta Road, rode along Civic Square and out onto Fort Road. She would ride via West Tilbury village. Aggie had what she wanted, her job back. She had her job and she had self-respect. That was priceless. She didn't need Mim's inheritance money for herself, she'd rather do something good with it. Thinking back to the night when she had gone with Sergeant Pavey to arrest John Parren, she tried to remember where they had stopped. It had been dark and now she wasn't sure she had the right house. Knocking at the door, she wondered what kind of reception she would get.

There was no answer. She knocked again. It was early, only around nine in the morning. Another knock, banging on the door. She heard a sound and the door opened. Penny Crabb stood there in a flimsy dressing gown, her deformed right eye gummed with old black make-up.

'What the hell do you want?' she spat. 'I haven't done anything.'

Aggie looked past her, saw a man slip through to the kitchen at the back of the house.

'You seem to have a strange man in your house, Penny. Is he an intruder? Should I go and speak to him, perhaps call Sergeant Pavey to arrest him?'

'Do what you want. He's gone now,' said Penny, yawning, turning away from the door. Aggie followed her inside to the front room where there was a card table and armchairs and it stank like the inside of the George and Dragon. The girl perched on the arm of a chair and lit a cigarette.

'Bit early, isn't it?' she said, picking the sleep out of her eye.

'Penny, I wanted to talk to you about something. Can I sit down?' The girl shrugged and Aggie sat. 'Penny, I want to help you. I'm in a position to set up a little business and I'd like you to come and work there. It's a laundry business. The money will be good, like in munitions, and you'll be able to come off the . . . be able to get some regular money doing something without having to do this.' Aggie looked around the room.

Penny hesitated. 'You wouldn't be able to pay me this kind of money,' she laughed.

'Maybe not, but Penny, you don't really want to be doing this, do you?'

Penny clenched her jaw and didn't reply.

'Penny, me and Arnie have got a spare room in our house

in East Tilbury village. We want you and Tilly to board with us until you get on your feet, and you can help get the business going, maybe it'll be a collective or something, you'll be able to save a bit and get yourself sorted out.'

'Why?'

Aggie shook her head, not understanding.

'Why are you asking me and Tills?'

'Because I'm worried about you and I want to get you out of this. You've no chance of a decent life this way, you'll not get married, have a family . . .'

Penny suddenly shouted up the stairs. 'Tilly, get yourself down here, will you?'

Aggie smiled at Penny and waited for Tilly to emerge, half asleep, from upstairs. 'Constable . . . What is it, Constable what?' said Penny.

'Constable Tucker, but call me Aggie when I'm not working.'

'She, Constable Tucker, wants to save us from all this,' said Penny, sarcastically.

Tilly rubbed her eyes and wiped her fingers on her nightdress. 'What?'

'Me and my husband are starting a laundry business and want you and Penny to come and work there and earn good money and there's a room in our house where you can board as well.'

Tilly scrunched up her face with confusion. 'What for? What do I want to work in a laundry for?'

'Because we will always need laundries,' said Aggie. 'Because whatever is happening with jobs now, a laundry is a good bet. And you won't have to do this any more.'

'I won't? What about my trial?'

'Well, doing this kind of work here isn't going to help your case, is it?' said Aggie, knowing that Tilly's trial for the wilful murder of her baby would be coming up in due course. 'If you had a proper, steady job at a laundry and you were boarding with a policewoman, that would probably help, I should think.'

'I'm doing it,' said Tilly to her friend, suddenly lucid. 'I'll work in a laundry.'

'All right, then,' said Penny, softening. 'All right. It's worth a try. Count me in.'

Aggie smiled to herself as she rode away. It meant a lot to her to help the girls. Their reputations were too far ruined to be able to go back home. They wouldn't be employed by anyone locally who knew them. Aggie was in a position to give them a second chance. And if she could save Tilly from being sentenced for murder, it might even mean she would save her very life.

She joined Muckingford Road at the junction with Blue Anchor Lane and decided to ride to Linford to check on the polling station there. The sub-inspector's comment rankled. It would have been nice to vote for the first time with the other women. They had been granted the vote under the Representation of the People Act. Weren't women from the working classes people too? Maybe the time would come when all women were allowed to vote.

She steered round a man walking down the road, perhaps he had got off the train at Low Street. His head was bandaged and she tried to look at him sideways as she passed but

337

couldn't see his face. Lloyd George was promising the injured a land fit for heroes. That wouldn't make any difference to the woman in Linford who had hanged herself, whose husband had the horrific facial injury. It might not make a difference to Arnie; he was a different man than the one she had married, inside and out.

The polling station in Linford was in the Methodist church on the main road. Aggie parked her bike there and got off to see. It was still early for working men to be voting, but there were a couple of disabled servicemen coming out and an elderly lady was on her own at the doorway, looking a little confused.

'Constable,' she said to Aggie. 'What do I do?'

Aggie didn't really know. She walked the lady inside and saw the polling booths set up behind screens. A man sitting at a table asked the lady her name. She disappeared behind the screen and Aggie smiled at the official, embarrassed to be excluded from the event. She walked out into the bright morning and saw the man with the bandaged head making his way along the road to the church. Frowning, she tried not to stare, but there was something about him that caught her interest. Her stomach turned over.

'Arnie?'

The man stopped. 'Oh, Aggs, it's you.' He came to her and they embraced. 'Sorry, love, I can't see very well.'

'What are you doing out of hospital? Are you all right? Have you had your operation?'

'Yes, I'm all right, I asked the hospital if I could . . . I just wanted to come and vote.'

'Vote? Did you?'

He nodded. 'I wanted to come and vote for Mim. I wanted her to get her vote, Aggs.'

Aggie stared at her husband. He had come all this way with a bandaged face, and was likely in a lot of pain, to do something wonderful for Mim. He was going to give his own first vote to her.

'Will you come in with me, Aggs?'

She nodded. 'Victoria couldn't run as a candidate, did you know?'

'I thought if I saw Victoria's name, I'd vote for her, if I didn't then it'd be Labour, because Mim talked about Labour.'

'Yes, that's it.' Aggie took his arm and they went in together to give Mim her vote.

Acknowledgements

Thank you to: my editor Maddie West, Thalia Proctor and the team at Sphere, my agent Laura Longrigg at MBA, Julia Silk, beta readers Louise Ryder and Mark Wilsher, my writing group, Allie Burns and Tanya Gupta and friends and family for supporting my writing, especially Mia, Molly and Kevin.

Invaluable research resources included exhibitions and archives, so thanks to the Thurrock Museum volunteers and staff, memories of local Thurrock people, Ruth Hunwick of the Old Palmerians, Susan Yates of the Thurrock Historical Society, Thurrock Libraries' Gazette archives and Thurrock Historical Society Journal Panorama archives. I also used maps and local history books and the many brilliant books about life during the Great War, including those that chronicled the terrible sacrifices made by men and the fascinating story of the first women police.

A grateful acknowledgement to the courageous women munitions workers, who proved to the country that women could do 'men's work'. Many women and men lost their lives in munitions factory accidents and explosions, including Ada Jane Wakeling, who died in a fire at Kynoch Explosives factory on 11th September, 1918.

Dear Reader,

I hope you have enjoyed reading *The Copperettes at War*.

Before I started researching this book, I guess I thought there must have been a time when women weren't allowed to be a part of the police force. It was fascinating to learn about the circumstances that led to this changing. 1918 is such an interesting year, historically: the end of a period of time when women had a first chance to show what they were capable of, only for it all to be taken away when war came to an end. It wasn't only a time of social change in terms of gender, but also in terms of class. It must have taken a lot to 'trespass' into another class's territory. I enjoyed going back in time and giving Aggie that chance.

As is ever the case, there is a healthy dollop of artistic licence to make the story work as a novel. Although German aeroplane raids ceased in May 1918, I let a couple more slip through, to work with the timeline of the story and to illustrate how German bombers were a threat in 1918 despite the popular conception that the First World War was about overseas trench warfare and not direct attacks on the home front.

I'd love to hear what you think of Aggie's journey and Mim's story. If you have a second, please leave a quick review online – it only needs to be a couple of words to make a real difference to a new book.

Many thanks again,

Sue x

https://www.facebook.com/SueWilsherWriter

Loved *The Copperettes at War*?
Check out Sue's other uplifting and
moving sagas set in 1950s Essex

Essex, 1959

Flo earns her money as a scrubber, cleaning the cruise ships
and dreaming of a day when she might sail away from her
life in the Dwellings, the squalid tenements of Tilbury docks.
Then the Blundell family are evicted from their home.

Fred, Flo's husband, finds work at Monday's, a utopian
factory town. Suddenly, it seems like everything is on
the up for Flo Blundell and her children. Even Jeanie,
Flo's sulking teenage daughter, seems to be thawing a
little in her shiny new surroundings. But when Flo's
abusive husband Fred starts drinking again, he jeopardises
the family's chance to escape poverty for good.

**Flo is faced with a terrible decision. Must she
fight to keep her family together? Or could she
strive for the life of her dreams – the kind of life
she could have when her ship comes in?**

Tilbury, 1950s

The Empire is a pub run by Vi, Doris's mother. When Doris falls pregnant out of marriage, she is kicked out of the house and forced to fend for herself.

Desperate to look after her daughter, Doris finds refuge in Southend and takes a job in a factory, hoping for a better life. When she finds herself cast out one night, Doris has nowhere to go but home – back to Tilbury. But she's still not welcome there and once again has to look for shelter and work.

Homeless and as a single mother, life is tough for Doris. And it becomes harder when she helps a neighbour, Claude, to find a new life in Britain. Now Doris must decide where her heart lies . . .

The munitions girls
have their own war to win.

The
Tilbury
Poppies

SUE WILSHER

Essex, 1916

Lily is a housemaid up at St Clere's Hall. But times are
changing with the outbreak of war. With a husband
bent on signing up for the trenches and a lecherous
master of the house, Lily is forced to leave.

Doing her bit for the war effort – and bringing in more
money for the family – Lily goes to work in a factory
making explosives to send to the trenches. It's a hard job.
The munitionettes must face terrible working conditions,
the constant danger of accidents and air strikes and a
patronising, self-serving boss. And then someone she never
wanted to see there arrives. Lady Charlotte, the pampered
daughter of the Hall, joins the factory as a supervisor . . .

**Lily and Charlotte have choices they never had
before – but in the shadow of the Great War, can the
factory girls work together for a better future?**